Nicola Marsh is
multi-award-win
than losing herse
a previous life, s
raising two dashing heroes, whipping up delish meals,
cheering on her footy team and writing—her dream
job. And she chats on social media. A lot. Come say
hi! Instagram, Twitter, Facebook—she's there! Also
find her at nicolamarsh.com.

J. Margot Critch currently lives in St John's,
Newfoundland, with her husband, Brian, and their
two little buddies, Simon and Chibs. She spends equal
amounts of time writing, listening to Jimmy Buffett's
music and looking out at the ocean—all the while
trying to decide if she wants coffee or a margarita.

STRIPPED

NICOLA MARSH

SWEET AS SIN

J. MARGOT CRITCH

MILLS & BOON

First Published in Great Britain 2019
by Mills & Boon, an imprint of HarperCollins*Publishers*
1 London Bridge Street, London, SE1 9GF

Stripped © 2019 Nicola Marsh

Sweet as Sin © 2019 J. Margot Critch

ISBN: 978-0-263-27374-8

MIX
Paper from
responsible sources
FSC C007454

This book is produced from independently certified FSC™ paper
to ensure responsible forest management.
For more information visit www.harpercollins.co.uk/green.

Printed and bound in Spain
by CPI, Barcelona

STRIPPED

NICOLA MARSH

MILLS & BOON

For my friend Tina,
who's always up for a trip to Chaddie
and never complains when I drag her through Mecca
or Sephora.

Love our lunches!

CHAPTER ONE

Hart

I'M NURSING MY third bourbon when Kevin barges into my office without knocking.

'Thought I'd find you here,' he says, helping himself to a double shot and joining me in the leather armchairs around the coffee table.

'Not a great deduction on your part, considering I've been sitting here every night for the past two weeks.'

'You're a sarcastic bastard.' He raises his glass to me before tipping it back and draining half in one gulp. 'Your grandfather was the same. The great Ralfe Rochester took shit from nobody.'

My throat tightens, like it does every time anyone mentions Pa. It has been three long weeks since the funeral here on Gem Island, his favourite island in the Whitsundays, four since he died—without me beside him. Pa wasn't just sarcastic; he was a stubborn old bastard too.

He should've called me; should've told me about

the ongoing heart-valve problems. But he didn't and he dropped dead before I could tell him half of what I should've. Like how much he changed my life. Like how much I owed him. Like how much I loved him despite doing my best to prove otherwise since he found me.

He died not knowing how I felt about him and that's something I'll have to live with every single day.

'He'd be proud of what you're doing here.' Kevin gestures around the monstrous office, with an entire glass wall overlooking the resort and the ocean beyond. 'This hotel has always been his favourite.'

I know. It's the only reason I'm stuck on this godforsaken island and not back in Buenos Aires or Brooklyn or Bangladesh, working behind the scenes to set up infrastructure for foster kids. Those kids need me like I'd once needed Pa. He found me at sixteen, took me in, nurtured me. He gave me everything. And what did I do in return?

Pretended I didn't need him. Acted like an ungrateful prick every time he reached out. Did a lame-ass job with the role he assigned me in the company.

Abandoned him.

I should've been here when he died, held his hand and given him whatever comfort I could. Instead, he died alone, his heart giving out just like the docs said it would. Yeah, Pa was stubborn to a fault. Guess I know where I get it from.

'I intend to get this place noticed.' I swirl the bourbon, staring at it until my eyes blur. It's easier than looking up and meeting Pa's right-hand man's eyes and seeing pity. It's a wasted emotion and I don't stomach it, never have. That's one of the things Pa first said to me, how he admired my resilience, how I didn't wallow in self-pity.

I didn't tell him that feeling sorry for myself had been belted out of me in the first foster family I'd grown up in. Attacks I'd deliberately provoked to prove my defiance meant more than their disdain. *Fuck 'em all* had been my motto growing up. Still is.

'Do you want me at the meeting with the new PR firm in the morning?'

I shake my head. As much as I appreciate Kevin's input I need to start doing things for myself. I need to get this business back on track. The extent of Pa's failing health has revealed itself in the company's bottom line and it isn't pretty. I can do this for him, even if being tied to a desk for the foreseeable future is the last thing I want. Maybe if I'd been a better grandson I would've known how dire things were and stepped up earlier.

I've been so goddamn angry at myself for it. It's been a rough four weeks dealing with my grief and discovering the extent of the company's problems and I haven't hidden my irritation well. I've snapped at staff, been abrupt to the point of rudeness with the board and almost sacked a decade-long employee for daring to question me.

I'm not proud of my behaviour, so when Kevin tactfully suggested I take a daily dose of happy pills—translated to snap the fuck out of it—I knew what I had to do. Shelve my guilt at being a poor excuse for a grandson. Make up for it by focussing on restoring the hotel chain to its former glory. Then appoint a great manager and hit the road like I always do.

'I'd rather meet the PR rep on my own, then when her boss arrives maybe the four of us can get together later tomorrow?'

'Fine by me.' Kevin tosses back the rest of his drink. 'Anything else you need?'

'Kev, you're my PA, not my butler.' I point at the door. 'The night is young. Go mingle.'

'I could say the same about you.' He hesitates, a wry grin creasing his face. 'Maybe that's why you're so grumpy. When's the last time you got laid?'

Too long ago to count, not that I'm interested. I've got too much to focus on. Like ensuring I pay back all Pa gave me, even if he won't know it. But I'll know, deep down in that place no one has ever touched, and for now that will have to be enough.

Besides, I don't date. I seek pleasure on occasion but most women shy away from me. They take one look at my permanent glower and either run or think they can redeem me. I'm not amenable to the latter.

'Hey.' Kevin snaps his fingers in my face. 'If it takes you this long to figure out how long since you've done the deed, it's been too long.'

'Done the deed? What are you, thirteen?'

'Fifty this year and proud of it.' He wiggles the third finger on his left hand. 'And this gold band says

I can get laid whenever and however many times I want.'

'It also says your wife carries your balls in her handbag.'

Kevin guffaws and I find myself laughing along with him. I rarely laugh. The occasional chuckle, maybe. But the cities I live in, surrounded by the poor and vulnerable, don't make me feel like smiling much, let alone laughing.

Pa understood my need to help kids like me. He recognised my restlessness after I'd completed my economics degree and worked alongside him in the hotel business for two years. He'd been grooming me and I'd done my damnedest to make him proud. But it hadn't been enough and he was man enough to let me go. Sure, I'd accepted a token position. Hotel Quality Control. Basically, an invented position akin to a mystery shopper where I'd travelled the world, checking into the company's hotels, and reporting back on everything from cleanliness of the linen to room service.

Pa swore my feedback mattered, that he instigated measures to improve hotel failings. I think I could've written my monthly reports in Mandarin and he wouldn't have noticed, that's how much faith he had in me.

I owe him. Big time.

'On that note, I better go find my balls.' Kevin stands and stretches his arms overhead. 'Let me know how the meeting in the morning goes.'

'Shall do.' I salute, glad that I have a guy like Kevin to lead me through the maze.

Being Pa's assistant for thirty years ensures he knows everything there is to know. He's invaluable to me. More like a mate, even though he's old enough to be my dad.

Considering the mammoth task of getting this resort back on track, I'm glad he's giving me a hand.

I need all the help I can get.

CHAPTER TWO

Daisy

'I'LL HAVE THE most colourful cocktail on the menu, please.'

I point at the chalkboard behind the bar like a pro, when in fact I get tipsy after one glass of wine.

The cute barman who bears a passing resemblance to a young Mel Gibson flashes me a grin, like he knows exactly how much of a phoney I am, before turning away to grab a multitude of bottles.

If all that alcohol is going into my cocktail, I'm in trouble. I don't care. This is my first night on Gem Island, one of the jewels in the Whitsundays, and I'm about to do a kickass PR job for the most enigmatic man on the planet.

I've done my research. He's an introvert who prefers travelling the world doing a menial job in Ralfe Rochester's hotel empire to following in his illustrious grandfather's footsteps. He has a limited social media presence. There's nothing to suggest he'll be a capable replacement for one of Australia's famous hoteliers who died recently, leaving Hart his sole heir.

According to my research, the Rochester business empire is floundering, which is where I come in. If I can make the Rochester hotels attractive to clientele, it'll be a massive coup professionally and one step closer to my goal: starting my own PR firm.

'Here you go.' The barman places a giant martini glass in front of me, filled with a pale purple liquid that has a sprig of lavender floating in it. 'Go easy. It's strong.'

'Thanks, what is it?' I feign nonchalance as I pick up the glass, swirling it like an expert.

'It's a Gorgeous Gem, one of my award winners.'

I look suitably impressed and he continues. 'Vodka, white rum, coconut, house-made lavender syrup, lychee juice, lemon juice and a secret ingredient I can't reveal.' He leans across the bar, close enough that I realise he smells as delicious as his cocktail. 'If I told you, I'd have to kill you.'

He winks and I hide how flustered I am by taking a big sip. Bad move. Catastrophic. Because I choke and cough and splutter, demonstrating I'm lousy with alcohol and a hopeless flirt.

He chuckles. 'Let me know when you want another.'

Try never, I refrain from saying, taking a more cautious sip this time. It's amazing: fruity and sweet, with a powerful kick. I take a bigger sip, enjoying the buzz. Who knows, I might even order another?

Alf, my boss, isn't arriving until tomorrow, so to-night I can relax.

I never do this back home in Brisbane. Not for the last twelve months, since my engagement to Casper imploded. Our engagement lasted three months, dou-bling the time I'd dated him. Turns out the perfect guy on paper isn't so perfect to live with.

Thoughts of Casper make me skol the rest of my cocktail. It burns my throat but man, I feel good. Better than good. Freaking invincible. Filled with false bravado, I order another.

'Thanks.' I flash him my best dazzling smile when he places it in front of me and he returns it with the slightest shake of his head, as if he knows what a lightweight I am when it comes to drinking.

As for the flirting part, he's already moved on to two girls barely out of their teens, leaving me feel-ing ancient at twenty-seven.

I raise the glass in his direction in a silent cheer. Your loss, buddy boy, I think, downing half the glass before I realise how fast the alcohol has affected my brain if I'm contemplating flirting with a stranger. I don't do that. I'm wildly out of practice. I've been on one date since Casper and that was a disaster, my one and only foray into a dating app. The guy turned out to be fifteen years older than his profile pic, and had lost all his hair along with his sense of humour. He'd been dour and sleazy, a terrible combination. I'm better off sticking to my career.

'Cheers to that,' I mutter, downing the rest of my cocktail and signing the tab.

When I stand, I sway a little. A short walk along the beach to clear my head might be in order. I have grand plans for my first night on Gem Island: room service, any movie featuring Ryan Gosling, and a bath. I'm living it up.

I follow the path from the bar towards the beach. Tea-light candles placed on palm fronds light the way and add a nice touch. This place is gorgeous. Romantic. Pity I'm flying solo and intend on staying that way for the foreseeable future.

I stumble at the end of the path and fall headlong onto the sand. It cushions my fall and I can't help but giggle. A giggle that turns into a full-blown laugh as I imagine how I look: on hands and knees, imitating my best cat yoga posture. Thankfully my ankle length maxi dress hides the bits I'd like to keep hidden but it's not a good look.

A pair of feet appears in my line of vision. Designer shoes. Dark tan. Scuffed, like they've been worn for ever and are the owner's favourite.

'Need a hand?'

The voice is deep, edgy, invoking an instant sense of annoyance. Like my putting a dent in the sand has somehow pissed him off. But at least he's stuck out his hand because with my head spinning from those lethal cocktails I seriously doubt my ability to stand on my own.

'Thanks.' I take the hand on offer and allow him to pull me to my feet.

My first impressions in the flickering firelight cast by tall torches: black hair long enough to be unconventional, dark eyes that could be indigo or brown, sardonic twist to his lips. Nice lips. Hot lips. Crap, I sound like an idiot even in my own head. Drunk and dumb. Not a good combination.

He looks vaguely familiar but I can't place him. He drops my hand quickly, like he'll catch girl cooties if he hangs on too long.

'That last step is a killer.' He sounds disapproving as he points to a gap between the pavers and the sand.

'Yeah.' Way to go with the scintillating response. So I say something even more mortifying. 'I think it's the killer cocktails at this resort that are more dangerous than any step.'

'You're drunk?' His eyebrow rises, making him rather rakish. I don't like bad boys as a rule but I'm willing to make an exception in his case. Crap, definitely the vodka, rum and whatever other alcohol I consumed in that cocktail earlier making me see things that aren't there. Rakish? Where did I even pull that from?

'Not drunk, just happy.' I grin to prove it but he doesn't smile back. In fact, he stares at my mouth with an intensity that leaves me a tad uncomfortable.

'You shouldn't be walking out here alone if you're feeling under the weather.'

Damn, now he sounds like Casper, lecturing me on what to do or not to do. Though Casper extended his alpha asshole-ness to telling me what to wear, what to cook, what to say in front of his stockbroker cronies. I've had enough of guys telling me what to do to last a lifetime.

So I snap back, 'I'm fine,' which only serves to raise his other eyebrow.

I wince. 'Sorry, it's been a long…year.'

It might have been my decision to end my engagement but I was still hurt. Disillusioned. Exhausted. Throwing myself into work seemed like the only solution at the time but after jumping through proverbial hoops for Alf for twelve months I'm still no closer to a promotion. Considering he's an old family friend who did my dad a favour in hiring me in the first place, it's awkward.

'I know the feeling.' He drags a hand through his hair, mussing it further, and now he's staring at the ocean, like he wants to swim out and never come back.

I rarely do things on impulse. I'm the good daughter, the good employee, the good girl. Everyone can rely on good old Daisy Adler.

But with this brooding stranger on a balmy beach, I take a risk.

'Want to take a walk?' Now it's his turn to stare at my outstretched hand. 'I'm Daisy, by the way.'

His brow furrows as he glares at me with disapproval. 'Hart.'

Oh, no. Hell no. This is *Hart Rochester*? It's an uncommon name so I can't imagine him being anyone other than the guy I have to work with. I have screwed up so badly. His first impression of me is a drunk who can't stand up after a cocktail or two.

And I can't hide my identity. It's only going to

make it harder when we meet in the morning. So I aim for levity.

'I'm your new PR person.' I force a laugh that sounds inane. 'I'm really not drunk. I'm a lightweight with alcohol because I rarely drink and those cocktails are strong.'

'I don't think anything.'

His stare is intense and unwavering, and I'm increasingly uncomfortable: it's like being looked at under a microscope, like he can see every one of my flaws.

To make matters worse, I realise my hand is still outstretched. Mentally cursing my inebriated bravado I start to lower it and am startled when he takes hold of it, his grip firm, decisive.

'If you still want to take that walk, there's an alcove at the end of the beach where you get a great view of some of the surrounding islands. It might give you a feel for the place before we start working together,' he says, tugging my hand so I fall into step alongside him. 'And just so you know, this handholding means nothing. I just prefer my PR person to be ready to hit the ground running tomorrow in the office and not hit the ground literally, again, tonight.'

I chuckle at his dry response but he doesn't join in. This is so weird. In any other circumstances this could be misconstrued as romantic but he's dour and I'm flustered and we're like two robots trudging through the sand.

It's crazy. I'm here to work. Though perhaps for one night I can just live in the moment without second-guessing every damn thing I do. Perfection comes at a high price and I've been paying it my entire life.

'I can hear you thinking,' he says, squeezing my hand lightly. It sends an unexpected tingle up my arm, a mild, pleasant shock.

'Just mulling over ways to showcase the parts of the resort we've passed.'

Great, now I sound like a kiss-ass, but I need to do something to focus on the professional when the pressure of his hand holding mine is making me feel things I shouldn't.

I'm hot all over and it has nothing to do with the temperate tropical night.

Once again, we fall silent and after a few minutes we reach the end of the beach, step around an outcrop and he points at the sea with his free hand.

'Can you see the lights from the other islands?'

'I can see a glow.' I've been wearing my contacts all day and my eyes are gritty and tired; I have no hope of seeing individual specks of light.

'I love this spot.'

'You come here often?'

The corners of his mouth curve upwards. 'Are you trying a pick-up line on me?'

I laugh. 'No.'

'Pity.' His gaze drops to my mouth again and I can't resist flicking my tongue out to moisten my lip. Not in any practiced move to attract, but a simple reflex action to a guy like him staring at me like he wants to taste my lip gloss.

After what feels like an eternity he drags his gaze back to mine. 'We should head back.'

'Yeah, we should.'

But neither of us move, trapped in some weird alternate universe where two strangers meet on a beach one night, know they can't flirt because of an upcoming professional work arrangement, but can't seem to tear themselves apart.

The wind gusts, blowing strands of hair into my face, and before I can tuck them behind my ear he does it for me. A strangely intimate gesture that makes me hold my breath. Then again, we're still holding hands so he's just being helpful. It's all rather bizarre.

His fingertips graze my earlobe and I gasp as a bolt of unexpected longing shoots through me. They drift lower, along my neck, my jaw, tracing the curve of my cheek. It's like he's trying to commit me to memory, which is ludicrous. I'm far from memorable.

His fingertips are roughened, calloused almost. They prickle my skin, setting nerve endings alight. My breathing becomes laboured, shorter, as he steps closer and I can smell him. Not aftershave exactly but a clean, crisp citrus blended with something subtler. Body wash? Shaving cream? Whatever it is, I want to devour it. Him. Whatever.

This is so wrong. I need to step away. Now. I swear my brain computes the instruction but my feet don't co-operate. So I try a few deep breaths. Wrong move. Catastrophic, as that citrus blend fills my lungs, sending messages to the rest of me, messages like 'you need to taste him now'.

I will him to move away, to be the sane one for both of us. Instead, he edges closer and I'm gone. Falling headlong into a monumentally stupid decision I know I'll regret but I'm powerless to stop.

I step even closer.

Filled with a daring I rarely possess, I eyeball him. I can't read his expression. The angle of the moon has cast his face in shadows. But he hasn't moved, his hand still cupping my cheek, and I know I have to do this before I chalk it up to yet another regret in my life.

Standing on tiptoes, I press my lips to his. Gently. Tentatively. Testing him. Me. I have no freaking clue.

He angles his head and I can't hold back. The alcohol has loosened my usual constraints and I'm a woman possessed.

I plaster myself against him and start to kiss him in earnest. Our mouths open and the first touch of his tongue on mine makes me moan. He takes control, deepening the kiss to the point where I can't breathe. I don't care. I want more.

His hands caress my back in a long, slow sweep, like he's exploring every bump of my vertebrae, before he squeezes my ass. It makes me a little crazy. I hook a leg around his waist, eager to get closer. My head's spinning a little, whether from the alcohol or his expert kisses I have no idea.

His hand slides from my ass along my thigh. My maxi dress has hiked up and when he grazes the skin behind my knee I tremble. It makes me pause. What the hell am I doing, making out with Hart Rochester on a beach, flinging myself at him like I'm more than ready to lie down on the sand and spread my legs?

It's a sobering thought, screwing up a campaign I need to go well, and I'm not sure if he senses my reluctance or I pull away first but suddenly we're apart and I'm smoothing my dress down, heat making my cheeks burn.

'That was unacceptable on so many levels.' My voice is husky and I clear it. 'I'm sorry for being unprofessional.'

I expect him to say the same. Instead, he says, 'Let's head back.'

There's no inflection in his tone, no hint of annoyance or anger. Like the last few minutes never happened.

Regret, quickly tempered with mortification, makes me turn away before he can see how his curt dismissal adds to my embarrassment. Crazy, because it's not his fault: I flung myself at him. But with him behaving like that make-out session never happened I'm thrust back into a familiar role of taking whatever is dished out. I don't like it.

So I break into a jog, desperate to get away and nurse my humiliation in peace.

He calls out, 'Hey, Daisy, wait up,' but I don't stop. I keep going.

I'm done looking back.

CHAPTER THREE

Hart

I SHOULD GO after Daisy. Smooth things over, placate her, give her a spiel about how the kiss meant nothing, to forget it.

Instead, I stand here with a dumbass grin on my face.

I know why I deliberately provoked her into that kiss. I've done it my entire life, since my dad dumped me in the foster system: push people to the edge so they can hate me first.

With Daisy, it backfired, big time.

I'd had a hard-on since I first saw her sprawled on the sand, her ass in the air. It's why I accepted her invitation for a walk even after she revealed her identity and I knew we'd be working together.

For me, our transient working relationship is perfect, because even if I do fuck her like I want to—the insistent throb in my dick won't let up—it won't mean anything. Just the way I like it.

So I needled her, accepting her invitation for a walk when I knew she'd hate me for it because I

should know better considering our impending working relationship. I expected her to bristle, to push me
away, to be appalled. The part where she reacted by
flinging herself at me? Not in the plan.

Fuck, she was a turn-on. A confident woman not
afraid to go after what she wants, even if that happens to be me, the guy working alongside her for the
next few weeks.

I should go after her and try to salvage the wreck-
age of this unexpected night before we meet in the
morning. Put her at ease. But then I remember the
way she devoured me, the way she felt me up, and
my damn face feels like it's going to crack with my
smug grin.

I'm rock hard, my balls throbbing. If all my blood
hadn't drained south I'd use half a brain cell and go
after her, if only with the intention to invite her back
to my room to finish what we started.

I watch her fleeing up the beach until she reaches
the resort gates and enters. Only then do I follow at
a sedate pace.

My grin fades the closer I get to the resort, the
weight of what I'm facing in the upcoming weeks
making my feet drag.

I'm nobody's saviour, least of all Pa's. But this
hotel business is his legacy and, for reasons I can
only blame on declining health, profit margins for
his pride and joy have plummeted.

I need to change all that.

It's the least I can do before I fuck off again.

Several couples stroll past, so wrapped up in each

other they don't notice me. A family, husband and wife, with twin boys about seven, are laughing by the water's edge, kicking at the incoming waves, sending sea spray high into the air, drenching each other.

It's late, the kids should be in bed, but as I watch the family having fun with a complete disregard for so-called society norms on child-raising, an ache starts in my chest and spreads outwards.

The complete innocence of the boys disarms me; their complete trust in their parents. I had that once. An expectation that the adults responsible for me would be dependable; an illusion ripped away the first time I got whacked across the side of the head for taking the last piece of bread, age three.

And the next time, when my dad took a belt to my butt for accidentally knocking over his beer bottle, I was four.

And the next, when a social worker didn't believe me when I told her I was locked in a cupboard at night so I wouldn't sneak off, I was six and in my first foster home.

I learned after that. Adults would never look after me. They would never hug me or care for me or love me.

So I did my best to make them hate me.

It ensured I didn't get close to anyone. Knowing my shoddy behaviour would have the desired result was the one thing I could control in a crumbling world I despised.

I never trusted anyone and despite how hard Pa tried, I couldn't let him into that hidden part of me, the part of me that wondered would he, too, eventually cast me aside.

One of the boys lets out a squeal and it pierces my reminiscing. I blink, surprised by the dampness in my eyes.

Shit, I'm turning into a sissy. Tears are wasted. The only good thing my father taught me before he dumped me at Social Services was to 'harden the fuck up'. Apparently a snivelling five-year-old had never been in his plans after my mum shot through shortly after my birth. I'm surprised the mean prick kept me around that long.

With a shake of my head, I turn my back on the happy family and head for the resort. I have a shit-load of work to do and the sooner I get started, the sooner I can leave this place and its unwelcome, maudlin memories behind.

CHAPTER FOUR

Daisy

MY HEAD HURTS. I shouldn't have drunk those cocktails last night. I shouldn't have done a lot of things, starting with downing those Gorgeous Gems like cordial and ending with snogging Hart Rochester on the beach.

I have a presentation to nail shortly and the painkillers I took with OJ half an hour ago haven't kicked in. Facing Hart after I practically mounted him will be hard enough without the drummer boy in my head practising his cymbal crashes.

I've done my research. I'm prepared. But unless I can pretend that kiss never happened, I'm in deep doo-doo.

I never should've run away. He called out to me too and I didn't stop. I acted like some crazy hormonal teen when I should've been mature and blasé, as he was.

Adults kiss all the time. We were attracted, we gave into it, shit happens. But by running away like some mortified ingénue, I made more of it rather than dismissing it as a casual sexual impulse.

Maybe I can joke about it when I see him shortly. Something witty and fabulous that will clear the air and ensure he takes me seriously when I present my plans to him.

Only one problem: I can't think of one goddamn thing to say beyond, 'I'm an idiot for flinging myself at you but you're a great kisser.'

Nope, not going to happen. I would've been nervous before this meeting regardless because I'm always like this before a presentation. Edgy and tense despite knowing I've considered every contingency.

My plans to promote this resort on Gem Island are foolproof. Starting with getting the new CEO, a renowned recluse, on board with a major social media ad campaign. It won't be easy convincing him. If anything, the disparaging media surrounding the hotel giant's fall from grace makes my job harder.

Ralfe Rochester's failing health fails his shareholders.
The prodigal grandson returns to manage the teetering family business.
Has the Rochester empire lost its Hart?

I'm up for the challenge, but Hart's minimal experience in this business and his lack of an online social profile means I'm in for a fight.

Hart needs me but what he doesn't know is that I need him just as badly. I need a final gold star on my CV before I consider going out on my own. I want to be the woman who puts Rochester Hotels and Gem Island back on the tourism map.

Starting now.

Tucking my portfolio and laptop tighter under my arm, I shut the door to my villa and follow the frangipani-lined stone path to the main building. Reception staff smile in greeting as I traverse the polished stone tiles. Lush palms in terracotta pots are placed alongside cream and cobalt cushioned cane sofas. Floral arrangements featuring local tropical flowers—the Queensland Black Orchid, the Powderpuff Lilly-Pilly and the Giant Palm Lily—throw splashes of colour, adding to the overall sense of understated elegance.

It won't take much to make this place noticeable amid the plethora of Whitsunday resorts. The owner may be another story. While Kevin gave me a rundown of the basics over the phone I garnered more information from what he didn't say than what he did.

Hart will be a challenge. His email responses to mine have been terse. I expect my clients to be more forthcoming, especially when we'll be working together.

I'm about to knock on a glass door leading to the office area when the concierge nearby waves me through.

'He's waiting for you.'

'Thanks,' I say, with a quick glance at my watch. I'm ten minutes early so I hope Hart values punctuality. With nerves making my knees wobble at our first confrontation since the awkwardness of last night, I need all the brownie points I can get.

The door to the sole office is open so I knock and push it when I hear a short, sharp, 'Come in.'

Taking a steadying breath, I fix a smile on my face and enter the office.

To discover Hart Rochester glaring at me with ill-concealed disapprobation.

His disapproval washes over me and the blood drains from my face. I can't move. My feet are soldered to the floor as embarrassment swamps me.

So much for witty banter to dismiss what happened last night.

A deep frown slashes his brow as he waves me in. 'Come in, Daisy, and let's get started.'

For a warped second I flashback to last night and think of the many ways we can get started. Before giving myself a mental slap upside the head.

I need to nail this job. Not this client.

I had my whole intro spiel worked out as I crossed the lobby on my way to his office. Something along the lines of, 'That was bizarre what happened last night, me running off like that after a kiss that meant nothing. So let's get down to work.'

But if he exuded powerful sexual vibes last night, I'm totally disarmed by seeing him again. He's wearing a crisp pale blue shirt, with the top two buttons undone and his shirtsleeves rolled up to his elbows.

The shirt is tight, like his impressive torso doesn't like being confined, and I can't help but remember how hard those muscles felt last night.

His hair is tousled and it's lighter than I thought: a lovely sorrel brown with caramel streaks from the sun rather than a hairdresser's foil.

And those vivid indigo eyes…damn, even if they radiate condemnation, they're striking.

I settle for a lame, 'I'm looking forward to working with you.'

One of his eyebrows rises, imperious and condescending, like he seriously doubts my work ethic after last night.

I don't blame him as I cross the office and place my paraphernalia on the desk. He's silent, meaning I'll have to broach the awkwardness of last night.

I try to come up with something droll and lighthearted when he says, 'Last night was an anomaly. You need to forget it. I have.'

Right. Got the message loud and clear. Asshole.

Totally unfair, because that's exactly what I want him to do, but his curt dismissal irks more than it should.

When he continues to stare at me, for a horrifying second I wonder if I spoke out loud. But he gestures at the seat opposite and I try not to collapse into it in relief.

'I've taken a look at the preliminaries you emailed and I have some questions.'

'That's what I'm here for.' I clasp my hands in my lap, doing my best to appear cool and professional, while all I can think is, You are *the* hottest guy I've ever kissed.

'The PR campaign for the resort is clear-cut but I need clarification on your ideas for making the brand more marketable.' He jabs a finger at my portfolio. 'You mentioned a more elaborate presentation? Do you want to run through it before I work through my questions?'

'Yes.' I sound like an idiot, answering with a monosyllabic affirmative, so I busy myself flipping open my laptop and trying to ignore his impenetrable stare.

He's making me uncomfortable, staring at me like he can't work me out. Join the club. How can he dismiss that kiss last night like it meant nothing?

Technically, it did, a random brief hook-up between two adults on a moonlit beach that probably happens every night of the week on an island like this; an unfortunate blip in our upcoming working relationship, a moment of cocktail-driven madness. So what was his excuse?

'You're overthinking this.'

My fingers stall on the keyboard as I'm bringing up my presentation. He's undermined me with his casual observation.

'Aren't you the least bit uncomfortable?'

I throw it out there, expecting him to shut me down. Then again, he's the one who's brought it up again and I'd rather confront the invisible tap-dancing elephant in the room than have to work in this tension-fraught environment for the foreseeable future.

'Maybe.' He shrugs, drawing his business shirt taut across his broad shoulders. 'But it happened. We can't change it. So what's the point of overanalysing it? We're adults. We acted on impulse. Why worry?'

I'm not worried, other than by an insistent hankering to do more than kiss him, and I can't help but look at his lips and remember how they felt moving against mine.

'Don't do that,' he says, his voice barely above a low growl.

'Do what?'

I muster my best innocent act when in fact I'm slightly peeved. He wants to dismiss the kiss, fine. But there's something in his tone that makes me feel belittled when it was pretty damn fantastic.

'Stare at me like you want a repeat.'

He's saying all the right things but I glimpse hunger in his eyes, a desire that matches my own. Crap, we're in trouble. For despite our protestations there's a powerful undercurrent between us. I can feel it, an insistent throb where I want him most.

I wriggle in my seat. It doesn't ease. Yep, trouble. So I settle for funny to ease the tension between us. I hold up my palm and mimic writing on it. 'Got it. Memo to Daisy. No more kissing hot guys on the beach.'

His eyes blaze with lust and I clench my thighs together, swamped with a ferocious heat like I've stepped too close to a smouldering volcano. After a long pause, he drawls, 'Nice to know you think I'm hot.'

That's the problem with being a smart-ass. Sometimes my mouth runs ahead of my brain. I should've omitted the part about him being hot.

'What I think is you need me to make you look good so let's start.'

'I need you to make this resort look good.' He leans forward, rests his forearms on the desk, smug and insufferable. 'I'm doing just fine without your help.'

Heat creeps into my cheeks, scorching and utterly embarrassing. I should've turned tail and run the moment I entered this office. But I need to ensure this job is the best work I've ever done and if that means battling wits with this inscrutable man, I'll do it.

Maybe I'm playing this all wrong? If I acknowledge what happened in a fun way, perhaps we can move on to work?

'Look, we really need to move past this. I acted on impulse last night, something I never do, and it was a kiss, nothing major.' His eyes widen, as if he can't believe I'm being so blunt. 'As for the debate regarding your hotness, I'm not in the habit of kissing random guys I just meet. I ended my engagement a year ago and haven't dated much, so considering the way we went at it last night I guess my libido classifies you as hot even if I don't want to acknowledge it myself.'

That's another thing that happens when I'm floundering. Verbal diarrhoea. It's too late to take it all back and he's gaping at me in open-mouthed shock.

I bite my bottom lip and start typing, bringing up

my presentation. 'Now we've got all that uncomfort-ableness out of the way, let's get to work.'

I could kiss him—again—when he nods. But he doesn't stop staring during my entire spiel and I've never been more grateful for my obsession with prep-aration, because if I didn't have slides I wouldn't have been able to speak.

I blather about social media campaigns and photo shoots and upgrading websites. I manage to sound halfway intelligent but the intensity of his stare is unnerving.

When I give my final spiel about a newsletter blitz to tourism boards around the world, I'm ready to snap my laptop shut and bolt.

'Your work is excellent.' He steeples his fingers and rests them on the desk in front of him, channel-ling a guy double his age. 'But you can forget about doing most of what you just said.'

I struggle to hide my shock. 'What do you mean?'

'I won't do it.'

With those four little words, I realise I'm in for the fight of my life.

CHAPTER FIVE

Hart

THE POCKET ROCKET is gaping at me in a most unladylike manner. Her hazel eyes glitter, the gold and green flecks glowing like cut glass when she's angry. I saw it earlier, when I dismissed that kiss as nothing. A crock of shit considering the memory kept me up all night.

When she walked into my office full of bright-eyed optimism I was stunned by the irrational urge to bend her over my desk. I don't give in to impulse as a rule so the fact her boldness bamboozled me last night into making out on the beach had already put me on edge this morning. But I'd chalked it up to a brief encounter that meant little, until Daisy strutted in here and I remembered exactly how good she tasted…

I hid my reaction well. I'm a master of the poker face. No one can get a read on me. Only Pa has ever seen the real me—to a point.

How he had the patience to coax my angry, recalcitrant sixteen-year-old self into a new life I'll never know. After discovering my existence, a wiser man would've thrown money at the problem. But Pa insisted I live with him: sent me to the best school for the final two years of my studies, funded my university degree, gave me everything.

But all that didn't make much of an impression: it was his unswerving faith in me, despite not really knowing me, that made me eventually trust him. I wish I'd realised it sooner and that I'd had the guts to tell him.

'What do you mean you won't do it?' She bristles like an indignant echidna, making her even cuter. Her honey-blonde hair is piled on top of her head in a loose topknot, to add extra height I assume. She's five foot two max, with the kind of curves that beg for a man's touch. I obliged for an all too brief time last night and now we're working together I can't touch her despite the urge to do just that.

It makes me extra tetchy. 'Unless you're hard of hearing, I mean exactly that. I won't do social media. It's not my thing, posting nonsensical, egotistical garbage for all the world to see in the hope of making people "like my brand".'

I make those annoying inverted comma signs with my fingers that I hate. 'And I'm not doing photo shoots to promote the resort. Focus on the scenery, the ocean, the island, the resort's many drawcards, that's it.'

I jab a finger in her direction. 'And no way in hell will you get me doing live podcasts or videoconferencing on the beach.'

If she was bristling after my initial refusal she's practically livid now. A vibrant pink stains her cheeks, making her eyes glow even more, and her hands are clenched so tightly I can see her knuckles pop where she's resting them on the desk.

When she forces a sickly-sweet smile, I know I'm not going to like what she says next. 'That's a pity, considering you were more than willing to do other stuff on the beach last night.'

Wham. She's hit me in a weak spot: my foolish attraction to her. It's wrong, fantasising about this woman, especially when she's working under me.

Fuck, bad analogy, and my dick hardens.

I have to admit, she's gutsy. A lesser woman would back down and defer to me because of my wealth and status. I'm the CEO of fifteen five-star hotels around the country and the media have been all over the story of Pa's passing and my return home to fill his proverbial shoes. It's why I hired this PR firm—because reports haven't been favourable.

The media dug into Pa's health decline and the accompanying effect on the hotels, making wrongful assumptions and generally painting him as an incompetent old fool who wouldn't move into the twenty-first century. Bookings at all the hotels plummeted as a result, as if morons think the hotels will close their doors unexpectedly at any minute. Gem Island has taken the worst hit and considering it was always Pa's favourite, it jolted me into doing something proactive.

Enter Daisy Adler, with her too-tight black power

suit better suited to a city glass tower, her immaculate make-up, her towering stilettos and those expressive eyes that sucked me into a vortex I have no intention of going near again.

She's smart. Her ideas are original and clear-cut. I need her to make the Rochester brand look good. So I'll have to say the C word, something I hate.

'I'm willing to compromise.'

The last word sticks in my throat. I don't do well working alongside other people. With my foster-kid charities around the world I have full autonomy. I work better that way. Not many people know about my involvement in establishing outreach centres in high-risk cities and I prefer to keep it that way. The last thing I need is my face bandied around as part of the Rochester empire and scaring off kids who might see me as a rich prick flinging his cash around rather than a guy who was once like them willing to give them a break.

I don't need accolades or publicity for what I do for those kids. I don't expect anything in return.

I help them because it's a way to pay my dues.

'You're willing to compromise? Lucky me.' She claps her hands, her sarcasm making me want to laugh out loud.

I've never met a woman like her. Isn't she at all intimidated?

'I could fire you. You know that, right?'

She doesn't blink. 'You can but you won't, because you need me to make you look good.'

Her snooty gaze sweeps me from my head to my

torso. 'And it's going to be a tough enough job without you vetoing everything.'

I bark out a laugh. I can't help it. She's feisty and mouthy and bold, unlike any woman I've ever met.

The girls I knew growing up in the foster system were defiant, but I always saw through to the underlying fear. It was like looking in a mirror. Later, when I began to move in Pa's social circles, the women were deferent yet calculating, impressed by wealth more than anything else.

Daisy is…unique. She's not scared of me, she's not embarrassed, and she's not backing down.

'I'm glad you find me amusing.' Her anger has faded, replaced by something more alarming: daring.

I see it in the brash way she meets my gaze, unflinching and questioning. And her mouth has relaxed, the corners curled up like she's about to smile.

'I find you many things, but amusing is low on the list.'

Those beguiling flecks in her eyes glow again but with heat this time, not anger. 'Do tell.'

I can't do this. I shouldn't do this. But I've never backed down from anything in my life and I'm not about to start now, no matter that I should.

'You're confident. Overly so.'

She remains silent, one eyebrow arched in provocation, and I continue.

'I also find you surprisingly impertinent for someone who's technically an employee of mine for the foreseeable future.'

The other eyebrow arches. 'There's a difference

between being impertinent and articulate. I'm the latter, in case you were wondering.'

'There you go, being insolent again.'

She rolls her eyes and I stifle another chuckle.

'And at the risk of going over old ground when we said we wouldn't, you're also incredibly attractive.'

'Hey.' She waggles her finger at me. 'You chastised me for looking at your mouth earlier so you can't say stuff like that.'

'You asked me to give you a list. I'm doing that.' I shrug. 'What's the big deal?'

She doesn't buy my guileless smile. Smart girl.

'I'll email you what I've just presented.' She closes her laptop, slips it into her portfolio and stands. 'I recommend you take another look and we reconvene this afternoon.'

I should let her get away with her abrupt reversion to professionalism but where's the fun in that? Not much amuses me these days and I haven't laughed in forever. Daisy Adler, with her swiftly changing faces—audacious to prim, teasing to business-like— has managed to get me doing both over the last thirty minutes.

'Maybe we should make it dusk and take another walk along the beach?'

Those sensational glossed lips compress into a thin line. 'I'll see you back here at two.'

With that, she tucks her portfolio under her arm and stalks towards the door, back ramrod straight. Her ass is divine and I remember palming it last night. How it filled my hands. Soft yet firm. Pliable.

As if sensing my thoughts she stops at the door to glance over her shoulder, shooting me a disapproving glare.

I can't help but grin as she slams the door on her way out.

CHAPTER SIX

Daisy

I CAN'T BELIEVE IT.

Hart caved.

Well, technically he's only agreed to doing a few shots around the resort but it's a start. I'll have him agreeing to the rest before he can say 'I'm a contradictory jerk'. Because he is. The way he stared down his nose at me one minute, then flirted with me the next... I could've slapped him.

Instead, I had to play nice. Especially when he said he had the power to fire me. That gave me a fright. But I took a risk. Rather than back down as he would have expected, I goaded him further and it worked. I'd pitched to guys like him in the past: they respected courage so I showed no fear.

Unfortunately, it semi-backfired when he found my boldness a bit of a turn-on, if the way he looked at me was any indication. He switched from moody to intrigued, like he couldn't figure me out.

Confronting the guy I kissed was bad enough.

My quick mental argument between my logical side and my inner vixen when I entered his office went something like this:

Why the hell does Hart Rochester have to be the hottie you kissed? What's so special about him that he makes you want to shuck your panties? What the hell were you thinking?

Well, I wasn't. He's a seriously good kisser and he's hot and I'm in a man drought so I couldn't help myself despite having to work with him. Damn, he looks fine. Better than I remembered in the semi-darkness last night. I wonder how unprofessional it would be to lie on his desk and ask him to take me now?

Thankfully I managed to appear calm and coherent during my presentation. But I was ultra aware of him throughout, staring at me with those enigmatic eyes that shield his every thought. Only when he lightened up did I see a glimpse of how he could be if he let go: funny, interested, alive.

The latter had me spooked because when I'd first entered his office and we'd got past the awkwardness of our kiss, I'd seen a man sitting behind a desk who appeared like a robot. Like he was going through the motions. Like he didn't want to be here.

I'm good at my job but no amount of positive PR will make an ounce of difference if he looks like that in the rebranding material I have planned. Which is why I'm here to ensure he lightens the hell up.

'How about this for a few casual shots?' I hand

him one of the outfits I asked him to bring down to the cabanas circling the pool.

He stares at the red polo and navy shorts like I've given him a chicken suit to wear. I expect him to baulk. Instead, he shrugs and glances around. 'Where should I change?'

I refrain from rolling my eyes, just. He's deliberately making this as hard as humanly possible and my patience is wearing thin, considering we've been at this for an hour.

I tap my bottom lip, pretending to think. 'I don't know, Einstein, maybe in one of the cabanas?'

'But the material is flimsy, you'll see everything.' He ducks his head to murmur in my ear. 'Or is that your intention, perv?'

I bite back a laugh. 'Trust me, Sweet-Cheeks, if I wanted to see everything it wouldn't be out here.'

'Then where would it be?'

He hasn't moved, deliberately staying close enough to taunt me, so I respond in kind. 'Somewhere private, because I don't like an audience for what I have in mind.'

He makes an odd strangling sound and backs away. Go me.

I deliberately avert my gaze when he enters the nearest cabana. But I'm only human, and insanely attracted to this smart-mouthed guy, so I risk a peek.

Bad move. While I can't see anything per se, I see enough. The angling of the sun ensures light pours through the cabana's canvas, casting his shadow against the opposite wall. He has his back to me and I see him slip off his shirt and pants, leaving him silhouetted like a goddamn Adonis. Broad shoulders, tapered waist, long, lean legs.

My mouth goes dry as he half turns and I see the rest: an obvious bulge in his jocks. Nice to know I'm not the only one turned on. I continue staring as he steps into the shorts, hikes them up and pulls the polo over his head. I'm hot, flushed from head to foot. Damn island heat. My excuse and I'm sticking to it.

Thankfully the photographer is busy changing lenses and doesn't notice my flustered state as I reach for a water bottle from the cooler nearby and roll it across my forehead.

'Heat getting to you?'

I jump and almost upend the bottle. He's snuck up behind me, the ratfink. His tone is silky smooth, as if he knows I've been perving on him.

I turn and glare at him, annoyed by his smug grin and knowing eyes, and I realise something. If he'd changed in the cabana on the other side of us, the sun wouldn't have cast him in shadow. Which could only mean one thing.

He wanted me to watch.

Two can play this game and I have a sneaking suspicion I'll be better at it than him.

'Yeah, it's incredibly hot here.' This time I roll the bottle across my upper chest, where the condensation transfers onto my skin.

He's riveted, staring at my chest like he wants to lick off the water droplets. The thought alone is enough to make my hand shake. I changed into a sundress after our meeting. It's not particularly low-cut but what skin that is exposed is now moist and he can't stop staring at it.

'You're…' He drags his gaze off my chest and meets my eyes. His pupils are dilated amid all that gorgeous blue. I'm definitely winning this battle.

'What?'

I eyeball him, daring him to articulate what's going on here. Disappointingly, he mutters something unintelligible and turns away, missing my victorious fist pump.

'I can see your reflection,' he says, sounding amused rather than annoyed, as I belatedly realise we're standing near the trendy glass-enclosed pool-side bar.

'Good. Then you'll know how absolutely pumped I am that this photo shoot is going so well.'

He turns back to me. His pupils have returned to normal and he looks way too controlled. I'll fix that. I'm not done with payback for that little cabana stunt yet.

'Where do you want me next?'

I flash him an innocent smile. 'If you're after the PG version, I'd like you to strike a casual pose over by the bar.'

He swallows. 'And if I want the R version?'

I lean closer and his sharp intake of breath indicates he isn't as controlled as he appears. 'You'll have to be a lot nicer to me.'

I will him to say he does want it, that, despite our

logical agreement to forget that kiss, he isn't averse to doing it again and a whole lot more.

I brace for him to fob me off and put an end to our verbal sparring.

'I thought we agreed not to do this,' he says, sounding gruff.

'We're just flirting. It's healthy.'

'The thing is, if you push me too far, it won't stop there.'

I resist doing a fist pump again. 'Promises, promises.'

He swipes a hand over his face, like he wants to eradicate my presence altogether. 'This is a dumb idea.'

'There are dumber.' I hold up my hand and start ticking off a list by lowering my fingers. 'Leg warmers. Crimped hair. Scrunchies. Acid-wash jeans—'

'As much as I like hearing that you're an eighties aficionado, can you be serious for one damn second?'

Okay, maybe I've pushed him too far because now he looks plain tortured. 'I don't like mixing business with pleasure.'

I shrug. 'Me either. But we're both adults. I'm pretty sure we can separate what happens out here from what could happen in there.'

I point over his shoulder towards the luxurious villas scattered among the lush tropical gardens. 'Or do you prefer it on the beach only?'

'Fuck,' he mutters, dragging a hand through his hair, ensuring I'll have to smooth it before the next batch of photos is taken.

He's conflicted. I see it in the shadows scudding across his eyes like storm clouds, in the wry twist of his mouth. He wants me but doesn't want to relinquish control.

So I take pity on him. 'The photographer's ready to start shooting again, so why don't you head to the bar?'

He locks eyes with me and I glimpse something that gives me hope: indecision. 'This isn't over.'

'I'm counting on it.' I wave him away with a dazzling smile. I hope it hides how damn uncertain I am about this too.

CHAPTER SEVEN

Hart

IT'S BEEN TOO long since I got laid. I need to remedy that pronto if all I can think about is taking my PR rep up against the nearest wall.

She's driving me insane.

I know it's wrong. It will muddy our working relationship. Then again, she won't be on the island for long. Four weeks max. Why can't we indulge this thing between us, and walk away unscathed at the end?

Because I'm a realist and know that the clean breakup after casual sex is a myth. A fucking fairytale.

I've never been involved with a woman, even physically, for longer than a week. It doesn't make me a man-whore. It makes me smart. Women I screw know the score. We're in it for a short time not a long time. Pure physical release. Fun.

Yet I have a feeling that even if I spell it out for Daisy she's the kind of girl to get under a guy's skin. I like the way she doesn't back down, the way she fires back quips, the way she fills out a dress. Yeah,

I'm a shallow, narcissistic prick but I can't stop thinking about her and I have a feeling I'll be a mess until I slake my thirst for her.

Kevin bollocked me after the shoot because I hadn't looked over the next quarter's projections and bookings are still falling. I wish I could shoulder the blame. I'd happily announce to the hotelier world I'm a nomadic hippy destined to run Pa's empire into the ground. I'd do anything to stop the muckraking press from besmirching Pa any more than they already have. And that means I'll take the Rochester hotels back to the top. I'll show them.

One thing not many people know about me: I never give up. I may not want this role thrust upon me but I'll be damned if I screw it up and let Pa down—more than I already have over the years. I have a plan: regain consumer confidence in the Rochester brand, install quality management hierarchy, then leave.

I can't be tied to a desk. It'll kill me. I've tried it before, after Pa invested in me. Back then I worked alongside him for two years after earning my degree, putting on a game face, as if running hotels was what I was born to do.

Pa saw straight through me. He invented a meaningless job for me, ensuring I could travel as much as I wanted but still be semi-attached to the company. I mucked that up, focussing more on the foster kids outreach stuff than my bogus hotel job. It makes me feel even guiltier that I let him down, that the one job he entrusted me with I didn't do properly. I felt like a fraud; still do.

I'll never understand how the gruff tycoon welcomed me into his life and gave me what I craved most: a family. He's been my emotional touchstone for so long—my only one—that since he passed away I'm dead inside.

Until Daisy.

She's the first person to make me feel anything other than repressed and shut off, even if it is only lust. I'd be a fool not to capitalise on it. She's joining me shortly, on the pretext of scouting more locations for her bloody photo shoots to make the hotel brand more likeable in some media blitz. She's insistent I need to be seen as part of the new brand to instil confidence in consumers and restore faith.

What a crock of shit. She's wasting her time. I have one of those faces that tends to scare off everyone. But I need this campaign to work if I want to escape the desk and return to what I like doing best: helping kids like me. Wary, resentful, terrified kids abandoned to foster systems around the world. They need me even if they don't know it, like I needed someone way back when.

Pa was my saviour, but at sixteen I'd already seen too much and endured too much, way more than any child should. Some people say I have a god complex. I don't. I'm not narcissistic enough to think I can control everything around me, but when it comes to those kids I'll do my damnedest to make sure they have a better life than I did for the first sixteen years of mine.

I hear humming and something akin to lightness makes the tension in my chest ease. Daisy definitely has a thing for the eighties because as she nears the caves she breaks into a Rolling Stones classic, off-tune yet endearing.

I smile. It feels foreign because I don't do it a lot. Yeah, a sizzling sexual encounter with this bold, quirky woman is just what I need to take the edge off and get me refocussed on the job at hand.

She pauses at the entrance, shielding her eyes to peer into the gloom.

'Over here.' I wave, knowing the exact moment she sees me, because her face lights up. It shouldn't. I'm no good for her. Not in the way a girl like her expects. But I wouldn't have asked her to meet me here if I didn't have more than work on my mind and I'm done lying to myself.

I want Daisy.

'You're not going to leave me here at high tide, hoping I'll wash out to sea?' She steps into the cave and lowers her hand, her head swivelling as she turns a full three-sixty. 'Wow, this is spectacular.'

'I thought you might like it. For the shoot,' I add, hating how clipped I sound, like I'd rather be doing anything other than this. I'm not a people person, never have been, and it irks that I'm so fucking horny for this woman I sound gruffer than usual. 'In another few hours when the sun sets the light in here is fantastic.'

'It's like something out of a fairytale.' She stops spinning and her eyes are wide and bright. Fuck. I'm not the knight in shining armour someone like her deserves. I should get the fuck out of here now. But my cock has other ideas. 'How did you find this place?'

'It was my go-to place when Pa first brought me to the island.'

Why the hell did I blurt out something so honest? Some of the light in her gaze fades at my terse response and I hope she'll gloss over it.

'When was that?'

No such luck. 'He discovered I existed when I was sixteen, so around my seventeenth birthday.'

She wants to ask more. I can see the blatant curiosity all over her face. But she surprises me. 'This would've been a perfect hideaway for a teen.'

I nod, characteristically uncomfortable discussing anything regarding my past. 'I'd bring a book, some snacks, and hang out. I liked the peace.'

After growing up in foster homes where yelling was often the main method of communication, I thought I'd discovered paradise in this cave. I haven't been back here for a decade and now I regret asking her to meet me here. It means too much and I'm overwhelmed. My throat tightens and there's a constricted band around my head, squeezing until it aches.

'What's wrong?'

Damn, so much for my famed poker face. 'Let's go scout a few more locations.'

If she registers my sudden panic she doesn't show it. But she does something far more frightening. She crosses the distance between us to stand in front of me, close enough I can smell the resort's signature exotic fruity body wash, a heady blend of strawberries, lime and coconut. I want to gobble her up.

'At the risk of sounding crazy, I'm all about the ambience of places. How a house feels, whether it's good or bad, that kind of thing. And this cave feels incredible, so I'd like to hang out for a bit.'

'You're right, you're crazy.'

I don't want to stay. Not with her standing too close and staring at me like she can see all the way down to my soul.

'So I've been told.'

I hear a hint of vulnerability in her voice and it slays me. I don't want to ask. I shouldn't. But I find my stupid damn mouth not working in sync with my head.

'Want to talk about it?'

'Not really,' she says, but her expression says different, like she's swallowed a lemon.

'Guy troubles?'

Belatedly, I remember what she blurted when we were both uncomfortable during our first meeting in my office, something about ending an engagement and not dating much since. I'm an idiot for asking something so personal when all I want to do is escape this place right now.

'Something like that.' She sighs and it makes me want to cuddle her. 'I was engaged to a jerk. Typical good-on-paper guy who's very different once you have to live with him.'

'Good on paper?'

She gives a wry chuckle devoid of amusement. 'The type of guy every woman would love to be with. Financially stable, owns his own house, charming, confident, good-looking.'

'Like me, you mean?'

'You're far from charming.' She looks at me, but she's not really seeing me. She's caught up in memories of some dickhead who hurt her.

'So what happened?'

'The usual. Once I moved in he became a demanding, control-freak bore. So I left after three months.' She's not telling me everything, her voice is high and tight, and she shakes her head, as if trying to clear it. 'Best decision I ever made. That was a year ago and I haven't looked back.'

'Single and loving it?'

'Something like that.'

But she doesn't sound like she loves it. She sounds morose and sad, courtesy of my stupid questioning. So I do something even stupider. I reach for her and haul her into my arms. She's smaller than I remembered from that night on the beach. Then again, we didn't do much hugging then. It was more a pawing.

Initially stiff and resistant, she soon melts into me, her cheek resting against my chest. It feels weird. When a woman's in my arms I'm not offering comfort. It's a prelude to sex and the mere thought of getting down and dirty with Daisy has my cock hardening.

I try to ease my hips away before she thinks I'm a callous prick only out for one thing. Which I am, but now isn't the time, not when she's like this.

Why the hell did I have to pry? I never do that. I don't give a shit about other people's problems because I've always had enough of my own. And then I have to go and hug her…what the fuck?

She resists and tightens her arms around me, then presses against me. She lifts her head slowly and looks up. I've succeeded. The sadness has gone. I should be glad. But what I see has the potential to undo me far quicker: burning desire.

Her eyes glow with it and when her tongue flicks out to moisten her bottom lip I'm a goner.

I claim her mouth like I've yearned to do since the first illicit taste two nights ago. I've never clashed teeth with any woman, but with Daisy I'm too eager and our incisors bump. Either she doesn't care or she doesn't notice because that tempting tongue sweeps into my mouth demanding attention. I give it to her. Our tongues tangle and explore, so fucking hot.

She moans in the back of her throat while hooking a leg around my waist. I grind against her, indicating where I'll be very soon unless she stops me. She doesn't and I know this will end how I hoped: with me deep inside her.

But I need to make sure this isn't the monumental screw-up I know it is. So I wrench my mouth from hers and drag in breaths to ease the tightness in my chest.

'Are you sure you want this?'

A coy smile curves her lips and I want to claim them all over again. 'I have a hankering for some sexual sorbet.'

'You're into kinky shit?'

She laughs. 'I haven't had sex since Casper so you're going to cleanse my sexual palate, so to speak. Break my drought, that kind of thing.'

I snort. 'Your dickhead ex was named after a ghost?'

She laughs and I feel the corners of my mouth twitching to do the same. If I don't smile very often I laugh even less.

'This doesn't have to mean anything other than physical release. I want you. You want me. Let's not complicate this.' She taps my ass with her foot—she still has her leg hooked around me—and I realise I'm wasting time talking and thinking. She's articulated exactly what I want. 'Give me my sorbet, now.'

In response, I slide my hands under her dress and encounter warm, round ass. I love that she's a thong girl. I hoist her up and she wraps her other leg around my waist. She's so light and when she buries her face in the crook of my neck I feel like some superhero rescuing the damsel in distress. It unnerves me. I couldn't rescue myself when I was a kid, I can never be the type of guy a woman depends on.

I lower her to the smooth sand at the back of the cave, on the exact spot I used to sit as a teen. Our mouths fuse again, hungry and demanding, as my hands knead her ass until she moans. I drag my fingers through her cleft, through the wetness of her folds, until I reach the nub I'm searching for.

Her pussy is so wet and my cock pulses with each circle of my thumb on her clit. Around and around until she's panting and writhing beneath me.

'So…good,' she murmurs, her hips arching as I slip a finger inside her, another, mimicking what my cock is yearning to do.

She writhes and arches and comes apart on a low groan, which surprises me. I pegged her for a screamer because she's loud when she talks. But there's something infinitely sexier about that groan, like it's been dragged up from deep within.

I unzip and make quick work of a condom, sliding into her while her eyes are still closed, her lips curved in a small sated smile.

She's tight and the friction against my cock is so fucking good. Her eyes snap open when I slide out and plunge in again, burying myself to the hilt.

I can't decipher the emotion in her eyes and I don't want to. So I pick up the pace, pounding into her over and over, craving a mind-blanking release. I don't want to think, I just want to feel the assured dazedness when I come.

She angles her hips and I'm a goner. My balls contract as I thrust in one last time and the oblivion takes over. Mindless, unadulterated pleasure, swamping me in a wave I don't want to resurface from.

I'm not a cuddler, never have been. Even hugging makes me uncomfortable. But Daisy's arms are clasped around me and I grit my teeth against the urge to disengage quickly.

When she continues to stare at me like I've delivered her the world on a platter, I scowl. 'Consider your palate cleansed.'

It's a shitty thing to say, the worst. She pales. I should be glad. I want her to think I'm a heartless prick that emotionally withdraws as soon as the deed is done.

But as I glimpse the hurt in her eyes, all I can think is, You're the biggest dumb-fuck ever.

CHAPTER EIGHT

Daisy

ALF ARRIVED AN hour ago and I've been holed up in a conference room giving him a rundown of what's happened on the island so far. I haven't told my boss everything for obvious reasons.

Like the fact I had hot cave sex with our client yesterday afternoon.

This job means everything to me. I need to start acting like it. Though as Alf drones on about profit margins I tune out, already envisioning my own logo with a cute daisy on it.

The campaign is progressing well, considering Hart initially baulked at the PR I'd outlined to use him as part of Rochester's new brand. We got some great shots around the pool yesterday, BC.

Before Cave.

After our sizzling interlude we were stilted and awkward, and couldn't get away from each other fast enough. I'd expected it but it still hurt. Crazy, considering he was excellent sorbet. Fresh and fabulous, completely cleansing me of Casper. Exactly what I'd wanted.

So why do I feel so hollow?

'Daisy, pay attention.' Alf snaps his fingers in my face. 'I've already met with the client and he's happy, so I'll be flying out in the morning and leaving this in your hands.'

'So what's new?' I want to ask. Alf does nothing but delegate. One of the perks of being the boss, which is exactly why I want to be one.

I've paid my dues long enough.

As Alf regularly implies, I wouldn't have this job if it hadn't been for my father. Dear old Dad was in Alf's marketing classes at uni and used the friendship card to land me this job. I didn't mind at the time because I was desperate to land my first job and eager for experience. Five years later, I know something else Dad gave me—the life lesson to never, ever quit—is wearing thin.

I've almost done it many times over the last twelve months but each and every time I'd hear Dad's voice in my ear: 'Adlers never quit, sweetheart. We never give up. We see things through, no matter how difficult or challenging.'

He drilled me in the family motto from the time I could walk and I know it's the only thing that has prevented me from handing in my resignation to Alf.

That, and the fact I quit on my engagement twelve months ago and I don't want to add my job to that less than illustrious list. I know in my gut I did the right thing leaving Casper, that I could never be the kind of woman a guy like him demands, but the fact remains I still left, ignoring my insistent voice of reason that maybe I should've tried harder, maybe I should've been more accommodating, maybe I should've been…more.

My family didn't say much when I left Casper but I saw the disappointment in their eyes, labelling me a quitter. The stupid thing is, I can live with that. But it's hard to admit, even to myself, that deep down I feel like I walked away too easily in my personal life so no way in hell I'll do the same in my professional one. I'm sticking with Alf until I nail this Gem Island job. Who knows, maybe he'll give me a promotion and I won't feel compelled to leave. And maybe the reef sharks circling the island will grow wings too.

As for my performance, I'd just bet Mr Rochester is happy with it, considering I spread my legs for him yesterday.

Okay, now I'm really being an idiot, labelling myself as some eager bimbo. I didn't bonk him to get ahead in my job, I screwed him because I've never been so attracted to a guy before and I wanted to see what it felt like to have sex without emotional entanglement.

Turns out I don't do so well having sex like a man.

Silly, because he gave me exactly what I wanted. The problem is, I want it again. While I'd never done it on the sand or in a cave, I wonder what it will be like on the luxurious bed in my villa, where we can do it more than once.

I'm not a sex maniac. My year-long drought is testament to that. Even with Casper, it didn't bother me if he was tired. We had a routine, Wednesdays and Saturdays, and it quickly became rote even though we hadn't been dating all that long when we moved in together. Before him I'd had three boyfriends, each lasting a few months tops.

Sex is fun with the right guy, and until now I thought I'd already had it. Turns out my previous boyfriends and one narcissistic fiancé weren't so great in the sack after all.

Damn Hart Rochester for making me want more than sorbet. One scoop isn't enough: I want the whole damn tub, with sprinkles on top.

'Is there a problem, Daisy?'

Lost in my musings, I wonder how much I've missed of Alf's ramblings. I occasionally tune out but not to this extent and I certainly don't fantasise about guys during our work discussions. My cheeks are hot and I struggle not to squirm in my seat like I've been caught red-handed doing something naughty.

'No, Alf, all good. I'm just envisaging how I can up the ante with the campaign.'

'Excellent.' He rubs his hands together. 'Keep this up for a few more years and who knows? I might give you a promotion.'

WTF? I've been doing a stellar job for the last five years with minimal input from him. He'll criticise for the sake of it, trying to find fault when there isn't any. He metes out measly pay rises annually and acts like he's giving me an extra ten grand. He takes all the credit for my ideas in meetings and is generally a pompous ass that needs to make better use of deodorant.

I want to tell him where he can stick his job and that after Gem Island I'll be giving myself a promotion far away from him but I settle for a sedate smile, knowing I'll need to pop a heartburn pill or two later.

I won't walk away, not this time.

I almost cheer when there's a knock on the door and Hart strolls in. Alf fawns over him, effusive and embarrassing. Hart's discomfort is obvious when Alf slaps him on the back and he steps away. Predictably, Alf doesn't notice.

Alf nudges Hart again. 'I'll leave you in Daisy's capable hands. She's not too shabby at her job because I taught her everything she knows.'

My fixed smile doesn't slip until Alf waddles out of the room, when I slump in relief.

'That guy's an asshole,' Hart says, staring at me with raised eyebrows when I smother a snort.

'He's not so bad.'

He's worse but I'd never badmouth my boss behind his back. I wave Hart towards the chair next to me so we can get started on the next stage of the campaign.

'Loyalty, I admire that.' He points to the clearly labelled manila folders laid out in front of us. 'From what I've seen so far, your work is excellent. You've done your research, your presentation was kickass and your notes are impeccable. Why don't you go out on your own?'

The last thing I would ever do is tell a client my plans. It's unprofessional. Then again, I've already done unprofessional things with this particular client, what's one more?

'It has crossed my mind. But that whole loyalty thing…' I shrug, wondering what he'd think of the real reason why I won't walk away. 'Alf gave me my first job. I've learned a lot.'

He studies me intently, like he knows I'm not telling him everything. 'There's a difference between blind loyalty and hiding your talents where they're unappreciated.'

How the hell does he do that, articulate my doubts?

'Who knows what will happen when I increase bookings across your chain of hotels? A big tick on my CV is always handy if I do decide to branch out.'

'You've got a great work ethic.' He nods, the admiration in his gaze making me want to preen. 'Though we both know that making someone like me an identifiable part of the Rochester brand is what will really have clients clamouring for your PR services.'

'I didn't want to state the obvious,' I say, with a self-deprecating shrug that makes the corners of his mouth twitch.

An awkward silence descends, as I knew it inevitably would after how we parted yesterday. 'Consider your palate cleansed' was the last thing he said to me. True, but it was the way he said it that was the biggest let-down after the great sex: like it meant little and he couldn't wait to escape me.

Following an embarrassing crying jag in the shower afterwards, I was determined to put my game face on when we next met. But as the silence stretches I know I'll have to broach the subject of what we did in that cave.

I clear my throat. 'Yesterday was an aberration that shouldn't have happened. We're working together and it complicates things—'

'Don't do that,' he snaps, a deep frown grooving his brows. 'You've got nothing to apologise for.'

I'm so taken aback at his harsh tone I'm not sure how to respond.

He grimaces. 'Sorry, it's a pet hate. Don't ever back down or apologise for something that isn't your fault.'

Ah…so that's what's bugging him. He thinks he took advantage of me somehow? I need to disabuse him of this notion because it's far from the truth.

'You think what happened yesterday was all you?'

His frown deepens. 'Of course. I lured you to the cave on the pretext of work, knowing I wouldn't be able to keep my hands off you after our little sparring session by the pool earlier.'

'Oh.'

Call me naïve but I didn't suspect a thing.

'Yeah. Oh.' A faint pink tinges his cheeks, like he's embarrassed. 'Considering my spiel after our kiss on the beach that it wouldn't happen again, I do something like that.'

'As I recall, there were two people doing the fucking in that cave.'

Now it's his turn to be shocked as his jaw drops and I place my finger under his chin and shut it.

'I don't know why you feel guilty about what happened. It was stupendous, just what I wanted, so don't beat yourself up.'

I'm tempted to say more, like how much I'd like to do it again, but I wisely keep my mouth shut. I can't allow this unexpected infatuation to derail my plans to make this the best job I've ever done.

'Now that we've got that out of the way, why don't you take a look at this campaign I've brainstormed and let me know what you think?'

I slide a folder across to him, silently willing him to drop the subject.

We had hot sex.

In a cave.

Shit happens.

But as he flicks through the sheets of paper and I study him, I know my plan to keep my hands off him will be sorely tempted over the next few weeks.

CHAPTER NINE

Hart

'THOUGHT I'D FIND you here.' Kevin sidles up to me, like he expects I'll push him off the cliff.

This is the highest point of Gem Island and until now I've avoided coming here. If the cave was my go-to place, this was Pa's. I remember him bringing me here when I first arrived on the island as a starstruck sixteen-year-old who'd never been off the mainland.

He told me the truth—how he made a mistake cutting off contact from my mum when she fell in with the wrong crowd at nineteen, how he stubbornly resisted her call for help two years later, how he didn't know I existed until he received a letter from her the day she died, stating she'd had a kid and how she'd abandoned him. Pa was always a straight shooter and as I lowered my carefully erected barriers and let myself depend on someone for the first time in my life, I learned that maybe there was something to this family caper after all.

I resent him for not telling me he'd been having heart problems but I understand why he did it. In his own twisted way, he was probably punishing himself for not being there for my mum when she died and he wanted to die alone too.

'I haven't been up here since we tossed his ashes.'

Kevin makes an odd garbled sound in his throat. 'Me neither. But this was the spot he did his best thinking and I assumed you'd be doing the same.'

His presumption annoys me. 'I'm not my grandfather.'

'I know you're not, kid, but I sure as hell see a lot of similarities.'

Utter bullshit, because Pa and I are nothing alike. He was noble and driven and a stickler for tradition. I can't wait to shrug off the weight of this responsibility and leave it all behind.

'Have you come here to lecture me over the fuckup with the Darwin hotel? Because having the entire kitchen staff go on strike because Pa was too stubborn to listen to their wage demands was not my fault.'

'No.' Kevin sighs. 'I came here to tell you to stop beating yourself up. You haven't done this job for years and even back then you were barely a kid out of university being stuck behind a desk you didn't want.'

'Not much has changed except I'm older.'

'Nobody's expecting you to fill Ralfe's shoes, but it would be nice if you could try them on for size for however long you're here.'

With that he turns and walks away. I should call him back, make light of his analogy, but his name sticks in my throat. I've told him my plans to improve the profile of the hotels and restore consumer faith. I guess Pa and I are alike in one respect: Pa was a private person who hated change and preferred to keep out of the limelight. He resisted modernisation and relied on the family name to keep profits soaring.

It didn't work and part of my plan is to move the Rochester brand into the twenty-first century. To try new ideas, to use PR in a way that the hotels' profiles will be what everyone talks about: the go-to place for tourists, families and businessmen alike.

It's a solid plan that Daisy is on board with. But once that's done I'm out of here. Kevin understands. He's a good guy. But how can I expect him to have faith in me when I'm filled with a self-loathing I can't shake no matter how hard I try?

It has been five days since I fucked Daisy in that cave. Five long, excruciating days where I've thrown myself into work and jacked off in the shower at night before falling into bed, sleep eluding me.

She's all I can think about and the screw-up with me not following up with the Darwin hotel's staffing wages is a direct result. It has me re-evaluating the wisdom in keeping my distance.

Not that it seems to affect her. She's been proficient and professional, polite during our regular meetings, while all I can think about is how her lips feel and how she tastes and that sexy groan when she comes.

It's killing me.

We need to talk. I've had short-term flings before, when I've been in Chicago or Chennai or Cairo, with co-workers who've known the score. Each of those times we worked hard during the day and fucked at night, knowing it would end in a few weeks. Easy, no-fuss arrangements with a clear end date.

I want that with Daisy.

My mobile buzzes in my pocket, a reminder that we have another meeting scheduled to start in fifteen minutes.

I have two options: continue as I have been, an introverted recluse working behind closed doors while I focus on fixing Pa's mistakes and refusing help, or ask if Daisy's up for a fling.

I know which of the options I would prefer and I hope she does too.

CHAPTER TEN

Daisy

I SIT AT a table for six at the resort's cliff-top bar and wait for Hart. I avoid the cosier tables because I don't want to bump knees with Hart considering we've already bumped uglies.

I've chosen this spot because I want to show him the preliminary shots the photographer has taken and how I've incorporated them into a snazzy slideshow to take the place of a header on the website.

I've also chosen it because I need fresh air. I'm sick of being stuck inside, doing my best to avoid Hart. Our daily meetings have been brief and impersonal. I should be rapt. He's giving me plenty of leeway on the campaign, has approved all my ideas and come up with some stellar contributions of his own. For someone who loathes social media he's forward-thinking and innovative, and working with someone who's so focussed on success is invigorating.

But all the fake smiling I'm doing is making my face ache and our brittle politeness is at breaking point. I can feel the tension simmering between us, like an invisible wire stretched taut, ready to snap.

It's driving me freaking nuts.

The six-two ripped waiter deposits an iced coffee on the table. I smile my thanks and sign for it, including a generous tip. One thing this resort has going for it: extremely cute wait-staff. Must be a prerequisite, to have modelling experience.

I take a sip and savour the icy sweetness. I need the caffeine hit, considering I've slept poorly all week and it has nothing to do with the cloud-like mattresses and perfect pillows. I see the cause of my insomnia striding towards me like he has places to be, long, confident strides I envy. Being a shorty means I have to practically scamper when we're walking alongside each other.

'This is a surprising change of meeting venue,' he says, taking a seat opposite.

'It's good to shake things up.'

'I couldn't agree more.' He pins me with a direct stare that has me wondering if he's talking about something other than where we meet.

Heat flushes my cheeks and I reach for my laptop in desperation, needing him to focus on anything but me. 'I want you to check out this proposed update for the website.'

He reaches out, his fingertip grazing my top lip, and I let out an embarrassing yelp.

'What are you doing?'

'You had a bit of cream from the iced coffee.' He

holds up his finger, studies the minute glob of cream, before popping it into his mouth and sucking.

I inhale sharply and my thighs clench together. It's the most blatantly erotic thing I've ever seen.

'Mmm…good.' He stares at my mouth again, like he's coming back for seconds and I scuttle back in my chair.

'What's going on?'

'We need to talk.' He reaches over and closes my laptop, leaving me under no illusions it's about work. Like I had any doubt after that cream incident.

'Are you breaking up with me?' I deadpan, increasingly confused by his changing moods.

One minute he's all business and avoiding me, the next he's staring at me like he wants to impersonate a caveman again.

'I want you to hear me out.'

I nod my agreement but rather than his perpetual glower fading, his frown lines deepen.

'This arrangement isn't working for me.'

My heart plummets. I can't lose this job. It means too much. The last cruel taunt that Casper flung in my face was that I'd never make it on my own, either in or out of the boardroom. He laughed at my dreams to open my own PR agency, one of the many reasons why I dumped him. He mocked me to the point I began to doubt myself.

Which is why I need to do this. I need to do a killer job on this campaign and hang my eponymous shingle ASAP to a prove a point, not just to the world but to the biggest doubter ever: me.

That's what I hate most about Casper: he made me lose myself. I loved him blindly and threw myself wholeheartedly into our relationship, not realising until it was too late that he was sapping me mentally and emotionally. He liked to control everything, from where and when we ate to who we socialised with. He distanced me from my family, my friends, and I happily sacrificed so much because I thought he adored me as much as I did him.

It took me too long to figure out he wasn't as emotionally invested as me and that I was yet another object in his perfectly timetabled life: it was time for him to marry and I was a convenient choice.

Though it wasn't until he started belittling my choices and demonstrating an underlying cruelly dominant streak that he frightened me and I realised I had to escape.

Love doesn't suit me. It made me give up too much. It made me lose confidence in myself and deep down I know that's the real reason I won't quit my job even though I yearn to.

Maybe I'm not as good as I think?

Casper sapped my confidence to the extent I doubt everything and it's this residual lack of assurance that is keeping me tethered to Alf.

I want to move past it, which is why doing a stellar job on this campaign will go a long way to securing what I want most: to be a competent, admired professional ready to take on the world.

I hated the woman I became with Casper. A woman who'd never take charge of her sexuality, the way I did with Hart. I felt so empowered after that kiss on the beach and later, screwing him in that cave.

I like who I'm evolving into: stronger, bolder, in control. Until this guy lays a finger on me and then I unravel.

'Daisy, are you listening?' He snaps his fingers in front of my face. 'I said this arrangement isn't working for me.'

'I thought you were happy with my work—'

'It's not that.' The grooves bracketing his mouth deepen and I hear a muttered 'fuck' under his breath. 'I can't stop thinking about you. It's distracting and affecting my work.'

Join the club, buddy.

I remain mute, curious as to where he's going with this.

'What do you think about a clear-cut short-term arrangement, where we indulge our passion?'

He sounds so formal, so old-fashioned, that I want to laugh. Some of my amusement must show on my too readable face because his mouth compresses into a thin line.

'You find my proposal funny?'

'Just the delivery. You sound like you've stepped out of the Austen era.'

The glower intensifies. He's not amused. 'Would you prefer if I said I want to fuck you every which way until you have to leave?'

Another wave of heat flushes my body. I'm too young for menopause but if this is what it's like I'm not looking forward to it.

'I prefer blunt,' I manage to say, resisting the urge to fan my face.

'Me too.' He rests his elbows on the table and leans forward. 'So what do you think? Is it doable?'

He's very doable.

I can string this out, make him squirm, but it's not my style. I'm tired of this push-pull game between us. I haven't let it affect my work yet because I'm too damn determined to show Alf what I'm capable of. But the sleepless nights will eventually catch up with me; there's only so much caffeine can do.

So I mimic his pose and inadvertently give him a glimpse of cleavage in the V of my top. His gaze rivets to it like an alarm laser homing in on an intruder. He has it bad. Good to know I'm not the only one.

I wave my hand in front of his face and his gaze instantly snaps up to mine.

'Don't make me beg,' he growls, his deep voice sending a shiver of excitement through me.

'It could be fun…'

I guffaw as his jaw clenches, like he's using every ounce of willpower not to vault the table and be on me in a second.

'What's it to be, Daisy? You in?'

He rests his forearms on the table, and his pinkie grazes the sensitive skin on the inside of my wrist.

I let out a gasp, knowing I don't have to respond, he has his answer right there.

But I nod anyway. 'I'm in.'

CHAPTER ELEVEN

Hart

I HATE WEAKNESS. I learned a valuable lesson when I entered my first foster home that if you show weakness you're a goner. Back then I cried because the older kids got ice cream after dinner and I didn't. I earned a hard smack on the backs of my legs with a metre-long wooden ruler that left bruises, so I never showed any kind of emotion after that other than anger. My deliberate fury served me well, alienating people before they could hurt me.

My sullen silences following my sudden rages meant I kept people at bay. They thought I had some kind of learning difficulty or behavioural issues. Not one person—foster parents, social workers, psychologists, teachers—figured out why I preferred to remain silent when I wasn't enraged. They labelled me hostile and surly. Nobody took the time to delve into why a young kid could be so antagonistic. It suited me, holding everyone at arm's length, disappointing them before they could do the same to me. Nobody cared.

Until Pa.

Somehow he took one look at my obstinate expression and knew. He didn't tolerate my moodiness and did everything in his power to make me laugh, from screening corny old movies I'd never heard of in his theatre room, to telling the worst jokes on the planet. I eventually thawed after eight long months, toning down my explosive temper, but what he never knew was it wasn't the jokes or the movies that made me perk up but his constant, unswerving attention.

Not once did he dismiss me as being irrelevant or stupid. Not once did he mock me for not knowing the difference between a fork and a seafood tine. He really *looked* at me and to this day I have no idea what he saw in my saturnine, ornery teen self.

The esteem I held him in was proven the day I set foot on this yacht. Because I couldn't swim I had a deep-seated fear of water. The fact that an older foster kid had held my head underwater in the bath when I'd been eight went some way to explaining my phobia. Pa didn't push but with his encouragement I eventually relented and took swimming lessons.

When I finally agreed to go out on his yacht he treated it as a monumental achievement, ignoring the fact I wouldn't remove my life jacket or the way I sat rigid in the stern, my knuckles white from clutching onto the railing.

Thankfully I've moved on from that terrifying day and I'm taking Daisy out on the water today.

It's just the two of us on the yacht and while this is technically a work jaunt, there'll be plenty of time for play when we anchor later.

I don't usually woo women but there's something indefinable about her that makes me want to impress.

'I've never been on a yacht before,' she says, reclining in the seat next to me. 'I'm impressed.'

'I thought you said the ghost was wealthy?'

She laughed. 'Casper had a lot of money but he preferred to see zeros growing in his bank account.'

'Tight-ass.'

'Yep.' She pokes me in the arm. 'Please don't spoil my first sailing trip by mentioning my ex.'

'Noted.'

I'm usually taciturn with women. Most find it a turn-on, always up for the challenge of figuring out what makes me tick. They like brooding and reserved, and I don't have the energy to be anything other than myself.

But I can't resist Daisy and those light-hearted smiles. She's shooting me one right now and for a second my chest tightens.

Her hair is loose, the sun highlighting the golden strands among the brown. She's snagged it with one hand so the wind doesn't blow it around her face. I want to see it wild in the gale that's picking up. Same with the dress she's wearing. I wouldn't mind seeing the skirt flip up. It's a red and white striped knee-length number that flares at the hem. It's riding up her thighs and I openly stare at her tanned legs.

'How big is it?'

'We're talking about the yacht, yeah?'

She rolls her eyes and flashes me another smile. 'Yeah.'

She's making me spar, which I like way too much to be good for me. But with fresh air filling my lungs, the rumble of the powerful engine beneath my feet, and a pretty girl by my side, I feel like I'm king of the world.

'It's forty-four foot, with a spacious living room, a fully equipped galley.' I pause for emphasis. 'And a killer master bedroom.'

'Oh?' She shoots me a flirty glance from beneath her lashes. 'Good to hear about the galley because I'm starving. You can whip me up a gourmet meal when we anchor.'

'The captain doesn't cook, the first mate does that and you're it today.'

'I burn water so unless you're teasing, we're going to go hungry today.'

'I can cook,' I admit, refraining from telling her that if I hadn't learned young I wouldn't have eaten. In the first two foster homes I was shunted to it was every man, woman and child for themselves, with the kids eating leftovers. The last before Pa found me was an eye-opener, with the family welcoming me as one of their own. I've never forgotten the meals I ate there: cottage pie, mac and cheese, chicken stir-fry, real comfort food that I enjoy to this day.

She winks. 'For what it's worth, I think a captain in the kitchen is pretty hot.'

'It's a galley on a yacht.' I sound like a dickhead

correcting her but I have to, either that or give in to the irrational urge to drop anchor when we've barely left the shore, drag her downstairs and give her a tour of the master bedroom she'll never forget.

'Kitchen, galley, whatever, as long as you're cooking in an apron, I'm there.' She rests her arms along the back of her seat and tilts her face to the sun. This time, my cock thickens with how badly I want her.

What the hell am I doing, drawing out the inevitable like some kind of torturous foreplay? She's agreed to a fling. I could be back at the resort right now, holed up in a villa with her naked. Instead, I'm prolonging this because she seems like the type of woman who enjoys the chase. Crazy, when technically I've already caught her.

'Why the frown?'

I glance at her and consciously blank my expression. 'I lied.'

'About?'

'I said today was about showing you the number one spot to take the best shot of the island but it's more than that. What we did in that cave was hot and since you agreed to this fling all I can think about is fucking you, but I don't want to be a douche who's all about the sex so I wanted to take you out and show you the sights today.'

Her hand flies to her mouth in mock horror. 'Don't tell me this is a D.A.T.E.?'

'I don't date.'

Her eyebrow quirks, calling me on my BS, and I begrudgingly add, 'Maybe.'

'Be still my beating heart.' She presses her hand to her chest, drawing my attention to a tantalising hint of cleavage.

Fuck the best vantage spot. I need to have her, now.

'There's a sheltered cove around the next outcrop, we'll anchor there.' I sound gruff and clear my throat. I clench the wheel so damn hard my knuckles stand out but I need to hold on tight to prevent myself from making a grab for her.

Her eyebrow rises. 'Are we at the spot already?'

'No, but I can't wait a moment longer to be inside you.'

Her mouth opens in a surprised O.

'I'm blunt. You'll get used to it.'

She tilts her head, studying me, as I belatedly realise that was a dumb thing to say. She shouldn't get used to me. She won't be around long enough. Besides, I don't want her hanging around to the extent she figures me out.

'Do you always say exactly what you're thinking?'

I shrug. 'I don't have time for games. If I want something, I go after it. If I like something, I admit it. Why lie?'

'Are you sure you have a Y chromosome?'

'Not all guys are liars, only the shitheads.'

She barks out a laugh. 'Well said. But in my experience it's rare to find an honest guy.'

'That Casper prick really did a number on you, didn't he?'

I expect her to rebuke me for bringing up the dickhead's name again. Instead, she gnaws on her bottom lip, making me push the lever to speed up. The sooner we get to that cove, the better.

'I don't understand how a guy can be so great one minute, then turn into a complete jerk the next.'

I don't want to ask. I don't want to know anything about her past relationships. All I care about is here and now. But I find myself asking regardless, 'Is that what happened?'

She nods, placing her hand over her eyes to shield them from the sun as she looks up at me. 'He treated me like a queen at the start, which is why I fell hard and fast. We got engaged after only three months and I moved in a week later. That's when things changed.'

She shakes her head, as if trying to dislodge a nasty memory. 'We moved away from my family so I couldn't see them as much. Spent all our time socialising with his friends, not mine. He started telling me what to wear, what to say, how to behave. Controlling everything.'

My hands tighten on the wheel again. I want to punch this dickhead in the mouth. 'He was abusive?'

'No, but I didn't stick around to find out what would have happened if I didn't do exactly as he said.' She lifts her head in defiance. Good girl.

'Smart. You're better off without him.'

'Not according to my family.'

I slow down as we round the outcrop of rocks. I can see the cove and I steer towards it. 'What's their problem?'

'The Adlers have this motto of never giving up.

We don't quit, it's not the done thing.' I hear a soft sigh that makes me want to hold her. 'Plus the same old cliché reasons. I'm the eldest of three daughters and have always been their touchstone. Perfect daughter, perfect sister, who became the perfect girlfriend and the perfect worker.' She makes a gagging sound. 'Turns out the guy I chose wasn't so perfect and I'm wondering if I'm kowtowing to a boss who undervalues me as some kind of retribution.'

'That's why this job is so important to you.'

'Yep. Doing a stellar PR campaign for your resort.' She shoots me a coy glance. 'And you will give me the kudos I need to consider going out on my own.'

'So you're basically using me for my name and my body,' I deadpan, relieved when she laughs.

'Hey, I think there are two bodies around here doing the using.'

Her gaze starts at my chest and drifts lower in a slow, leisurely perusal that makes me feel like she's stripped off my polo and shorts and left me naked.

'Whatever you're thinking, I like it.' I ease the yacht into the mouth of the cove and drop anchor.

'I'm thinking I've never felt this carefree,' she says, sounding wistful. 'It's tiring after a while, living up to expectations.'

'I know.'

The admission slips from my lips before I can censor it and I know, I just know, she's going to ask what I mean. Damn.

'Your grandfather?'

She homes in on the one subject I don't want to discuss but I can't cut her off without sounding rude. Besides, she's opened up about her ex and family; I'm only responding in kind.

'Yeah. I tried to be the grandson he wanted but I wasn't cut out to run an empire.' I grimace, the familiar feeling of unworthiness making me want to thump something. 'Ironic, considering that's exactly what I have to do now that he's gone.'

'I think you're wrong,' she says softly, reaching out to lay a hand on my forearm. 'You're exactly the kind of grandson he would've wanted. You're dedicated and loyal and hard-working, as evidenced by you being here when it's obvious your passion lies elsewhere.'

How the hell did she do that, read me so easily?

'Is it that obvious?'

'You travel the world when you could've been behind a desk all these years, so yeah, I guess.' She hesitates. 'I researched you. I know you were working for your grandfather but I came upon an article that mentioned you did some charity work for kids?'

Fuck, this is why I don't do conversation. Or dates. Discussing what I do in my own time isn't for public consumption and I don't need her treating me like some goddamn knight.

I shift my arm so her hand dislodges. Irrationally, I miss her touch. 'Any dickhead can don a suit, crunch numbers and issue orders.'

'You're underestimating yourself.' She folds her hands in her lap, the prim posture not detracting from her subtle sexiness one iota. 'You're a brilliant CEO.'

Thankfully she hasn't pushed for answers about my behind-the-scenes work with foster kids.

'Yeah, so brilliant I need to perform miracles to reverse the chain's downward spiral.' I eyeball her. 'And why you're here, remember?' I snort, showing exactly what I think of anyone having the tough job of using me to make the Rochester brand more appealing. 'You're a miracle worker if you can instil consumer confidence in *me*.'

I'm used to people not liking me; to making people not like me. It's what I've always done. But my bitterness is audible and the corners of her mouth droop. I've soured the mood. Typical.

'Want a tour of the yacht?' I hold out my hand to her, willing her to take it and forget our conversation. This is why I don't do deep and meaningful. It brings nothing but regret.

'Sure.'

I exhale in relief when she places her hand in mine and I tug her to her feet. I should release her hand. It's too...romantic, standing close on the bridge of the yacht, holding hands, staring into each other's eyes.

But I don't. Instead, I duck my head to brush a kiss across her lips, a promise of what's to come.

CHAPTER TWELVE

Daisy

THE MASTER STATEROOM is bigger than I expect. Pale wood cupboards and bedside tables, a cushioned curved love seat under the porthole window and a king-size bed covered in a lemon and blue bedspread with matching scatter pillows. I stare at the bed, imagining Hart doing all sorts of wicked things to me.

He's gripping my hand tightly, like he's expecting me to make a run for it. I figure I don't have to tell him there won't be a 'woman overboard' situation today, not when I'm so hot for him I can barely see straight.

It's not good, the way we bonded up on deck. Sharing snippets of our past. Chatting. Joking around. He's way too charming when he lowers his barriers and I find myself considering ways to make him do it more.

I can't get close to this man. It can only end badly for me. Aloof, reserved, hands-off, he's the kind of guy who would screw with my mind if I got too close, making me want to solve all his problems and make all the hurt go away. I've already lost too much of myself in the past getting caught up in a guy's life and trying to change the unchangeable—never again.

Hart is nothing more than my sexual sorbet. I must keep telling myself that and stay clear of personal topics. Because that underlying vulnerability I glimpse every time he mentions his grandfather slays me.

I know why I'm indulging this fling. Hart is the complete opposite of any guy I've ever been with. I like that he's dark and brooding and mostly silent. Words are frivolous and wasted on him. Which explains why I practically hang on his every one whenever he speaks.

With what he revealed up on deck it's obvious he doesn't want to be here, taking his grandfather's place as head of the hotel conglomerate. He'll leave once the business is stabilised, back to his altruistic work with kids. It's a noble cause. Which makes it harder to understand why he doesn't want to talk about it. It's like he has a hate-on for the world and doesn't give a crap, when he obviously does.

I can't fathom how tough it must've been growing up in the foster system, but that was a long time ago. He speaks highly of his grandfather so I assume they had a good relationship. In fact, he wouldn't be back here assuming control if they hadn't.

So why is he so damn grim all the time?

I don't have time to ponder when I hear the door close and he comes to stand behind me. His body doesn't touch mine but I can feel the heat radiating off him. I'm hot from head to toe, knowing I'm in way over my head but powerless to stop.

When we had sex in the cave it was spontaneous and wild and hedonistic. Today is different. Revealing snippets of ourselves has made us more aware of each other. I saw it in the way he looked at me up on deck and I'm sure my expression mirrored his: like I'd made assumptions about him, only to find there's so much more simmering beneath his glowering surface.

He takes a step closer and rests his hands on my waist. I burn beneath his touch, my stomach falling away when he kisses the back of my neck. A soft kiss that grazes my skin and sends a shiver of sheer want through me.

His hands slide down over my hips and bunch my skirt, then his palms are on my skin. I quiver and lean back against him, grateful for the support considering my knees are wobbly.

'You feel so good,' he murmurs in my ear, nipping the lobe as his palms slide higher. 'Smooth. Hot.'

Wait until he hits my really hot spot.

I don't have long to wait as he hooks his thumbs into the elastic of my panties and eases them down. I like that he's taking things slow this time, in contrast to our frantic sex in the cave. I've fantasised about this, about being with him with a bed in the vicinity, and I'm so turned on from his simple touch I can't see straight.

My senses are heightened, not being able to see

him. I can't get a read on him if I can't see him and not knowing where he's going to touch me next is so hot.

As he slides my panties down he kneels. I know this because my back is suddenly cold and his hands return to my waist, gently insistent in turning me around.

When I do I gasp because he's staring at me with adoration. This stubborn, recalcitrant man is on his knees in front of me, relinquishing control, ready to give me pleasure. It's incredibly heady stuff for a girl like me, who thinks all the talk of prolonged foreplay in magazines is a myth.

'Beautiful,' he says, leaning forward to kiss me *there*.

I whimper.

I sense him smile as his tongue darts out and zeroes in on my clit, making me clutch the top of his head for balance.

He licks me over and over, his tongue delving and probing and driving me wild with an expertise that is definitely no myth. Hart is giving me the best head of my life and it's real.

Pleasure snakes through me as he laps at my clit, short, sharp strokes designed to drive me over the edge. It usually takes me a while to come this way but as my muscles clench and the ripples of release shimmer, I realise it's no fault of mine, and everything to do with the guy.

His hands grab my ass, anchoring me, as his tongue circles me faster and faster, and I'm gone.

Writhing against this mouth. Tugging on his hair. Screaming my release as I buck against him, wanting this exquisite pleasure to never end.

My knees buckle but he's there, standing, and holding my ass he lifts me onto the love seat. It's the perfect height and I wrap my legs around him.

His expression is fierce as he unzips, like he's hell-bent on pleasuring me. He won't get any protests. But we haven't spoken since he gave me the best orgasm of my life and I have no idea if I should thank him or return the favour.

'I've wanted to fuck you since we set foot on this yacht.' His tone is barely above a growl and it reverberates deep inside where I want him most.

'Then do it.'

I tilt my chin up in defiance and spread my legs. His hungry gaze zeroes in on where I want him to be. My breathing is shallow, my nipples so hard they hurt, my skirt is rucked up and I've never felt so wanton.

I watch him tear open a foil and roll on a condom like he has all the time in the world. Either he's teasing me or he has the self-control of a monk.

I wriggle closer until I'm teetering on the edge of the love seat. Sensing my desperation, he claims my mouth in a kiss that defies logic. His tongue plunders my mouth, ravaging me with a precision that makes me go a little wild.

I claw at him, trying to gain purchase, grasping at his chest, his shoulders. And just when I'm on the verge of begging, he slides inside. Full and long and thick, making me gasp with the depth of his penetration, making me crave everything he's willing to give.

I tear my mouth away so I can watch, leaning back on my outstretched arms. My boldness is a turn-on if his reaction is any indication: he withdraws slowly, inch by exquisite inch, before thrusting into me hard. Over and over until I'm panting, desperately clinging to the edge of sanity, the pleasure is that intense.

My muscles tense and I writhe, eager for release. His gaze, smouldering and confident, locks on mine as he lifts my butt slightly and changes the angle of his hips, driving into me with calculated precision.

He hits my sweet spot and I come apart, wave after wave of soul-searing release swamping me until I'm floating.

He groans a moment later but I'm oblivious, lost, stunned.

I'm boneless when he lifts me and lays me on the bed. I don't expect a cuddle. I'm not that naïve. We're indulging in a sexual fling and it's stupendous.

But when he stares at me, an inscrutable expression in those fathomless eyes, I feel compelled to say something to articulate how freaking fantastic that was.

However, as I try to come up with something suitably light-hearted, a wave of nausea washes over me.

Crap.

While I was upright the rocking boat didn't bother me but now that I'm lying down my stupid body is registering the change in posture. Repeated ear infections as a kid ensure I'm not a great traveller and motion sickness can be a problem.

I'd been fine with the boat moving while standing but now, with it anchored and bobbing and me horizontal, I'm in trouble.

My stomach gripes and a cold sweat breaks out over my body. Hell. This isn't going to be pretty.

'I'm sorry,' I manage to say, surging off the bed and making it to the bathroom just in time.

I slam the door and bend over the toilet, retching. It's not good. That tropical fruit salad I had for breakfast was a bad idea.

I try to stand but my body has other ideas and I retch again and again until nothing is left. Weak and woozy, I finally push to a stand and prop myself on the basin. Glancing in the mirror is a mistake. I look like shit, a weird grey-green colour with watery eyes.

Groaning, I splash water on my face and rinse my mouth out. I open the glass cabinet and thankfully there are fresh toiletries there. I tear open a plastic-covered toothbrush, squeeze a dollop of paste from a mini dispenser and brush my teeth. Only then do I start to feel slightly human again.

This time when I look in the mirror the green has given way to pale but I feel better. Time to face Hart and explain my humiliating bolt from the bedroom.

I open the bathroom door and he's pacing, his expression formidable. When he spies me, he takes two steps towards me then stops, as if he doesn't want to get too close.

'Are you okay?'

I nod and wrinkle my nose. 'Sorry about that.'

His eyes turn flinty. 'You have nothing to apologise for.'

Too late, I remember he has a weird thing for apologising when it isn't one's fault.

I point at my ears. 'These go wonky sometimes so when I lie down on a moving vessel...' I mimic barfing. 'It's not pretty.'

He doesn't say anything for an eternity and when he moves it's so swift he startles me. He pulls me into his arms, one hand clasping me tight at the waist, the other cradling the back of my head against his chest.

I feel his heart thudding against my cheek and it's disarming how much I like being comforted. I'm under no illusion that's what he's doing. He may be a man of few words but his actions speak volumes and he looked tortured when I opened the bathroom door.

'I'm okay,' I murmur, when he finally releases me. 'Though I feel like an idiot for disrupting your plans to spoon me.'

I smile, hoping my joke will alleviate the tension bracketing his mouth. It doesn't.

With a final glower, he stalks out of the cabin and slams the door.

CHAPTER THIRTEEN

Hart

I'M IN HELL.

I don't do emotions. I don't do closeness. And I certainly don't do comforting, but I indulged in all three and am reeling because of it.

I hated hearing her retch. I wanted to barge into the head and do something to help but I couldn't, gripped by a foreign helplessness when I'm usually decisive. Then to make matters worse she opened the door, I took one look at her wan face and a surge of protectiveness made me hold her, wanting to do anything to make things better for her.

I'm not that guy.

I can't be any woman's fucking hero.

So I dragged my sorry ass up here, drew the anchor and we're moving again. The faster we get to the other island, the best vantage for Gem Island, the better.

I hear a footfall behind me, followed by a murmured, 'Hey.'

'Hey.' I will myself not to turn, waiting for her to climb the few steps up to the bridge.

Like the bastard I am, I studiously avoid looking at her, still shaken by my feelings back in the cabin.

'Why the hell did you run back there?' She sounds confused rather than angry, with just a hint of uncertainty. It's like a slug to the gut all over again.

'I thought you needed time to recover,' I say, brusque to the point of rudeness.

'Bullshit.'

God, I love her boldness.

'Leave it alone,' I grit out. She'll think I'm a selfish prick, treating her with disdain after great sex. Then again, I should be glad to alienate her considering how out of sorts I'm feeling.

'The hell I will,' she snaps, her signature brashness making me smirk. 'And what's so damn funny?'

'I'm a dick and you don't hold back in calling me out on it.' I risk a glance at her and she's frowning, but colour has returned to her cheeks.

When she made an odd sound on the bed I thought it was excitement for more, until I took one look at her sickly green face. I was seasick the first time Pa took me out on the yacht so I know the signs. I wanted to make it easier for her because I know how shitty it felt, that's all, but my urge to protect has made me feel off kilter ever since.

'At least you acknowledge you're a dick.' She sounds begrudgingly admiring but is still frowning.

'I'm in this for the fuck-fest, I've made that more

than clear. If you're expecting hearts and flowers crap, it's not me.'

Her eyebrow arch is signature. 'You think I'll be scared off because you're an emotionless drone?'

'Just saying it how it is.'

She makes a cute snorting sound. 'You don't need to spell out we're just sex, I know that.' Her eyes sparkle with mischief. 'But FYI, holding me after I've barfed may be misconstrued as you actually having a heart.'

'Don't spread the news around.'

My flippancy earns her first genuine smile since she came back on deck.

But it fades all too soon. 'Seriously, I get it. This is a fling. Nothing more. But it's inevitable we're going to bond a little beyond the obvious.' She shoots a pointed look at my groin and my dick hardens. 'So don't freak out when it happens. Because it will. And I want to have more of that sensational sex and you going all strong and silent isn't helping.'

Damn, I admire her bluntness. She's the female version of me.

'Bonding isn't my style but yeah, you're right. We're working together, we're fucking, it's bound to happen.'

The corners of her mouth twitch when I add, 'Just don't go getting any ideas.'

'Like what? That you might actually care beneath that frosty exterior?'

'Hey, watch it, all this sentimental crap is making me want to barf and we both can't be fighting for the porcelain bowl.'

She laughs as I intend. 'There must be other toilets on this floating palace.'

'They're called heads on a marine vessel.'

A slow blush steals across her cheeks. 'Speaking of head…damn, you're good at it.'

Her sense of humour kills me as much as the rest of her. She's so goddamn addictive and I'm in serious trouble. Because, despite my protestations that I don't bond, we already have. First the phenomenal sex, then my urge to hold her. Emotions are for saps and I turned mine off a long time ago.

Focussing on sex is more my style. 'I can't wait to get you on dry land.'

'Why wait?' She bats her eyelashes. 'I'm fine while the boat is moving, I just can't lie down.'

'And who's going to steer?' I lower my voice. 'Because trust me, babe, when I'm deep inside you, as you well know, I want all my focus on you.'

I watch her throat convulse in a swallow. 'Okay.'

We fall silent but it's comfortable. Another surprise, because when I date women all they want to do is talk when we're not fucking, incessant chatter for the hell of it; endless inane questions that do my head in. It's why I don't usually date the same woman twice. Because after one date they feel entitled to delve and I don't want that.

If I wanted some woman to stick her nose into my business twenty-four-seven I'd get married.

Never going to happen.

When the silence stretches to five minutes I risk a quick sideways glance, sorry I did. She has her face tilted to the sun, eyes closed, a small secretive smile playing about her mouth. A woman enjoying the day on a beautiful yacht under the perfect Queensland sun, a beguiling mix of angel and vixen, like she knows something I don't.

Lust slams me like a punch to the jaw, ferocious and startling, before the inevitable emptiness sets in. I can't want her this much. I don't want to know what's behind that smile. I won't get too attached to my island fuck-buddy.

Stick to the plan, dickhead, and you'll be fine.

I have to be.

CHAPTER FOURTEEN

Daisy

I CAN'T LIE. I'm glad to be back on terra firma.

'What do you think, landlubber?'

How does he do that, home in on exactly what I'm thinking yet again? He gestures at the stunning vista before us, squaring his shoulders in pride, like he manually constructed Gem Island by hand.

'You're right. This is the perfect spot to take pictures of the island for the revamped brochures and online advertising.' I squint a little. 'Though to be honest, it's almost too picture perfect. Tourists will think all that cerulean ocean and lush greenery is digitally enhanced.'

'Isn't the whole point of PR to talk up the place so they come and see for themselves?'

'Yeah, but this…' I sigh, wishing I could be so lucky as to live and work here permanently. Hart has that opportunity but he can't wait to escape. Madness. 'It takes your breath away.'

'I thought that was me.'

I chuckle. I love a dry sense of humour and he has one of the best when he lets his guard down, which isn't often enough. 'Keep telling yourself that, stud.'

'I didn't hear any complaints earlier,' he murmurs, his deep voice so damn compelling I feel it all the way down to where he had his tongue buried on the boat.

'I've praised you enough for that.' I sound priggish and toss my hair for good measure.

He laughs, a genuine bellow that startles some parakeets out of a nearby palm tree. 'You can never praise a guy enough for his prowess. We're a bunch of egotistical Neanderthals that way.'

Enjoying our sparring more by the minute, I respond, 'Well, just so you know, I don't give praise lightly and there's a *lot* of difference in prowess between Neanderthals.'

'Then I'm flattered.'

'You should be.'

His expression is relaxed, almost serene, and at complete odds with his perpetual glower. All this playful banter about him giving me the best head of my life has me focussing on his mouth and remembering…

'You're easy to read, you know that?'

I drag my eyes from his mouth to find him staring at me, wild-eyed, like he did back on the boat right before we went down to the cabin.

'So I've been told.' I circle my face with a fingertip. 'Open book here.'

'We all have secrets,' he says, eyeing me with an

intensity that makes me want to tear off my clothes. 'And I don't give a shit. All I care about right now is fucking you.'

His husky response ripples over me like a physical caress and my skin pebbles. My nipples are tight peaks, begging for attention. But I know it can't be all about me, not this time.

I glance around the secluded slice of beach hugging the south side of this tiny island. He moored at a jetty about a mile away and we walked along a rough-hewn rocky path between lush, jungle-like foliage to get here. It's uninhabited, owned by some preservation society determined to protect islands in the Whitsundays.

I've never been gladder for the conservationist cause because if we're alone in paradise I know exactly what to do.

'Come with me.' I grab his hand and tug on it. An eyebrow rises but he lets me drag him higher up the beach towards the tree line.

When we reach the shade of the palms, I glance around one last time, nerves making me second-guess this wild decision. But we're completely alone and unless there are some serious badass zoom lenses on a satellite far above, no one can see what I'm about to do.

'What is it about island heat that makes me so damn horny?' He doesn't answer my rhetorical question as I release his hand and reach for his zipper, his eyes wide, his expression solemn.

'Fuck,' he mutters as I lower his zip carefully, delighting in his tortured expression.

This is going to be fun. I undo the top button of his shorts, then slide my hand inside his jocks.

Velvet steel. Soft and hard. Perfect.

He moans as I take his cock out and kneel. The head brushes my cheek and I turn, swiping it with my tongue.

'Fuck, Daisy…'

'You will, later,' I say, before taking him into my mouth.

He tastes salty, musky, delicious. I work my hand up and down his shaft in time with my mouth, an easy rhythm that makes me feel confident and empowered.

He starts to thrust and we work in sync, my tongue swirling while my hand pumps, over and over until he's muttering incoherently.

It's heady stuff, knowing I can make a commanding guy come undone. It's incredibly empowering, and I squeeze and suck harder at the same time, relishing his moans.

'Daisy…' His cry is raw as he comes in a hot rush, followed by a long, drawn-out guttural groan that is so damn honest I feel like a queen.

I ease away and when I stand he's staring at me like I've bestowed the greatest gift.

'You are phenomenal.' He cups my face, the intensity of his stare beginning to unnerve me.

Oddly bashful, I try not to squirm. 'One good head deserves another.'

The corners of his mouth lift. 'You're mixing up your metaphors or analogies or whatever it is.'

'I'd rather we continue to mix business with pleasure.'

I need to get away, to put some distance between us, because I can't stand the way he's looking at me.

Like I matter.

I got the message loud and clear on the boat: we're sex, nothing more. He's my sorbet. That's it. Any bonding is superficial at best. I want it this way.

So why do I get the feeling that having scorching sex with this guy has the potential to lead to complications neither of us want?

CHAPTER FIFTEEN

Hart

I'M IN SO much fucking trouble.

Drowning, in way over my head, and it's got nothing to do with the water surrounding us as we head back to Gem Island.

Sex has served me well. Uncomplicated, no strings, a release. That's what this thing with Daisy is supposed to be but the reality is getting…complicated.

I'll take all the earth-shattering blowjobs she cares to dish out but I can't deal with my irrational reaction whenever I'm near her.

Like a quickie isn't enough.

The sex is phenomenal and that's part of the attraction, I get it. But her feistiness in not copping my bullshit arouses me as much as her hot curves. And that's not a good thing. Indulging in mutually satisfying sex is one thing; wanting to know more about her is quite another.

I can't believe she confronted me after my freak out when I comforted her in the cabin. Worse, she knows we've bonded beyond the physical today despite all protestations to the contrary.

I can't let her get too close. My head's in the game about this being just sex, but is hers? She's saying all the right things but I'm wary. I need to re-establish distance. So I've turned mute.

She's abandoned me on the bridge in favour of taking a seat in the shade starboard. Said she wanted a nana nap, determined to stay vertical to do it after her earlier hurl. But I know better. She got tired of my silence. Hell, I'm sick of myself in this kind of mood.

Pa knew to leave me alone when I was like this. He never pushed or questioned, he respected my need for quiet. I should be thankful Daisy is the same, but I can't help wonder what's going on in that pretty head of hers.

Is she regretting hooking up with me?

Is she really okay with this casual arrangement?

Is she expecting more of today: more talk, more revelations, just *more*?

I need to maintain my distance for a while. Regain perspective. Ensure I'm hardened to the riot of uncharacteristic emotions whirling through me like a cyclone.

I usually don't *feel* much of anything. I'm not emotionally stunted, I'm dead inside. I had to be, to cope with the horrors of my past. Feigning lack of interest worked with my first foster father, a sadistic bastard who forced me to call him Dad, when enduring a beating with a metal rod or being flayed with a whip, the only way to survive was to detach myself. It soon became a habit.

My next foster family was uninterested rather than nasty and my last was great, but by then I was thirteen and already closed off.

Only Pa got through to me and that was because he was as bull-headed as me: he never gave up. He pushed until I had no option but to let him in. But now he's gone and it's all too easy to revert to what I know best: disengaging.

As we dock at Gem Island's marina it has to start now. I ignore her as I kill the engine and tie up, only acknowledging her presence when I give her a hand up onto the dock.

'Thanks.' She shoots me a tentative smile and I glimpse confusion in her eyes.

She must think I'm a crackpot; my moods swing that erratically. I don't care. I need to do this. Self-preservation has always come first for me.

'Will I see you tonight?'

I hate how my first response is 'hell yeah' so I say the exact opposite. 'Sorry, I've got a shitload of work to do after skiving today.'

'Understood.' She pins me with an astute stare. 'Before I set up the online media profiles, I need to clarify one thing.'

Relieved she's reverted to professional, I say, 'What's that?'

'What to include in your bio.' She hesitates, before tilting her chin up. 'You didn't respond earlier when I mentioned your charity work with kids—'

'I don't want any of that mentioned,' I snap, feeling like a bastard when she recoils. 'Focus on the hotels, that's it. My work with foster kids is off-limits, got it?'

'Fine.' But it's not. Her jaw clenches and her eyes shoot daggers. 'I'll get the staff profiles done and I'll organise the photographer to get across to that island tomorrow.'

'You do that.'

I feign lack of interest to prevent her asking further questions I'd rather not answer and predictably she draws her shoulders back like she's preparing for battle. But I don't want to fight. I want to be left the hell alone so I don't do something I'll regret—like blurt out exactly how much I want her but without all the accompanying complications.

'I get that you're not a people person.' She folds her arms and glares at me with contempt. 'But if my research is correct and you do spend time with kids, they smell bullshit a mile away. So that means you're just rude and tetchy around me. And you know what my response to that is?'

Before I can berate her for mentioning the kids again, she flips me the bird and stalks away, leaving me filled with admiration and clamping down on the urge to run after her.

CHAPTER SIXTEEN

Daisy

I HAVE A lot of work to do. Emails to answer, final approvals on campaigns to be given. However, when I get back to my villa, I head straight for the shower.

I need to wash off the day.

If only memories could be as easily soaped and slicked away as the sweat clinging to my skin in this infernal humidity. But I can't get bloody Hart out of my head. He's the most infuriating, boorish, moody guy I've ever met.

I still want him more than ever.

Flipping off a client isn't the smartest thing to do but I was so mad on the dock I could've easily shoved him into the water and hoped he choked on a lungful of it.

He can be so attentive one minute and a frosty asshole the next. I'd like to say I'm done but that would make me a liar. I want more of the mind-blowing sex and his talented tongue. I just need to get my head around the fact he's an irritable jerk and focus on the physical stuff.

I can do this.

Besides, sorbet isn't always sweet. It can be tart and edgy but in the end it achieves the same result: leaving the palate cleansed. Hart is my sorbet, so no more shared confidences or moments of intimacy. We have sex, we enjoy it, that's it.

Humming a song about being a woman and being able to roar, I towel off and slip into my PJs. Room service as I work sounds perfect tonight. Staying in has the added bonus of not running into Hart and possibly strangling him despite my vow to view him as a giant, lickable scoop in a cone.

I deal with emails first. It takes thirty minutes and I only stop towards the end to order Moreton Bay bug ravioli and a deconstructed strawberry parfait. Considering I emptied my stomach contents on the yacht, I'm hoping it doesn't take too long.

I'm absorbed in compiling a diplomatic response to Alf's latest demands when there's a knock on the door. My stomach growls in anticipation and I run towards it.

However, when I open it, I'm not served with ravioli and parfait.

I get sorbet instead.

'What are you doing here?'

Hunger makes me grouchy and Hart's taken aback at my less than cordial greeting. What did he expect, for me to throw out the welcome mat after the way he chastised me on the dock for asking a simple question?

'Can I come in?' he asks, but he's not looking at

my face. He's checking out my attire and I resist the urge to put my hands on my hips and give a shimmy for good measure.

'I'm not dressed for company,' I say, sounding suitably snooty.

'Get changed.' That damnably kissable mouth quirks into a half-grin. 'Or take them off.'

Heat arrows between my legs, damn him.

'My PJs are staying on.' I jerk a thumb over my shoulder. 'Besides, I'm working.'

He's still staring at my outfit. 'Are those ice-cream cones?'

I shrug. 'What can I say? I love the stuff.'

'Sorbet in particular.' His voice turns husky and I'm reminded by exactly how yummy he is.

'You really have to go—'

'But aren't you hungry?'

I sigh and lean against the door. 'I'm not in the mood for word games—'

'I passed the waiter with your order and seeing as we were both headed in the same direction...' He pulls a trolley out from behind the neatly trimmed hedge shielding one villa from another. 'Your dinner.'

'Bring it in please,' I say begrudgingly, because I really am starving and the thing looks like it weighs a tonne. Even with his impressive biceps he struggles with manoeuvring it over the incline into the villa.

After he positions it near the desk, he turns to me. 'Do I get a tip?'

'Yeah, be good to your PR whiz.'

He gives me a lopsided smile. 'I thought the PR whiz prefers it if I'm bad.' He leans in closer and I grit my teeth against the urge to bury my face in his neck. 'Very, very bad.'

'Enough.' I put up a hand. Like that's going to stop him if he wants to come closer. 'I'm mad at you.'

'I know. And I deserve it.' He shakes his head and his mouth downturns into its signature moue. 'I came to apologise.'

I won't make it easy for him, despite his hangdog expression. 'How noble of you.'

He winces. 'I've been a prick because it's who I am and I don't like getting personal and I've fucked this up badly.'

Okay, so his gut-honest declaration gets to me a little.

'Just so you know, I'm not a fan of roller coasters. Never have been. They make me barf worse than stationary boats. So this temperamental thing you've got going on followed by lame-ass apologies?' I make a slicing action across my neck. 'I've had it up to here. It's not going to cut it.'

His hangdog expression makes me want to hug him. 'Yeah, I know. Can we talk?'

I shouldn't waver. I should abandon talk altogether when it comes to this lunatic and focus on the physical. But he's staring at me with those big puppy eyes, practically pleading with me to hear him out, so I relent. I'm a wuss like that.

'Fine.' I shut the door and gesture to the comfy-cushioned cane sofa. 'Knock yourself out.'

'I was way out of line when I snapped at you down on the dock in relation to my work with kids.'

'Yeah, you were.'

I wait until he sits so I can sit opposite. The last thing I need is to have him too close on the sofa.

'What I'm about to tell you is private and can't appear anywhere in relation to the hotels, got it?'

I refrain from rolling my eyes at him for stating the obvious and settle for a nod.

'I do a lot of behind the scenes work for foster kids around the world, setting up outreach centres so they have a safe place to go when needed.'

He glances away but not before I glimpse pain, the kind of soul-deep agony I have no hope of understanding. 'It's public knowledge I was a foster kid when Pa found me. He gave me so much that I like to pay it forward with other kids.'

He taps his chest. 'I know what they're going through because I've been there, done that. And I don't need fucking praise from anybody for it, so that's why I prefer to keep it private.'

There's so much more he's not telling me. I see it in the compressed lips, in the bunched shoulders, in the rigid neck. He's hurting and it's more than pity for the kids he empathises with.

But I've learned my lesson. I'm not going to push. I'm stunned he's shared this much with me and for now it'll have to do.

'I hate having to explain myself to you…' He shakes his head, his mouth so twisted it's like I'm torturing him with nipple clamps. Not that I know

what that's like. I've heard. Online. As part of research for the PR I did on a sex-toy store. 'We both
know the score. We're fucking, that's it. But this just
feels way too complicated.'

My heart sinks. 'It doesn't have to be.'

He waves his hand between us. 'The fact I'm here
apologising for my behaviour when I hate doing that
is testament that this is more than sex.'

He's right, damn him.

So I need to get this back onto an even keel, by
doing something we both understand: focussing on
our sexual attraction.

'Don't sweat it. We both know you coming here
and sustaining a dent in your alpha armour is your
warped version of foreplay.'

'Dammit, you're making this difficult,' he growls
and only then do I allow a smile.

The moment he sees my smug grin his shoulders
relax and he slumps back in the sofa. 'You're toying with me.'

'Just a little?' I hold up my thumb and forefinger
an inch apart and he chuckles.

'Am I forgiven?'

'Yeah, but only because I'm too hungry to continue this conversation.' I pad across the room to
where he's set up the trolley. 'You hungry?'

'I'm good.'

'Great, because I'm too ravenous to share. Here's
the plan. I'm going to shovel this ravioli and strawberry parfait into my mouth as fast as humanly possible, then I'm going to do some work.'

'But what if you feel like sorbet after eating all that?'

His tone is silky smooth, rippling over me like a caress. My skin pebbles into tiny goose bumps and my nipples harden to tight peaks, immediately drawing his gaze.

'Some of your ice-cream cones seem to have a cherry on top,' he says, with a wicked smirk.

I laugh and he joins in. 'Okay, you can stay.'

'Good.' His eyes darken as they sweep over me. 'Because you're not the only one with a sweet tooth and I have a sudden hankering for some ice cream.'

Heat flushes my cheeks as I remember exactly how good he is at licking. 'You know, we've never had sorbet in bed. It might be fun.'

'That's what I'm thinking.'

He's thinking a lot more than that by the lascivious glint in his eyes.

I swoon a little. I'm light-headed from hunger. My excuse and I'm sticking to it.

'Eat,' he commands and I do as I'm told while he slouches on my sofa and flips through the magazines on the coffee table.

The ravioli is divine, succulent slivers of Moreton Bay bugs encased in handmade pasta and covered in white wine sauce. The deconstructed parfait is just as good, with strawberries, meringue, cream, lemon curd and a berry coulis artfully arranged on a triangular white plate.

Only when I'm done do I glance up to find him watching me, his gaze riveted to my mouth.

'What? Do I have something on my lip?'

'Not yet, but you're about to.' He launches himself off the sofa and I yelp, pushing back from the trolley and skittering around the work desk. The villa isn't small but it's not built for chasing either and I'm soon cornered by a big, hulking, brute of a man with one thing on his mind.

Luckily it's the same thing that's on mine.

'I know a good way to work off that meal,' he says, leaning forward to brush a kiss across my cheek.

His lips are like a feather grazing my skin, barely there but making me shiver with the slightest touch. He trails butterfly kisses along my jaw towards my ear.

'By the way, that blowjob blew my mind,' he whispers, flicking my lobe with his tongue so his warm breath fans it and makes me bite down on my bottom lip to stop from whimpering. 'You give great head.'

'So do you,' I manage to say. It comes out a high-pitched squeak as he places his hands on my waist and lightly guides me towards the bed.

I'm taking mincing steps backwards but he's not in any hurry, every step punctuated by a kiss: on the point of my shoulder, on my collarbone, on my jaw.

It's pure exquisite torture because I want that talented mouth on me in other, more sensitive areas.

The backs of my knees hit the bed and he steadies me when I fall backwards.

'These really are very cute,' he says, plucking at the hem of my pyjama top.

'Wouldn't you prefer sexy?'

'What's underneath is all the sexy I need.' He tugs at the hem and peels the top off, his gaze zeroing in on my breasts. 'Oh, yeah, so fucking sexy.'

I don't move because I sense he wants to take this slow and I'm rewarded when he places his hands on my shoulders and slides them lower. Over my biceps, my elbows, my forearms. He reaches my hands and covers them with his. He guides them towards my breasts.

'I want to see you do this.'

His thumbs and forefingers are over mine, guiding me, rolling my nipples. I'm doing it under his instruction and it's so damn hot I feel dampness between my legs.

'Don't stop,' he says as his hands slide lower, fingertips fluttering over my ribcage, dipping in at my waist, skirting my hips before delving into the elastic of my shorts.

He pushes them down and they fall, pooling at my feet. I kick them away and suck in a breath when his hands palm my ass. He kneads while watching me play with my nipples, his lips slightly parted, his breathing shallow.

I throb with wanting him but he makes me wait. Dipping a finger into the cleft of my ass while sliding the other hand around to the front.

I arch my pelvis forward and he tut-tuts. 'Not so fast.'

'I need...you.'

'And you'll have me, but I want to play first.'

He slides a finger into me and I moan.

'So fucking wet.' His voice is rough and he stares at me in a daze as he continues to finger me. In and out. A low leisurely pace like he has all the time in the world to make me come.

I'm not that patient.

I've never done this before, tweaking my nipples while a guy tries to get me off and it's super hot. But I'm naked and he has too many clothes on. I want to feel his skin against mine. I want it all.

I unbutton his shirt with fumbling fingers and he shrugs it off without stopping what he's doing, expertly swapping hands.

'My, my, you're talented.'

The corner of his mouth kicks up. 'I thought you would've already figured that out by now.'

'I figure flattery will get me everywhere so the more I pile it on, the better you'll be.'

'High expectations. I can live with that.' He watches me unsnap his button and unzip.

My heart pounds as I take him in hand and squeeze. He growls in response and I feel it all the way down to my toes. He lowers me onto the bed and I'm left hovering on the edge, cloying at an orgasm that's just out of reach.

'Patience,' he says, reading my mind as he shucks off his boxers and trousers. 'We're taking it slow tonight, remember?'

'Get back here.' I scoot backwards up the bed and pat it. He doesn't need to be asked twice.

He lowers himself over me, propping himself up on his elbows and caging me with his impressive biceps. I arch my pelvis, so needy. He chuckles and nips my neck, his bite treading a fine line between pleasure and pain.

'I love how you smell,' he murmurs, trailing his nose against my skin.

'And taste.' He swipes his tongue from my collarbone to my ear, a long lick that sends a shiver of desperation through me.

'I need you inside me now.'

When he looks at me with an amused quirk of his brow, I add a demure, 'Please.'

He pushes off me momentarily and that foil ripping is the sweetest sound I've ever heard. We have all night to do slow. But he's driven me mad with his push-pull behaviour and now I want to show him exactly how good we are together—between the sheets, of course.

I watch him roll on the condom. It's beyond erotic because I know what taking him in my hand feels like. The strength of him. The length. The breadth. Magnificent.

But he's not done toying with me yet. He rests his hands on my thighs and gently pries them apart. My legs fall open willingly. I know what's coming and my nerve endings zap in anticipation. He's very, very good at this.

His stubble tickles the inside of my thighs as he

kisses his way towards where I want him most. I wriggle impatiently and he murmurs something that sounds like 'fuck me'.

'Believe me, that's all I want to do,' I whisper, ending on a moan when he swirls his tongue over my clit.

He lifts his mouth. 'Better?'

'More,' I demand, and give a little shimmy for emphasis.

His impish smile tells me I'm about to get exactly what I wish for, as he dips his head and devours me.

Little teasing licks, stronger swipes, nips and kisses and then he starts sucking. I'm gone, my body winding tighter and higher until I'm flying, the power of my orgasm blinding me to everything but him.

Before I float back to my body he's inside me. A long, smooth thrust that's decadent and divine.

'You feel so good,' I murmur, grabbing onto his shoulders, winding my legs around his waist.

'Right back at you.'

Our gazes lock as he starts to move. Exquisitely, torturously, slow. I never knew I had a G spot until he slides his hands under my ass and lifts me slightly, so I'm locked around him with my legs in the tightest fit possible.

He's taking his time, hitting that damn spot with every single thrust and I'm starting to go a little crazy, the pleasure so intense it borders on pain.

I dig my nails into his shoulders when he changes the angle again, the slightest shift making me gasp. I want to plead with him to end this exquisite torture and he must see something in my eyes because he moves faster. Pounding into me until I can't breathe, the tension clawing at my body is that great. It builds and spirals until I'm blown apart in a detonation of pleasure so intense I feel tears burning my eyes.

Thankfully he doesn't see because he lowers his head the moment before he comes on a bellow that makes the hairs on the back of my neck snap to attention.

Neither of us speak.

There's nothing to say.

Besides, how can I articulate the most terrifying thought?

You've ruined me for other men.

CHAPTER SEVENTEEN

Hart

I'VE NEVER SPENT the night with a woman.

It's disarming to discover I want to despite every self-preservation mechanism in my body telling me to do the opposite and run from this villa as fast as humanly possible.

Daisy asked me to stay and after the way I treated her earlier today I can't say no.

'I didn't pick you for a cuddler,' she says, glancing up at me from the crook of my shoulder where her head currently rests.

'I'm not.' I sound gruff and temper it with. 'But I can't get enough of you and I'll be ready for round two shortly.'

'Only twice?' She whacks me playfully on the chest. 'Don't forget you're spending the night, mister, so I expect you to double that tally at least.'

'Done,' I say, tightening my hold on her.

She snuggles in tighter and, surprisingly, that insistent urge to bolt fades.

What's so bad about staying the night, ensuring I wake up with an armful of hot woman? It's not like she's slipping a gold band on my finger or anything.

'Want to hear something funny?'

I'm not a talker in bed either. Once the deed is done I'm out of bed so I can get home, usually to a hotel room. But that's another anomaly tonight: I don't mind her ramblings.

'Sure.'

'I've never had a holiday fling.' Her chuckle borders on a girly giggle. 'And even though technically I'm working, I'm at a fabulous resort with a hot guy so it feels like a holiday.'

'You won't say that when I make you work overtime to get my campaign out to the masses ASAP.'

She waves away my concern. 'You know I'm good at what I do so let me have this indulgent fantasy for a while.'

I drop a kiss on her forehead. Man, I am such a sucker. She tilts her head up and flashes me an approving smile that makes me feel like a god.

'Can we play twenty questions?'

'No.'

I've already revealed too much and I don't like the way she looks at me when I do, like she can see all the way down to the dark part of me where I lock away my innermost shame.

'Too bad, because I want to play.' She tweaks my nipple and I swat her hand away. 'What's your favourite colour?'

'Pink.'

Her nose scrunches. 'No, it's not.'

'It is.' I trail a fingertip from between her tits to her navel. 'The gorgeous blushing pink of your skin after you come.'

The same pink suffuses her cheeks now. 'You're not going to turn every question into a sexual innuendo, are you?'

'Possibly.'

Especially if it saves me from revealing any more. 'What's your favourite car?'

She's not going to be deterred so I decide to play nice for a while. 'I don't own one but if I did it would be a Ford Mustang.'

'Convertible?'

'Of course.'

She nods in approval. 'Nice choice. How old were you when you lost your virginity?'

'Now who's turning things sexual?'

She shrugs and the sheet covering her top half dips. Bonus. 'I'm curious.'

'Fifteen.'

'That's young.'

'An older woman took advantage of me.'

A frown appears between her brows and I smooth it away. 'Not in the way you're thinking. I was living in Melbourne at the time, in a really great foster home. The parents had a kid of their own and fostered another three for a time. The eldest foster daughter was seventeen and one of her friends in the same year at school...well, let's say she found me rather appealing.'

'So you like older women?'

'How old are you?'

'Twenty-seven.'

'Then the answer is no.'

Her smile is cute and coy and utterly irresistible, like the rest of her. 'What's your biggest regret?'

The lightness of the last few minutes fades as I recall the exact moment I'll regret for the rest of my life.

Pa called me the night before he died. We talked sport, the economy and an upcoming car rally. He never pressured me into returning to work alongside him but that night I heard something in his voice, a fatigue that tainted everything he said. I felt like shit and didn't sleep much after that call—an insomnia that only intensified when I got another call the next day, informing me Pa died.

Not telling him I'd planned on coming home to surprise him the following week was the biggest regret of my life.

But I can't tell Daisy that so I settle for a lame, 'Not being drafted to play for the Sydney Swans.'

'Were you that good at playing footy?'

'No.'

'Idiot.' She whacks me again on the chest but this time her palm rests there, directly over my heart. Too close. Way too close. 'If you could wish for one thing, what would it be?'

Inexplicably, my throat tightens. I've never liked the 'what if' game. What if my mum had stuck around? What if my dad hadn't abandoned me? What if one of my foster parents had seen past my angry exterior and understood I was inherently good? What if Pa had found me sooner? What if I could've been the grandson he wanted, to stand by his side and rule his empire and tell him how much he really meant to me?

I hate what ifs. They're for suckers.

'I'd wish we could stay in bed all night long.'

She patted my chest. 'I already intend on making that wish come true.'

'Good. Then let's start now...'

CHAPTER EIGHTEEN

Daisy

I'M EXHAUSTED. I feel hung-over when I haven't had a drop to drink. I blame Hart and his insatiable sexual appetite.

The guy is a sex god.

Even now, at ten past nine after a scant three hours of sleep, I remember the feel of his hands and mouth on me, the rasping of his stubble against my inner thighs, the hardness of him inside me.

I am in no shape for an impromptu meeting with Alf.

He landed on the island an hour ago and texted me to meet him in the conference room at nine. While I dragged myself out of bed leaving a sated Hart sleeping and made it here two minutes early, Alf hasn't appeared. Typical.

I slick a coral lipstick over my lips, check my calf-length navy shift is respectable and sit at the conference table. I've brought my notepad and laptop because I have no idea what this meeting is about.

I'm used to these senseless meetings where he'll try to reassert his control when we both know I'm the one doing all the work and keeping his company afloat. It's one of the major reasons I'm contemplating resigning to start my own business.

If only he'd give me a well-deserved promotion, I'd be happy. Quitting isn't high on my priority list but if he leaves me no choice... I hate thinking about walking away from a second commitment in a year.

I flick through the latest campaign update for Hart, loving how it's all coming together.

Alf blusters into the room at nine-fifteen, no apology for his tardiness. 'I need to talk to you.'

'What about? I sent through the latest campaign specs—'

'I know what you're up to and I won't stand for it.' He jabs a pudgy finger in my direction before collapsing into a nearby seat. 'It's unprofessional.'

My heart stalls before I give myself a mental kick. He can't know I'm contemplating leaving. I'm not dumb enough to sabotage my job even if I am tiring of the lack of recognition. He's fishing.

Mustering my best acting skills, the ones I use on a daily basis to pretend I actually respect this doofus, I fix a polite smile on my face. 'I don't understand what you're referring to.'

He slams his palms down on the table so hard I jump. 'Don't act so damn naïve. You're up to something with my clients.'

I try to remember if I've slipped up with any of my

recent jobs and come up with nothing. He's definitely trying to psych me out or probe for information.

'Can you be more specific—?'

'This is a bloody outrage! You sitting there like butter won't melt in your mouth when I know you're screwing me over, you conniving c—'

'That's enough!' Hart's booming voice makes me jump for the second time in as many minutes and I swivel in my chair to find he's entered through the side door.

He's red-faced, scowling, and his shoulders are so rigid I could stack bricks on them.

Alf's expression crumples. 'I was going to say cow—'

'I don't give a fuck what you were going to say, you don't call a lady names in the first place.' He strides towards us like an avenging angel and looms over Alf, who is doing his best to shrink into his seat and disappear. 'And you certainly don't make half-assed accusations to an employee without proof. Now apologise.'

Alf crosses his arms and his mouth compresses into a thin, twisted line. He's never apologised for his shitty behaviour towards me in the past so this will be a first, which I'll probably pay for later. Maybe it's time to move on from contemplating leaving to actually doing it.

'A client in Brisbane mentioned something about your lackadaisical approach on his job—'

'That doesn't sound like an apology to me.' Hart perches on the table in front of Alf, ensuring he towers over him. 'And you'd better make it good because if you don't I will personally fund this talented young woman's solo foray into PR so she never works for your slimy ass again.'

Alf gapes like a goldfish and I sit on my hands to stop from applauding.

Hart, my hero.

It doesn't take Alf long to reassemble his wits. Nothing keeps his big mouth shut for long. 'I'm sorry,' he mumbles, staring at some point over my shoulder.

Hart leans forward so he's almost in Alf's face. 'If you don't make a better job of it than that, I will sack you right now and give my entire business to Daisy Adler.'

I assume it's an empty bluff but I stare at Hart like he's a knight come to rescue me. I want to clamber all over him and hug him tight but that would only undermine my professional stance and ensure I get fired rather than an apology.

Predictably, the threat of losing money works. Alf sits straighter and actually looks at me this time. 'I shouldn't have jumped to conclusions, Daisy, I'm sorry.'

Hart's frown deepens and Alf adds, 'You're doing an excellent job.'

'She certainly is.' I don't need Hart's affirmation but it helps, as a warm glow of pride spreads in my chest.

Sure, I get clients thanking me after I finish a campaign but it's usually Alf who receives the accolades because he makes out he's the brains behind our unit.

One day we'll be in competition for business and I can't wait to go up against him.

'Is there anything else you need to discuss or can I confer with my PR rep on where my campaign is at?' Hart clasps his hands and rests them on his thighs, instantly drawing my attention to his quads and evoking a memory of how I stroked them in the early hours of the morning.

Heat flushes my face and as if sensing my thoughts he switches his potent gaze from Alf to me. I feign a cough and he smirks, knowing exactly how he affects me.

'No, I don't need to be here for you to meet with Daisy.' Alf struggles to his feet, considering his ass is wedged in the chair. 'I've seen what she's come up with for your island so far and it's very promising.'

It's better than promising and we both know it, but I'm used to his pompous proclamations. Hart isn't.

'Her work is extraordinary,' he says, standing next to Alf, presumably to help shove him out of the door. 'I'm more than satisfied.'

'Good, good,' Alf starts to bluster again, out of his depth and intimidated but trying not to show it. 'I'll leave you to it.'

Neither of us speak as Alf shuffles out of the door, suitably cowed. Only when the door closes do I allow myself the luxury of touching Hart. A hand resting on his forearm that can't be misconstrued if anyone happens to come into the conference room.

'Thank you. No one's ever stood up for me like that before.'

He makes a disparaging sound, half snort, half grunt. 'I hate bullies.'

His vehemence magnifies the three little words, making them sound like an unsavoury curse.

'Personal experience?'

The questions pops out before I can stop it and he rears back like I've poked him in the eye, dislodging my hand in the process.

'I lived in the foster system for eleven years, what do you think?'

'I think I should know better by now not to ask such personal questions but I can't help myself.'

He eyeballs me with blatant wariness. 'Why?'

'Because I'm a glutton for punishment? Or maybe I'm just interested in you beyond your dick?'

If my bluntness startles him he doesn't show it. Then again, I don't think much would dislodge that poker face. He's a master at it. The only time I remotely get a read on him is after we've had sex and even then only for an all too brief moment before he emotionally withdraws and yanks down the proverbial shutters.

He swipes a hand over his face and sinks into the chair next to me. 'That asshole got me riled up. I shouldn't take it out on you.'

'Especially when I was so nice to you last night.' I bat my eyelashes at him and he smiles as I intend.

'You weren't nice, you were naughty.' He leans across to nip my ear. 'Very naughty.'

'That's only because you were and I was trying to keep up.' I drop my gaze to his lap. 'And speaking of up...'

He groans. 'Stop. I have to walk out of here shortly and I can't do it sporting a boner.'

'A massive boner,' I add, with a grin.

'So you've said.' He shuffles in his seat. 'You know the way to a man's heart is to compliment the size of his cock.'

'Hey, I'm just telling the truth.' I hold my hands wide. 'That's one mighty impressive appendage you've got, mister.'

When he allows himself to smile, it melts away the residual tension and transforms him from handsome to head-turningly gorgeous.

He hasn't answered my personal question about being bullied but I let it drop. We're good together when we banter like this and I'm a fool to want to delve. He's an expert at deflecting the hard stuff, as evidenced when we played twenty questions last night. If I learned anything in my short engagement to Casper, it's to not push for something that isn't there.

'As much as I'd like to continue this scintillating conversation, I do need to work.' I point at my laptop. 'I've got a stack of online marketing sites to contact and a bunch of high-end magazines to harass for advertising space.'

I hold my hand up and start ticking off tasks on my fingers. 'I have to give final approval to the photographer's shots around the island. I need to ensure the new website is ready for launch by the end of the week. The podcast interviews you've done need to be vetted. And that's just for starters.'

He's staring at me like I'm some kind of magician; it's disarming.

'You really are determined to make me look good.'

'Isn't that what you're paying me for?' I wrinkle my nose. 'Or paying Alf, more to the point?'

'You need to quit and start your own business.'

I stiffen, before forcing my shoulders to relax. He makes walking away sound so easy but what he doesn't know is my confidence is a bluff. I can wow clients with my skills but what if it's tougher on my own? What if no one wants to take a chance on a start-up? What if I end up floundering, like I have been emotionally for the last year?

Casper really did a number on me and while I pretend I'm fine, I harbour doubts I'm not good enough in all aspects of my life… Mucking up professionally will be the last straw.

I can't quit my job, not until my self-belief is stronger. Any time now would be great.

'It's not that simple.'

'Yeah, it is.' He points to my notes on the desk. 'You know what you're doing. You're smart and switched on. You should do it.'

Easy for him to sound confident when he has the Rochester millions backing him. Even if he flounders in his new role he won't be left feeling a useless failure.

But I don't say any of that. Instead, I point to the

large window on the far side of the room, where I can see a stunning view of the resort's lush gardens and the marina beyond. 'Thanks, I'll keep that in mind. In the meantime, I'm almost done with the PR on making your resort more appealing, because that out there sells itself.'

'Great.' He glances away and an uncomfortable silence descends.

'What's wrong?'

He takes another few seconds to respond. 'Nothing. We can discuss it another time.'

Uh-oh. 'But you're happy with my work, right?'

'Absolutely.' He shoots me a tight smile. 'It's just an idea I had on the way over here but I'd prefer you wrap things up on the resort's PR, then we'll talk.'

'Phew.' I make an exaggerated swipe of my brow. 'Okay, sounds good.'

'I'll leave you to it.'

Before he stands I touch his hand, just because I want to. 'Things are all good with us, yeah?'

'Yeah.' He glances around and out of the window, as if ensuring we're alone, before swooping in for a quick kiss. 'Though you should've woken me this morning.'

'Why, when I was having so much fun watching you sleep?'

I trace the back of his hand with my fingertip, over the tendons, the knuckles, his long fingers. It's an intimate gesture and he doesn't shy away.

'That's rather stalkerish,' he says, turning his hand over so we're palm to palm.

'Then consider me your stalker for the brief time I have left on the island.' I make a scary *woo-woo* sound. 'You have been warned.'

He cracks a grin but his heart's not in it. Something is wrong but before I can grill him further he gives my hand a squeeze and stands.

'I'll see you later.'

'You can count on it…' But my response fades because he's already at the door like he can't get away from me fast enough.

After last night I know we're okay. We're going to have fun after hours for however much longer I'm here, a few days max. That's what happens when I do too good a job, it wraps up earlier than expected.

But Hart is hiding myriad secrets and I need to accept that I'm not the woman he'll divulge them to.

CHAPTER NINETEEN

Hart

LATER THAT AFTERNOON, Daisy sends me the final website design so I can approve it before it goes live.

It's phenomenal.

She's super talented, like I told her asshole boss, and will do well if she decides to branch out on her own. The new website is easy to navigate, with clear-cut links to bookings, villas, facilities, attractions and a gallery that would make any tourist want to get here as soon as humanly possible.

She's made Gem Island *the* place to be and the resort look like a haven. She's even managed to make me look good and that's saying something. I have no doubt that once this website goes live and she ramps up the social media campaign, bookings will start to increase for the first time since Pa's death.

But as I scroll through the fancy new website I'm struck again by how this place would be perfect for what I have in mind. It's a radical idea that doesn't fit with the island's glamorous image. I mentioned it to Pa once and he shot me down before I finished articulating it.

I know it's a good idea. Not for the PR but for what it will give to those kids who are doing it tough like I once did. It's my way of giving back.

I'm sick and tired of dealing with the same issues over and over. No matter which city in the world I visit, no matter the age of the kids, they're all facing the same fears. Fear of being shunted from home to home, fear of foster parents and siblings, fear of losing everything and ending up on the streets, fear of abuse, fear of bullies.

I should've known Daisy would home in on my comment about bullies. That's what set me off when I entered the conference room and saw that boss of hers berating her. Something inside me snapped, catapulting me back in time to when I was eight, in my first home, and an older foster sibling was standing over me, yelling in my face, jabbing his finger into my chest, trying to get me to fight back.

I despise bullies.

Thankfully Daisy didn't probe when I switched our conversation to light-hearted. I like that about her. She's refreshing and fun and genuine. And she'll be leaving shortly. I should be relieved. I'm not. I'm already imagining how empty this place will be without her, which is crazy considering I have no plans to stick around long-term either.

I've had a few applicants for the role of island manager but none have the experience to run a resort of this magnitude. I'm leaning towards offering Kevin the job but he vetoed the idea when I first mentioned it shortly after Pa's funeral.

Then again, I didn't exactly couch my offer in appealing terms, virtually asking him to step up so I wouldn't have to. This time will be different. I'll put together an attractive package, one he can't say no to. I'll formally interview him, on the pretext that he's up against a host of super-qualified candidates. Yeah, he won't be able to say no.

The sooner Kevin assumes managerial duties, the sooner I can leave. But not before implementing my plan with Daisy's help. For my idea to have an impact I'll need the right PR and I know just the woman for the job.

My gaze is drawn to the computer screen again. She's a whiz. I fire off an email telling her so and asking her to meet me here in an hour. It gives me time to draw up a rough outline of what I envisage for the older villas at the back of the property.

When I hear a knock on my door I glance at the time in the top corner of my screen, surprised to see sixty minutes have flown by. I get like this when I'm passionate about something and making lives easier for the kids I deal with is my new priority.

'Come in,' I call out and the door swings open. I'm prepared to see Daisy; I'm not prepared for the tightening in my chest. It's an unusual feeling, part heartburn part breathlessness, like I'm an asthmatic who indulges in one too many burritos. Stupid, because my breathing is fine and I hate Mexican food.

I don't like that the awful burn in my chest makes

a mockery of my previous belief that I'm dead inside, that I don't feel anything, because there's an inherent quality to this amazing woman that makes me feel *something*, no matter how much I don't want to admit it.

I pegged it as lust initially. Lust is good. Lust is slaked. Lust fades and can be chalked up to a memorable fantasy to be dredged up when I'm an old man.

But that burn intensifies as she enters my office, her smile light, her eyes bright, her pale pink silk sundress swishing around her shapely calves, making her look carefree in a way I can never be.

The burn has to be lust. It's all it can ever be.

'You wanted to see me?' She closes the door and sashays across my office, working it.

I want to vault my desk, grab her and take her up against the nearest wall.

'Yeah, thanks for coming.' I stand and move around my desk, gesturing at the leather sofas in the far corner. 'Let's have a seat.'

Some of her sassiness fades. She's shooting me glances from beneath her lashes, like she's uncertain and nervous.

'Don't worry, this is a good thing.'

'Okay.' She sits and clasps her hands in her lap, oddly straitlaced when I've seen her naked and wanton and willing.

'I have an idea. For the island.'

I have no trouble articulating my thoughts usually but this project is too close to home and I'm oddly reluctant to divulge it for fear of her judging; or worse, seeing right through me.

'For the ad campaign?' A tiny frown appears between her brows. 'But we've already finalised everything. Adding changes now will only delay the launch.'

'I think it's worth it.'

I sit opposite so I can see her reaction. I've always depended on my gut reactions to any situation and I've never been steered wrong.

'Go on.' She relaxes slightly and leans back into the sofa.

'On your first tour of the resort, do you remember the older villas situated down by the lagoon?'

She nods. 'The ones that you want to renovate?'

'Yeah.' Here goes nothing. I'm not used to bouncing my ideas off others. I make a decision, I stick to it. But her expertise can only help in this case. 'I want to designate those villas for a new foster kids programme I want to develop. Where kids and their foster families can come to the island for a few days of R&R. A weekly rotation, where different families come from all around the world for some much deserved time out. We have eight villas so that's thirty-two families a month, three hundred and eighty-four a year who can benefit.'

The words tumble out in a rush. 'So many of the kids I see have never left their cities let alone had a holiday. And the men and women who foster are the same. These people would benefit greatly from a programme like this.'

I search her face for some clue that she gets it; gets me. But she blinks a few times, like she's trying to hide her surprise or come up with a response that I'll like.

My heart sinks and I let out a breath I'm unaware I'm holding. Her lack of enthusiasm says it all. Her first instinctive reaction is that my idea sucks.

Disappointment filters through me. I thought she'd seen beneath my brusque exterior to the real me, no matter how many times I've tried to hide from her.

I can't blame her. It's what I wanted, to hold her at arm's length, to not reveal too much. I brought this on myself. So why does it feel like a kick in the guts?

'I think it's a fabulous idea.' She sounds stilted, like she's choosing her words carefully, and I'm disappointed all over again.

'But?'

'The relaunch is ready to go and this will delay it. Is that what you want?'

Damn her for sounding so logical. She's right. I'm running on adrenalin, eager to get the redevelopment happening, but I can't derail the plans to make the resort viable again. It's what we've been busting our asses to achieve.

'Isn't there some way we can incorporate the programme into the new campaign?'

She shakes her head, the frown between her brows deepening. 'I don't think that's a good idea.'

'Why?'

'Because the campaign we've created focuses on the glamour of Gem Island, the high-end luxury for the discerning traveller. You can't muddy the message with a cause.'

A cause. She makes it sound like helping foster kids is akin to offering the devil a week's free accommodation.

Her eyes brighten and she snaps her fingers. 'Unless we utilise all those shots we took of you, the ones you vetoed. That way, we can put a face to the kids' holiday programme—'

'No.' I hold up my hands. 'No fucking way.'

I can't be the poster boy for this programme. It's not why I'm doing it, for the recognition. I need to stay behind the scenes as usual, ensuring the focus stays where it needs to be: on the kids.

Her nose gets this cute crinkle on the bridge when she's disapproving. 'We can make this work. The foster kids' holiday programme can be an adjunct to what we've already done. An offshoot of the campaign, but it will only work if you're the face of it to bring both aspects together in a cohesive way—'

'What part of no can't you understand?'

My hands bunch into fists and I take a deep breath, willing my anger to subside. I must be going mad. A few moments ago I was disappointed she didn't jump at my idea, now I'm furious because her enthusiasm is overriding common sense.

Her cheeks flush and it's not because she's excited. Disapproval tightens her mouth. 'You initially took me by surprise and I couldn't see how this would work with the new campaign as it currently stands, but with the tweaking I suggest I think this is a great idea. You hired me to do the PR for Gem Island's resort and we've made a great team. Why can't you see that enhancing the campaign by featuring you in it is a good thing?'

I grit my teeth against the urge to blurt the truth. 'Because no one gives a fuck who I am. Those kids don't identify with me. They'll see me as some rich prick flinging his cash around for the sake of a tax deduction. They won't understand. Nobody will...'

I've said too much and, predictably, she stares at me with pity. I fucking hate it.

'I want you to do a separate PR campaign for the holiday villas. That's it.'

She glares at me like I've insulted her. 'You've trusted my professional opinion until now. Why won't you trust me on this?'

'This isn't about trust, it's about business. You said it yourself. The campaign is ready to launch. I made a mistake trying to rush this. I don't want to damage the brand you've tried to create for the island so let's wait.'

'"Damage the brand?"' she mimics, her eyes widening in outrage. 'Can you hear yourself? You sound like a judgemental idiot.'

She puffs up like one of the fish Pa told me to avoid at all costs because of their deadly poison. 'Your idea is brilliant and I wish I'd had it myself.' She snorts. 'Can't you see I want to make this happen and we can do it sooner rather than later if you agree to do it my way?'

'Did you just call me an idiot?'

'No, just that you sounded like one.' This is not good but we're both riled now and too far gone to back down. 'Why are you being so stubborn about this? Why can't you acknowledge that I'm the expert when it comes to PR and you should take my advice on board?'

'I would if it wasn't crap advice,' I yell, hating this out-of-control feeling.

I learned to control my anger issues after Pa took me in. I soon figured that he wouldn't put up with my moody crap and no matter how hard I tried to push him away he wouldn't leave me alone. No good ever comes of letting anyone else see your weakness. But she's pushed me too far and I can't rein it in.

'I can't believe you're so gung-ho that you won't listen to reason—'

'We'll discuss this when you calm down.' She stands, shooting me a last scathing glare before stalking to the door.

Who the hell does she think she is, scolding me like I'm a goddamn child?

'Don't you dare walk out on me—'

She slams the door on her way out.

CHAPTER TWENTY

Daisy

I'M FUMING. SO damn mad that I'm shaking from head to foot. My head spins like I've stepped off a whirling carnival ride and my legs wobble. I make it to the garden before I collapse onto a bench and stare up at the sky, willing the sting of tears to abate.

I won't cry, not over him.

The stupid thing is, I think his idea for the foster kids is brilliant, the act of a selfless man who wants to help the less fortunate. But he's wrong about not utilising himself as the face of the campaign. I could give him a thousand reasons why it's perfect but he wouldn't let me speak. He lost his temper and took it as a personal affront that I voiced an opinion at odds with his own. That's what made me so damn mad, that in the moment when he wouldn't listen to me or hear me out, he reminded me of Casper and the many times I felt useless; like my opinion didn't matter or what I wanted was irrelevant.

It's this residual lack of confidence that is making me stick with Alf when I should take a risk and start my own PR company. I hate that Casper's cruel and calculated campaign to bind me to him has resulted in this: me feeling vulnerable and weak despite knowing I'm right. So when Hart did the same thing, dismissing my opinion as meaningless, I had to get out of there.

Something niggles at the back of my mind…*a personal affront…*

Crap, I've been an idiot. Of course he's taken all this as personal. He was one of those kids who probably never had a holiday, who only dreamed of visiting a tropical island. To those kids, spending time on Gem Island would be as unattainable as flying to the moon.

This idea would be as personal as it gets and that's probably why he's so reluctant to put himself out there for the campaign.

Stifling a groan, I straighten and dab at the corners of my eyes with my pinkies. I take deep breaths, steadying my resolve. I'll have to tread lightly when I go back in. I have to. We need to resolve this now. And considering it's obviously a hot button for him I need to present rational, sensible responses so he understands my point of view.

I stand and give my arms and legs a little shake. My legs are steadier as I walk back towards his office. Thankfully there's no one around. I would've died of mortification if they'd witnessed my slamming-door tantrum and subsequent crawl back.

I knock once but don't wait for a response. Why

give him the opportunity to tell me where I can stick my apology?

I open the door and he's exactly where I left him, sitting on the couch. But his head is in his hands and his shoulders are slumped. He's defeated.

I did this.

I brought this powerful, commanding man to his knees.

I feel sick to my stomach.

He doesn't speak as I close the door and approach, my steps tentative as I struggle to come up with something sensible that won't inflame the situation.

I sit beside him and he stands, moving towards his desk where he props himself, butt on the edge. He folds his arms in the classic defensive posture and I know I'm going to have to do some serious grovelling to get this back on track.

'I shouldn't have stormed out like that. I'm sorry.'

'And I shouldn't have yelled at you.'

His tone is cold and I resist the urge to rub my arms. 'We'll discuss this another time—'

'No, we need to get it sorted now.' I try to sound calm and rational but my voice quavers, undermining my authority. I know PR, he doesn't. I need to make him see sense. 'You hired me to do a job and you've been nothing but happy. So you need to listen when I say that using you as the face of the holiday project for foster kids is a brilliant idea.'

'In your opinion.'

'Of course it's in my bloody opinion,' I snap, instantly regretting my outburst when he smirks, as if he expects nothing less. 'Look, for what it's worth, I understand your concern, about you being rich now and those kids potentially not identifying with you. But you were one of them once and if we play up that angle while showcasing this fabulous resort, it'll gel nicely—'

'Thanks for stating the obvious, that I was one of them once.' He slow claps and my palm itches to wipe that smart-ass smirk off his face.

'You need to listen to reason—'

'No, you need to listen to me,' he says, fury darkening his eyes to ebony. 'I'm not asking you to make this work without me in the campaign. I'm telling you. Use the new campaign you devised and tack on the kids' holiday programme.'

'And what if I say I won't do it?'

It's stupid calling his bluff and I know it the moment I fling the taunt at him. I'm an idiot. I can't afford to ruin this campaign before it's launched. It would mean I'm stuck with Alf until some other project this big comes along and that could be for ever. I need to salvage this situation before it's too late.

'If you won't do it, there's the door.' He shrugs. 'Use it.'

His nonchalance is galling. He's ready to replace me without a qualm. I'm not egotistical but I've worked in marketing long enough to know not everyone has the same flair as me. Casper sapped my confidence; I'm not letting Hart do the same.

'Do you always use threats to get what you want?'

His gaze shifts away. 'I'm the client and I get final say. I thought you were okay with that.'

'I am.' A sigh escapes my lips. I can't fight him. I've put too much work into this campaign already. But his attitude disappoints me more than it should: he's like Casper, demanding and commanding, knowing I'll back down.

My chest aches with the knowledge that I may have put my trust in the wrong man again.

'We'll do it your way.'

'You don't have to sound so thrilled about it.' His mouth kicks up into a wry grin but I don't return it.

I'm hurting when I shouldn't be. I've made the ultimate mistake: feeling too much for my fling.

At what point did the sex and the work become more?

Every muscle in my body tightens, preparing for a flee response. I need to escape this office before I say something I'll regret.

'What's wrong?' He stalks towards me and stops within touching distance, too damn close. 'And don't say nothing.'

My lips compress so I don't blurt what I'm feeling and how he's hurt me with his casual undermining.

To my surprise, he laughs. 'Honey, the silent game you're playing? I invented it. Whenever a foster parent taunted me or a sibling pushed me around, I learned to bottle up my rage.' He shakes his head. 'Sure, I exploded a few times to make a point, but I discovered that silent rage works so much better than getting physical.'

He reaches out to capture a strand of my hair and I swat his hand away. 'So you see, I can out-silent you. I'm a stubborn bastard that way.'

Damn him for hitting me in a weak spot: my thirst to know more about him.

'How many foster parents did you have?'

I expect him not to answer and evade anything personal as usual, but to my surprise he meets my curious gaze.

'Three. When my dad dumped me with Social Services, I was six. That first home was really crappy, the parents were only fostering for the money so it was pretty brutal. Two older siblings who'd been shunted between homes too many times already. I hated it...'

A lump forms in my throat at the thought of this amazing man being abandoned by his father so young.

I remain silent, expecting him to do the same after revealing so much but once again, he surprises me.

'I was there until I was ten, then got moved to another home, much better parents who already had three kids of their own, but...'

'But?' I prompt.

'But by then it was too late. I'd become too hardened, too sceptical, too cut off from everyone.' A vein throbs at his temple as his jaw clenches. 'They were okay people but couldn't tolerate my shitty behaviour, so I eventually got shipped off to my third home in Melbourne, a really nice family who got through to me a little. I lived with them for a few years, then Pa discovered I existed.' He shrugs as if his childhood ordeal means little. 'You know the rest.'

Actually, I don't. I don't know why he's beating himself up by sticking around in a job he obviously loathes. I don't know why he's so reluctant to keep his charity work secret. And I sure as hell don't know why I feel more for this damaged man than I should.

'Let me guess. The Adlers are one big, happy family.'

He doesn't sound bitter. In fact, he sounds almost curious, like he actually gives a crap about me. Wishful thinking.

'Yeah, I guess I'm one of the lucky ones. Mum and Dad still idolise one another, my two younger sisters are in long-term relationships.' I hook my fingers into devil horns and place them on my head. 'Since I quit my engagement, I'm the baddie of the family.'

He reaches for my hand and I let him clasp it, his warmth a comfort. I'm still a topsy-turvy mess over the realisation that I've somehow moved beyond just sex and actually feel something for Hart, but his firm grip brings me back to the reality of how much I like him touching me.

'It's okay to walk away when something isn't right for you. Sometimes, strength in our convictions is all we have.'

Such a simple proclamation with such profound results.

He's right.

Why has it taken me so long to realise it?

And why do I need him to spell it out for me to make me believe it?

'Thank you.'

I turn towards him, slip my hand out of his and cup his face.

'For what?'

'Telling me what I needed to hear.'

Our gazes lock and I know in that instant that he feels it too. *This.* Whatever this is.

It's bigger than sex and island flings and work.

It's tenuous and fleeting but it's there just the same, binding us when neither of us wants it.

'Hart...' I search for the words to make him understand that we've moved beyond fuck-buddies, but before I can speak he slams his mouth onto mine, hard and fast.

I would've fallen if he didn't haul me against him, pinning me between his thighs. I'm mad at him for silencing me this way, for his cowardice in not wanting to confront the obvious, but my momentary struggle is for show only. Because the second his lips sear mine, I'm gone. Swept up in a tide of passion and unwilling to surface.

I open my mouth to lodge a mock protest and he takes it as a blatant invitation to sweep his tongue into my mouth. With a resigned groan I meet him halfway, our tongues tangling as his hands slide under my skirt.

He plucks at my thong, toying with the elastic, before ripping it clean away. I'm embarrassingly wet, so turned on by his powerful display of control that I want to lie on his desk and spread my legs for him.

He wrenches his mouth from mine and stares at me like I'm death by chocolate, lemon meringue pie and sticky date pudding all rolled into one.

'Turn around.'

I swallow a moan and do as he says.

'Rest your hands on my desk.'

I do it and feel my skirt being hiked up, exposing my ass to him.

I hear him unzip and the tearing of foil. He's taking too long and I wiggle my hips impatiently. Then he's there, rock hard, nudging my cleft.

He bites the back of my neck, a playful nip followed by the teasing lap of his tongue, making me tremble in anticipation. His hand slides around to the front and he zeroes in on my clit without preamble.

This isn't going to be slow. We both want it fast, a way to release our tension. Maybe it's easier this way, showing rather than telling, using our bodies as a way to communicate what we already know: we're good together.

As he circles my clit he slides into me and I gasp. It's like this every time, him filling me to perfection and making me crave more.

He withdraws and I push my hips back, needing him inside me again. He obliges by driving into me with such force I fall forward a little.

I rest my forearms on the desk as he pounds into me, fingering me at the same time. It's wild and wanton and beyond anything I've ever felt before.

I glance over my shoulder. He's glassy-eyed, his mouth hanging open slightly as he stares at where he's driving in to me.

I stand on tiptoes in response, knowing it will change the angle and he's a goner, a man possessed as he pumps into me, my own climax clawing at the last of my control as I let myself go and just *feel*.

My keen of release melds with his roar and my head falls forward, thumping the desk. I don't feel a thing. The ripples of pleasure take a while to subside and I cling to the precious feeling, knowing that all too soon we'll need to talk. But I let him lift my torso gently and cradle me from behind.

For now, it's enough.

CHAPTER TWENTY-ONE

Hart

I'M NOT PROUD of what happened in my office three hours ago.

I'm a fuckwit.

Still repeating the same mistakes over and over. I've always dealt with my avoidance issues like that: not by fucking the nearest hot woman but by deflecting. And in Daisy's case, the result of me blabbing too much information meant I deflected by using sex to distract.

One minute we were oversharing, the next I had to shut her up and we did it doggy style on my desk.

I'll never be able to work on this thing again without remembering.

'Fuck.' I swipe a hand over my face. Yeah, like that's going to wipe away the memory.

She was so hot leaning over my desk, her ass in the air. My cock stiffens just thinking about it but I can't afford to get distracted again. Not this time.

We didn't resolve anything. Not the important stuff anyway. The work, sure. She acquiesced to my demands. But when we started talking about the other stuff... I sensed the shift, saw it in her eyes, felt it all the way down to my frozen fucking heart.

I'm in over my head and she's right there alongside me, drowning.

She left to go tidy herself up, and I've been hiding behind my desk ever since. I take the coward's way out by sending her a text, citing that I have business to take care of for the rest of the day. She responds with a terse 'fine' but we both know it isn't.

We need to talk. I don't want to. That's what the sex was about, making sure I prevented her from asking the tough questions I didn't want to contemplate let alone answer, and ensuring I kept my big mouth shut so I didn't blab any more than I already had.

I refocus on the proposal on the screen. I've crunched some numbers, contacted the appropriate governing bodies and laid it out in a clear, easy-to-read format.

This holiday programme is going to kick ass.

Imagining the joy of the foster kids when they first land on the island, I choke up and press the pads of my fingers to my eyes. That damn stinging must be from staring at the screen too long.

I blink several times and take a few steadying breaths. Better. But as I stare at the screen again, at the pictures of kids on Australia's most reputable website for families wanting to foster, I'm catapulted back in time.

'We're going away,' my foster mum said, packing a hamper with bread, peanut butter, chocolate-chip

cookies and tiny bottles of lemonade—treats we never had.

Deni was a good foster mum compared to my first, but she always favoured her three biological kids over me: snotty-nosed twin girls a year older than me and a boy, the eldest by two years. I never understood why she fostered me three years ago. Bringing a ten-year-old into an already struggling family seemed dumb to me. I guess she did it for the government money.

'Where are we going?'

She stared at me with incredulity, like she couldn't believe I could ask such a stupid question. 'We're going to Coffs Harbour. You're staying here.'

My stomach roiled and the rotten apple I'd eaten for lunch threatened to launch up into my throat and out. She was taking her precious kids on holiday and leaving me behind. I shouldn't be surprised. Yet another disappointment in a long line. But for once I'd thought I might be welcomed here. I might even be liked.

'My sister from Cairns has rented a house for us. I haven't seen her in a decade and there's only room for four of us.'

'That's okay,' I said, embarrassed when my voice broke a tad. It had to be the onset of early puberty and nothing to do with the sadness making me want to bawl. 'I can take care of myself.'

'Actually, you can't,' she said, her furtive glance away alerting me to the fact that if I didn't like the news about their impending trip, I'd like what she

was about to say even less. 'You can't stay alone so you'll be moved on.'

Moved on...

I knew what that meant. I'd be sent back into the government home until they found me another placement with another deadbeat mother with another host of problems.

I glanced at the computer screen on the desk in the corner of the kitchen. She'd obviously been doing an online search for Coffs Harbour and the images on the screen featured palm trees, white sand and a blue ocean that looked digitally enhanced.

I'd never had a holiday and at that moment I yearned to go so badly I ached, like that time I had the flu.

'You're a good kid, Hart, you'll be fine,' she said, sounding gruff as she turned away to finish packing the hamper.

'No, I'm not!' I yelled, punching the hamper so that it toppled and landed upside down on the floor. 'I'm bad and that's why you're sending me back.' I stomped on the loaf of bread on the floor, flattening it, as she stared at me with pity. 'I hate you!'

I pushed through the back door and slammed it so hard the glass pane beside it cracked. I seethed until I reached my go-to place, a bicycle shed at the farthest corner of the stupid high school I'd just started at, where I sat in the deserted shed and cried...

I blink several times and lift my fingers to my cheeks, shocked to find them damp. I've dealt with my past and I moved on a long time ago but it catches up with me at the oddest of moments.

Pa made up for lost time when he found me. I tried to feign disinterest in holidays but he took me to Hong Kong, Tokyo and Mumbai in our first year together, then London, Dubai and Paris the next. Despite pretending nothing impressed me, I lapped up every fact I learned in each new city and when I wasn't able to hide my interest he showed me more.

Once I started to trust him a little, I opened myself up to learning more about his world and it seemed natural to follow in his footsteps when I finished school. Doing a business degree was his idea, as was my part-time job in the flagship hotel in Brisbane. I did everything from concierge duties to valet parking, getting a feel for how a hotel ran from the ground up.

When I did an internship in the hotel's business centre while completing my degree, Pa was the happiest I'd ever seen him. It made what I had to do all the harder because I knew even then that I couldn't be the man he wanted me to be. Being stuck behind a desk, ordering people around, delegating the shitty jobs I didn't want to do myself, I would hate every minute of it.

I knew what I wanted to do. Work behind the scenes, helping kids like me reach their potential despite the hardships they faced along the way. But I continued to toe the company line until I became so miserable Pa demanded I tell him what the hell was going on. I told him the truth; I owed him that much. And the kicker was that he understood, and he invented the hotel quality control job so I could travel while ostensibly still carrying on the Rochester name in the business. He gave me his blessing to follow my dream.

'Dammit.' I thump the desk and the penholder tips, spilling its contents onto the floor. There's a framed photo of Pa and me next to it, taken on my first visit to Gem Island. I'm a gangly sixteen-year-old, uncertain and glum, Pa has his arm around me, pride in his grin.

I'll never understand how he accepted me so unreservedly, welcoming me into his life and his heart.

That's what my holiday project for foster kids is all about. Giving them the kind of awe-inspiring experience that I had the first time I set foot on this island.

I want them to feel welcome and wanted and warm for one week in their lives, something to hold onto when times get tough, something to remember.

I ignore the pens and return my attention to the computer screen.

I refuse to be the face of this campaign and I'm launching this programme, with Daisy's help.

And once she's done, our liaison will be over.

Simple.

At least, it should be. So why does the thought of never seeing her again make me want to smash something?

CHAPTER TWENTY-TWO

Daisy

I'M A WUSS. A weakling. I should never have let Hart distract me in his office yesterday but the moment he kissed me all my questions evaporated under the onslaught of his charisma. If that's what I'm calling scintillating sex these days.

It was so freaking hot doing it on his desk, our heightened emotions adding to the frantic edge.

I can't let it happen again.

I allowed myself to be distracted once before, when the man I thought I loved captured my attention and ensured he controlled it, while I slowly but surely lost pieces of myself. Casper influenced my opinions, my likes, my goals, while making it sound like I wanted those things along the way. His subtle way of controlling me meant I lost sight of the important stuff, just like I lost sight of it yesterday thanks to Hart.

I hate making comparisons between the two men but Hart too is demanding and dismissed my opinions like they meant nothing. One minute I was smarting, the next he opened up about his past and I was catapulted straight into a depth of feeling I've been avoiding ever since this fling started up.

I wanted to confront him about it, to see if he'd be honest about our deepening attraction, but he distracted me in the hottest of ways...

The sex might have been phenomenal, but it pulled my focus from where it had to be: seeing how far he was willing to go to admit we've moved beyond the sex.

I don't like that I allowed myself to slip back into old patterns of behaviour, to be distracted because of my feelings for a man. It doesn't bode well for me and it makes me resent him for doing it.

We didn't say much afterwards. I had to take a call from Alf, cited work, and bolted. He texted me thirty minutes later saying he had international teleconferences for the rest of the day.

And he hasn't contacted me since.

Not that I expect him to but... I call bullshit because I did expect to hear from him last night. In fact, I listened for a knock on my villa door for half the night before falling into a restless sleep.

The mature thing to do would be for me to contact him: a blasé text, a call, a drop-in at his office. I've buried myself in work all day instead, ensuring the suitable adjustments Hart requested to the Gem Island campaign about to go live are the best they can be. I'm not exactly thrilled that I can't feature him front and centre of his proposed holiday programme, but considering the mock-ups, I'm pleased with how everything has turned out—my best work yet.

I was on the verge of emailing the lot to Hart for final approval when Alf dumped a shitload of work on me. He's punishing me for having Hart treat him like a subordinate. He has forwarded emails from five potential new clients, requesting quotes for their needs. This, on top of putting the finishing touches on Hart's campaign.

I pulled up my resignation letter after his fourth email of the morning with its excessive demands. It's ready to go, if and when I ever gather the courage to send it.

But every time I read it, I get a hollow feeling in my gut and I hear Dad's voice in my ear: 'Adlers don't quit, honey.' Dad will be disappointed, no matter how hard I try to explain that I'm done with Alf treating me like slave labour for little reward. He's already shattered that I ended my engagement. While he didn't use the Q word on me then, I know by the shared glances with Mum that they think I quit on a relationship rather than hanging on for the long haul.

That hurt, having my own parents not trusting me enough to make a sound decision that affects my future. Wait until they hear I'm contemplating quitting my job too. I don't like when they don't have faith in me, in my judgements as a grown woman. But not half as much as I hate not having complete confidence in myself. Even after the stellar job I've done on this campaign and the positive feedback from Hart, I still doubt myself. Wondering if I'll make it on my own. Reluctant to take the next step to professional independence.

I think some of that bitterness influenced the way I behaved with Hart yesterday, when he didn't trust me enough to know what's best for his island and his holiday programme idea.

I was so mad at his lack of faith in me... I was so tempted to fire off a curt outline of what he needs to do if he wants the Rochester brand to be successful, but I'm not done with Hart yet so I didn't.

I'm not done with Hart.

Professionally, I am. The campaign will be ready to launch first thing tomorrow morning once he gives the final go-ahead. And he will, considering I acquiesced to his hare-brained idea to tack the foster kids programme onto it without using himself to bring both campaigns together in a seamless transition.

But being done with Hart professionally is a far cry from being ready to walk away from him personally. Despite my determination to view us only as island sex-buddies, the thought of flying back to the mainland in a day or two is making me feel like crap.

Crazy, considering I knew this had an end date when we started up. It's exactly what I wanted. Short-term gain with none of the long-term pain. Sorbet, remember?

But what if one or two scoops aren't enough?

What if I want the whole damn sundae with a cherry on top?

Not going to happen, but for an indulgent moment I allow myself to fantasise about what it would be like to stay. If I finally believe in myself enough to resign and start my own firm, I can work with clients around the world remotely. And if a job needs a face-to-face meeting, I can do that too. What I can't 'do' is Hart if we're not together and the thought of not having him hold me or be inside me is enough to send me into withdrawals before I've even left.

An email pings into my inbox. It's him.

My pulse races as I open it. Read it.

'What the fuck…?' I reread it, to make sure I'm not making a mistake.

I'm not. Hart has outlined succinctly what will happen once his precious bloody campaign goes live.

Absolutely nothing.

He's saying goodbye and effectively ending us in a fucking email!

I won't let him get away with this.

I fire back a polite response, asking him to meet me in the conference room in half an hour to discuss his email. I deliberately choose the venue, knowing that we can't meet in an intimate place for fear of our rampant sexual attraction getting out of control again.

This time, not even his wicked mouth, his talented fingers or his impressive appendage will derail me.

His response is quick, confirming the meeting. Good. I have thirty minutes to prepare myself for a confrontation I have every intention of winning.

I arrive at the conference room with three minutes to spare. He's already there, looking surprisingly dishevelled with his pants creased, his shirtsleeves rolled up, the top two buttons undone and dark shadows circling his eyes. Good to know he had a rotten night's sleep too.

'Hi.' I breeze into the room, giving the door a little kick to shut it, before joining him at the table where he's glaring at me like a foe.

'You read my email?' I nod and his jaw clenches as he slams his hands into his pockets, before taking a seat opposite me. 'If so, what did you want to see me about?'

No preamble, no small talk, no acknowledging the simmering tension buzzing between us even now.

'Yes, I read it, and I call bullshit.'

He places both his hands palm down on the table and leans forward, his glower formidable. 'Don't do this, Daisy. It's easier this way.'

'Easier for you, you mean?' I try to scoff and it comes out an embarrassing snort. 'As hard as you tried to dismiss us in that email as being nothing beyond a professional partnership, I think you need to confess.'

His lips thin as his frown deepens. 'To what?'

'Actually giving a damn.' I point to his heart. 'And feeling something rather than pretending you don't.'

'You don't know the first thing about me,' he snarls, his upper lip curling as he rears back like I've prodded him. 'I don't feel a thing—'

'Oh, yeah? Then what's this?' I swipe my phone to bring up the amended campaign, featuring a sidebar with the foster kids camp. 'You want to help these kids in a way you wished someone had helped you, and that proves you care—'

'Maybe about the kids,' he roars, crimson creeping up his neck. 'But what's that got to do with you?'

That hurts. A hell of a lot. I want to walk out of here and not look back, like he wants me to.

He's trying to undermine me, like Casper undercut me every chance he got during our relationship. Having a guy I actually care about treat me the same way…it kills me.

So I go on the offensive.

'Is this how you were with your grandfather? Pushing him away until he had no choice but to let you go? If so, I feel sorry for you. You like to blame everyone for your misfortune rather than face up to your past and your abandonment issues with your dad and—'

'Stop!' he bellows, his face a concentration in devastation.

He's hurting, an unimaginable pain that makes my throat tighten. Maybe I've gone too far but I had to try to make him face the reality that he has a woman who hates quitting, a woman willing to stick around, a woman who's crazy about him. But by the way he's staring at me, he'll never forgive me for verbalising my pop psychology in an attempt to get him to open up about his feelings.

'Hart, listen—'

'Get the fuck out of here.' His outburst echoes through the room and I try to hide my dismay.

'You don't mean that,' I say, doing my best to stay calm.

I lay my hands out, palm up. 'I care about you—'

'What we had is called fucking. Don't mistake it for something it's not.'

He's staring at me with barely concealed dislike and a tiny part of my heart cracks at that moment.

He's gone too far and there's no coming back from this.

'That's a low blow.' I stand and take a few steps back, willing my feet to step and not run like I want to. 'I pegged you for many things, a coward wasn't one of them.'

I turn my back on him and walk towards the door.

'Launch the website as we previously agreed.' It's a barked order from a man who has retreated emotionally and is treating me like the hired subordinate I am.

It's not his fault I feel cheap and used, because we both agreed to a fling. But I felt the same way when I walked out on Casper: like I'd given him a tiny piece of my soul that I'd never get back.

'Okay.' My voice is amazingly calm considering I'm a wreck inside.

I continue striding towards the door. I need him to stop me, to hold me, to comfort me. To admit he's made a mistake. To tell me he feels the same way I do. To apologise for being a cold, heartless jerk.

I will him to do it.

When he doesn't I know we're officially over.

I wait until I reach the shadows of the towering palms outside my villa to let my tears fall.

CHAPTER TWENTY-THREE

Hart

I'VE GONE TOO FAR.

But there's no turning back.

I knew what I was doing when I deliberately taunted Daisy in such a crass way. I knew she'd walk away. It's what I wanted. Because the moment she articulated exactly how I feel, like she could see right through me, I had to end it.

'Is this how you were with your grandfather? Pushing him away until he had no choice but to let you go? If so, I feel sorry for you. You like to blame everyone for your misfortune rather than face up to your past and your abandonment issues...'

It wouldn't have mattered what she said after that, I had to drive her away. Belittling what we shared was guaranteed to do that.

I'm a fool. I've been so hell-bent on proving that all we had was great sex that I didn't see the moment it moved beyond that. I'm also a coward because rather than explain why I can't take this thing between us further, I deliberately let her think otherwise.

She'll think I used her. She'll think I'm an A-grade prick. I should be glad. Yet all I feel is hollow inside and my face is numb, like all those times I had to pretend being ignored or bullied or abused meant nothing.

There's a knock at the office door and Kevin sticks his head around it. 'You wanted to see me?'

'Yeah, come in.'

I need to forge ahead with my plans, sooner rather than later.

'Are you okay?' He sits on the other side of my desk and I determinedly try to ignore the memory of Daisy and me and what we did there. 'You look awful.'

'Just tired.'

Wisely, Kevin doesn't call me on the bullshit even though he continues to stare at me with blatant curiosity. 'What's up?'

'I've made a decision regarding the general manager position here on the island.'

His eyebrows shoot up. 'But you haven't interviewed anyone yet.'

'I've scoured the applicants' CVs and done remote interviews by videoconferencing.'

'Right.' Disappointment downturns his mouth, which gives me hope that he'll jump at the opportunity I'm about to offer him.

'But none of the applicants impressed me as much as you do, so I'd like to offer you the position.'

Kevin's jaw drops before he quickly shuts it and straightens. 'You're serious?'

'One hundred per cent.' I gesture at the office. 'I know you refused when I first offered you the position but since I've been here I've watched you and I can't think of a better candidate. You've spent enough time alongside Pa, three frigging decades. You know how this place operates better than anyone else. I can't think of a more capable manager to ensure the Gem Island resort moves forward and continues to grow.'

'I won't refuse this time. Besides, the missus kicked my ass after I did the first time.' He grins like I've handed him the keys to the kingdom and holds out his hand. 'Thanks, mate. I won't let you down.'

'I know you won't.' I shake his hand, relieved the first part of my plan has gone so smoothly. 'There's just one hitch.'

'What is it?'

'You need to start now.'

He laughs. 'Nice one.'

'I'm not kidding. I need to fly to Melbourne shortly and I'm not sure how long I'll be gone. And if all goes well down there I may not be back for a while.'

Confusion creases his brow. 'I don't understand. We haven't launched the new website yet—'

'Daisy's handling that. It will go live tomorrow morning, along with a bunch of pre-recorded podcasts and trailers shot around the island over the last week.'

'So Daisy's sticking around but you're leaving?'

I don't like where this is going. I thought we were discreet but Kevin sounds like he knows.

'Yes.'

I don't offer more than a curt affirmation, hoping he'll leave it at that.

'But I thought...' He gives a rueful chuckle. 'Never mind.'

Relieved that Kevin isn't probing, I turn my computer screen so he can see what I've been working on. 'This is the reason I'm going to Melbourne. To meet with the founder of the Australian foster kids association and get the ball rolling on my idea.'

Kevin peruses the screen, reading quickly, before meeting my gaze head-on. 'What do you have in mind?'

'You know those old villas at the back of the property?'

He nods.

'I want to turn those into a holiday destination for foster kids and their families. Give them something that most never have, time away from the drudgery of their lives. Open up new horizons. Let them see there's more to life.'

'Wow, impressive.'

Kevin's audible admiration encourages me to continue.

'I want it up and running sooner rather than later, and I want to advertise the fact. But Daisy didn't agree initially.'

'What do you mean?'

'I wanted to add this onto the resort's main website so when prospective families look this place up they can see what's on offer. She agreed, but only if I'm the face of both campaigns to pull them together.'

'Sounds sensible—'

'It's not.' I shake my head, residual anger making me grit my teeth. 'I'm a private person. I don't want my face bandied around as some do-gooder. So the kids' programme needs to be an adjunct of what we've already come up with.'

A small frown appears between his brows. 'Isn't that muddying the message?'

My expression tightens but I give him a chance to elaborate.

'I mean, the whole aim of this PR campaign was to re-establish faith in consumers that the Rochester brand is being reinvigorated and going from strength to strength despite your grandfather's death. We want to promote the hell out of his island, use it as some kind of flagship resort, increase bookings by fifty per cent, and to do all that you hired a PR firm.'

Annoyed by his logic telling me nothing I don't already know, I say, 'And your point is?'

'While I think your idea for foster families is brilliant, I agree with Daisy. To make all this work cohesively, the rebranding and your idea, we need to make you the new face of the brand.'

I open my mouth to respond and he holds up his hand. I should be outraged but all I can think is he'll make a damn fine manager.

'I don't mean that to sound snobby or to reflect badly on the foster programme at all, but I think we have a great opportunity here to do something for those kids and why would you want to rush it without giving the programme due diligence?'

I nod, begrudgingly admitting he's made a valid point. 'I'm not trying to rush anything but the way I see it, why not make use of the launch to gain free publicity rather than having to duplicate all over again when the programme is up and running?'

'But won't you just have a vague outline of the programme if you add it onto the new website, with a "coming soon" label? Is that really the publicity you want when you could make a much bigger impact when there's actually something to see and links to bookings? Unless your ugly mug is plastered all over the website, only then will everyone know what you represent. High-end glamour for tourists and generous lodgings for kids in need.'

Fuck, he's making sense.

'You're right, but we're going ahead as planned.' I thump my desk in frustration and he jumps. 'Sorry. I fucked up with Daisy over this.'

'She's a professional, she'll do what's best for the Rochester brand.'

Yeah, but what about what's best for me?

I've never had anyone see through me the way she did. Even Pa didn't know the root of my problems and why I could never fully trust him. But she mentioned my abandonment issues with my dad like they were the most obvious thing in the world and the moment she said it, everything seemed so clear. My residual resentment, my quickness to push people away, my repressed emotions... I still blame my dad even though I dismissed him years ago as having no relevance in my life whatsoever.

Daisy helped me gain clarity and how did I repay her? By pushing her away like I do with everyone else. My gut churns and I grimace.

Kevin chuckles. 'I knew I was right. You two are an item.'

'We're not...' The automatic refusal dies on my lips.

We're something, but I don't know how to label what we are. Were. Considering I've fucked up deliberately.

'She's a nice girl. Good head on her shoulders.' He snickers. 'And anyone can see you two combust whenever you're near each other.'

'Is it that obvious?'

'Yeah, though only if you're looking for it.' He taps his chest. 'I'm an old gossip from way back. Your grandfather always said so and now that he's gone I've switched my busybody ways onto you.'

He pauses and stares at me with open speculation. 'So what are you going to do?'

I know what the right thing to do is. Go and find Daisy and apologise, yet again, for my appalling behaviour.

But what will that solve? She's about to leave like everyone else has in my life; starting with dear old dad who's done a stellar job of fucking me up for life.

Even Pa, who I let into my heart, left me. Through no fault of his own, and it's irrational to feel this way, but it hurts so much harder when I actually care about the person who leaves.

And I care about Daisy.

I need to leave before she does.

It's my only option.

'I'm flying to Melbourne as planned to set up the programme properly with the governing bodies, then I'll investigate further options for the PR.'

Sadly, it won't be with Daisy because I know after I've fucked up this badly she'll never want to work with me again.

Kevin's eyebrows rise again. 'You won't consult with Daisy before you leave?'

No way in hell.

I can't see her again because I'm at risk of wavering and seeing her in person will make my resolve crumble.

This has to end, on my terms.

'I'll consider all options when it comes to the PR for this programme.'

Kevin makes an odd disapproving sound that I ignore.

'I'm taking off within the hour so I'll leave all this in your capable hands.' I stand and offer him my hand, needing to get the hell out of here before he asks any more probing questions. 'I'll be in touch and feel free to contact me if there's any problems.'

'Shall do.' He shakes my hand, a powerful squeeze that tells me more than any words do. I admire a man with a strong handshake. It hints at hidden power. 'And good luck with your kids project.'

'Thanks.'

I'm looking forward to getting my idea off the ground but I can't shake the feeling that I've made a major mistake with Daisy. And I have no frigging clue how to fix it.

CHAPTER TWENTY-FOUR

Daisy

I WORK LIKE a maniac for the next few hours after my confrontation with Hart. It's the only way to ensure I don't curl up in a ball and rock forward and backwards.

He's hurt me. Badly.

And I brought it on myself.

I'm the stupid one for developing a full-blown crush. I'm the idiot who fell for him. I'm the moron for believing I had the power to invoke a change.

Men don't change. Any woman worth her XX chromosomes knows that. But I foolishly believed otherwise and now I'm paying the price.

I did the same with Casper—trying to invoke subtle changes in the hope he'd love me the way I loved him. But nothing I did was ever enough and I'm now dealing with the same emptiness, like my heart has been drained and stuck back in my body for purely biological reasons. It's aching. Not a metaphorical ache but a full-on pain in my chest that won't quit.

It makes me work harder because focussing on work rather than my stupidity can only help.

After three solid hours, my work is done. The Gem Island campaign is complete. All I need to do is hit a few buttons for the website and the preloaded social media posts to go live and I'm set to go.

But I need the client's final approval to do that; a physical signature on company documentation.

Damn. The last thing I want to do is face him again but I'll keep this professional: get the go-ahead, thank him for his business and be on my way.

However, when I reach his office, he's not there and his right-hand man, Kevin, is behind Hart's desk.

'Hi, Kevin. Is Hart around?'

'No, sorry, he's gone to Melbourne.'

Shock makes me almost drop my laptop. 'When?'

'He left a few hours ago.' He hesitates, as if evaluating the wisdom of saying more. 'And I don't know when he's coming back.'

My heart plummets and I know it has more to do with how appalled I am that he'd leave things so badly between us than wondering how he'll sign off on the campaign now.

'He's a headstrong young man, but I'm guessing you already know that?'

Kevin beckons me in and I step into the office, trying to avoid looking at the desk where our mutual anger sparked sensational sex.

'He certainly does have strong opinions,' I eventually say when Kevin stares at me expectantly.

'For what it's worth, I've never seen him look as happy as he has these last couple of weeks.'

Heat flushes my cheeks. Kevin knows? I can't imagine Hart telling him so that means we've been too obvious despite trying to keep our fling under wraps.

'Being back on the island has probably helped,' I say, my nonchalance failing when Kevin flashes a knowing grin.

'I think his happiness had more to do with you than Gem Island.' Kevin leans back in his chair, his expression that of a benevolent god controlling his minions. 'You've been good for him and he needs a woman like you in his life.'

I remain mute, not willing to corroborate his theory in case he's fishing for information regarding his boss.

'You're as strong-willed as him. You'll stand up to him and not take any of his crap. He needs that.'

I finally break. 'What he needs is a swift kick up the ass.'

Kevin laughs. 'See what I mean? You're perfect for him.'

Unfortunately, only two of us feel that way and we're both currently in this office.

'I need to discuss business.' I also need to get this conversation back on track because dwelling on what can never be isn't helping my already fragile state. 'If Hart's not around, can you help me?'

He nods. 'I'm the new general manager, so sure.'

'You're in charge?'

Wow, Hart really has done a runner. I shouldn't be surprised. It's exactly how I'd expect him to deal with anything unpleasant. We've been doing the

weird push-pull dance for a while now and this ultimate withdrawal should cement what I already know.

He's not a keeper.

Then again, he never professed to be one. He
warned me right from the start and I agreed because
I couldn't keep my hands off him. More fool me for
expecting things from a guy, things he was never
willing to give.

'I sure am, so what can I help you with?'

I place my laptop on the desk, flip open the cover
and type in my password, while sliding the paperwork
out of my bag. 'The campaign is ready to go live but
I need final approval and only the client can do that.'

Kevin stares at the screen for an eternity before
shaking his head. 'I'm sorry, I can't approve this.'

WTF? I've put in countless hours of work on this
project, it's the best work I've ever done and I need
this job to finish successfully. It can't stall now.

'What do you mean?'

Kevin closes down my screen. 'What I mean is,
even though I'm the new general manager, I can't
give final approval on a project that is essentially
Hart's baby. He needs to approve this, not me.'

He's looking way too smug and for a moment I
wonder if this is some lame ploy to push us together.

'But I need his physical signature on the paperwork.'

'Then I really think you should get his approval
in person.'

And I really think Chris Hemsworth should be
my personal butler for a week. Neither is going to
happen.

But I ask the question regardless. 'Why?'

'Because if you give up on him now you'll be yet another in a long line of people who've given up on him and we both know you're not a quitter. If you were, you would've already left the island the first time he tried to push you away.'

I gape, stunned by his insight.

It shifts the cogs in my head…is that why Hart left, so he could leave first? Does he feel something too? Has this been more than a fling? And the biggie, what will happen if I do as Kevin suggests?

I've already put myself out there for a guy before. I followed Casper: to a new suburb, to a new house, to a new life. I was the perfect fiancée and he crapped on my dreams regardless.

He took what I gave and more, with no regard for what I really wanted. And when I tried to articulate my dreams, my needs, he laughed in my face.

My folks are wrong. I didn't quit on Casper; I made a calculated choice for self-preservation. I should do the same now. Going after Hart isn't a smart move. He's emotionally closed-off and I don't have the energy to make a guy like me. Been there, done that, had the three-carat whopper to prove it.

I can't do it again: risk losing another piece of myself. Especially not with a guy who's already made it more than clear he doesn't want me. I'm many things, but a masochist isn't one of them.

I've always done the right thing my entire life. My parents relied on me to set a good example for my two younger sisters. My sisters used me as a buffer between their antics and my folks. Casper must've taken one look at me and thought 'perfect trophy wife' he could easily control and jerk around.

Being perfect isn't always a good thing, but isn't that what my fling with Hart was all about? A long-overdue, much-needed shot at being bad?

Following him would be beyond pathetic.

I can't do it.

But if what Kevin says is true, am I willing to fall into Hart's stereotype, that I'll leave him like all the rest?

I flung his abandonment issues in his face as a way to shake things up, to get him to admit the truth: that he's emotionally repressed and too damn scared to take a risk on us. Then I envisaged reassuring him and professing my feelings and…who knows after that?

But he didn't give me a chance. He shut me down verbally and now he's shut me down by leaving, ensuring we're over.

What if I prove to him we're not by showing him I won't quit on us?

'You're a smart girl, Daisy. You'll do what's right, for both of you.' Kevin makes a grand show of glancing at his watch. 'Now if you don't mind, the new general manager has some other tasks to approve.'

I knew it.

He's pushing us together.

But I'm not angry any more. I think he's right. I am smart.

Time to start acting like it.

CHAPTER TWENTY-FIVE

Hart

MY MEETING WITH the founder of the foster kids association goes to plan. He's blown away by my idea and will do anything he can to help get it off the ground. We brainstorm for several hours and when I leave his office in Collins Street I'm happy.

Okay, happy may be stretching the truth. I'm optimistic. There's a vast difference. I should know, I've rarely been happy. The last time was...an image of us in bed, Daisy curled into my side while teasing and joking, springs to mind.

Yeah, that was the last time I was truly happy and it sucks that I'll never have that again.

I stride down Collins Street, past the boutiques and restaurants and theatres. It's been years since I've been to Melbourne but I barely notice the changes. It's a concrete jungle, like many cities around the world. Glitz and glamour on the surface, hiding a seedy underbelly where homeless sleep in doorways and kids roam the streets in search of a better place to live.

I was fostered here, the third family I was with. They lived in North Melbourne, an older couple with one kid, a boy about my age, Erik. I was thirteen at the time, going through the awkwardness of puberty and struggling at a new high school, but the Pendleburys were good people. They were footy mad and dragged me to watch their beloved Kangaroos every weekend. And while the Aussie Rules game itself didn't interest me much, I grew to cherish those weekly outings to the football.

For the simple fact we felt like a real family.

During those few hours we crammed into the stadium with other supporters I'd sit with the Pendleburys and forget I was a ring-in, living with them for goodness knew how long. They'd ply me and Erik with home-made sandwiches and cakes, packets of chips and small rectangular juice boxes better suited to younger kids. I never complained. I never told Barb that I hated ham sandwiches and disliked cream in my cupcakes. I took everything she dished out gratefully because, amid the cheers and boos and feeding frenzy, I felt like I belonged.

Then Pa found me and my life transformed but I never forgot the footy-mad Pendleburys and the way they made me feel…safe for those years I lived with them.

As I turn into Swanston Street and head towards the iconic Flinders Street Station two blocks away, I'm plagued by the oddest feeling: restlessness.

I thought that by coming here and throwing myself into the new project I'd be suitably distracted.

But there's not much more I can do in person here. Usually, I'd welcome this edginess. It ensures I keep moving from place to place and don't allow myself to get attached to anything or anyone. I welcome it.

So why can't I summon up the enthusiasm to head to the airport and board a flight to Sydney?

I organised it after my meeting concluded, to keep momentum going for the project. I have a meeting scheduled there first thing in the morning. Then who knows? I might tour every capital city to ensure kids from all over the country have access to a holiday on Gem Island.

Yeah, it's doable. After Sydney I'll do a capital hop: Hobart, Adelaide, Perth, Darwin, with Brisbane last. I'm well aware of why I'll visit Queensland's capital last: Daisy lives there and the longer I stay away, the less likely I'll feel compelled to look her up.

In this case, I intend for absence not to make the heart grow fonder.

I grab a takeout coffee at a trendy café in Federation Square before hailing a taxi. I'm travelling light, though may have to buy a suitcase and a few more items of clothing if I'm planning a tour around the country that's longer than a week.

Pa used to laugh at me for my frugal packing whenever we travelled. He never understood my lack of need for things. Then again, he wouldn't have understood a lot of things about me.

Like how I kept a backpack in the back of my closet, packed with the barest necessities, in case I had to leave on short notice. It had happened before, when I'd escaped out of a bedroom window to avoid the heavy hand of my dad and hidden under a tree in the backyard.

Like how I rarely slept well, born of years of not closing my eyes due to fear of what may attack me in the darkness.

Like how I always kept snack bars in the pockets of all my suits because I never ever wanted to feel starvation clawing at my belly again.

Pa was great but I hid so much of myself from him. And if I couldn't truly be honest with the one man who meant everything to me, how can I ever presume to have a real relationship with a woman?

Annoyed how my thoughts keep drifting back to Daisy, I snatch a quick nap in the back of the taxi, only waking when we pull up outside the airport terminal.

'Last stop, Tullamarine,' the taxi driver says, punching in some numbers to calculate the final fare. I hand him a hundred-dollar bill and don't wait for the change.

'Thanks, mate,' he yells, but I'm already gone, seeking refuge in the air-conditioned terminal, eager to board my next flight.

My mobile rings before I make it through security. I hold my breath until I see it's Kevin's number on the screen.

My disappointment is acute and I clamp it down as I answer. 'Hey, Kevin, how's things?'

'All good here. How's Melbourne?'

'The same from what I can tell. Now I'm off to Sydney.'

'Are you serious?'

I don't understand Kevin's audible panic.

'Yeah, the meeting went well here so I'm heading off to another meeting in Sydney.'

'But…you can't…damn.' Kevin blows out a breath. 'I've stuffed up.'

He's barely been in the job twenty-four hours and my heart sinks. I have high expectations of Kevin. I need him to do a stellar job so I'm free to return to doing what I do best: travel the world, help foster kids and maintain ties to nobody.

'What have you done?'

'I think I may have sent Daisy on a wild goose chase.'

His answer does nothing to clear up the situation but I latch onto her name. Just hearing it makes my heart pound faster.

'Where is she?'

'Coming to see you in Melbourne.'

'What?'

I hold the phone away from my ear and stare at it. Yeah, like that's going to change what I just heard. 'Why the fuck would you do something as stupid as that?'

'Because she cares about you and you care about her.' He sounds defensive and oddly huffy. 'Besides, she needs your final approval for the campaign.'

'But you could've signed off on that…wait a minute, didn't the site go live this morning?'

I grit my teeth in frustration, knowing the answer before he speaks. I haven't had time to check the new website for Gem Island, what with being caught up in that meeting for hours. If it hasn't gone live, I won't be happy.

'No, it's not live yet. I figured a day's delay wouldn't be that big a deal so I told Daisy she needed your approval—'

'Why would you do that?'

But I already know. Kevin's trying to play matchmaker.

'Because you need a shove in the right direction and hopefully when she catches up with you, you'll do the right thing.'

'Did anybody ever tell you you're an interfering old busybody?'

'Your grandfather, all the time. For the record, it didn't stop me.' He snickers. 'You need to call her. Tell her where you are.'

I sigh, not in the mood for games. 'I will. And you need to butt the hell out of my private life.'

'But I was trying to get your snazzy new campaign approved. This has nothing to do with your personal—'

'You're a very bad liar as well as an interfering prick. I'll be in touch.'

I end the call and stare at the screen again. I don't use a screensaver, preferring to see functional apps against a black background.

Right now I know what needs to be done. I should

punch in the numbers I've memorised and speak to Daisy.

Instead, I slip the phone into my pocket and head through security.

I'll email her.

Later.

CHAPTER TWENTY-SIX

Daisy

I WAIT UNTIL my plane lands in Melbourne and I disembark before firing up my mobile to call Hart.

I have it all planned out. We'll meet at some public café in the heart of the city, far away from the temptation of hotel rooms and anything remotely resembling intimacy. I'll say our meeting is business but use it as a way to suss out how he's feeling.

Because all I can think about since Kevin mentioned it is how this amazing, infuriating man has such low expectations of other people.

Everybody leaves him; I'd already figured that much out. And considering my track record, he probably thinks I'll leave too. If I walked out on an engagement, what's tethering me to him? I need to confront the man and make him understand that I don't quit on the things that really matter.

I wait until I'm clear of the crowds disembarking before I hit the call button. It rings but the oddest thing happens. Rather than hearing the ringtone through my phone, I hear his signature tone, a honking horn, nearby.

It has to be a coincidence because a billion people would have that same ringtone but as I turn to seek the source of the sound, I lock eyes with Hart.

He's staring at me with horror and I laugh. He's definitely not happy to see me.

'Leaving Melbourne already?' I glance up at the board, which states the flight I've disembarked is leaving for Sydney in another hour. 'Let me guess, you heard I was coming.'

'Not everything revolves around you,' he says, grouchy as ever, but I see the fear in his eyes.

What is he afraid of? That I might actually make sense if he hears me out? That we could actually be happy beyond a fling? That I'll jump him in a public place?

'In case you were wondering, I did fly to Melbourne to talk to you face to face.'

When he doesn't speak, I point to my bag. 'The new campaign can't go live until you sign off on it.'

'You could've emailed me.'

'Yes, but I also need a physical signature. Company policy. Alf's stipulation, not mine.' As expected, he's not going to make this easy for me. 'Besides, where's the fun in that?'

He shakes his head, his lips compressed. 'I don't understand why you're here. I was a rude asshole to you and I left without apologising. You should be furious.'

'I am.' I stare at his neck. 'I'm imagining strangling you with my bare hands right now.'

'So why are you really here?'

'Already told you, I need your signature for final approval.' I gesture at a row of nearby seats that is vacant. 'Can we sit and get this over with?'

Because the sooner I take care of business, the sooner I can tell him the truth. That I'm crazy about him and not willing to end things between us. Not like this.

I slip my laptop out of its case and flip open the lid. We don't speak as it fires up and it's an awkward silence filled with too much unsaid. But I'm aware of him with every cell of my body. We're not touching but his thigh is close enough to mine that I want to reach out and stroke it. His strong forearms are resting on his thighs, with those capable hands...

I swallow to ease the dryness in my throat. The memory of what he can do with those hands...heat creeps into my cheeks.

I can smell him too, that signature citrus aftershave, so crisp, so fresh, I want to bury my face in his neck and guzzle until I've had my fill.

'Are you all right?'

'Yes, fine,' I mutter, the heat in my cheeks worsening. 'You know me. Must be a bit of residual motion sickness from the flight.'

His eyebrows rise in blatant scepticism. I don't blame him. I wouldn't buy my lame-ass excuse either.

Thankfully the screen flares to life and I swipe my thumb across the mouse pad to bring up the firm's retainer agreement.

'You've already seen the final product so all I

need is your electronic signature here and on the printed copy.'

He stares at the document on the laptop screen, expressionless. 'What if I don't sign?'

I rein in another impulse to strangle him. Closely followed by confusion. If he doesn't sign, the campaign won't go live…is that what he wants? Does he want to keep me alongside working with him? I hate second-guessing myself and I hate him for making me feel this discombobulated.

'What do you mean?'

'Nothing.' He touches my arm. It doesn't reassure me. 'I'll sign.'

I swipe my brow in mock exaggeration. 'Phew. For a minute there I thought I'd resigned for nothing.'

He rears back. 'What the—?'

'I quit my job. Yesterday.'

I shrug like it means little when in fact I'm terrified I did the wrong thing on a whim to follow my heart.

'But that means you won't get credit for this campaign and can't advertise the fact you were brilliant on it with your new business—'

'Some things are more important.'

I eyeball him, daring him to articulate what we both know.

I did this for him.

He capitulates first, tearing his eyes away to stare at the screen, muttering, 'Fuck.'

I suck in a breath, mustering my courage to lay it all on the line, well aware he could break my heart again but needing to do this regardless.

'I did this for us, in case you were wondering. I had no idea how long it would take me to find you if you didn't answer my calls so I quit, allowing me to follow you for as long as it takes to—'

'This is crazy. *You're* crazy.' He glares at me, wild-eyed and frantic. 'How could you do this? Your dream is to have your own PR company—'

'My dream is to be happy.'

It always has been. I just didn't know what could make me truly happy until I fell for this infuriating man.

'And you think I can make you happy?' He swipes his hand over his face, but not before I glimpse the sheer horror. 'Fuck, Daisy, I can't be responsible for your happiness, not when I'm so screwed up.'

'Who says?'

'I do!' His voice rises and several passengers nearby glance across at us, sporting matching expressions of concern.

I don't care. All I focus on is Hart and making him understand we can work if he faces his fears and gives us a chance.

'Listen, we can—'

'No, you listen. I can't be the man you want me to be. You deserve the best.' His voice breaks a little. 'And that's not me.'

Tears well in my eyes but I can't show weakness. I have to be strong enough for the both of us.

'I won't leave you,' I say, so softly he has to lean towards me to hear it. 'I'm not a quitter. You know that. It's been ingrained in me since birth. I don't give up easily.'

'Yeah? You quit your engagement to that dickhead named after a ghost and you just quit your job, so what's to say you won't do the same to me?'

He has a point. 'I can't give you a guarantee. You know life doesn't work like that. But I'm willing to take a chance because I believe in us. Can't you?'

He doesn't speak and I see the inner battle he wages play out across his face. Terror. Hope. Regret. Anxiety.

When he finally lays a hand over mine where it rests on my thigh, I know I've won.

'Do me a favour. Come with me to Sydney. See for yourself why I'm so fucked up. Then make your decision.'

Okay, so my relief is short-lived. But I can do this. He wants to scare me away? Let him try.

'Do you really think I'll change my mind?' I lean in close to murmur in his ear. 'I want you.'

He squeezes my hand and releases it. 'You're confusing sex for something more—'

'Don't do that.' I jab him in the chest, hard. 'Don't belittle what we have.'

To his credit, he nods, his expression sheepish. 'Fine. So we've got something beyond the phenomenal sex. But I don't do relationships. I never have.'

'That's because you're too busy running at the slightest sign of commitment.' I sigh and sidle closer to him so our arms and thighs are touching. 'Tell me why you left the island so quickly.'

He glances at me before his gaze shifts away. Guilty. 'I needed to meet with the founder of the foster kids association—'

'The real reason.' I nudge him gently with my shoulder.

He takes an eternity to answer and I hold my breath, willing him to admit the truth. 'Because I realised I started to feel more than physical attraction for you and I ran first before you could.'

'Better.' I exhale in relief and flash a smile. 'Not your rationale but the fact you actually admitted it.'

'It doesn't change anything,' he says, folding his arms and leaning away from me. 'I'm not the guy for you.'

'Why don't you let me be the judge of that?' I jerk my head at the screen. 'Now sign off on this so I can get your fabulous, whiz-bang campaign up and running, then I can organise my last-minute seat on this flight.'

He startles, like he doesn't expect I'll be boarding with him. 'I doubt you'll get on this flight.'

I make a grand show of looking around the boarding gate area, where there are many seats vacant. 'Really?'

He huffs out a breath. 'I'm making you do this, it's only fair I buy your ticket.'

'Fine. I'm unemployed at the moment and last-minute tickets cost a fortune.'

If he's surprised by my quick capitulation he doesn't show it. 'Here. Let me sign off, then I'll book you a ticket online.'

I slide my laptop across to him, drumming my fingers impatiently against my leg. I want him to do this fast so he doesn't change his mind, because the fact he actually wants me to accompany him to Sydney, albeit to scare me off, is huge. I didn't expect it. I thought I'd have to do a lot more cajoling—once I actually caught up with him, that is. I envisaged more resistance, less cooperation.

'There. Signed. I'll do the hard copy later.' He hands me back the laptop and slides his mobile out of his pocket.

He eyes my radiant smile with suspicion as he swipes his finger across the screen, pulling up the relevant website to book me a ticket. He frowns and my heart sinks. I'm not getting on this flight.

When he flips the mobile towards me so I can see, I beam.

'Sorry to disappoint but it looks like I'm coming with you to Sydney.'

His frown deepens. 'So it seems.'

'Is it too much to hope I scored a seat next to you?'

He rolls his eyes but I glimpse the glimmer of a smile. 'Unfortunately, I have to put up with you next to me for the full one-hour-twenty-minute flight.'

'Yahoo.' I do a little dance with my hands clasped, arms outstretched and shoulders rolling.

His frown vanishes. 'See? You're definitely crazy.'

'Crazy about you,' I murmur, hoping he can see how much he means to me in my eyes.

When he leans forward to brush a kiss across my lips, I sigh.

I'm one step closer to that elusive happiness.

CHAPTER TWENTY-SEVEN

Hart

I SHOULD NEVER have agreed to this.

I should've lied and told Daisy the flight was booked. Then I could've avoided this pure torture.

We're thirty minutes into the flight, with less than an hour to go. I doubt I'll make it, what with her constant touching. I have no idea if its deliberate, her idea of making me see what I'm missing out on, or accidental, but whatever the reason it's driving me slowly but surely insane.

She's flirting too and I can only hold out so long. I'm a guy after all and she's a sexy woman I've had the pleasure of being inside, of licking, of tasting, of hearing the sounds she makes when she comes.

My cock is rigid and has been since she sat next to me. I'm a lost cause.

'Nuts?'

My balls throb. You have no idea, I want to respond as she offers me a packet of cashews and I try not to shy away.

She's leaning over, pushing her breast against my arm, and I grit my teeth.

'No, thanks.' I stare straight ahead and return the tray to its upright position. Big mistake, as her gaze drops to my groin, where I'm sporting a massive boner clearly outlined by my pants.

'Wow,' she says, pushing her breast a tad harder against my arm, leaving me in no doubt her whole touching routine has been deliberate. 'I sure wish I could help you with that.'

Her saucy taunt evokes an image of her doing just that. Taking me into her mouth. Stroking me with her talented tongue. Sucking.

I make a half-strangled sound and she has the audacity to laugh.

'Pity it's not an international flight, we could've indulged in a little mile-high action.' She straightens and I instantly miss the feel of her breast pressed against me. 'Maybe we could fly to Auckland next time?' She winks. 'Three and a half hours should just about do it.'

'Stop. You're killing me.' I shift in my seat. It does nothing to relieve the ache in my balls. I reach for a magazine to hide my hard-on before I give the flight attendants an eyeful too.

'Not yet, but give me a little one-on-one time and—'

I kiss her. It's the only way I can think to shut her up. But I haven't thought it through because the moment her mouth opens beneath mine I'm a goner. Lost in the relentless pull between us, the yearning to possess, the craving that won't be satisfied with just a kiss.

When her tongue darts forward and touches mine I wrench my mouth away, desperate for air, desperate for more. There's a discreet cough and a disapproving glare from the older couple across the aisle, while the male flight attendant handing out drinks a few seats up gives me a thumbs up.

'Well, that was unexpected.' She dabs at her lips with her fingertips, her eyes wide, her skin flushed. 'Now I really wish we were on an international flight.'

'Stop with the flirting.' I make a zipping motion over my lips. 'No banter until we land.'

'Then it's no holds barred?'

I groan and press my fingertips to my temples. 'I've got a headache.'

'Yeah, but which head is aching?'

I manage a rueful chuckle and she grins, as we share a moment of complete and utter sync the likes of which I never imagined having with a woman.

Seeing her again, having her this close, sparring with her, has made me realise how much I'll miss her when it's over for good. And it will be. I'll make sure of it.

She won't listen to me. She doesn't believe me when I say I'm no good for her. So I'll have to show her.

It's the only thing I could think of on the spur of the moment when she kept haranguing me. To take her to the place where I spent a lot of time growing up so she can see for herself why kids like me become closed off and eventually push away anyone who's foolish enough to get close.

I'm not a complete idiot. I know my heart is fissured and open to her a tad. But I can never give myself one hundred per cent, not in the way she expects and deserves.

That's what gets to me the most in our fucked-up scenario. She's so damn deserving of the perfect guy, the perfect house, the perfect dream, but she doesn't know it.

She's fallen for me, like I have for her, but whereas I'm tough enough to make the smart choice and walk away, she has visions of happily-ever-after.

I'll show her in Sydney that there's no such thing.

'You've gone all quiet.' She bumps me with her shoulder. 'Are you imagining all the ways I can relieve your tension?'

My cock throbs. 'You promised no more flirting on this flight.'

She holds her hands up and feigns surprise. 'Hey, I was just talking about a massage. Can I help it if you hear innuendo in every single thing I say?'

'You are incorrigible.'

'Why thank you.' She does a mock curtsy in her seat, her grin making her eyes sparkle, and it hits me.

I may think it's going to be easy walking away from Daisy.

I may know it's the smart choice for both of us.

But when it comes to actually ending this for good, it's going to rip my fucking heart out.

CHAPTER TWENTY-EIGHT

Daisy

I DON'T PLAY FAIR.

I've done everything in my power to tease Hart on the flight from Melbourne and as we touch down in Sydney I feel like flinging my arms high overhead in victory.

I wanted to show him what he's missing out on by not giving us a chance. I achieved my goal, plus got an added bonus of seeing visual proof that he still wants me as badly as I want him. Though seeing his boner proved somewhat problematic for me, making me practically squirm with wanting to do something about it.

I might have talked the talk but inside I was burning up. I've never experienced such lust before, the kind of craving for a guy that's irrational and confrontational and utterly sensational.

I don't envision doing naughty things with men on planes as a rule but sitting next to Hart, deliberately brushing up against him, taunting him, only served to ratchet up my own desire to unbearable levels.

We join the taxi rank outside the airport and are soon ensconced in air-conditioned comfort. I haven't been to Sydney for years and I forgot the humidity makes my hair resemble a frizz ball.

He hasn't said much since we disembarked but I can see the tension in his rigid neck muscles, and in the clench of his jaw. Maybe I've pushed him too far but I don't care. He needs his stubborn ass kicked for being so closed off to the possibility of us.

'Where are we going?'

'You'll see.'

I snort my disgust. 'You know this grand plan of yours to push me away isn't going to work, right?'

He stares straight ahead like he hasn't even heard me.

I poke him in the arm. 'Hey, I'm talking to you.'

He slowly turns his head, like looking me in the eye is the last thing he wants to do, and when I see his expression I know why. He's in pain. The kind of pain I know well because it's exactly what I felt back on Gem Island when I discovered he'd left without a word.

'This isn't a game.' He's gutted, the agony in his eyes making me want to undo my seat belt and fling myself into his arms. 'I need you to understand where I came from, why I am the way I am, why I can't give you anything.'

'I'm not asking for anything.' I place my hand

on his thigh. 'I only want time to explore what we started on the island. That's it. No expectations.'

He stares at my hand like it's scorching him, before covering it with his with obvious reluctance. 'There are always expectations.'

I squeeze his thigh and he flinches. 'Okay, how's this for expectations? I *expect* you to finish what we started on the plane. I *expect* you to make me scream because I'm on edge. And if you're really determined to end this within the next hour or so, I *expect* you to take me somewhere right now so we can give this fling/relationship/whatever-you-want-to-call-it the proper send-off it deserves.'

His hand grips mine so tight I feel the tendons crunching. I don't complain. Because I see my outburst has sparked something within him. His eyes glow like polished glass before his gaze drops to my mouth.

He wants this. Wants me.

'Yep, you're fucking killing me,' he mutters, before he leans forward and directs the driver to an address in Darlinghurst.

'You'd better be taking me to a hotel,' I murmur beneath my breath and when he sits back, he shoots me a glance that's pure wickedness.

'And you'd better put that mouth to other uses besides giving me a hard time when we get to the hotel,' he says, his tone tinged with reluctant amusement.

'Oh, I will. Trust me.' I slide my hand higher on his thigh and he clamps down on it before I hit the jackpot.

'You are in so much trouble,' he mutters, but as we lock gazes—molten heat tinged with excitement—I can't wait to get into trouble of the good kind.

He turns his hand over, palm up, and intertwines his fingers with mine. We sit in silence and hold hands for the rest of the fifteen-minute drive. I don't mind. I like the quiet. It gives me a chance to formulate what I'm going to say later, when he inevitably tries to push me away.

I'm deep in thought when we pull up outside a hotel. It's rather ramshackle and nothing like the five-star place I imagined. Not because I'm a snob or because I expect Hart to fork out a fortune for a quickie because he's rich, but it's surprising he would want this to be where we have fantastic reunion sex.

Unless…he's really serious about this being a rousing send-off and doesn't particularly care where we do it.

The thought saddens me but I paste a smile on my face as he pays the driver and helps me out of the taxi. He hasn't released my hand and is staring at me, looking for some kind of judgement perhaps?

'Ready?' I squeeze his hand and I glimpse a flicker of disappointment.

Oh, yeah, bringing me here is part of his grand plan to alienate me but I'll be damned if I give him the satisfaction.

'Absolutely,' he says, with less conviction, as we stroll into the foyer.

It's nothing like I expect and at complete odds with the seedy exterior. The owners have stuck with an old-world charm theme, from the black and white tessellated tiles on the floor to the gleaming brass lamps casting light over crimson velvet sofas strategically placed throughout.

It's not a large space but it exudes a welcome cosiness and I experience a twang of jealousy at the thought of Hart knowing to come here and with whom he might have been here in the past.

'Give me a minute.' He releases my hand and approaches the sole reception staff behind the desk, a sixty-something brassy blonde who wouldn't look out of place draped across one of the sofas in a flapper dress.

He slides across his credit card, signs a slip of paper and pockets a key. An actual old-fashioned key, not the plastic swipe cards that most modern hotels favour these days.

It's madness, because I instigated this, but I'm struck by a sudden case of nerves. The moment I emailed Alf my resignation I set these events in motion. Finding Hart. Following my heart.

But what if I'm wrong?

What if this is nothing more to him than a last, quick fuck?

If he truly won't let me into his heart and his life?

'We're on the second floor. There are no functional elevators. We need to take the stairs.' He holds out his hand and I know without a doubt that he's giving me an out. One last chance to turn tail and run.

I stare at his palm: the strong lifeline, the weaker

marriage lines and those long, strong fingers that have strummed every inch of me.

A blinding fear makes me tremble imperceptibly.

But I can't turn back now.

I have to know that I've given it all I can.

I can't quit now when I've come this far.

'Pity we have to take the stairs because I don't want you tiring yourself out.' I place my hand in his and he tugs me hard so that I stumble and land flush against him.

'Are you questioning my stamina?'

He presses his boner against me, grinds against me a little.

'No, but I'm questioning your sanity in teasing me down here when we could be upstairs, already naked.'

He lowers his head and nibbles on my neck, my skin breaking out in instant goose bumps. 'You know all that teasing on the plane? I'm going to make you pay.'

'Promises, promises,' I whisper in his ear, a second before I bite the lobe a tad hard.

He doesn't even flinch but I hear a low moan. 'Come on.'

We walk, fast, towards the ornate staircase that winds between the three floors in a sweeping circle.

'You couldn't have chosen a room on the ground floor?' I ask as we hit the first at a fair pace.

'I didn't want anyone to hear you scream when I lick you out.'

There's no suitable verbal response to that but the

dampness between my legs makes me want to sprint. We skip every second step and arrive at the second floor panting, but I don't think it's from the exertion.

'Room two-twenty-two,' he says, almost heading the wrong way in his hurry to get me naked. At least, that's what I hope.

'It's to the left.' I point at the directions posted on the wall in front of us and he mutters a curse before we take off in the opposite direction.

We're almost running by the time we reach the room, at the end of a long hallway. He jabs the key in the lock, misses the first time and I chuckle. He shoots me a filthy look before trying again and this time the relic slides in and turns first try.

He pushes open the solid mahogany door and waits until I pass before letting it close. I barely have time to register a smallish room that resembles a brothel from the fifties—crimson carpet, drapes and bed-spread, with purple lamp shades, recliner and vinyl-topped desk, and gold accenting everywhere—before he's on me. Grabbing my wrists and lifting them overhead. Pinning me to the wall. His body flush against mine.

It's exactly what I want.

'You drive me wild,' he mutters, claiming my mouth in a searing kiss that sizzles all the way down to where I want him most.

My nipples peak, craving the relief only his mouth can give. As if reading my mind he dips his head and nips them through the cotton of my shirt, a sharp bite that's more pleasure than pain.

I can't keep still. I writhe against him, my hips undulating of their own accord. He holds my wrists overhead with one hand and uses the other to rip open my shirt. Thank goodness for pop stud buttons.

Then his mouth is on me. On my collarbone, my chest and finally my nipples when he flicks my bra hooks open at the back.

He laves and licks and sucks, moving from right to left, leaving the nipples rigid and wet. Then he blows the faintest puff of air on them and I'm arching off the wall.

'Please, Hart…don't make me beg.'

The corner of his mouth crooks. 'Might be kind of fun.'

'No. You. Inside me. Now.'

I'm bossy and petulant and he laughs.

'Okay.' He releases my wrists and they fall limply to my side. I'm tingling, though I doubt it's from the lack of circulation. Because it's spreading all over my body, starting from my breasts that he's staring at like the best damn thing he's ever seen, all the way down to my toes.

'But first, I must do this.' He drops to his knees and eases my skirt and panties down in one go. There's no waiting, no preamble; his mouth is on me and I let out a moan.

He tongues my clit with the perfect pressure, the perfect rhythm, just freaking perfect… I've been on the edge since the taxi ride and my muscles quickly tense, the pleasure spiralling out of control as my orgasm hits like a freight train, making my knees buckle.

I have no idea I'm bucking until he steadies my hips with his hands and places an almost chaste kiss above my bikini line.

Then he's unzipping and sheathing and inside me. Hard and long and thick, a wistful sigh escaping my lips.

I want this all the time.

I want him all the time.

Not just because of how he makes me feel, like no other man can ever fulfil me this way, but because I deserve this.

I deserve him, no matter how damn unworthy he thinks he is.

His mouth covers mine in a soft kiss that defies the way he's pounding into me. In and out. So hard. So good. Over and over until I'm climbing again, winding tighter and tighter, ready to come apart.

My thighs tremble and he changes the angle of our joined pelvises by bending his knees a little. It's enough to push me over as I groan into his mouth. It drives him a little nuts as he thrusts into me so hard I'm now standing on tiptoes, my head clunking the wall.

I don't think it registers because he's devouring me with his mouth and a second later he comes, wrenching his mouth from mine to stare at me like I've given him the greatest gift.

It's disarming, the intensity of his stare. I can't get a read on it and as we stand there, with him still inside me, our bodies slick with sweat, our chests heaving with the effort of dragging air into our lungs, I don't know what confuses me more. The fact his expression is fearful and hesitant while his eyes are adoring and tender or the fact I'm terrified of discovering that in following my heart I may have lost him anyway.

CHAPTER TWENTY-NINE

Hart

I'M HANGING ONTO my sanity by a thread.

I never should've allowed Daisy to lead me astray.

Fuck, I sound like some naïve kid. What a joke. From the moment I laid eyes on her at the airport in Melbourne I wanted her with a ferocity that shakes my belief system to the core.

I deliberately chose a hotel near the Cross so that we could walk to the skate ramp afterwards. But now that the time has come, I'm reluctant. I'd rather stay in this hotel room for ever.

Which is enough to propel me out of bed and into the shower and out onto the street faster than I can blink.

Daisy knows I'm running. She hasn't called me on it because she's too high on loved-up endorphins. But she will. And I'm dreading it. The moment when I finally reveal my true self she'll be let down like all the rest and she'll bolt.

I'm counting on it.

'Is it far?'

'No.' I'm monosyllabic and have been since we left the hotel on foot five minutes ago.

'So do I get a clue about this great revelation?'

'No.'

'A man of few words. I like it.'

I shoot her a scathing glare and it bounces off her like the rays of sunshine glinting off her hair. It's been a long day and dusk will fall soon but she looks as fresh as a...well, as a daisy. Shit, even my thoughts are turning corny.

'Does nothing I say faze you?'

'No.' She pauses and her cheeky grin is infectious. 'There. How do you like a one-word answer?'

'Love it.'

'Liar,' she says and takes my hand. I let her. While I want to drive her away permanently, if I can make this as painless as possible for her I will.

We round the corner, walk another block and we're there. A grungy skate ramp tucked into the back streets of Australia's seediest suburb, renowned for its pimps and hookers and drugs. King's Cross always draws a crowd, from curious tourists to bucks' parties looking for a good time. But its faux glitz hides a multitude of sins and I've seen them all.

The kids that hang out here are hiding from something or running from something or both. I know I was.

We stop on the outskirts, behind a half-collapsed chain-link fence. Not much has changed. There's a rectangular patch of cracked concrete to the left, with one basketball hoop at the far end, and a bunch of ramps of varying heights to the right. Kids cluster around both ends. Some are on skateboards, some are passing a basketball back and forth, all sport the same wary expressions with darting eyes and permanent scowls.

'What is this place?'

'An escape for kids, mostly foster, a few runaways.' I point to a small tin shed near the hoop. 'That's where the drug deals get done.' I wave towards an alley that snakes behind the ramps. 'And that's where the creeps gutter crawl to pick up the kids willing to do anything for money.'

To her credit she doesn't recoil like I expect but the sadness down-turning her mouth and the pity in her eyes guts me.

'You used to hang out here.'

It's a statement, but I know there's a bunch of questions hovering. I want her to ask. I want to shock her. I want to drive her away.

'Yeah, I hung out here every chance I got. I was eleven. Living in a nightmare and the kids here were the only ones who got me.'

She squeezes my hand. 'Tell me about the nightmare.'

I don't want to talk. Talking achieves nothing. How many dumb-ass psychologists have tried to get me to open up? Countless but they were useless. I fed them the usual trite drivel: I'm sad because I don't have parents; I'm mad because I have to live with a bunch of strangers who don't give a shit about me;

I'm bad because it gets me attention. They offered trite platitudes, not having a clue as to the emptiness that made my chest ache on a daily basis.

She's looking at me expectantly and I have to give her something now that I've started down this track.

'It's the usual nightmare for kids like me. Channelling anger to push people away and scare them into thinking I was a badass before they hurt me. Being labelled a troublemaker because of it. Doing all kinds of bad shit to ensure I kept them at arm's length. Ensuring I hurt them before they hurt me.'

'You must've tolerated so much.' She leans into me, resting her head on my bicep. She doesn't offer a pity-filled apology, which surprises me. 'I know this doesn't make up for what you went through, but you're an amazingly strong man and I think your experiences have shaped you.'

They sure have. But not in a good way. I can't shake the instinct to run. It's ingrained now. It's who I am. Not even Pa's unswerving and undeserving faith swayed me. He did everything in his power to make me stay: he trusted me, he adored me, he loved me. I ran anyway.

He hid it well but I gutted him and I'll end up doing the same to Daisy. I'm doing her a favour in pushing her away first. Much easier if I end this now.

'See those kids shooting hoops?'

She nods, her cheek brushing my arm. It feels nice, having her this close. I make the most of it because it won't be for much longer.

'They'll end up beating the crap out of each other soon.'

'Why?'

'Because anger festers and builds and trying to blow off steam throwing a basketball around isn't enough.'

As if on cue, a puny kid with straggly hair shoves a bigger boy square in the chest and it's on. The boys push and punch, fists flying, with the occasional kick thrown in.

Daisy gasps as one of the kids falls to the ground and another kicks him in the guts, leaving him clutching his stomach and rolling around. The fight breaks up after that and they resume dribbling the ball, passing it, and shooting. The kid on the ground pushes to his feet after a few moments and joins in.

'You wanted me to stop that, didn't you?'

She glances up at me and the tears in her eyes slug me. 'Yeah.'

'It would've only inflamed them, having an older dude step in.' I bark out a laugh devoid of amusement. 'Trust me, I know. Been there, done that, still have the scars to prove it.'

'Is that how you got that scar on your hip? And the one on your lower back?'

She sounds on the verge of tears, which slays me, but it's what I want: for her to understand why we can never be together.

'Yeah. I was wrestling with a mean kid on the ground and a passer-by tried to intervene. The fight got worse, knives came out, I got nicked twice.'

Her hand flies to her mouth. 'You were stabbed?'

'More like glancing blows with the pointy end but it hurt like the devil.'

She buries her face in my chest and I'm left with no option but to hold her. I want to dip my face to her hair and inhale so badly that I feel light-headed but I resist.

I need her to be appalled so I keep talking.

'What happened to me with that knife didn't hurt half as much as constantly being called a bunch of names I can't repeat, or forever being told you're fucking worthless so that soon you believe it, or being so fucking angry at my shitty life that I beat up on any kid I could whenever I could—'

'Stop.' She pushes off my chest and tilts her head to look up at me. Her cheeks are tear-stained, her eyes bloodshot. 'I get it. You think I'll be repulsed by what you went through so I won't want to be with you any more.'

She shakes her head and more tears seep out of the corners of her eyes. 'But I l-like you and hearing all this breaks my heart.'

That makes two of us, because I know walking away from Daisy is going to be the hardest thing I've ever done.

'I'm telling you this so you understand why I can never be in a relationship.' I take her face in my hands, cupping gently, splaying my fingers wide over her ears so she hears what I have to say. 'I'm broken inside. I can't forget the horrors no matter how hard I try. And I've tried. Professionals, meds, nothing worked. So I cope the best I can by helping kids like me. It soothes something inside me but it will never ever fix me.'

Tears trickle down her cheeks and drip onto my thumbs. 'You don't need to be fixed. You need to allow someone in—'

'Please don't tell me what I need.' I release her and step back, starting the process to distance myself. It hurts like a bastard, far worse than the sting of those knife wounds. 'I know I can't give anything more of myself than I already have. And yeah, I admit it's been a lot more than sex between us. And I feel more for you than I ever have for any other woman. But I can't do this, Daisy.'

My throat tightens but I force the words out. 'I can't be the man you want.'

I turn away and swipe a hand across my eyes so she doesn't see the evidence of how badly I wish things were different.

'I brought Pa here once, to show him where I came from—'

'No, you brought him here to push him away like you're trying to do to me.' She lays a hand on my shoulder and spins me back round to face her. 'How did he react?'

'Appalled, like you, but he tried to hide it.' I bark out a laugh. 'He had the audacity to try and turn our visit into a happy memory for me.' I point to the hoops. 'He made me wait until most of the kids left, then we shot a little one-on-one.'

The memory makes me choke up. 'He was a good man and I didn't do right by him either.'

'He loved you. Sometimes that has to be enough.'

Startled, I search her eyes for answers and end up losing myself in the shimmer of her tears. I need to pull her out of this fanciful dream where the two of us end up together.

'You were right, by the way. About my issues stemming from my dad abandoning me.' My gaze drifts to the fence and the kids beyond it. 'The moment he dumped me is the first time I lost trust in everybody and I've never been able to regain it.'

I point to the hoop in the distance. 'Even that day Pa tried so hard to make this place better for me, he disappointed me, because he never truly understood why I brought him here.'

Confusion creases her brow. 'To push him away, right?'

I shake my head, tapping my chest. 'Not just that. I needed him to validate what I'd been through, to acknowledge that it all started with his daughter abandoning me, hell, maybe to even take some of the blame. Which is ridiculous, I know that, but I had so many years of pent-up frustration that I needed him to be my saviour and when he didn't live up to my expectations when I brought him here… I kind of lost faith in anything good happening for me, ever.'

She's staring at me, wide-eyed, and what I see terrifies me more than anything: acceptance, understanding, with a healthy dose of pity thrown in.

'Maybe part of the guilt you harbour surrounding your grandfather and not being good enough for him is misplaced.' She hesitates, before continuing. 'Maybe you regret not being as close to him as you would've liked? That what happened here, him disappointing you, is your way of justifying that?'

I hate how damn insightful she is and in that moment, I realise she's right. If Pa and I were as close as I thought, I would've been there for him at the end; and before that, for all those years when I abandoned him before he could do the same to me.

'But just so you know, you are worthy.' She presses her hand to my heart. 'And I won't let you down.'

I want to believe her, I really do. I've tried so hard to push her away yet she's still here and for a moment I contemplate giving in.

I can let go of a lifetime's resentment and fear right now. I can let her in. I can have belief that she won't disappoint me, that she won't quit on me, that she won't abandon me.

I want to do it. She's helped lead me to this moment.

I open my mouth to speak but the words don't come. My throat is tight, clogged with the fear of taking a leap of faith.

Instead, I shake my head and her quiet sob undoes me completely.

I hold out my hand, waiting until she takes it before we start walking away from my past and into a future filled with lifelong uncertainty.

CHAPTER THIRTY

Daisy

HART THINKS HE knows me but he doesn't; especially the part where I don't quit. Ever. Sure, I've told him repeatedly but he doesn't believe me. He's a sceptic. Considering what he's showed me at the skate park, I don't blame him.

As we walk back to the hotel I don't argue or plead with him. It's not the time. His emotions are raw and I can't talk past the tears clogging my throat, so we stride in silence. He's walking fast, like he can't wait to ditch me, and I keep up because I'm too scared that if I release his hand he'll bolt.

He has revealed so much of himself, expecting me to walk away. But I can't. I won't.

I love him.

I don't give up on the people I love.

He has taught me that.

Not my family, not me, him. By doing his utmost to push me away, he's opened my eyes to how determined I can be when I really want something.

He expects me to walk away so I'll prove my love to him by doing the exact opposite. I won't quit. Not this time.

I won't give up on Hart like all the other people in his life.

When we reach the hotel, he pauses outside and tries to slip his hand out of mine. I tighten my grip.

Adlers don't quit, Daisy. I've never been so happy to hear Dad's annoying voice in my head. It gives me the courage to face the next ten minutes; such a short snapshot in time but one that will shape my future. Our future, hopefully.

'I need to show you something up in the room and then if you still want to leave, you can leave.' I sound remarkably calm for someone wanting to blubber because I'm filled with uncertainty and fear.

Hart's past has shaped him, I get that, like mine has influenced me. I want him in my life. Not because I see him as some challenge not to quit from, but because he makes me feel happier than I've ever been. Despite his moods and his recalcitrance, I know deep down he's the one I want to be with and that's worth fighting for.

If I wasted my time and energy fighting for Casper and our empty relationship, I'm certainly willing to do whatever it takes to convince Hart we're meant to be.

'Come upstairs, for a minute.' I tug on his hand, more insistently this time.

He stares at me for an eternity, his eyes inscrutable. 'I can't—'

'You owe me that much.'

'Fuck.' He wrenches his gaze away and stares over my shoulder, indecision twisting his mouth.

When he doesn't make a move to leave I squeeze his hand. 'Come on. It won't take long.'

It's too early for relief, not until I see this through until the end, but at least we climb those interminable stairs to our room, where I've left my stuff including my laptop.

When we enter the room I release his hand and wish I could take a quick swig from the minibar for fortitude.

He doesn't sit and I don't either as I fire up my laptop on the desk in the corner.

'Whatever you're doing, Daisy, it won't work—'

'Shut up and look at this.'

I swivel the screen towards him and type furiously for a moment, bringing up the relevant information.

Then I let him look and read and absorb.

I hear a muttered, 'Fuck,' followed by, 'When did you do all this?'

'On Gem Island, after our last meeting.' Buoyed by the wonder in his eyes, I continue. 'I could tell you'd never budge on your stance to stay out of the limelight, despite the fact you're a PR dream to tie in the resort with your kids' holiday programme, so I agreed to do it your way. But I knew melding both our visions had potential and came up with this. What do you think?'

'But it must've taken you hours…' He shakes his head, unable to tear his gaze from the screen.

'I didn't sleep.' I shrug like it means little when in reality it means everything. 'I wanted to show you what happens when we compromise.'

'Why?'

'Because we're great together, professionally and personally.' I take a deep breath and blow it out. 'I wanted to prove to you that I listen. That I take everything you say on board. That I make informed decisions. That even when I fear I'm not good enough and the doubts creep in, I'm still willing to keep the faith and invest in something worth believing in.'

He's frowning, staring at me with blatant wariness. 'What are you saying?'

'That I'm just as vulnerable as you, that I've had to overcome my own fears of unworthiness even to be here again after the way you ended things on the island. And I've heard everything you've said, now and down at the skate park. And my decision is you.' I step towards him and lay my hand on his chest, over his heart. 'I choose you.'

Shock renders him immobile and he gapes, before shaking his head. 'I'm no good for you—'

I fling myself at Hart, cutting off his words by plastering my mouth to his. He half pushes me away but then he's kissing me back, hot and deep and frantic.

He backs me up until my butt hits the desk and cups my ass so I can do a little leap and wrap my legs around his waist.

I hang on tight as our tongues duel, slow, sensual sweeps that make me moan. He's consuming me, like he can't get enough. I know the feeling well.

When he wrenches his mouth from mine, we're breathing hard, my butt is sore from perching on the sharp edge of the desk and my thighs have cramped where they're clasped around his waist.

I don't care. He's a man of few words so the fact he's still here and kissing me means more than anything he can say. At least, I hope it is, and that wasn't a stupendously hot goodbye kiss.

I lower my legs and he helps me into a standing position, then takes my hand and walks to the sofa. He sits and tugs me down next to him. We're holding hands but he can't look at me and my hopes plummet.

'I need to tell you a bunch of stuff and I need you to listen,' he murmurs, his voice barely above a croak.

'Okay.'

'When my dad gave up on me, I was devastated and ended up pushing people away first before they hurt me. Pa never gave up on me but you're right, I never truly let him in…and I have to live with that regret every single fucking day.' He's staring at some folksy print of the Harbour Bridge on the far wall, but not really seeing it, his eyes glazed with pain. 'I don't know if I'm capable of love, let alone giving a woman like you what you need.'

Blinking back tears, I say, 'What do you think I need?'

'Everything.' His head falls forward and I bite my bottom lip to stop the sobs threatening to spill out.

'There's only one thing I really need and that's you.'

I can't stem the tears any longer and they trickle down my cheeks.

'Fuck, don't cry, not because of me.' He bundles me into his arms and I let go, the sobs bubbling up from deep within, wave after wave until I'm drained and clinging to him.

I eventually quieten and he eases back, his expression stricken, his eyes dark with pain.

'I will hurt you,' he says. 'I will push you away and be grumpy and be a total asshole, because I'm so fucking scared you'll leave me and that will kill me...' He clears his throat and his eyes, those beautiful eyes, fill with tears. 'Because for the first time in my life I think I know what love is.'

The ache in my chest expands until I'm filled with it. Hope.

'I haven't slept much so I don't think this is a dream, but just in case...' I pinch him on the arm, hard.

'Ow. Easy, babe, that'll leave a bruise.' His hands slide down my arms, up my waist, up my torso, over my shoulders, where they come to rest, his touch light.

He stares at me for an eternity, like he's trying to memorise my features. 'Did you hear what I said?'

'I heard. And for the record, I get it. You push people away as a protective mechanism and it's so ingrained you can't shake it.' My fingertips graze his cheek. 'I'm sorry that you didn't get the chance to truly open up to your grandfather. And I hate all the horrors you had to endure growing up. But I'm here. I love you. And I won't leave you.'

He stiffens, his neck muscles protruding. 'You're insane to love someone like me.'

I grin like a lunatic. 'Yeah, I am, crazy in love.'

'Fuck me,' he mutters, but his lips curl into a soft smile that wipes years off his face. 'I guess that's okay because I think I love you too.'

My heart leaps and my stomach goes into free fall. 'Not exactly a rousing endorsement but I'll take it.'

His expression is dazed, like he's just woken up, and he shakes his head. 'I never thought you'd take a chance on an emotionally stunted asshole that has done everything in his power to push you away since we first met.'

'You're not emotionally stunted,' I deadpan.

He grins at my quip. 'You know, during all the time I hung out with foster kids, during all my travels, even during the good times with Pa, I never felt as comfortable as I do with you.'

He blinks but he can't hide the tenderness that almost undoes me. 'You're truly unique, Daisy, because I don't want to run from you.' He thumps his chest with one hand. 'In here. For the first time ever, I want to take a risk on someone, because I feel... safe when I'm with you, and that has never, ever happened before.'

Of course I blubber again. I can't help myself, as tears leak out of my eyes.

'So I'll make a deal with you. I won't push you away any more, and I'll love you as best I can, if you promise to tell me if you're not happy or if you want out.' He clasps my chin and eyeballs me. 'I need to know if you want to leave me.'

'Deal,' I murmur, burying my face in his chest and wrapping my arms tight around his waist.

He hugs me back and we sit there, locked in our first purely honest embrace.

The first of many.

EPILOGUE

Hart

I TAKE DAISY'S hand as we step onto the beach. It reminds me of the first time I offered her my hand on this very spot seven months ago.

'Who would've thought my emotional recluse would have a romantic streak a mile long?' She swings our linked hands, her expression pure mischief. 'I mean, there's only so many dusk walks along the perfect beach a girl can take.'

'You love it,' I say, enjoying our banter now as much as I did when we met.

'And you love checking out your handiwork.'

She knows me too well. Since the holiday programme for foster kids launched a week ago, we've taken a stroll along the beach every night at this time, so I can check on the first batch of visitors.

Daisy has accused me of being like an overprotective father but I can't help it. I want the best for these kids because they deserve a break.

It took months to renovate the old villas, which

gave Daisy time to launch our campaign in spectacular fashion. I even let her use several shots of me so I'm the unofficial poster boy for this. The response has been overwhelming and the Gem Island Kids Vacation Club is booked solid for the next eighteen months. So many families and kids craving a slice of paradise and a break from their daily drudgery, even for an all too brief week.

'Don't you mean *our* handiwork?' I drop a peck on her cheek. 'I couldn't have done all this without you.'

'BS and you know it. You did this.' She pats my chest over my heart. 'Straight from here.'

'We did it,' I reaffirm, enjoying being part of a team for once in my life.

The terror that I'll eventually lose her hasn't left me. I don't think it ever will because it's as much a part of me as those damn knife scars.

But I'm getting better. With each passing day that I wake up to see her smiling face on the pillow next to me, the fear is abating. I can live with it. I can't live without her.

'Come on, you sentimental thing.' She tugs on my hand and we fall into step; in sync, in love, so damn much it hurts.

As we near the end of the beach I hear kids' laughter and it's the sweetest sound ever. There's a bunch of them, about fourteen of varying ages, playing cricket in the garden behind the villas where they back onto the beach.

I hear good-natured ribbing and more laughter, and damned if I don't want to cry.

'You did good,' she says, sliding her arm around my waist. 'And I love you, every big-hearted, generous inch of you.'

Her complete and utter devotion makes me want to cry more, so I dip my head to whisper in her ear, 'I have some very generous inches waiting for you to appreciate when we get to the cave.'

'Sex maniac.' She laughs and snuggles in tighter.

'Yeah, but I'm your sex maniac, for however long you want.'

'How about for ever?'

'Sounds like a plan.'

My voice breaks a little and she knows, the sheen in her eyes as we lock gazes telling me that maybe, just maybe, I can believe in for ever, with her.

* * * * *

SWEET AS SIN

J. MARGOT CRITCH

MILLS & BOON

For my own romance hero, Brian, the man who sits somewhere comfortably between an alpha and a cinnamon bun. There is a bit of you in every hero I write about—the guy next door, the nerd, the goofball, the bad boy, the protector, the powerful businessman.

Without your unending love and support I wouldn't be able to live my dream. Thank you for loving me, making me laugh, putting up with me, and being my best friend, my inspiration, and all-around favourite person.

I love you. And your butt.

CHAPTER ONE

ALEX FISCHER LEANED back and spread his arms along the back of the couch and scanned the night-club around him. There were hundreds of gorgeous women in high heels and short dresses, flawless makeup and hair, and his hopes for the evening were high. Peeling his gaze away from the crowded dance floor, he looked at his friend Gabe, who sat across from him in the VIP area of Swerve night-club, and poured them each a couple of fingers of bourbon.

"Thanks," Alex said, taking his, leaning in so Gabe could hear him over the music. "This couch used to be a lot more crowded," he said, referring to their buddies Brett and Rafael, who used to join them at their nightclub, carousing, drinking, club-hopping, hooking up with women. Since they had met their women and fallen in love, they hadn't joined them in the activities of the young, rich, good-looking single man.

"Yeah," Gabe said, and snickered. "Now that Brett and Raf are sufficiently neutered, it seems like it's just you and me. And Alana, when we can pull her away from Di Terrestres."

Alex brought his glass to his lips and sipped the fine spirit as Gabe reached into his breast pocket and withdrew his phone.

"Oh hell," Gabe muttered, reading the screen of his phone.

"Anything wrong?"

"Oh nothing. Just one of my clients having a crisis at—" he checked his watch "—nine fifteen on a Friday night."

"You're on the clock?"

"Aren't we always?"

Alex frowned. "I thought we were hanging out."

"So did I," Gabe told him, taking one more wistful look around the club. "But I have to take care of this tonight. I'll text you tomorrow." When Alex stood, Gabe held his hand out. "Why don't you stick around? Enjoy the booth, finish the bourbon, find someone to share it with you. No sense in it going to waste." He gestured to the dance floor with a nod of his chin. "Get into a little trouble," he said with a wink.

"Maybe I will," Alex agreed, sitting back on the leather banquette. He could take Gabe's advice and get into some trouble, but he wasn't sure he wanted to do it on his own. He scrolled through the mental list of his closest friends, the rest of The Brotherhood. The five of them had formed the group out of college. With similar goals of running the Las Vegas business and nightlife scene, they'd realized that they were stronger as a unit and had joined forces, using their own specialties to bring them all to the top. It was Alana, the only female member of the group, who'd come up with the name, as a nod to the legends of secret societies of the powerful and wealthy throughout the country. While neither Alex nor his friends donned robes and performed rituals, The Brotherhood worked together to run their tied businesses and make decisions as a group.

Once driven by power and success, it seemed like each member of The Brotherhood was finding true love, settling down, getting married, blah, blah, blah... So Brett and Rafael were both at home with their women; Alana working at their club, Di Terrestres, even though they'd hired managers; and Gabe had just bowed out of partying in favor of work.

They were growing up, and as they pressed onward into their thirties, a part of him yearned for the old days. But every night, while Brett and Raf went home to their gorgeous partners, Alex still went home to his cold, empty condo, which overlooked Las Vegas Boulevard. All the revelry below did not match the sullen loneliness of his thirty-six-hundred square feet in the sky. Alex looked around the packed club, at the women in their minuscule dresses, gyrating, bumping and grinding against one another on the dance floor. More than one cast interested looks in his direction as he sat alone on the VIP couch. Maybe a little "trouble" was exactly what he needed.

Finishing the bourbon in his glass in one swallow, Alex headed for the dance floor, his eyes sharp and focused as he looked over the women in attendance. And there were many who were just his type— blonde, gorgeous, tall, fit, *generously proportioned*.

But there was one woman in the crowd that caught his attention, and she stopped him dead in his tracks. She was easily the sexiest woman in the club, moving with a confidence that came from always being the most beautiful woman in any room. The woman swiveled her hips to the music, keeping time with the beat. But there was something familiar about the dark-haired beauty, in a short skirt that stopped just below the round curve of her ample ass and perched on high stilettos, dancing with some guy, grinding against him as they moved. His hands found her waist, pulling her closer. She was stunning in a gold satin backless shirt; the only thing holding it on her body were the thin ties at her neck and lower back. She spun around, so she'd faced him briefly before turning her back on him again. Her breasts moved unencumbered under the loose material, proving she definitely was not wearing any kind of bra.

Every other woman in the club fell away as Alex got closer to her. It didn't matter to him that the siren was dancing with another man, she wouldn't be for much longer. He was a couple of yards away before her face came into view. The large brown eyes, and full red lips were those of a woman he knew.

Fuck, it was Maria.

Rafael's sister—*his best friend's* sister—looking like complete, unadulterated, absolutely sinful sex that made his dick stand upright at attention. She might have been twenty-six, but he'd never seen her dressed like that, moving like that. How had she transformed from the good, sweet young woman he knew into the vixen in front of him?

What the fuck is she doing here?

He stalked over to her as anger, possessiveness and a lust he didn't quite understand coursed through him, each feeling warring for dominance. Her eyes widened in surprise when she saw him, but the guy she was dancing with didn't seem to notice his presence at all until he pulled the other man's hands from Maria's body. "Think again, kid," Alex sneered.

"What the fuck?" The young bro came up to Alex, his ego injured, looking for a fight, even though Alex outsized him by at least eight inches and one hundred pounds of muscle. The kid was clearly somehow stupider than he looked in his polo shirt and khakis. *Who even dresses like that anymore?*

"Get out of here," Alex told him. The kid looked like he might stand his ground, but just as Alex suspected, he didn't put up a fight and backed away. Even though a girl, *a woman*, like Maria would be worth dying for. But instead of realizing that, the young asshole looked Maria up and down, then glared at Alex before he backed away into the darkness of the club.

"What the hell, Alex?" Maria yelled over the music, smacking him in the chest, hard. Her small fist bounced off his pec.

But he was undeterred. "What do you think you're doing here? Dressed like that." He stared down at her, trying to ignore the way her smooth exposed skin made him feel, and the way his body tightened in response. He tried to push it back. He couldn't be attracted to Maria.

But Maria didn't seem to notice his turmoil and was squarely focused on being pissed at him. "Well, I *was* dancing with a cute guy, before you rudely interrupted." She was mad. Alex recognized the pout of her lips, an expression she made when she was unhappy or when he and Rafael would pick on her as kids. She folded her arms across her chest, and the action plumped her breasts, pushing them up the low neckline of her shirt.

"Who was that guy?"

Her shrug was full of attitude. "I don't know. I just met him."

His eyes drifted south, watching the movements of her breasts, before he forced them back to her face. "Are you here alone?"

"No, I'm with my girlfriends." She gestured vaguely over her shoulder.

"Well, where are they?"

"They're *around*. What's it to you, Alex?"

"Have you been drinking?"

"Well, I am at a nightclub," she said, looking at him, as if it was obvious.

He grabbed her arm. "Come on. We're getting out of here."

She pulled back and wrenched away from his grip. "No, I'm not going anywhere. I'm here with my friends. And I *was* having a good time until you rudely interrupted."

"Go get them. I'm calling you a car."

"Fuck you, Alex." Admirably, she stood her ground, not backing down from him. He looked around and could see that they were starting to catch the attention of the bouncers and staff.

"Maria." He leaned in, whispering near her ear. "Come on. We're leaving." Looking around them, he didn't miss the way that every guy in the place looked at Maria like she was a lamb in a lion's den. *A stubborn, immovable lamb.* Relenting, he sighed. "Fine. If you aren't leaving, then neither am I." There was no way in hell he was going to walk out of that club while she was dressed like that.

She huffed and turned on her stiletto-clad heel and stomped away from him, toward two other women he assumed were her friends who stood at a table. He tried to ignore the way Maria's ass shifted and her hips swayed under her skirt, or the flex of her toned thigh and calf muscles with every step. Grumbling to himself, frustrated, he went back to the VIP area and poured himself another drink. "Jesus."

"Need anything else, Mr. Fischer?" the cocktail waitress asked him, within twenty seconds of his returning to his table.

Not taking his eyes off Maria, he shook his head. She was facing away from him, but every few seconds, she would look at him over her shoulder. Her large dark eyes were hot, burning him across the crowded nightclub, and her full lips pouted, teasing him, egging him on. Saluting her with his glass, he knocked back the bourbon in one large swallow.

He'd known Maria for years. When he was a child, the Martinez family had saved his life. He'd moved in with the family and out of his slum after his mother's death and his father's incarceration, and he never looked back. Alex owed Maria's family everything, and whether she wanted him to or not, he would look out for her—make sure she stayed safe, and that certainly didn't mean entertaining any of the thoughts he currently had in his mind.

Maria could feel Alex's gaze on her back. Just who in the hell did he think he was? She was just trying to have some fun with her friends, Beth and Anna, dance with some good-looking guys, have them buy her some drinks. But of course, she couldn't go anywhere in Las Vegas without being seen and coddled by one of Rafael's overprotective friends. She was twenty-six years old, and completely sick of being treated like a fucking child. It was the curse of being the youngest daughter in a strict, Latino Catholic family. They loved her, and God knew her family was more important to her than anything else, but their watchful eyes were burdensome.

Thankfully, her parents had at least finally recognized that she was an adult. But Rafael was another issue. He flat-out refused to even remotely acknowledge the fact that she was no longer a child. She was a grown woman, she'd seen firsthand all of the terrible things that could happen to a woman, and she knew how to protect herself from those who would wish to do her harm. Since graduating from college, she'd spent months at a time on humanitarian missions with various groups like the Red Cross and Doctors Without Borders in areas ravaged by war, disease and natural disasters. Her eyes had been opened to how dangerous the world could be when people were desperate and willing to do anything to survive. But in the mind of her stubborn brother, she was still a naive kid. Hell, she would be an eighty-year-old woman, and he would still be calling her his baby sister.

Alex's closeness to her brother, and the fact that he had basically been raised in her home, meant that she should probably think of him as her brother, too. But she hadn't. They'd grown up together, and while she'd always had a bit of a crush on him, somewhere along the way he'd ceased to be the gross boy who'd teased and picked on her, and had become the strong, gorgeous man who lit her every desire on fire.

"Maria, who was the hottie?" Beth asked, breaking through her thoughts. Maria blinked and realized that she was still looking at Alex, who was staring right back.

"Alex. A friend of my brother's."

"He is seriously the best-looking guy in here." Maria watched her friend as she sized up Alex from across the room. "And he can't keep his eyes off you. Why don't you go for it? Crawl up on all that muscle."

It certainly wasn't beyond the thoughts that Maria

had had about Alex. The man was a certified hunk. She may have spent thousands of hours in the middle of the night, in bed everywhere from Las Vegas to Haiti to the Middle East in the midst of fantasies about Alex Fischer. Those strong shoulders, the rippling muscles of his back and the bulge in his pants. "Believe me, I would," she said, her breath pushing out from her constricting lungs. "But there's no chance. He still thinks of me only as a kid, Rafael's little sister." A *good girl.* That was how everyone thought of her. Sure, she was a good person, but she also had a wicked streak that she heartily embraced every chance she got.

Oblivious to the conversation Maria and her friends had been having, some guy took the opportunity to join them, sidling up close to Maria, wrapping his arm low around her waist. He said something stupid about her *culo,* and she rolled her eyes. *Idiot.* God, she'd had enough of men imposing themselves on her, and her patience was at an all-time low. *Can't a woman just go out and have fun with her friends?* She pulled his arm away from her. "You'd better get out of here, *pendejo.* Before I kick *your culo* all over this club." She didn't need Alex to scare off idiot guys. She could more than handle herself.

But he didn't walk away; instead, he somehow sidled closer. "Ooh, fiery, I like that."

The guy had no idea. She'd learned a long time ago while on missions how to deal with chauvinists, catcallers, guys who attempted to touch her uninvited. It wasn't pretty. She'd seen some real dangerous men in her time. This frat boy in his Old Navy chambray shirt and chinos didn't interest or scare her. "Listen, man, I'm not playing. Back off!" She turned away from him, trying to talk to her girlfriends.

When the guy laughed and grabbed her ass, Maria whipped around and grasped the guy's fingers in a grip that twisted his wrist, causing him severe pain. He cried out, and everyone in the near vicinity looked in their direction. A bouncer moved close, but he didn't stop her. "You know you shouldn't go around touching people without their permission, don't you?" She twisted her hand, and as she pinched a nerve ending, he screamed in pain. "So what do you say? Will you get the fuck out of here, or do I have to break your fingers?"

"Fine, I'll go," the guy wailed. She let him go and he cradled his injured hand. "Crazy bitch."

"What was that?" she challenged, not backing down. "I don't think I heard you." There was one thing she hated and that was misogynistic, predatory assholes. He hadn't backed down when she said no, so she literally took matters into her own hands. Hopefully the guy learned his lesson, but if not, she would gladly teach him again.

"Is there a problem?" Alex asked her, suddenly appearing at her side, but turned his attention to the guy as he retreated. He started to follow, but Maria held him back.

"No, I've got this," she said as the other guy slunk

out of view, disappearing into the crowd. "I don't need a bodyguard, you know."

"So I saw. That was pretty impressive." He took her hand in his. His large fingers dwarfed hers and she felt the full-body tremor that traveled throughout her, starting with his touch, radiating to her core. "Are you okay?"

"I'm fine," she managed to say as he inspected her fingers while she watched his face.

Alex turned her hand over and frowned. "You broke a nail."

She looked down and saw that the recently manicured nail on her index finger had cracked off. The manicure had been expensive, and she frowned that it was ruined, but she covered her annoyance with a cool laugh. At least she hoped it was. "It's no worse off than his pride, though. So, now that you can see I know how to look after myself, you can leave."

"That's where you're wrong. I'm not going anywhere." He smiled, turning on the charm. "Maria, I'm very sorry I interrupted your dance earlier and ruined your fun," he said. She was skeptical that he was sorry at all. "So I want to make amends." Pointing to the VIP area, he leaned in, speaking mostly to Beth and Anna. "Ladies, I've got a booth in the VIP area over there, and I'd love for you all to join me."

She knew that his offer wasn't just to be nice, that there was something else happening behind that devilish smile. But before she could say anything, her friends all nodded in agreement.

"Hell yeah, let's go," Beth said, and Maria watched,

annoyed as Alex stood between them, cupped his palms around their elbows and led them toward the VIP area, leaving Maria standing alone.

Alex took several steps before it looked like he finally realized she wasn't following. He turned to face her, his lips turning upward in a grin, knowing he'd won. "Coming, Maria?"

Alex had come up on her and steamrollered her plans to have fun with her friends. Hell, there were a lot of places worse than the VIP area of one of the hottest clubs in Las Vegas. She knew what he was doing. But that didn't mean she couldn't play a game of her own. Maybe it was the opportunity to do something she'd always wanted to do.

"Yeah. Sure."

Alex escorted Maria's friends to the VIP area. But the women who flanked him didn't hold his interest like the woman who trailed them stubbornly. Beth and Anna, as they'd introduced themselves, sat on one end of the semicircle couch. He waited until Maria took a seat next to them, and he sat next to her, again trying not to focus on the way her breasts shifted under her shirt as she moved, settling into the couch, or the way her skirt rode even farther up, revealing more of her tanned thighs. She was curvy, every inch of her body incredible, and he wanted to put his mouth and hands on her and discover her every secret. He blinked and then quickly looked away, hoping to banish the image from his mind.

Beth plucked the drink menu from the center of

the low table in front of them and when the waitress came over to the table, she ordered a round of shots for them all. In just a couple of minutes, the cocktail waitress returned and placed a shot glass containing some kind of purple liquid in front of each of them.

Alex looked at the shots with a frown, and considered passing on what looked like little more than liquid candy, but then he shrugged. Who was he to turn down a round of shots with a trio of gorgeous women? So, raising his glass with them, he downed the shot.

His swallow was followed by a grimace. The thing was sweet, pure grape-flavored sugar, and he shuddered and felt his stomach try to revolt against it. To temper the sweetness, he took a mouthful of bourbon. The heat pleasantly covered the purple haze, and he sipped again for good measure. He leaned back with his glass and easily slung his arm over the back of the couch, above Maria, just inches away from what he believed must be the smoothest skin he'd ever desired to touch. He just hoped that he looked more casual than he felt.

She smiled and moved in closer to him, close enough to press her thigh against his, and he stiffened in response to her nearness.

"Don't think I don't know what you're doing," she said.

Alex shrugged. "What do you think I'm doing?"

"You're seducing my friends with bottle service so they'll stay close and then you can keep your eyes on me."

Maria was good.

"And let me guess, you've already called Rafa and told him I'm here, and you promised to watch out for me, right?"

She was really good. He hadn't called Raf yet, not wanting to interrupt his night with Jessica, but he'd honestly thought about it.

Alex said nothing but sipped his bourbon again. He could feel the alcohol start to warm him pleasantly from the inside. At least he hoped it was the alcohol, and not Maria's effect on his anatomy.

The waitress approached. "Another round, ladies?"

Alex withdrew his black charge card and passed it to her. "This'll cover it. And get the women whatever they want."

The waitress took Alex's card while the three of them tried to decide which $1,000 bottle of champagne they wanted. He laughed and leaned in, telling them they should probably order one of each. They wholeheartedly agreed.

"You're going to regret that decision," Maria said to him with a laugh. "You don't know the damage this group can do when we have girls' night out."

Alex shrugged and smiled. He'd spent more money on way more frivolous items. It wasn't an issue for him. He might have come from humble beginnings, but he and The Brotherhood had made themselves each quite a small fortune. He had the money, and knowing that his future was secured, he liked to spend it. Their eyes widened as the waitress brought the first bottle of champagne. He remembered being young, just out of grad school, MBA in hand and broke as a joke.

Maria and her friends were nice girls—*women*, he reminded himself. He knew that they worked hard together at the community center, and they deserved to be treated. Sure, Alex would be down a little cash, but a black-card-funded night in a VIP booth at a hot club probably wasn't an everyday occurrence for them. He wanted the women to enjoy themselves, no matter what the cost. And maybe Maria had been right—as long as her friends were in his VIP booth, he knew that she wasn't going anywhere. "Just have fun," he told them, and remembering Gabe's words earlier that evening, he smiled. "Get into a little bit of trouble."

CHAPTER TWO

AN HOUR AND copious amounts of champagne later, Alex still sat back in the booth and watched the three women dance together, rubbing their bodies against one another like girlfriends did, turning their backs on and completely shutting down every guy who tried to interject himself—not that Alex would have let it happen either way. No more greasy dudes would be putting their hands on Maria, or any of them.

With a chuckle, he remembered seeing her almost break that one asshole's wrist. Maria obviously wasn't the helpless young woman he'd believed her to be. She was strong and tough and most definitely knew how to hold her own.

Alex toyed briefly with the idea of leaving. Maria would be fine. But there was something else that kept him in his seat. He was perfectly content to watch Maria as she put her arms over her head and swiveled her hips seductively. He wasn't strong enough to ignore her, and he focused his gaze on her sexy movements, the way she flipped her long hair and closed her eyes, as though the music traveled throughout her body and she felt the notes on an erotic level. His posture stiffened on the leather couch as he watched her, and interest stirred his dick. The rest of the club fell away, and he saw only her, as her hips swayed and she pushed her palms down her front to her thighs as she bent over slightly, not-so-subtly pushing her ass in his direction. He added *twerking* to Maria's list of talents.

His heart battered the inside of his rib cage, and he swallowed roughly. His dick stood at full attention as he watched his best friend's sister move seductively in the middle of the dance floor. With her back to him, she looked over her shoulder, and her eyes connected with his. As if she could read his mind, her lips quirked upward into a sly smile, and she winked. And she soon broke off from the group and walked over to him, her steps even and confident and in time with the beat of the music as she somehow balanced on her precarious stiletto heels. Maria leaned over him, resting her forearms on his shoulders, her red lips just inches from his. Alex tried not to look down the gap of loose material at the front of her shirt. He was unsuccessful, and he couldn't help but get an eyeful of her smooth round breasts underneath her shirt. His hands clenched into fists, fighting the urge to reach up and cup them in his hands.

"Hey, my eyes are up here," she admonished.

His eyes snapped back to hers. "So they are."

Her fingers pushed into his hair, tickling the back of his neck. "You know, if you're going to be my shadow all night, you might as well come dance with me."

"I don't think so." Alex shook his head, but it was a jerky movement as he struggled with control. "I thought you were mad at me."

"Come on," she pleaded. "I'm having too much fun to be mad. And you can make it up to me by dancing with me. You owe me a dance, you know."

"How so?"

"I was dancing with a guy when you so rudely interrupted. You should take his place."

"I think I did you a favor. That guy was a loser."

"How do you know that?"

"Because he walked away from you without a fight."

Her eyes widened. "Would you have fought for me?"

Alex answered without hesitation. "There's no question." She smiled down at him, and their eyes met. "Okay, fine. Just one dance."

She grasped his wrist with both hands, and he allowed her to pull him up and drag him toward the dancers. They didn't join her friends, but instead found a dark corner on the dance floor. The music vibrated through the crowd, and all the bodies on the dance floor pressed together, bringing them closer, pushing Maria against him. Gabe's parting remarks had been about finding some trouble. But Alex hadn't counted on this. He was already in too deep, and he knew it.

Maria turned to face him. She rotated her hips and

raised her arms above her head, swaying in time to the music. He didn't know how Maria, who'd always been a "good girl," had learned to move that way. His body tensed, and he tried to fight his physical reaction to her.

Her eyes never left his, drawing him in so that the rest of the club disappeared. And even though Alex knew it was wrong, his libido was now in firm control. He couldn't pull himself away, couldn't stop himself, and he pressed closer. It was just him and Maria. She turned around, facing away from him, and bumped her ass against his groin. A shock traveled throughout him, and she did it again. Unconsciously, he dropped a hand to her hip and held her in place as she danced, continuing to grind her ass against his dick, and there was no way she missed the fact that he was rock hard. Perhaps it was the alcohol, the driving beat, the lights, the crowd, that had lowered his inhibitions and debilitated his common sense. But she was a beautiful woman, and she was warm, and he wanted her. There was no denying that.

Without thinking—his brain hadn't even entered the equation, and he was moving on primal instinct—his hand moved around her front and flattened against her stomach below her belly button. His groin was in control, and even though he knew he should stop, he didn't. He knew what he wanted. And whether it was wrong or not, what he wanted was Maria Martinez.

He pulled her close, so that her back pressed into his chest and she made contact with his hard dick.

Maria turned in his arms to face him, so his hand rested high on the curve of that deliciously round ass. Looking down at her, he was reminded that he was dancing with, had his hands on, was holding close, his best friend's sister. Maria. But as much as he knew that he should push away from her, he didn't want to. And instead of being smart, he pulled her closer. In her dangerously high heels, the top of her head only came up to his nose. He inhaled, pulling in the light, airy scent of her perfume, and he closed his eyes and savored it.

Why didn't he know she smelled so amazing?

Who was he kidding—Alex had known exactly how amazing she smelled. He'd known for years. Only now would he let himself accept it. While his eyes were closed, she wedged his thigh between both of hers, straddling it, sliding herself up and down, her hips moving to the beat of the sultry music. Her touch was so damn hot, he had to look down to make sure she wasn't singeing a hole right through his pants.

Already sentenced to hell for what he was doing, Alex said a silent prayer and grasped Maria's waist, small in his hands, and instead of pushing her away, he used his hold on her to swivel her body, rotating her hips, so that she ground against him more fully. Her lips parted, and he could see the heavy rise and fall of her chest. She was turned on just as much as he was. She wrapped her arms around his neck and pulled closer, almost lifting herself off the dance floor, putting her mouth near his ear. Over the music he heard a small gasp that escaped her lips as he thrust his thigh against her. It was all so wrong. He knew he was violating the guy code—*no sisters!* But he couldn't bring himself to push Maria away. Goddammit, he wanted to hear that sigh again. He thrust his leg again, against the unmistakable heat of her pussy, rubbing her where he knew she needed it. The sigh became a moan. And her lips found the side of his neck, kissing his pulse point, which he knew was racing. He kept going. The muscles of his thigh continued to rub against her. He kept pace until her heavy breath stilled and her thigh muscles clenched around his. She threw her head back and exhaled roughly as small tremors still coursed throughout her body. He refused to take his eyes away from her as she came.

And then the reality of what he was doing struck him. He froze in spot as he regained his senses. Maria smiled up at him, and she winked, clearly more relaxed than he was. His heart beat even faster as a deep sense of shame settled over him. He was with Maria. And he'd made her come on a crowded dance floor.

Alex's eyes dropped to Maria's mouth, her full lips, that damned cupid's bow that she'd covered in red lipstick, looked so delicious, and he wanted a taste. They stopped dancing, isolated in their dark corner, isolated from the rest of the dance floor, oblivious to everyone, everything. Both of them were breathing heavily, and with each breath she took, her full breasts brushed his chest. The air between them crackled with electricity, and he knew he had to push away from her before he burned himself, or her.

"Maria," he whispered. He reached out and swiped his thumb over her lips. The lipstick somehow didn't smudge. Her lips parted, and she drew his thumb into her mouth. She sucked him, stroked him with her tongue. The air rushed from Alex's chest, and his knees almost buckled. He closed his eyes and let himself feel her and wonder what it would be like to be fully surrounded with her heat. "Fuck, Maria," he muttered. He needed to get away, but there was no way he could part from her. He was trapped on the crowded dance floor. Frozen in place; needing to get out of there, but completely helpless to her. Alex had been with his share of women, but he'd never been so enraptured by one, and he knew he was in trouble.

Maria hummed around his thumb, the vibration waved throughout him, and he couldn't handle it anymore. He pulled his digit from her mouth and before he could change his mind, he quickly replaced it with his lips. He took her bottom lip between his teeth and nibbled lightly until her lips parted, all the invitation he needed for his tongue to find hers, stroking against it. Tasting her. She was sweeter than anything he'd ever tasted, and he gripped her hips tightly, his fingertips digging in before they moved around to cup her ass in his palms.

It was wrong, but goddammit, he didn't care. He owed Rafael more than to be making out with his sister on a dance floor. But still he briefly toyed with how easily he could get Maria out of the club and back to his place.

No! He couldn't do that. A moment of clarity flashed behind his eyes, and he realized what he'd just done. The lustful fog that had muddied his brain cleared, and no matter how much he wanted to go further with her, Alex knew he had to end it. He released Maria, letting her fall softly, so that she was standing on her own. She looked stunned. But he didn't look at the hurt in her eyes; instead, he took out his phone and messaged the car service that he and The Brotherhood kept on retainer for when they needed it. He ordered a town car to come pick up the women, and he looked at Maria. "I just called a car. Get your friends. You're going home."

CHAPTER THREE

"DID YOU HAVE fun last night?" Rafael asked, his tone casual and innocent, as they took their seats next to each other at their table at Thalia, one of The Brotherhood's restaurants, but Maria knew from experience that the conversation was beginning to exhibit all the earmarks of an interrogation.

The waiter slid in her chair, and Maria sat back and watched her brother. He wasn't the only one with an impassive poker face. Controlling her features, playing it cool, she wondered if he'd found out about the dance that she'd shared with Alex that brought her over the edge. She knew that there was no way Alex would have told him what had gone down between them. However, it wasn't impossible that someone else at the club may have seen them. Did he know that Alex had kissed her? Or anything else? "What do you mean?" she asked.

"Mr. Martinez," the waiter thankfully interrupted them. "The rest of the party will be along soon."

"Thanks, Nick," Rafael said. They were waiting for the rest of The Brotherhood. Rafael had convinced her to join him in their monthly dinners. "I meant exactly what I said. How was your night out with your friends?"

She shrugged. "It was fine," she told him, trying to keep her expression neutral. "Actually, Alex was there, and just so you know, he took the role of bodyguard very seriously."

"Oh really?" Rafael seemed surprised. "I saw him this morning, and he didn't mention seeing you. I've no doubt he took good care of you."

A wave of heat flushed throughout her, and she knew exactly how well Alex had "taken care of" her. She still remembered the way his lips felt on hers, how his tongue had stroked hers. He'd made her come, for God's sake. She'd never experienced anything quite like the wanton need she'd had for Alex. She had a wild streak, but she'd never had a guy get her off on a dance floor. And she wanted more like it. More Alex.

"What time did you get home last night?"

"Early enough, *Mom*," she assured him, even though she'd regretted the late hour when she'd woken up tired and hungover that morning. Working with the children at the community center had exhausted her and, with a pounding head, had been a challenge until lunchtime, when her hangover had finally subsided. But she wouldn't tell Rafael that. Not a chance. "I had fun. And despite having him loom over my shoulder, it was really nice hanging out with Alex again."

"I know you think I'm overbearing sometimes—"

"All the time. You have to learn to trust me."

"Maria, I do trust you. It's men I don't trust." When Maria rolled her eyes, he continued. "I worry about you. You don't know what it's like out there."

"I've traveled around the world, in some pretty dangerous areas. I think I can handle Las Vegas Boulevard." Maria scoffed. "And as a woman, I think I may have a better idea than you do what men are like and what it's like for us out there."

"I'm not going to win this argument, am I?"

"Do you ever?"

"No," he said with a laugh. "Fine." He raised his hands in surrender. "How is the new apartment?"

"I love it! Beth's a great roommate." Since she'd returned from her last mission in Haiti, getting her own place and moving out of her parents' house had been a priority. But with only her meager salary at the community center, as the rent became due each month, her savings had started to dwindle. She loved working at the center, but needed a better job, so she could continue paying her bills.

"It's not in a good neighborhood, you know."

"It's fine," Maria insisted. "It's close to the center, and Beth and I carpool. You know there have been hardly any home invasions or carjackings since I moved in."

Rafael rolled his eyes and smiled, knowing that Maria was making fun. "Okay, I'll drop it."

"Thank you. I'm grateful that you want to look after me, but you've got to let me go, you know. I have to live my own life."

"I know. But you'll always be my little sister. And I will always look out for you, ready to destroy anyone who messes with you."

She smiled. Maria loved her brother, even though he was frustrating and overbearing. "I appreciate that."

Their conversation was thankfully cut short when they were joined at the table by Brett and Rebecca. Then Jessica, Rafael's fiancée and mayor of Las Vegas, showed up, and Maria smiled watching her brother's face light up when she came into the room. Gabe and Alana, arrived next.

Alex came shortly after, apologizing for being late. Her breath halted in her throat as Alex took his place at the table across from her, at the only empty seat, barely looking at her. She watched him as he studied his menu—she couldn't get her fill. He was so incredibly sexy in his tailored black pants and white shirt, unbuttoned at his throat and the sleeves rolled up to his elbows, so she could see the black and gray tattoos that swirled over his forearms. Her throat dried, and she drank some wine to quench it.

"So, guys," Gabe started, looking in Alex and Alana's direction. "I'm eager to know all about this 'secret project' you guys are working on."

Alex and Alana made eye contact, and they both grinned. "Why do you want to know?" Alex asked.

"As your lawyer and business partner, it might be good for me to know if you're planning on doing anything that might lead to an indictment."

"Well, it isn't exactly a secret project." Alex's

voice lowered, and the rest of the table leaned in to listen. "But we're trying to keep it under wraps. At least for a while. The Brotherhood is getting into the hotel business."

"Really? What brought that on? The rooms at Di Terrestres aren't enough anymore?" Rebecca asked of the exclusive, erotic club the group owned.

"After the recent exposure given to Di Terrestres when that tape of Rafael and Jessica leaked, membership applications have tripled."

Rafael rolled his eyes. "Glad we could help," he said, wrapping his arm around Jessica's shoulders and pulling her closer. Their "help" had come in the form of a sex tape that had leaked of them in Rafael's private suite. The club where they'd been secretly recorded belonged to the entire group and allowed their high-end clientele to explore their desires in a safe, discreet environment. They'd thought that the leak would spell doom for the club, but instead, it had had the opposite effect. It had garnered a ton of interest and been more profitable than they could have imagined.

Alana laughed. "We don't have the capacity to accept everyone, even after the extreme vetting process we have. So we're expanding. A couple of weeks ago, Alex and I brainstormed over a whiteboard and a bottle of whiskey. And we came up with Hedo."

"Hedo?" Gabe asked.

"We want to take the erotically charged theme of the club and create a full-service hotel. The first adults-only playground in Las Vegas, right here on the Strip. Hedo will be a place where our guests can indulge in their fantasies. Each floor will have a distinct theme, and people can choose, depending on what they like. Unlike Di Terrestres, people won't have to be members. Anyone can come and partake. It'll draw people from all over the world, looking for some good, safe debauchery. You know, what they come to expect from the City of Sin. We're thinking hip, but seductive, sexy overtones. Something completely new to Las Vegas. Like a luxurious adult playground. Only the finest offerings, the most beautiful people, luxurious, handpicked tapestries and decor, the hottest DJs, everything that one would come to expect from a nightclub experience before they head up to their rooms."

Gabe nodded, a smile turning his lips upward. "I like it. Why all the secrecy?"

"You know nothing gets done in this city without everyone hearing about it. Alana and I want to keep it on the down-low for as long as possible. In case anyone else gets a similar idea. We've even got a property picked out to buy and develop." He leaned in closer, and lowered his voice, not wanting anyone else to hear the next part of their plan. "And that's just the first step in our plan to buy up, redevelop and revitalize the north end of the Strip."

"Lofty goals." Rafael nodded. "I'm on board. This is big."

"We're on track for The Brotherhood to be the next big name on the Strip. If we all focus on this one goal in the next several years, we can be bigger, better, *richer* than anyone who's ever had a piece of Las Vegas Boulevard. We're going to make everyone at this table a lot of money."

"Put me down for some of that." Gabe chuckled and extended his glass in cheers. "Let me know if you need anything."

Maria couldn't help but stare at Alex as he dived into talking about their new project. His passion and fire for his new hotel was infectious, and it spread around the table. She leaned closer. There was nothing sexier to her than a passionate man who could hold a group in the palm of his hand.

"And you should see the designs we came up with," Alana said. "Hedo's going to be amazing. Kind of a throwback to the hedonism of ancient Greece, and in keeping with the themes of our other businesses."

"Clothing optional," Alex added, cocking an eyebrow. "It's going to be large, but intimate. Very sexy. Especially since the increase we've seen in membership at Di Terrestres, we need more space and more services." He smiled at Rafael and Jessica. "And again, you guys, we can't thank you enough."

Rafael and Jessica shared a wry look, but they both laughed. While Maria had felt bad for Rafael and Jessica, having their privacy invaded by a local reporter, it had been refreshing seeing her older brother as something other than the serious and infallible golden child.

"But speaking about that," Rafael said, turning to Gabe. "I'm going to need that blind trust set up again. With the Senate run coming up, I need to be kept as clean as possible, which means not associating with you known degenerates."

"I don't know, Rafa," Maria interrupted. "Of the group, you're the only one with the leaked sex tape."

The rest of The Brotherhood laughed, and Maria heated when she heard Alex's chuckle over the others.

"Maria, I love you, but kindly shut up," Rafael said, pulling her close and dropping a fraternal kiss on the top of her head. He sobered. "Anyway, I've got to keep myself out of the headlines, so I'll still work with the businesses, but publicly, it needs to look like I'm taking a back seat." He turned to Alex and said, "Especially with that new hotel on the horizon."

"Don't worry about it. We've got it covered. And we'll help you out with your campaign in any way we can," Alex said. Maria could feel the bond between Alex and Rafael; it had always been there. Their eyes connected briefly, before he looked down and grasped his glass in his hand, bringing it to his lips and downing the drink.

Maria briefly let her mind wander as she thought about him. The illicit thoughts took over, and her fantasies ran rampant. She remembered the way his lips had whispered against hers, how his strong hands felt on her body. His hard thigh, as he guided her over it... Reality then made way to fantasy, as she imagined his naked body hovering over hers as he entered her—

"How are you, Maria? I haven't seen you in a while," Brett said from across the table, pulling her attention from Alex, and all of the dirty things she wanted to do to him and have him do to her.

She shook free mentally and quickly recovered. "I'm great," she told him. "I'm working at one of the community centers downtown. We're running breakfast, after-school and recreation programs. It's fun and fulfilling, but I still need to look for something that pays a little more." She looked around the table at some of the top earners in the city—hell, *the country*. She wondered how long it had been since any of them had worried about paying rent. Even though Rafael had offered to help her out financially, there was no way she would accept it.

"How's the job hunt going?" Alana asked.

"Tiresome. There aren't a lot of paying positions in community health. Lots of volunteer job and internships. Because heaven forbid people get paid for working. But I'm looking, pounding the pavement. I'll find something."

"I wanted her to come work for me," Rafael explained.

"But I refuse to because politics isn't my thing. And if I think he's overbearing now, I can't imagine him signing my paychecks."

"Payroll is all done electronically these days," he assured her, his voice wry. "I wouldn't have to sign anything."

"Why don't you come work for us at Collins/ Fischer?" Brett asked casually.

Maria's eyes widened and whipped to Alex's.

He played it cool, didn't react, even though she did. "What?"

"With the hotel project coming up, we've got a lot going on," Brett explained. "We'll need another assistant."

"But—" Alex tried to interrupt.

"Man, we talked about this earlier. I don't think we should stretch ourselves too thin," Brett said to Alex. "It would be great to have an assistant. We take on too much as it is." He turned back to her. "So how about it? You could start next week."

Maria glanced quickly at Alex, whose eyes burned, looking at her with the same intensity that they had the night before, but she wasn't sure which emotion was at play behind them. He gave nothing away, and Maria would have given anything to know what he was thinking.

She knew that working for Rafael's friends was just a step removed from working directly for her brother with how tightly their enterprises were interwoven. But who was she to turn down a job offer? "Uh, yeah, sure. I'd like that. Thanks."

"Awesome. That's great." Brett turned to Alex. "Isn't that great?"

"It's fantastic," Alex responded, his voice deadpan, obviously trying to look like he didn't care if she accepted the offer or not.

Maria smiled at what she knew was an act. *He wasn't so disinterested last night.* Maybe it was time to have a little fun. As the rest of the group conversed, she sat back in her chair and covertly slipped off her shoe. She extended her leg under the table until she felt the smooth material of Alex's pants against the pads of her toes. She felt him tense at the contact. Then she ran her foot up the outside of his calf. That got his attention as he sat up straight and blinked, his eyes gripping hers.

With the exception of the heavy breath that lifted his shoulders, Alex's reaction was unreadable, but he didn't push her away as she inched her foot up his leg, continuing her pace past his knee, moving to the inside of his thigh. Alex glared a warning at her. But she didn't heed it. Without anyone paying attention, she ventured farther up his thigh until she met his crotch. He was already hard, and from what she could feel, just as she'd felt the night before, he was quite large. There was no doubt that Alex wanted her, and it made her feel powerful. He might act like a tough guy, like he wasn't affected by her, but she knew it was a lie. She had the power, and she would use it to get what she wanted. And what she wanted was Alex.

While the rest of the people at the table chatted among themselves, she noticed how Alex tried to engage in the conversation and ignore her. But whether he wanted to or not, his attention just kept focusing on her. He took a drink from his water, and as her toes traced his rigid length, he coughed, earning him the attention of everyone at the table. He shoved her foot away, and she picked up her wine and smiled at her success behind her glass. *Who isn't interested now?*

"Excuse me, guys, I have to go to the ladies' room," Maria said, slipping her foot back into her shoe before she stood and walked away.

She met Alex's eyes as she sauntered away, making sure to put an extra bit of swivel into her hips. She knew Alex was watching when she turned the corner where the restrooms were located. She stood there, leaning against the wall, waiting.

Just as she'd suspected, she didn't have to wait long. Alex turned the corner, walking stiffly. He pushed his fingers through his hair. She'd frustrated him. "Maria, what was that about?"

"You didn't like it?" She looked down at his crotch, and she could see the bulge in his black pants. "It felt like you did. The way you liked what happened between us last night."

He ignored her question. "I don't know what you think happened last night."

"What do you think happened?"

"A mistake. One you'd better forget."

She shook her head. "I don't know if I can."

"Maria," he warned her, his voice dark and holding an amount of malice under all of the frustration. But despite the meanness in his voice, he took a step toward her, closing the distance between them. "You'd better be careful not to provoke me."

She squared her shoulders and pushed closer to him. The movement brought her nipples against his chest. They ached; her whole body wanted, needed him. She looked up into his eyes and wet her lips. His eyes followed the movement of her tongue. "Maybe

I want to provoke you," she whispered, putting her hand on his groin, and satisfied, she found him still hard. "It seems as if you might like it."

With a growl, he was on her. His hands cupped her cheeks and he pulled her lips to his. He kissed her again. It wasn't timid or slow. There was nothing shy or tentative about the touch of his lips on hers. Alex's mouth was hard and demanding, and he tasted rich, like bourbon, cigars, but those flavors were no more potent than the pure taste of Alex. She curled her fingers around the back of his head and threaded her hands in his hair, holding him in place. He pushed her to the wall and pressed his hips against her so that she could again feel his arousal against her stomach, as if she'd had any question of his desires. She wanted him. Wanted to feel his weight on top of her, feel him inside her. And she knew he wanted her, too.

Maria lifted her leg so that her inner thigh brushed against the outside of his. And he gripped her and pressed into her again. A moan passed from her mouth to his, and it turned into a surprised gasp when he dropped her leg and broke away from her. Stepping back, he put more than a foot of empty space between them.

"Jesus, I'm sorry." His voice was a rough whisper as he wiped his mouth with the back of his hand.

"I'm not."

"I shouldn't have done that."

"It's not like I wasn't a willing participant."

"I've got to get out of here. Go back to the table,

Maria," he ordered her through heavy breaths. "Your brother is waiting for you."

"You're leaving?"

"Fuck, I've got to stay away from you," he said, low, quiet, as if he were talking to himself.

"That's going to be hard, seeing as how I'll be working for you next week."

"You won't be working for me," he assured her. "You're Brett's assistant. Not mine."

"Alex, don't be ridiculous—"

He pointed a finger at her. "Don't, Maria." His whisper was fierce. "This can't be anything more. I've already crossed too many goddamn lines here with you. Just forget it ever happened."

"How can I forget it?" she said, pressing against him. "Alex, I've wanted you for so long, and now that I know how good it feels to kiss you, and touch you..." She ran her palm against his cock again. "How long and hard you are. It just makes me want more." She squeezed him through the silky material of his expensively tailored pants, and as he closed his eyes, his groan made her feel powerful. She stepped even closer. "Don't you want me, too?" she whispered against his throat, her lips skimming his stubble. The scratch electrified her, and she felt the jolt all the way to her core.

He hesitated—she could see the tightening of his jaw, the clenching of his fists, and she knew that he was trying to fight it. But from the way he exhaled through his flared nostrils, she knew that he was at war. And that between his common sense and libido, she knew which side was winning. He nodded, and triumph surged throughout her. "I do want you." He shoved her hand away. "But this can't happen," he said before he turned away from her and walked back into the dining room.

CHAPTER FOUR

ALEX WAS IRRITABLE before he even entered The BH, the office tower built and owned by The Brotherhood, the home and headquarters of Collins/Fischer and the rest of their enterprises, including, of course, Di Terrestres, which encompassed the entire bottom floor. Before he even set a foot out of the elevator and onto the floor of Collins/Fischer, he felt like staying inside and riding back down to the front lobby. A week had passed since Brett went ahead and hired Maria, and even though she had yet to start working there, he'd been a ball of tension since that evening.

He hadn't seen Maria since he'd followed her from the table at Thalia, but he didn't need to. Everywhere he went, he smelled her, could taste her on the air, as if she'd been permanently etched on his skin or tied to him, following him everywhere he went. It would be her first day at the office and even though their workloads would keep them busy and she would be assisting Brett, Alana and him on all of the work related to Hedo, he didn't know how he would manage to focus on anything knowing that she was in the building.

Alex looked up from the panel of buttons, still contemplating pushing the one marked with an *L*, and stared out the parted door at the clean titanium Collins/Fischer logo that faced him. "Goddammit," he muttered to himself. That was his name on the company's logo. He owned the fucking building. He'd worked his ass off to get where he was. He'd fought every adversary, every odd that had been stacked against him, and he'd persevered. If he couldn't handle having one woman in his vicinity, then he might as well quit his job and go back to where he'd come from, become his father. Instead, he took a deep breath, scrubbed his hand over his face and exited the elevator, stepping into the hallway.

Collins/Fischer, a normally loud and bustling company, was quiet. Of course it was; it was barely 7:00 a.m. And while Alex and Brett liked to get an early start, they didn't expect their staff to get in that early, and most waited until nine. Early morning was their quiet time to arrange their projects and coordinate their schedules for the day and upcoming week.

Alex yawned, and on the way to his office, it occurred to him that he'd forgotten to restock the coffee in his office. The fine Panamanian beans he'd been so pleased with had not lasted the week with the long hours he'd been putting in. He'd have to order more. Like, twenty pounds more. But until then, the communal office coffee would have to do.

He veered into the lunch room to his left instead of heading straight to his office.

He was stopped in his tracks, however, when he smelled the hints of a familiar spicy perfume, and he knew he wasn't alone in the room. His breath caught in his throat when Maria turned to face him, gorgeous in a crisp white blouse, and a high-waisted gray pencil skirt that hit just above her knees. The look was completed with her thick black hair tied back into a bun and cherry-red high heels. Her outfit might have been modest in cut, but it somehow seemed to show off her delicious curves rather than hide them. She looked like the star of every fantasy a man could have about a woman in an office setting.

Her red lips spread in a grin. "Hi, Alex. Or should I say *boss*?" she asked with a throaty purr that made him sweat through his suit.

Maria was going to be the death of him.

If Rafael didn't kill him first.

Alex nodded and walked past her to the espresso machine without returning her greeting. He busied himself preparing his own coffee, but he could feel her watching him. "What are you doing here?" he asked, not looking at her, trying to ignore his every response to her.

"I work here, remember?"

How could he forget? "What I mean is, it's early. People don't normally start showing up until at least eight thirty."

"Brett emailed me and asked me to be here early so he can get me started, and he wants me to sit in on your morning meeting. Then I have to meet with Alana to get caught up on what you guys are working on. You start early—it only makes sense for your assistant to do the same."

"You're Brett's assistant," he reminded her with a grumble. His voice was thick, rough, with desire. He needed time to ease into his day without having to worry about his dick getting hard, imagining laying her out on his desk.

But she didn't seem put off by his demeanor, and she laughed. "You're grumpy in the morning, Alex." Her high heels clicked on the floor as she walked over to a bank of cupboards, absently looking inside a couple, becoming acquainted with the room, before she moved closer to him still, opening the fridge. She bent at the waist and leaned in, putting her brown-bag lunch in a free space at the bottom. He looked over and took in the stellar view of her ass and the gray material stretching over her luscious curves. She stood, and Alex tried to look away, but he was like a man possessed, driven to her, unable to stop himself from coming up behind her. His fingers curled over her hips, gripping her, digging into her flesh.

He heard the shocked gasp exit her lips, and she fully straightened, bringing her back flush to his chest. "Alex." Her voice was a whisper, but it rang out in the empty room.

He bowed his head, placed his lips on her temple and spoke against her skin. "Maria, I'm not sure what you do to me, but I just can't resist you."

"Maybe I don't want you to resist."

He pushed his hips against her ass, certain that she couldn't mistake how hard he was. She was so warm and firm, but so goddamn soft. "We can't, though. I know it. You know it. This has already gone too far."

"I do know that. But I don't understand why. If we want each other, what's the harm?"

Alex knew one hundred reasons why not, but fuck him if he could think of one at that moment. Maria's body just felt so good against his. He lowered his head, and with her back still against his chest, she turned her face in his direction. Their lips were only millimeters apart. He could feel her breath, almost taste her...

A throat clearing behind them jolted Alex, and he separated himself from her. He turned around, half expecting to see Rafael, who also occupied office space on the top floor of the building. But it was Brett, his eyes narrowed and his eyebrows drawn together. He obviously hadn't misinterpreted what he'd walked in on. "Maria, I'm ready to start if you are."

Maria recovered immediately. She gave her new boss a big smile and, switching gears, she seemed completely unaffected by the moment she and Alex had just shared. "Okay, great." She walked away, leaving Alex standing by the refrigerator.

Brett stood aside, letting her leave first, before he turned his attention to Alex, raising his arm, blocking Alex's exit. "What exactly did I just walk in on?"

"It was nothing," he told him.

Brett clearly didn't buy it. "Is there anything I need to know here?"

"No, not a thing," Alex said, pushing past him. "Let's get started."

Maria sat in on the day's first meeting, where Brett and Alex went through their upcoming appointments, deciding who would represent the company at which functions, before moving to discuss the progress on their biggest projects. Besides the new hotel they were building, they still had their regular work ongoing, and she wasn't sure how they kept so many balls in the air, kept everything straight with only a couple of assistants—her and those employed by Alex and Alana. She sat next to Brett and across the table from Alex. Several times, she would try to catch his eye, but he refused to look at her. Her heart still pounded from their earlier encounter, and she could feel his hands on her and his desire as he'd pressed against her.

Alex stood. "I think that's everything. I've got to see Jessica at city hall. She's checking on the permits for Hedo," he said, rising from the desk and gathering his things.

"Expecting any problems with that?" Brett asked.

"There shouldn't be any holdups. I anticipate they'll go through pretty easily. And then it's just funding and investments, partnership agreements. The usual."

His phone beeped on the table, and he picked it up. He read the screen. "And that's Alana. She wants us all to get together tonight to discuss the designs. Working dinner?" he asked Brett, not looking at Maria.

"Ah hell, I can't tonight." Brett shook his head. "Rebecca's entertaining some clients, and she wants me on hand."

"I can stay," Maria said, getting both Alex's and Brett's attention. When neither man said anything, she tried to brush off the embarrassment of possibly speaking out of turn. But she wanted them to say yes. She wanted to be a valuable part of the team, and not just for her amazing ability to take notes and fetch coffee.

"That's not necessary." Alex held up a hand. "Me and Alana will be able to handle it. You should know that even though we have teams to handle a lot of the details, we like to personally do as much as possible. It's important for us to have a hand in and oversight over every part of the business."

"Makes sense," she said with a frown at being rejected by him, but she could also see the turmoil in Alex's eyes. He'd made it known how hard it was for him to just be around her, and she probably shouldn't hold it against him. "But if you're so involved, then you need as many trusted hands in this as possible, right?"

"That's right. Maria, that's a great idea." Brett turned to Alex. "If I can't be there personally, Maria will be a great stand-in. And she'll get a better handle on the project." A silence fell over the room, and she watched the showdown between the two men. Silent communication traveled between them and she only wished that someone would say something.

The next sound was Alex's sigh. "Fine," he muttered and turned to her. "You like sushi? We'll order in."

"Yeah. Sounds good."

Alex turned to leave but then glanced over his shoulder. "Be here at eight."

CHAPTER FIVE

IT WAS CLOSE to midnight by the time they finished up. Alex stood and stretched his back. He looked over at Maria, admiring her work ethic, especially seeing how it was her first day. She still looked beautiful, and no more worn than she had that morning, except for the fact that she had taken her long, luxurious hair down from her bun. And every time she pushed it behind her shoulders, he'd had to restrain himself from reaching out and threading his fingers through it.

"What did you think of your first late-night summit?" Alana asked her as they gathered their things.

"It was good. This is such an awesome project, I'm so glad to be working on it. I'm almost energized. It's late, but I don't think I'll be able to get to sleep yet." Alex caught the pointed look she shot in his direction.

"Why don't we go downstairs for a drink? I could certainly use one," Alana suggested.

"Downstairs?"

"Di Terrestres."

"I've never been there."

Alana's eyebrow raised. "No?"

"I've never been invited," Maria laughed. "Like Rafa would ever let me. I've heard about the sorts of things that happen there, though."

Alana shook her head. "Raf won't let you go? He's unbelievable."

Maria laughed. "Not unbelievable at all. He's so overprotective."

"Please let me be the one to tell him that I'm putting you on the permanent guest list."

Alex watched with interest. The women had known each other for years, but it looked as if an easy friendship was forming between them. Even on day one, Maria had easily become a member of the team. She fit in so well. If he could remember that she was just that—an employee, part of the team— then he may be able to forget his desirous inclinations toward her. Standing next to him, Maria bent over to retrieve her purse and bumped against him; whether it was inadvertent or not, he stiffened in response. Forget he wanted her? *Not fucking likely.*

"So, a drink?" Alana asked them both, leading them out of the conference room.

"I'd love to," Maria said.

They both looked at Alex expectantly. He always went downstairs for a drink or two to unwind after work. It would just look strange if he refused that night. "Yeah, sure. Let's go."

When Maria crossed the threshold of Di Terrestres, she felt like she'd entered another world. The light was low and cast a favorable gold shimmer on every surface and person in the room. It was after midnight on a Monday, but it didn't matter, there was still a crowd, and they danced seductively to the low music and kissed and touched in booths that lined the wall, watched over by nearly naked men and women who danced on platforms.

Maria was no prude, but she still looked around the room, eyes wide, as she saw the familiar faces of some of Las Vegas's, and America's, most notable people among the guests, engaging in acts that she couldn't believe weren't splashed over the gossip rags. Like her brother's own intimate encounter at the club had been. Alana and Alex seemed unaffected. Of course they were. It was their club, and they were more than accustomed to the overt eroticism around them.

"We're up here." Alex touched her arm and directed her up a small set of stairs to a table on a balcony that provided them with a view of the entire club. His touch sent electricity through her, and her toes curled inside her shoes. It was the first time he'd touched her since that morning in the lunch room, and she'd craved it.

"Quite a view up here," Maria commented as she took a seat next to Alex. "Like you can watch over all of your domain."

"Yeah, 'gods of the earth' and all that," Alana said, referring to the Latin name of the club.

"What actually goes on here? If I'm supposed to work for you, isn't it reasonable that I know what you do?"

Alana answered first. "We provide a place for like-minded individuals to gather, socialize, have a drink, without having to worry about being under the scrutiny of the press or anyone else."

Maria scoffed. "Come on. That sounds like the sanitized press release version you give the media. I've heard rumors." She gestured to the crowd below them. "I just want to hear it from you guys."

The waitress came with their drinks, and Maria caught the way that the woman looked Alex up and down. She couldn't blame her. A person wearing a blindfold could recognize that Alex was the sexiest man in the room. He had the ability to draw people in and commanded a power over everyone.

"As long as everything happens between consenting adults, we don't discourage physical exploration within our walls," Alana continued. "In fact, we welcome it. The more relaxed and confident people feel, the better time they'll have. And for the lofty membership price, we show people a good time."

She'd known about Di Terrestres' sexy reputation. Everyone did. But unless you were invited or paid the exorbitant membership fee, there was no way you were getting inside the door. The intensity of Alex's stare almost made her look away, but she didn't waver. "You guys are being purposefully vague," she said to both, but looked only at Alex. "And how do you show people a good time? Like, what specifically do you have set up here?"

He leaned forward as well, so that their faces, their lips, were only inches apart. Using every bit of restraint, she managed not to kiss him. "We have entertainment on the main floor almost every night—dancers, erotic performers. But it's our other facilities that keep people coming back. There are also such events as private parties, black-tie masquerades.

"But it's what we offer our most notable clients that makes us successful, so we have the bedroom suites that people can use for an additional cost, but our more VIP experience is tailored to each person's individual needs. We have rooms set up for exhibition and voyeurism, dominance and submission, group sex."

"Oh really?" She leaned in, resting her chin in her hand. "And I imagine that you've partaken in the facilities?"

Alex looked directly at her, and it felt like they'd left Alana completely out of the conversation. Maria wondered if the other woman could see the sexual tension between them. "Obviously."

"And what's your favorite?"

He shrugged. "I'll try anything once." His voice was smooth, whiskey-dark and sexy.

Alana cleared her throat, interrupting their conversation. When Maria turned away from Alex, she saw that Alana was indeed watching them. Her raised eyebrow showed that the moment had not been lost on her. She looked at her watch and pushed her glass away with a feigned yawn. "Well, it's officially late. I'm going to get out of here. Maria, you did good work today. It's going to be great having you on the team."

"Thanks. I'm really excited about it."

"Alex, we'll touch base in the morning?"

"Of course."

They both watched Alana leave, and when she was out of sight, Maria turned to Alex. "I really had a great day," she told him. "I'm excited to be working with you."

He smiled. "I'll admit, I was skeptical. But I'm glad Brett offered you the job. You're an excellent addition to the team."

She felt a blush color her cheeks, and she looked down at her glass of wine.

"But Alana was right. It's late. We should go."

Maria frowned. She wasn't tired. Not in the least. But as Alex stood, she did as well. She followed him down the staircase and onto the main floor of the club. As the night had progressed, the erotic acts around her had become more brazen. Heat flushed through her, and she wondered if it would be appropriate to play at the club or if Alana's adding her to the list was strictly for professional reasons. Alex had told her that he partook in the activities there, and just thinking about that made her desire skyrocket. She felt her panties grow moist, and she stopped walking, clenching her thighs together as a way to seek relief.

"You okay?" He turned to face her. The flush on his cheeks made her wonder if he was similarly affected by the acts going on around them. He looked desperate, impatient, as if he were just barely hanging on himself. Maybe he wasn't as cool as he let on. "Come on, let's go."

"What's your hurry?" she asked.

"It's late."

"Yeah, you already said that." She smiled and twirled a tendril of hair around her finger. "But you know what, Alex, I'm not tired."

"Well, I am," he told her. He clenched his fists and looked tense enough to burst free of his shirt.

"You don't look tired. So what's your plan here?" She took a step closer. "Are you trying to get me out of here so you can find some other woman to suck your dick? Or do you prefer a little bondage? Or maybe you want multiple women?"

"Stop." His voice was low, with a hard edge, but she carried on. Provoking him, pushing him. She was playing with fire, of course, because she knew that if Alex gave her an inch, if they allowed themselves to do exactly what both of them wanted, the flames would consume them both.

She stepped closer. They were chest to chest. "I haven't been able to think about much else but you since we kissed. I can't help but want more. You feel what's happening between us, I know you do."

Alex sighed. "I do. I want you too goddamn much. I want you so much that it physically hurts me."

She laughed, a short, light sound and she thought she saw him flinch. "If you want me, what's the problem? I want you, too, if I haven't made that known." She leaned closer, stepping on her toes to bring her lips within a hair's breadth of his.

She could tell that his restraint was razor thin. "Maria, don't. Don't push me," he said, pulling her hands to his cheeks and she felt his five o'clock shadow scratch against her smooth skin.

"Why not?"

"You're my best friend's sister."

"So?"

"If he found out anything—"

"He's not here right now, is he? Like you said, nobody talks about what happens here. He won't find out," she said as she unbuttoned the top button of his shirt. "He doesn't have to. It's none of his business."

Alex closed his eyes. She could see the resignation on his face. "Okay." He took her hand in his and pulled her away from the edge of the dance floor. But he didn't lead her to the exit. They turned a corner and stopped at a host stand in front of two sets of stairs. One that led up, the other down.

"Any rooms free, Andre?"

Andre handed him a plastic fob without giving her a second look. If he recognized her as Rafael's sister, he didn't mention it. "Number four."

"Thanks." Alex took the key and led her up the staircase.

Maria had questions, but she didn't dare say anything lest she break him free of whatever spell he was under. He led her to a door and used the electronic fob to unlock it. He opened the door and quickly ushered her inside.

The motion-sensor on the lights activated and the room was filled with low, muted lighting, reminiscent of candlelight. Maria looked around. They'd told her about the private rooms, but she wasn't sure what to expect. The room was small and comfortable and held minimal furniture, just an armoire and a large king-size bed, which was flanked by nightstands. She peeked through an open door to find a bathroom that contained a stand-up shower. There was also a small wet bar on the opposite wall that looked well-stocked. Alex stood in the center of the room, and they watched each other in silence, but Maria was certain she could hear their hearts beating in tandem, connected, from several feet apart.

They didn't touch, didn't speak, but she knew Alex, she had for years, and she could tell from the way he clenched his fists over and over and breathed heavily through flared nostrils that he was barely holding on to control. It finally hit her with a bolt that by the end of the night, she would know all the power that he harnessed under his tattoo-covered skin and that he normally kept retained in exquisitely tailored thousand-dollar suits. As if it were a tangible thing, she felt his intensity. The barely restrained masculinity, the strength that he possessed. He was hard, his posture rigid, and she wanted it all, even the anger, directed at her.

She heard Alex's deep breath as he broke away from the staring contest and walked to the small, fully stocked bar. "You want a drink?" he asked, his voice rough, turned away from her.

"Sure."

He poured her a glass of wine and two fingers of

bourbon for himself. He handed her drink over, his fingers grazing hers.

He drank his bourbon in one swallow and breathed out as he looked her up and down. "What am I going to do with you, Maria?"

Her eyes didn't waver. She sat on the edge of the bed and smoothed her hand over the soft blanket. "What do you want to do with me?"

He didn't answer, just poured another drink for himself, and she considered it a victory when he joined her on the bed.

She scooted closer and brought her knees under her, so that they touched his hard thigh. "You know, I'm not a kid. I'm a woman with my own body and my own desires. And I want you. Why is that so bad?"

"I've never known you to have a boyfriend or anything. I can't believe I'm asking this, but are you a virgin?"

"No," she told him, kind of surprised, although she shouldn't have been, that he would think that. "And in fact, I haven't been for quite a while." She put her hand on his thigh; the hard muscle flexed and tensed under her touch. "I might have gone to an all-girls high school and college—thanks Mom and Dad—but that doesn't mean there wasn't an opportunity to get off, hook up with guys...and girls."

"Girls?" He raised an eyebrow. "Oh really?"

"Hey, I'm a twenty-first century woman. I know what I like, and I know I'm allowed to get it." She waited for his next move, sipping from her glass.

Her breath caught when he put his hand on her bare knee. He exhaled roughly but didn't look at her. He rubbed her leg, and she watched his tattooed hand, the knuckles inscribed with the word *play*—as opposed to the one marked with *work*—as Alex made his way slowly up her thigh and under her skirt.

"God, Maria." His words were soft with his resigned sigh. "This is so goddamn wrong."

"Why is it so wrong? We're both adults. We know what we want. Why not just let it happen?"

"Fuck, if your brother finds out."

"Will you let it go? He doesn't have to find out anything," she whispered, parting her legs for him, opening up to him, allowing his fingers to travel farther upward.

His hand was high on her thigh, under her skirt, and going farther. Anticipation and his touch had wound her so tightly that when his fingertips toyed with the edge of her lace panties, she shuddered as a ragged breath was expelled from her lungs. She looked down, his hand under her skirt, smoothing her crease through her panties. When she looked back at him and saw that his eyes were also locked on his hand. Looking upward again, their eyes met as he sought approval, because they both knew that they could never go back. He would no longer be Alex Fischer, her brother's best friend, one of her current bosses. He would be her lover, at least for the night. She would have intimate knowledge of his body, and he hers.

Maria could tell that he was barely holding on,

just like she was. Years of buildup of wanting him would finally be unleashed. There would be no more mysteries about the powers of Alex, and yet she remained still, afraid to move in case she broke the spell. She just wanted him to press on, venture farther. His slow, methodical fingers might kill her.

With his other hand still holding his glass, he lifted it to his lips and drained it, and tossed the glass on the floor. "Oh what the hell," he said, quickly grabbing her by the waist and pulling her into his lap, and then rolling over so that he was lying on top of her.

She didn't have a chance to say anything before his lips crashed down on hers. He inserted himself between her spread legs, which wrapped around his hips and pulled him closer. She could feel the length of his hard cock against her hip, and she shook with anticipation of finally having it inside her.

He nipped her bottom lip before he trailed his lips across her jaw and down her throat. She let go of her grip on her wineglass and let it fall to the floor with a small *thud*. For only a second she thought of the remaining liquid spilling onto the carpet, but she forgot it when she pushed her fingers through his sandy-colored hair, pulling him closer, as he licked, tasted and bit his way down her chest. He took control of the buttons down the front of her blouse, opening them and then spreading her shirt open.

Alex kissed a trail down her torso as he exposed her flesh, inch by inch. He got off the bed and knelt on the floor. Wrapping his tattooed fingers around the outside of her thighs, he pulled her toward him, and then he ventured back under her skirt. He hooked his fingers around the waistband of her panties and pulled. She lifted her hips obligingly knowing exactly what was coming next, but simultaneously not believing it. He took the opportunity to unzip her skirt, and when he pulled it down, she was naked below the waist, and she could pinpoint the second when her tattoo caught his attention.

He smiled and looked up at her before he bowed his head to her hip bone and traced the text with his tongue. The air rushed out of her lungs as he looked up again and chuckled. *"Trouble?"* His eyebrow quirked at the word that she'd had permanently inked on her body.

She shrugged and smirked. "I got it in high school. As a good girl with a wicked streak, it seemed appropriate at the time."

"I think it's appropriate now. You are certainly trouble. It's written all over you," he said, tossing her underwear over his shoulder. "Do you have any more secrets? Or should I keep looking?"

"I've got a few things up my sleeve," she told him. "No more tattoos, but you can keep looking if you don't believe me."

"Challenge accepted. But first we've got to get you undressed."

Alex straightened, still kneeling in front of her, and she sat up, facing him. He was tall enough so that they were the same height. He reached behind her, unclasped her bra and pulled down the straps at her shoulders, peeling it from her body, her freed breasts falling into his waiting palms. He squeezed, cupped her, and she arched her back into his touch. "Alex."

He was still dressed, and she needed to change that. She wanted to get her hands all over that hot, hard body. But he leaned away from her touch.

"Not yet." His eyes raked over her, and he again crouched between her legs and leaned in so that he was just inches from her core. He parted her legs, draping them over his shoulders, swiping his tongue over the seam of her pussy. He went deeper, spreading her, and licked again, his tongue hitting every nerve ending along the way. Maria inhaled deeply and fell back, letting herself fully experience the way Alex's mouth felt on her. He moaned, and the vibration traveled from his throat into her body. He went deep and using his fingers, lips, tongue, he consumed her and she cried out, gripping his hair, pulling him close to her. Not letting him go until she began to feel the warmth start low inside her.

The waves of heat radiated, traveled, until she felt her thighs quiver and her toes curl. She pushed his head into the crevice of her thighs, as she came with a loud cry, taking all he offered, not knowing, or even caring, how he could breathe. She just wanted more.

When her fingers cramped, her grip on his dark blond hair loosened, and he crawled back up over her. Kissing her as he moved up her body, his fingers and lips tickling her ribs, running below the curve of her breast. He kissed her, her breasts, her throat, taking her mouth deeply, his tongue exploring hers, dancing with her. Never before had she been kissed so fully, so deeply, as if he were stealing the oxygen from her lungs.

She tasted him; the bourbon on his tongue mingled with her own flavor and, combined with his maleness, was a powerful, debilitating, intoxicating anesthetic. Any more, she would be drunk from him. But it still wasn't enough. She wrapped her arms around his shoulders trying to pull him closer, to get more, but he stopped and pulled back from her, looked her up and down. How she must have appeared to him, splayed on the bed, legs spread, panting for more of him—her hair and makeup must have been a mess.

But if Alex thought so, he didn't say as much. "Jesus, Maria," he whispered. "You're incredible. You're so fucking beautiful when you come."

She reached for him again, hooking her index finger under the waistband of his pants, pulling him forward. His pants tented with the huge erection behind it. "You don't know anything yet," she told him, palming his dick through his pants. From what she could feel, he was large, thick and hard. His hand caught hers before she pulled him too close. His eyes and the frown that marred his beautiful face told her that he was still at least a little unsure and conflicted. "Come on, Alex," she implored. "I want more."

"Fuck," he muttered, allowing himself to be pulled on top of her. "As long as I'm going to hell, I might as well enjoy the ride."

* * *

As Alex pressed Maria into the mattress, he knew that he was far from hell. Maria's body was a heaven that he'd never known before. He could taste her on his lips, her flavor sat heavy on his tongue, and he couldn't wait another second to be buried deep inside her. He kissed her, one of his hands on her cheek while the other unbuckled his belt and lowered his pants. His dick was out and then he moved his hips forward, pushing his shaft along her clit. It was glorious. She was so *close* to him. *Too close.* He was just a second away from plunging into her when he pulled his hips back.

"Shit," he whispered, his voice strained against the skin of her neck. Every movement was torture for him. Need clenched his chest, and it was hard to breathe.

"What?"

"I need to get a condom." He'd been so consumed that he almost forgot about his number one rule—always use protection. He knew he was clean—he was young and single and enjoyed a healthy sex life, he always used a condom, and was tested regularly—but there was no way he was going to take her without protecting her.

His gait was stiff and hurried, as he made his way to the armoire, the one that they kept stocked with onetime-use devices, anything that a guest would need—restraints, various sexual devices in their original packaging, along with a basket filled to the brim with an assortment of condoms next to neat rows of various massage oils and personal lubricant. He grabbed several condoms and returned to her on the bed.

Maria took a condom from his fingers and knelt on the bed, straddling his thighs. She ripped the foil and slowly, torturously, rolled the latex over his throbbing length. He hissed, pulling the air between his teeth, forcing his eyes to stay open, to watch her cover him. Alex wasn't sure why he'd waited so long to have her. This felt absolutely right. Having Maria touch him so intimately was more than he could have wanted.

Still on her knees, she crawled closer, bracing herself on his shoulder, she wrapped her fingers around his cock and he moaned at her touch and held his breath as she lowered herself over him, guiding him into her until she was fully seated in his lap. He almost came then and there. Maria was hot, tight, and he'd never experienced anything like it.

Maria reached behind her and put her palms on his knees and raised up using her thigh muscles, pushing her chest in his direction, until just his tip remained inside her, and then she slammed down on him again. He thrust into her, meeting her movements, knowing he wouldn't last long. He ground his teeth, trying to hold on, and dropped a hand to where their bodies met, finding her clit. He circled it with his thumb until she cried out and tightened around him, and it wasn't until she stilled that he let himself go. He threw his head back and squeezed his eyes shut as he came, filling the condom.

He took her by the waist, pulling her closer, kissing her, then he eased her off his lap before he stood and got rid of the spent latex. Watching her over his shoulder, he smiled as she stood, gloriously naked, and walked to the bathroom. And even though he'd just had one of the best orgasms of his life, he was amazed when his dick stirred with need for her again.

Fuck. He exhaled a heavy breath. He had just crossed a serious line. *Crossed?* He'd goddamn pole-vaulted over the fucking line. He couldn't even *see* the line from where he stood. Rafael was essentially his brother, and Alex owed the Martinez family, the only *real* family he'd ever known, everything. And how did he repay them? By fucking their daughter. Sure, he and Maria were both adults, able to live their own lives, but something about it still felt *wrong.* His dick twitched to life as the word *wrong* passed over his mind, as if what they'd just done was salacious, dirty. He heard the toilet flush and the water run in the bathroom before Maria strode naked toward him. By the time she reached him, he was again fully erect. The things he wanted to do with her might have been dirty, but they sure as hell weren't wrong.

She looked down in his lap and raised an eyebrow. "You're ready to go again?"

To answer her question, he grinned, took her hand and pulled her down into his lap. He kissed her and let her strip him of his shirt and pants.

They were both naked, bare flesh on flesh, and

he rolled her over on the bed so that he lay on top of her. As he kissed her, he smoothed his palms over her body—her shoulders, back, her incredible ass, breasts, pausing to tweak her nipples, earning him a lustful sigh. He could barely stand to take one hand away from her body to reach for another condom. He rolled it on and entered her again. This time was slower than the first, but no less powerful. Even though his heart drummed a staccato rhythm against his rib cage, he thrust into her in long, lazy strokes, taking his time with her, relishing the way she felt, sheathing him. Her grip tightened around his neck, and her breathing quickened. He already knew her tells, and she hummed, moaning something he didn't quite catch in Spanish. She clutched him, her nails raking across his shoulder, and she contracted around him in a blissful crescendo. He let go, felt his toes curl as he climaxed.

He rolled away from her and gathered her close as they both caught their breaths and let their heart rates return to normal. With his arms around Maria, he momentarily pushed aside all of his doubts. Nothing about holding her felt wrong.

CHAPTER SIX

THE NEXT MORNING, Maria arrived back to work at The BH. She was tired, but her night with Alex had left her invigorated. After they'd had sex twice, they dressed quietly, because having expended all the energy, dissipating the sexual tension, they'd found little else to say. Even though there was a conversation to be had, he'd walked her to her car and said good-night with a brief touch on her arm, instead of the kiss that she'd come to crave.

In the light of the early-morning sun, her body was sore but relaxed, and she smiled remembering how she came to be so achy. When she walked through the main entrance that led to the offices, she came upon Brett and Alex waiting for the elevator.

"Hey, Maria." Brett turned and greeted her with a smile. He was certainly more of a morning person than she was. Alex looked straight ahead, but she could see the minute movement of his stiffening as she got closer.

"Hi," she said, trying not to yawn. She looked over at Alex, who averted his eyes.

The elevator doors finally opened and the three of them stepped inside.

"How was last night?" Brett asked, looking down at the screen of his phone. Her eyes widened, and she and Alex made alarmed eye contact from either side of Brett.

"It was fine," Alex responded finally, obviously referring to their late night working with Alana. "I added everything we did to the cloud storage if you haven't had a chance to look at it yet."

"I haven't yet." He turned to Maria. "Thanks for filling in for me. We can go over everything you covered before we get down to work."

"Sounds good."

The elevator finally arrived at the top floor and they stepped outside.

"Maria, let's get started in a couple of minutes, all right?" Brett said, turning in the direction of his office.

"Yeah, sure. Sounds good."

"Maria, wait," Alex murmured, leaning close, wrapping his fingers around her elbow. "Can I see you for a moment?" He steered her into his office before she had a chance to respond.

As soon as they entered his office, he closed the door behind them. She knew what he wanted. "We have to talk about it, don't we?" she asked.

"We definitely do." His voice was gruff.

"Do you want to start?"

He shook his head and looked at her straight-on. For the first time she noticed that his eyes were red, and he hadn't shaved. He looked like hell but Alex at his worst still looked better than most people at their best. "I don't really know where to start besides to say that it shouldn't have happened."

"No?" Her left eyebrow cocked quizzically.

"Maria, I wasn't kidding when I said that even touching you was a huge betrayal to Rafael, your family. I was up all night, and the only explanation I can think of is that we got carried away. I've been working a lot. And you started this new job. We were drunk the first night we kissed. We let our libidos get the better of us." He slammed his palm down on the top of his desk. "It won't happen again."

Maria wasn't convinced. He said the words, but the way he looked at her—like he wanted to rip her clothing off and take her again—betrayed that. "Listen, Alex, us sleeping together was probably inappropriate, given the fact that I'm now working for you. But you need to get past all that 'betrayal to my family' stuff. I'm not beholden to my family. Sure, Rafa probably wouldn't be thrilled if he found out what happened between us. But it's also none of his goddamn business what either of us do."

"Yeah." His voice was a dark murmur. He looked her up and down. "But either way, it's over."

"That's too bad," she said, shrugging and standing. "We could have had a lot of fun." She walked to the door, then stopped and looked over her shoulder at him. "I just hope I can get out of here at a decent hour tonight. I have a date."

Maria could have laughed at the way Alex flinched. "A date?"

She nodded. "Yeah, a guy I know from my mission in Haiti texted me. We're grabbing dinner." Nathan had actually texted her a few days ago and had made a date to get together strictly as friends. But it seemed like too good way to drive Alex crazy.

Alex scowled. "He texted you to ask you out on a date?"

"Yeah," she said, trying not to smile at Alex's jealous reaction.

He shook his head. "Fucking kids," he muttered under his breath.

She tamped down the giggle that formed in her throat. "What's wrong with that?"

"What ever happened to calling a woman? What did his message say? *Hey, baby, DTF?*"

She laughed. "Oh my God, you're jealous!"

"Jealous?" He snorted. "Of some twentysomething, aged-out frat boy? Hardly."

Maria laughed. "How do you know he's a frat boy? He's a really nice guy."

"I'll bet he is. Guys that age, especially when they take women like you out, are hardly ever nice."

"And what, pray tell, is a woman like me?"

"One of those good girls," he explained. "He thinks you're naive, and he has ulterior motives."

"Is that what you think?" Her head tilted. "I thought I was *trouble*."

"You are trouble," he agreed, returning her sly

smile. "But it took me years to learn that. This guy has no idea what he's in for."

He *was* jealous. Maria laughed as she walked out, leaving Alex alone in his office. She had been successful in getting completely under his skin. Now she had to do everything she could to stay there.

CHAPTER SEVEN

THE WEEK PROGRESSED, and by Friday, Alex was tired, irritable and on edge. He had been successful in avoiding any one-on-one interactions with Maria. Not trusting himself to be in the same room with her, he stayed in his office or took meetings at other locations. But now he was feeling the tension. It was after seven in the evening—another twelve-hour day—and Alex threw down his pen. The incessant work and lack of sleep and abundance of caffeine were all finally catching up to him. His shoulders ached, and his eyes stung with fatigue. As evidenced by how they blurred when he looked at the numbers and words in front of him. It was time to call it a day.

He needed a drink, a cigar and a woman. On any other day, he might be tempted to go downstairs to Di Terrestres, find a willing woman or two, and work off a little tension. But since being with Maria and sharing those incredible hours with her, Alex had had no interest in any other woman. He wanted to blame the lack of enthusiasm on the workload, but deep inside, he knew that it was because of her.

He thought about Maria and wondered if she'd enjoyed her date earlier in the week, or if she had seen that guy again. All week, Alex had tortured himself with the images in his head of Maria kissing this mystery guy, going to bed with him... Frustrated, Alex exhaled deeply and clenched his fists in front of him. He had to forget about Maria. She deserved a good guy, someone who was better than him. Maybe this *nice guy* was the one for her. It was what she deserved. Not him.

But still, the thought of another man touching Maria made Alex sick.

So instead of leaving his office, he got back to work, digging into the rest of his to-do list, because there was always something that needed to be taken care of. Work had always been a convenient distraction from his past and current demons. One of the few things that chased away the memories and the darkness.

He checked his email and found several new ones that needed his attention. They could probably wait until Monday morning, but he might as well figure them out now. He started reading the first one, but was interrupted when his cell phone rang. Alex almost didn't answer it, but he recognized the number as an office at city hall. "Fischer," he said by way of greeting, hitting the speakerphone button so he could keep his hands free to reply to his emails.

"Hey, Alex, it's Neil from the permits office."

He knew Neil and liked the guy. They'd been working together for years; he'd hooked up Alex and the rest of The Brotherhood with permits and other documentation since they'd started in business. This was the latest in the day the man had ever called. He looked at the clock on his laptop. "Hey, Neil, what's up? For you to be calling me after seven on a Friday, I'm guessing it's not good news."

"You got that right."

Alex's fingers stilled over his keyboard. "What is it?"

"The permit for your new hotel has been stalled."

"What? Jessica—I mean, Mayor Morgan said it'd be fine, and we'd have no trouble as long as the paperwork was in order."

"And she was right to say that. At the time. Everything *was* fine. But now some people are accusing her of greasing the wheels for her boyfriend and his friends."

"That's bullshit. Everyone knows Jessica has too much integrity for that."

"You and I both know it, and so do most of the councillors. But some are claiming that the proposal is morally indecent—"

"It's just a fucking hotel."

"We know that, but based on the controversy last year, people automatically assume that it's some kind of brothel or something. And you know we don't allow that in Clark County."

Alex huffed out a frustrated breath. "So, what do we have to do?"

"My unofficial advice is to apply again. Maybe do some PR about the project and assure the people that they're mistaken about what you guys are doing. Keep the pressure on city hall, convince the holdout councillors. Come by next week. Attend the council meeting."

Alex scoffed. "Okay, so we have to make nice with a couple of people too prudish to allow an erotic hotel? Between us both, we have applications from at least three-quarters of the city council who want to join our private club waiting to be processed when we open the new place."

Neil laughed. "Well, it should be pretty easy, then. I know I don't regret my membership. But keep at it. This is just a bit of stumbling block. A small delay."

"I hate that word."

"I know, man. We all do. But like you said, being so late on a Friday, there's nothing we can do until Monday at the earliest."

"I know. Thanks for the heads-up, Neil."

"Any time. Let's get together some night. I've got some craps money burning a hole in my pocket."

Alex laughed, remembering their last time, carousing, drinking and dropping money on the Strip. "Yeah, let's do it. Let me know when is a good time for you."

Alex disconnected the call and the smile dropped immediately from his face, and he slammed his fist down on the desk. "Fuck!"

It was just a minor setback, but it could have huge implications on the project. If they couldn't get the permits in order, Hedo would be dead in the water. If word got out that they were having trouble getting started, suppliers and other investors would start to pull out. The dull ache behind his temple had become a mad throbbing as anger swelled within him.

He had to get out of his office, maybe take a play from Brett's book and cut back on the hours he put in. Although his friend had good reason to leave work early these days—a gorgeous wife waiting for him at home. Alex pictured his own empty penthouse condo, overlooking the Strip, and he didn't want to go home. Two of his friends, Brett and Rafael, had, despite the odds, found love and while Alex made fun of their now-quieter lifestyles, part of him was jealous. Not jealous in that he wanted a wife, or family, but jealous in that he'd never once experienced the unconditional love they shared with the women in their lives. But that's why he had ownership in Di Terrestres. No shortage of people who wanted to spend time with him.

He knew just how to get past the frustration. Like he always did. Good booze and even better sex. He stood from his desk and picked up his cell phone. He decided to hit up Di Terrestres after all, have a couple of drinks, and see if he could round up a gorgeous woman or two and see where the night took him. But even thoughts of naked women in one of the club's suites didn't do much to relieve his stress when the only woman he could think about was the one he'd told himself he couldn't have. Goddamn, he wanted Maria.

The night that they'd spent together earlier in the week was still with him. He normally didn't give his sexual encounters a second thought after they were over. But Maria was still with him. He could smell her, taste her, and whenever she plagued his thoughts, his dick got hard. So he'd stayed in his office, door firmly shut.

But putting Maria out of his mind was easier said than done. He could still feel her on his skin, and he itched to pull her body against his. Just one more time. But he couldn't allow it.

The problem was, it was impossible to forget she was there. Especially when he had to walk past her desk on his way to and from Brett's office. She always looked up at him, and she would smile, a knowing, sly smirk that he tried his hardest to ignore. But even avoiding eye contact didn't help him when her perfume tantalized his senses. The light citrusy notes hit him and would linger in his nostrils for the entire day.

But that night with Maria—it wasn't going to happen again.

"Fuck it," he muttered, now fully plagued with desire. He knew that he wouldn't get anything else done until he expelled the sexual tension that racked his body. Di Terrestres. He had to forget about Maria, replace her with memories of another hot, tight, perfect body. He sent a text to the VIP host, Andre, telling him what he was looking for. "Nope. Never again," he muttered to himself as he rode the elevators down to the club floor. It was still early in the evening, but people were beginning to trickle in. He nodded in greeting to many of the patrons before

looping around and going down the wide staircase
that led to the lower floors. The host in the VIP area
nodded and let him walk past. Alex looked at each
of the eight closed doors with little interest, each
one representing one of the more popular kinks and
secret indulgences of their VIP clientele. He knew
which one he was looking for, and walked into a
room almost at the end of the hallway.

The lights were dim and the music soft; the only
sounds were the loud moans of the two women sitting on the round bed in the middle of the room. They
were naked but for G-strings, kissing, touching each
other, just waiting for him to join them.

They were women who frequented the club. Alex
had met with them several times, and they always
had fun together. Both gorgeous, fun. They looked
at him expectantly. Alex took a step in the room,
trying to feign interest. Thinking that if he just got
into it he'd be fine, but he stopped. He didn't feel it,
and he knew he wouldn't be able to go through with
it. Something had changed within him. Maria had
changed him. He shook his head and stepped out of
reach of four manicured hands. "Sorry, ladies. My
mistake."

One woman's head cocked to the side, not used
to being refused by him. "Alex, are you serious?"

"Yeah, I'm sorry. I guess I'm just more tired than
I thought. I'm going to get out of your way. Have a
good night. If you need anything, don't forget to
let Andre know, okay? He'll take care of you." He
backed out of the room and shut the door.

Andre came up behind him. "Everything okay, Mr. Fischer?"

"Everything is fine. Thank you, Andre. But I realized that I have somewhere else to be." He knew exactly where he *wanted* to be—wrapped up in Maria's sweet body. His hands shook with need, frustration, confusion. And he tried to talk himself out of it. But as he'd heard the angel on his right shoulder tell him to be good, the devil on his left held more sway.

He took the elevator back up to the top floor to his office to get his things. He should just go to the gym, or home, have some drinks and veg out in front of the television until he passed out. He sent a message to his driver to come around to the front of the building. But he opened his door and came face-to-face with Maria.

From just looking at her, he felt lighter. Juxtaposed with the bad things in the world and every negative feeling that dredged up, Maria was a beacon of light that he hadn't realized that he needed.

"Alex," she said, and he loved the way she said his name.

"Maria." He tried to keep his tone casual. "Heading out?"

"Yeah, I'm meeting a friend for a few drinks."

"Another date?"

"Maybe. Why are you so interested?" Her voice was soft, melodious, but he knew they both felt the underlying sexual current that zapped between them. "Seeing as how you've been avoiding me all week."

His brain might be exhausted, but his body zinged

to life. Neither a workout nor the warmth of a bourbon buzz would suffice. Maria was all that would do. Alex looked around and saw they were alone in the hallway outside his office. Despite everything telling him not to, he moved in. "I want to see you," he whispered. "Why don't you come over to my place tonight? I feel like we should talk."

"What if my date goes late?" she challenged him. "What time do you go to bed?"

He tried not to scowl as he thought of how Maria's date could go late. He was tired of the games. And he resigned himself to the fact that he wanted only to end the night with her, no matter what. But he kept himself cool. "Come by whenever you want. I'll be up."

"Oh I'm sure you will be."

CHAPTER EIGHT

ALEX LEANED OVER the railing on his private balcony and puffed his cigar, thankful for his connections that let him get his hands on a supply of fine Cubans. He sniffed the smoke from the lit end, and it soothed him. Pensively, he watched the view below him. Even thirty-seven floors above Las Vegas Boulevard, he could still hear the noise, the music, the shouting, and feel the energy. In a move that not many native Las Vegans made, Alex chose to join wealthy tourists by buying a penthouse condo on the Strip. He never liked the quiet; he liked the distraction that was provided by the chaos, the noise and energy of one of the world's hottest party spots. And the fact that he could hit a blackjack table, get some drinks and then be home in time to watch Seth Meyers seemed perfect to him. Most nights, when he was home long enough to enjoy it, he reveled in it.

He sat directly in the lap of luxury. He liked the finest spirits, the best cigars, gourmet coffee and food, the finest things life had to offer. He worked his ass off for it. But he never forgot where he came from. His current life was miles away from where he'd started. A small, scared boy, alone and bundled up to go live with his best friend's family. But as he always did, he banished the memories and focused on his life now. He had a good life. He worked hard, but he also couldn't discount luck. Things could have turned out very differently for him. He could have grown up in the system. But the Martinez family had given him everything he needed—including the love and support he'd never had before.

He heard the buzzer from the lobby, signaling Maria's arrival. He'd already told the doorman to let her up immediately whenever she got there, regardless of the time. When the elevator doors parted, he saw Maria. She had changed out of the navy dress she'd been wearing at the office and was now wearing a pair of skinny jeans and a tank top. But even in her casual clothes, she looked just as beautiful and put together.

Without saying a word, he reached out for her and pulled her to him. His lips came down on hers, and it was the purest moment he'd experienced all day. Her lips parted instantly, and he took full advantage. His tongue sneaked into her mouth and found hers, swiping against it, tasting her. She moaned and pushed him away first.

From the rapid rise and fall of her chest, he could see that she was breathless. "I thought this wasn't going to happen again?"

"I was an idiot," he said; his voice was just a stolen breath. He let go of his grasp on her waist and took her wrists. He brought one to his mouth and placed a kiss on her pulse point.

He was rock hard, and as much as he wanted to push her down on the couch and have his way with her, he wanted her in his bed more. He wanted to savor her, see every bit of her, taste every inch of her smooth body. "Let's go to bed."

Maria followed Alex to his bedroom. Her heart was pounding, and she could barely hear anything else. She and Alex had been together before, but this felt different. They stood next to his huge bed. He cupped her face in his hands and drew her to him. His lips found hers, and instead of being domineering, forceful, his kiss was slow, searching, almost tentative, seeking permission.

Maria parted her lips, allowing him access. His tongue brushed against hers, and he shifted his position, taking the kiss deeper. With just one touch of his lips, he owned her entire body completely.

His hands lowered to the hem of her shirt and fisted in the material. She lifted her arms, allowing him to pull it over her head. He threw it on the floor and then loosened the button of her jeans and pulled them, along with her thong, down. Taking her hand, he helped her step free of them and guided her to lie on the mattress.

He looked down at her as she laid on the center of the bed, naked and exposed. Maria was confident about her body, but Alex's attentive gaze made her shiver. She crossed her arms over her middle, trying to hide.

"No," he whispered. "You're beautiful. Don't ever cover yourself up around me."

"Well, are you going to take off your clothes and join me, or just stand there and look at me all night?" Her body begged for his touch, but he seemed in no hurry to join her.

She watched, riveted, as his hands went to his front. His sure, capable fingers unfastened the buttons on his shirt. There was something about watching his hands, the strength he possessed in them. The tattooed knuckles that made way for full sleeves of dark ink that swirled up his corded wrists and forearms, and across his chest and shoulders, which were being revealed as he shed his shirt. She parted her lips and her eyes widened. They'd had sex before, but she hadn't been treated to the show of watching Alex slowly undress. He was sex in a hard, six-foot-five body.

Next came his pants, and he lowered the zipper and pushed them down. He'd left his underwear on, and her eyes went to the huge bulge that tented the designer briefs.

Alex knelt on the bed in front of her. She reached out for the band of his underwear, hoping to lower them, but he stopped her, taking her fingers in his. "Not yet." He made his way to the spot between her spread legs. "I'm hanging on by a thread here. The second these shorts come off, I'm going to be inside you."

Her breathing was heavy. "I don't see anything wrong with that."

He groaned. "Baby, I'm going to spend the night making love to you. I don't want it over in a couple of minutes."

He kissed her again and smoothed his hands down her shoulders and over her breasts. She sighed at the contact and pushed her chest against his hands. He leaned over her and captured one of her nipples between his lips and drew her in while his fingers toyed with the other, caressing her breast. He switched his attention, alternating between his mouth and fingers, plucking at her sensitive nipples and every nerve ending at her chest. Every touch sent a shock of pleasure to her core, and it made her desperate. She gripped the back of his head and wove her fingers in his dark blond hair, holding him closer, simultaneously wanting more of his touch and not being able to handle his attention.

When she knew she couldn't handle any more, he broke away and proceeded to kiss and lick his way down her midline. He traced the letters of her *Trouble* tattoo with his tongue and nibbled lightly on her hip, tickling her, forcing a giggle from her lips that contrasted with the heavy, potent air between them.

Chuckling against her skin, he kissed a trail to the apex of her thighs. He opened his mouth and closed it over her, his tongue and lips spreading her, delving deeply inside. He found her clit and sucked on it, and drove two fingers into her wanting body. His touch was expert, skilled, but it wasn't nearly enough. She thrust her hips against his hand and mouth. But he stayed the course and flattened a hand against her stomach, stilling her.

Her hands fisted in the blanket below her, and she arched her back away from the mattress as the thunderous orgasm overtook her body. He crawled his way back up her body, a satisfied, smug look on his face. "You're so sexy," he whispered against her lips. "If I could just watch you come for the rest of my life, I would die a happy man."

She moaned against him, smelling and tasting herself on his skin, mingled with his own intoxicating aroma. She needed no time after her orgasm; she wanted him again, and she pressed against him, dragging her sensitive pussy against the steel column of his dick, which was still trapped behind his briefs. She reached down and pushed them over his ass and pulled him closer. Their most intimate parts rubbed against each other, and without breaking away from her, he reached into the nearby nightstand and removed a condom. He wrapped himself and kicked his shorts off so that they were both completely nude.

Alex leaned back, aligned himself against her and pushed inside, filling her so completely that she found it difficult to breathe. His arms wrapped around her, and her legs encircled his hips, their bodies entwined. His hips pulled back and then pushed against her. His cock hit just the right spot inside her, making her see stars. She wasn't far from another breath-stopping, body-bending orgasm.

He moaned against her skin, his breath as hot

as his fiery touch. Every nerve ending in her body burned as he consumed her. Her hips met his, and the spot where they joined. She came again, and she could feel her internal muscles grip him, pull at him. He stilled above her and reached his own orgasm with a shout.

He rolled away with a puff of breath. He disposed of the condom and rolled back over to her. "Christ, Maria," he muttered, nuzzling her throat. "Maria," he repeated, as if chanting a repetitive prayer. "You're amazing."

She snuggled more closely to him and rested her head against his chest. Alex might have maintained that being together was wrong, but it certainly didn't feel wrong. She drifted off as Alex's heartbeat slowed and his fingers played with her hair.

CHAPTER NINE

WHEN MARIA WOKE up, the sky was still dark, and reaching out, she discovered that she was alone in Alex's bed. His side was cold. "Alex?" she called, and got no response.

With a frown, she pushed back the blankets, pulled one of Alex's T-shirts over her head and left his room, looking for him.

She sniffed, and followed the scent of cigar smoke as it wafted from the open sliding glass door that led to the balcony. Alex sat on a lounger, facing outward, shirtless, wearing a pair of pajama pants. He puffed a cigar and held a tumbler that contained a couple of fingers of an amber liquid. She knew it was the expensive bourbon that he loved. She watched him for a moment, a voyeur of his quiet, private moment, and she smiled. Classic Alex.

Before joining him on the balcony, she saw the humidor and decanter sitting on a table near the door, so she selected a cigar, expertly cut the tip, and poured herself a couple of fingers of bourbon. Then she walked outside, joining him on the balcony.

Even though they were almost forty stories up, they could still hear the noise of the Strip below them.

"Got a light?" she asked. He turned his head, looking surprised to see her there, but he smiled when she took the chair next to him and pulled it closer. He held up a silver lighter and flicked it. With the cigar in her mouth, she leaned in, puffing on her cigar as it lit.

"Cigars and bourbon?" he asked her. "You are certainly full of surprises."

She leaned back onto her own lounger, laughed and blew out some smoke. "You have no idea how often I hear that."

He looked her up and down, his gaze leaving a singed trail on her skin. "You'll freeze wearing that. Not that it doesn't look good on you."

"I'm fine. You'll keep me warm."

He grinned and puffed on his cigar. "How was your date tonight?" he asked her, casually, focusing on the cigar, flicking ash into the tray, trying to seem uninterested.

Initially she was confused, not knowing what he was talking about. But then she remembered that she'd had some drinks with Nathan, and they'd caught up, talked about old friends, memories in Haiti. But that was it. He could have taken her sky-diving or flown her to the Amalfi coast, but it drastically paled in comparison to the hours she'd just spent with Alex. "It was nice. We're just friends. There's no connection there. You know, no spark." Not like the sparks that were between her and the man sitting next to her. Those were stronger, brighter, more explosive than anything he'd ever experienced.

He nodded, not looking at her.

She felt the small smile as it formed on her lips. "You were jealous, weren't you?"

His bottom lip stuck out a little farther, and he shook his head. "No. I wouldn't be jealous of some guy who's just barely old enough to drink."

"I don't believe you." She swung her legs around to face him. "I think you were jealous." She leaned in closer. "Were you picturing me on a date with another guy? Were you picturing him touching me? Like you touched me?"

He snapped and turned to her. "I *know* another man couldn't touch you like I do. You're just goading me."

She leaned back, satisfied in the knowledge that she was right. He was jealous, and she'd gotten the reaction she wanted from him. She flicked her cigar ash into the tray that sat on the table between them. "So, did you actually want to discuss anything tonight? Or was it a ruse to get me here? Because I'm not sure what you're about to say, but if it's more of what you said to me the morning after we first slept together, I'm not interested in hearing it." He opened his mouth to respond, but Maria kept going. "I don't regret anything that has happened between us. Although judging by tonight, I don't think you do either."

He looked at her. "I don't regret it. I just know that

if Raf ever found out, he'd kill me, and he'd send you off to a nunnery."

She nodded. Her older brother was protective, stubborn and unwilling to mind his own business when it came to her living her life.

He turned to face her. "All week I tried to not think of you. I tried my damnedest to distract myself and put you out of my mind, but when I bumped into you today, it all came back to me. I wanted to see you. And I want to see you every day. But I know that your family won't approve. And I can't lose them, or Raf. He's like a brother to me."

"Why would you lose him, or any of them?"

"Because you're his sister," he said as if it was obvious to her.

"That's idiotic. You keep saying that, but shouldn't Rafa be happy that you, his best friend, a man he loves and trusts, would be involved with his sister?"

"It's not that simple," he insisted, taking a drink from his glass. "This is so fucked up. It's wrong. You know as well as I do that he wouldn't approve of someone like me dating someone like you. I'm hard, dark. I've lived through some things that shouldn't even touch you. You're so beautiful, and sweet, and good, and sexy. God help me, because I can't help myself. If Rafael finds out, he'll be pissed, and with The Brotherhood expanding our operations and Raf making his run for Senate, I can't afford to drive a wedge in the group. There's too much on the line for all of us."

"I understand that. You make me want to do wild

things, too. Why don't we just keep it private? What we do is no one's business but our own."

"Would you want to do that? You deserve better than that. You deserve a man who will take you out, show you off."

"Admittedly, it isn't ideal. But if it's what we have to do, at least until it's the right time to come clean, it could be kind of fun." He put her palm on his thigh, and it drifted upward, toward his lap. "Having this secret affair makes it feel kind of *illicit*, don't you think?"

His chuckle was low. "You're right about that."

She sipped the dark liquid in her glass and felt him staring at her. "What?" she asked, lowering her glass.

"We've known each other for years, but to think I didn't actually know anything about you."

"You try being the youngest daughter of a good, strict Catholic family. After so long of being expected to do only the *right things*, I rebelled hard in my teen years, and never looked back."

"I had no idea."

She shrugged. "I never got caught," she said, one corner of her mouth ticking upward. "It's why I moved out a little while ago. I needed my own space, away from my family. They love me, I know. But it's frustrating, you know, stifling. I'm an adult. It's like they're smothering me with love."

"Sounds nice. I've never known that," he muttered, and turned back to the watch the lights below them.

Maria frowned. Admittedly, she knew next to

nothing about Alex's life before he came to live with her family when she was little. She'd asked questions, but his past was a thing that people whispered about, and certainly not to her. She always wondered what sort of situation would cause a young boy to move away from his family, and she suddenly felt bad for complaining about her family because they were *too loving.* "I'm sorry, I'm an idiot. I shouldn't have said anything."

"Don't worry about it. I grew up with your parents, too. I know they're a little overwhelming. But it's only because they love you. It must be driving them crazy that they can't watch out for you twenty-four/seven."

"You have no idea," she said. "If I still lived at home, they'd be waiting up for me to play twenty questions. *'Where were you? Who were you with? Do you know how late it is?'*" Her voice mimicked her mother's tone. She sighed. It might be annoying, but she knew that it came from a place of love.

Alex laughed. "Don't forget, I've been on the receiving end of that interrogation as well."

A quiet fell over them. Maria turned to face him again. "How long have you been out here stewing while I slept?"

"I don't know. Do you want me to call you a car so you can go home?"

"No. Unless you want me to go." She held her breath, waiting for his response, not wanting to leave him, but she would if he wanted his space.

He smiled. "Not a chance."

Maria stubbed out her cigar in the ashtray and crawled over onto his lounger. Sitting across his lap, her arms encircled his neck and his tightened around her waist as she settled against him. His skin was chilled from the amount of time he'd spent outside, and she nuzzled close in an attempt to warm him.

"This is nice." She felt his nod against her head, and he put his lips to her temple in an achingly delicate touch that made her shiver, all the while feeling his dick harden against her.

His arms tightened around her. "Are you cold? We can go inside."

She shook her head. "No, I don't want to go anywhere else. I'm happy right here. I think we can keep each other warm."

He ran his fingertips down her back, until his palm smoothed over her butt. He squeezed her. "I think I have a couple of ideas of how we can do that."

"Oh yeah?"

He turned her in his lap so that she straddled him. He rested his hands on her thighs. She wasn't wearing anything under his shirt, and he hummed appreciatively when he discovered that. Using his thumb, he stroked her.

Closing her eyes, she fell forward, landing against his chest. He pushed one finger inside her, and she gasped.

Alex's breath was as ragged as her own, as he placed his lips against the outer shell of her ear. "I don't know, baby, you seem pretty hot to me."

CHAPTER TEN

"HAS THERE BEEN any movement on that permit issue?" Alana asked.

Alex exhaled a heavy breath. It was Monday evening, and he looked around the people at the table—Alana, Brett, Maria and their other two assistants, who were meeting to discuss the progress on Hedo. "No," he said. "I've been on the phone all day, and I've reapplied but Neil seems to think that it might just come down to us getting buddy-buddy with some of the councillors. I just don't like that any of this is having a blowback on Jessica. They're claiming that she's in our pocket."

"I was talking to her yesterday," Alana said. "She isn't concerned about it. The holdouts are a couple of old guys who have been giving her trouble since she took office last year. We can probably make them come around."

"Yeah, the sooner the better. It might take us the rest of the week, but we can't go any further until we get the permit. Hopefully we can keep the delay quiet before it starts making people nervous."

"Unlikely," Brett laughed. "We all know the Las Vegas business community spreads more gossip than an old women's sewing circle."

Alex looked across the table at Maria. She was staying quiet and taking notes on her tablet. She was wearing a high-collared shirt coupled with a scarf, and he knew it was because of the marks he'd left on her soft skin that weekend. In the three nights that they'd spent together, he'd had her every which way, all over his apartment. In his bed, on his couch, in the kitchen, in his shower, on the balcony...

His blood headed south, but they both kept their faces neutral as they made eye contact across the table. They had a massive secret. And no one else knew. Alex knew that she was just as thrilled by the secrecy as he was. She smiled, her brown eyes large and bright, just as they'd been that morning when she'd looked up at him from her position on her knees, in the shower, with her lips wrapped around his dick.

Brett started talking about something that Alex should have been listening to, as Maria was, since she diligently took notes on her tablet. But instead, Alex took out his phone and quickly dashed off a message to her.

I can't wait for this meeting to be over, so I can bend you over my desk and fuck you until you can't take it anymore.

He watched her. He knew when she saw the message on her tablet, because her eyes widened, and she looked at him and grinned. He smiled back, and they both turned their attention back to Brett. Alex's phone buzzed on the table, and he picked it up.

Good thing I didn't wear panties today.

Alex almost choked on his tongue, and with a fully hard dick, he tried to focus his attention back on Brett, to hear what his partner had to say. He saw that Brett's mouth was moving, but damn if he could hear any of the words. So he picked up his phone again. Forget bending you over my desk. I'm going to slide your skirt up and eat your pussy until you scream. But that's not all...

He knew she'd gotten his message when her head ticked to the side. And...?

I'm going to take your clothes off and fuck you hard on the floor, then I want you to ride me, so I can suck on your nipples while you bounce on my dick.

Maria blew out a ragged breath, and Alex thought he'd bested her. But when his phone screen lit up, he knew that she also had the same game in mind. At what point can I put your cock in my mouth? I want you to fill me until I feel it hitting the back of my throat. I want you to fuck my mouth until you come, and I swallow every drop of you.

Alex bit back a groan. He dashed out another message to her. Excuse yourself. Right now. I don't care what you say, just get your sweet ass downstairs to the club and get one of the suites. It was midday; the rooms should be mostly empty.

God, you're bossy. Now?

Right fucking now. Cancel all of your plans tonight, because you're mine for the rest of the night. When you get down there, take off your clothes, get on the bed and wait for me.

"You with us, man?"

Alex lifted his head from his phone and looked around the room and saw that everyone was watching him.

"Yeah, I'm here."

"Then you would know that we need to get our design ideas to the architectural engineers in two weeks."

"Yes."

"And I was wondering if we could all get together again tonight. Get some takeout and hammer it out?"

"Tonight? No, I have plans."

Brett blinked, and Alex knew that his friend could see through him. Alex didn't put work by the wayside just for social plans. "Nothing you can get out of?"

Alex shook his head no. "Afraid not." Brett and Alex watched each other for several tense beats before Brett shrugged. "All right, we'll worry about it tomorrow then, I guess."

"Sounds good," Alana confirmed with a quick couple of flicks, checking her calendar as Alex did the same. He was a bundle of unspent sexual need, and he looked at Maria.

"Excuse me, Brett. I'm sorry, but I have to leave." She cast a look at Alex. "I have an…appointment. Sorry I forgot to let you guys know—"

"Don't worry about that, Maria," Alex said, sitting back as casually as he could. "We might be *bossy*, but we aren't slave-drivers around here."

"Yeah, it's fine," Brett agreed, looking at his watch. "It's time we call it a day. Before you go, Maria, do we have everything in order for our New York trip tomorrow?"

Alex had forgotten the pair would be heading to the east coast tomorrow for the rest of the week. He wasn't sure how he'd be able to get through until Saturday, but all he knew was that he would have to make tonight worth it.

Maria smiled and left the room, no doubt on her way to Di Terrestres, to do just as he'd told her. Alex stood quickly, gathered up his phone, laptop and notepad and put them all in his shoulder bag, holding it in front of him so no one would see the tell-tale bulge behind his zipper. He managed to leave the room without anyone asking him any questions.

Alex made his way to the elevator, and his phone rang. It was Maria. "Hey."

"Alex—" She was breathless, as if she was hurrying.

"You okay?"

"Yes. No. I have to go."

"Where?"

"To the community center. There's a bit of a crisis with one of our regular kids. I have to get over there."

All of Alex's erotic plans for Maria came crashing down. But he knew that she was committed to her work for the center, whether she was a paid employee or a volunteer, and she had to go. "I didn't know you were still working there."

"I still volunteer there, Alex. They're still my kids. And my friends."

He nodded. Maria's compassion was admirable and unmatched. "Is everything okay? Any way I can help?"

"I can't get into it now, but it hopefully will be. It might be a late night. I'm sorry, Alex. I was hoping we could get together before I left for New York."

"Don't be sorry," he told her. "Go help people. I'll see you on Saturday at your parents' barbecue."

"Okay. I'll make this up to you, Alex," she said.

"You definitely will," he assured her.

CHAPTER ELEVEN

ALEX PARKED HIS car outside the Martinez home, the home where he'd spent his adolescence. The driveway was already mostly full, as it looked like he was one of the last to arrive for the extended family's weekly dinner. He turned off the car and bounded up the driveway. While he didn't get to attend every week, because work sometimes kept him away, he looked forward to the get-togethers, and this week was no different. But what put an extra bounce in his step was the prospect of seeing Maria. Her compact car was in the driveway, and a thrill shot through him. She'd been in New York for several days and he missed her. His heart beat for her, getting quicker with each step, as he came closer to seeing her again.

He pushed open the door and was greeted by the usual rush of noise and calamity that often accompanied their family gatherings. The house was full of loud, passionate people who all loved one another, and laughed and fought to prove it. Children ran around inside and out, and the women prepared food in the kitchen while the men were out back, minding the grill, or smoker, or roasting a pig or whatever the meat of the day was.

"Alex," Mrs. Martinez called to him across the house from her place overseeing the work in the kitchen. "There you are. I was afraid you weren't going to make it."

"I wouldn't miss it for the world."

"I just know how busy you all are, especially with this new hotel you're building."

Rafael came up behind him and put an ice-cold beer in his hand. "I know I haven't seen you or Maria in the past few weeks. You guys must be really burning the midnight oil."

He looked at Maria across the room. She raised a knowing eyebrow, and he shifted, attempting to covertly arrange himself behind his zipper. Since he started seeing Maria, he found himself with more inopportune erections than he had since his teen years.

"Outside?" Rafael asked, hooking a thumb toward the French doors that led to the backyard. "I want to talk to you."

"Yeah, sure," he said, reluctantly walking away from her. Alex couldn't read the look on his best friend's face. Did he know about him and Maria? Did he want to get him away from the family so he could kill him in private? They walked into the backyard, but instead of joining the rest of the men, Rafael led him to the quiet spot on the deck. Away from the noise and chaos of the house, they silently drank their beers. "How are the wedding plans going?" Alex asked.

"I have no idea," Rafael laughed. "Jess and her friend Ben are taking control of all the planning. I've just been tasked with showing up at the right place and time."

"Not a bad deal."

Rafael paused. "I also have to pick my best man. Are you game?"

"That means I get to plan the bachelor party, right?"

"That's about it, yeah."

Alex smiled, honored to have been asked to stand by his oldest friend as he married the woman he loved. He hadn't always approved of Rafael's relationship with Jessica, especially since they'd been in the middle of an election when their relationship had started, but he could see the positive effect she'd had on his best friend. "Well hell, I'm in."

"Thanks. There's no one I'd rather have up there with me."

Alex swallowed his beer past the lump in his throat. Rafael trusted him. They'd been so close that they considered themselves brothers. And how did Alex defile that trust? By taking his sister to bed and doing things with her that he could never tell Rafael. He looked up, and as if she had a beacon on her ass, he immediately knew when Maria was in the vicinity.

They watched her through the large glass door as she roughhoused with some of her young cousins. The doors and windows were closed and even though he couldn't hear her laughter, her joy, her love, as she played, was obvious.

"How's she working out with you guys?"

"Awesome," he said, trying to keep his face neutral. Although no part of him felt neutral when it came to Maria. "She's been an amazing addition to the team."

"I'm glad you've been showing her the ropes."

Ropes, there's an idea, Alex thought as Rafael kept talking, not hearing one goddamn word he said, watching Maria as she disappeared farther into the house.

He shook his head. "Does she seem different to you at all?" Rafael asked him.

Alex paused. "What do you mean?"

"I don't know. I think she's more distracted than usual. She's never available. And I know that you guys work a lot, but I wonder if she's spending her spare time with anyone."

"You think she's in a relationship?"

"I don't know. But I hope she's not being screwed around with by some guy. I don't even think she's ever been with a man."

False.

"But I hate to think some bastard is leading her on, breaking her heart. Just because she doesn't know how men work. I don't want anyone to take advantage of her."

Alex frowned. What would his friend think if he told him that *he* was the bastard? "I think she knows how to look after herself. She's smart. Maybe smarter and wiser than you give her credit for." Guilt surged through him. He'd never lied to Rafael, or any of his friends, before. He needed to come clean. Before he could stop the flow of words, his mouth opened. "Raf, I've got something to tell you—"

"Rafa!" one of Raf's aunts called from the house. "Jessica's here! Come help her unload the car!"

Rafael's smile was huge with word that his fiancée had arrived. "Be right there. This can wait, right?" he asked, referring to the bombshell that Alex was about to drop.

Alex nodded, feeling slightly relieved but frustrated at the same time.

"Coming," Raf called back. "Jessica is bringing a bunch of food. Want to give me a hand?"

Alex took a deep breath. "Yeah, sure." He had almost irrevocably changed his relationship with Rafael. He'd never been a coward, and he knew that any relationship he had with Maria counted on him being able to come out to her family. He had to tell Rafael, no matter the consequences.

As per Martinez family tradition, after dinner was finished, the kids all tuckered out, settled in the media room watching a movie, the older adults retired inside to the family room, while the younger adults lounged around the fire pit in the backyard. Soon the conversation turned to Alex's love life.

Maria's older sister, Dita, started. "So, Alex, are you seeing anyone now?"

Maria watched him as he tried to coolly play it off with a chuckle. "Come on, Dita, when am I *not* seeing anyone?"

"You're not getting any younger," she reminded him. "Isn't time you settled down? Find a nice woman like Rafa has?"

"When did you turn into your mother?"

"Yeah, I'm pretty sure Ma used that exact *nice woman* line on me before Jess and I got together," Rafael said, draping his arm over Jessica's shoulders.

Alex's eyes snapped to Maria's. She was enjoying her family's playing with Alex. "Yeah, Alex," she joined in. "Why not find a nice woman?"

He smiled. "Unfortunately, dear Maria, the nice ones don't want anything to do with me. The only ones attracted to a guy like me are one hundred percent *trouble*," he said, with a cocked eyebrow in her direction. "And I'm so very grateful for it." He laughed and stood, draining his beer bottle. "I'm going to head in and grab another beer. Anyone want anything?"

Several people requested refills and Maria jumped up as well. "I'll give you a hand."

He nodded, and she could feel his eyes run over her, like they always did when she was around him. And every time, she still felt the same thrill in her stomach at his attention. His gaze was heated, his attention focused on her. Maria wasn't sure how her family missed their connection, but they had moved the conversation on, oblivious, to talk about Rafa and Jessica's wedding plans.

They walked into the house together, and when they knew they weren't visible to her family out-side, they moved closer together, and Alex boldly dropped his hand to her lower back. Looking up at him, she smiled, and a silent message telegraphed as his fingertips drew little circles just above the curve of her ass.

Instead of stopping at the fridge to retrieve the beer bottles, Maria made a hard right and walked into the pantry. She reached out and snagged the front of his shirt and dragged him inside with her.

He kicked the door shut, pressing her to the wall. His mouth descended on hers and took her lips in a kiss so fiery it threatened to burn them both. His hands went lower, palming her breasts through her tank top. He drew down the strap and kissed her shoulder.

She broke away, putting a firm hand on his chest. Her breath puffed from her mouth as she tried her best to steady it. "We don't have time for that. If we're doing this here, it has to be now." That was true. They had limited time, and she wanted him. They had gone on a trip to grab beer. And she could hear the laughter and conversation of her parents and aunts and uncles in the nearby family room. All any of them had to do was walk into the pantry, and they'd find her and Alex together. It was risky, but everything about their relationship was risky.

"You're right," he breathed. He grasped her hips and turned her roughly, so she was facing away from him. He pushed her skirt over her hips, pulled down her satiny thong so it stopped midthigh. He kicked her ankles apart and cupped her from behind, allowing his middle finger to delve between her folds. She was soaked immediately, and he spread her moisture. Maria moaned and pushed back against his hand and he slipped a finger inside her, making her moan before he dipped another inside, causing her back to arch against him. He withdrew his fingers and spread her wetness upward, to the tight pucker of her ass. He pressed his thumb against her, and she gripped the shelf in front of her. He pulled a condom from his back pocket and quickly rolled it over himself. Then he positioned himself at her opening and slid effortlessly inside.

"Fuck, Maria," he cursed. She loved the coarse vibration of his voice, the way she made him swear, talk so dirty and crass to her.

He pulled his hips back and withdrew from her, leaving only the tip of his cock inside her before slamming deeply inside again.

She moaned, trying to stay quiet, but they both stilled when they heard laughter outside the pantry door. Two of her aunts had walked into the kitchen. He clamped his hand over her lips and held her close, burying his face in the crook of her neck and shoulder. His jagged breath was hot on her skin.

Maria could hear the women in the kitchen as they prepared coffee and dessert. With Alex's dick still inside her, she didn't know if she could hold on until they left. But apparently Alex had other ideas and when his hips pulled back again, she moaned into his hand as he entered her and kept going, finding a pace that had her clamping her lips shut, trying not to scream while her aunts chatted and laughed on the other side of the door.

He pulled his hips back and slammed them into place again, slapping against her ass with a fury that almost knocked them both forward. He firmed his stance, and then pumped in and out of her. He released her mouth, and his hand went around her, and he found her clit again. He circled it until she met his thrusts. Their movements were fast, jerking, until Maria threw her head back on his shoulder. Alex craned his neck, kissing her, swallowing the cries of pleasure from her orgasm as the women finally left the kitchen. She felt her intimate grip on his member squeeze him, and it was enough for him to finish as he slammed into her once more, his muscles flexing and tensing as he came. She milked him, felt him spasm, filling the condom, until his grip on her loosened.

He withdrew from her, and they straightened their clothes while he got rid of the condom, tossing it into the small nearby garbage can and covering it with some paper towels. "They're going to wonder what happened to us," he told her.

"We'll think of something," she told him. "Think they'd believe us if we said we got lost?"

"In your childhood home? Probably not."

She picked up a nearby unopened bottle of tequila. "How about some margaritas?"

He chuckled. "Yeah, sure."

She opened the door and came face-to-face with Jessica, her future sister-in-law. There was no telling how long she'd been standing outside or how much she'd heard. "Hey, Jess."

"We were wondering what happened to you guys. What, did you get lost or something?" Maria didn't miss the questioning in the narrowing of her eyes, suspicious of what she'd walked in on.

Maria laughed lightly, trying to hide her guilt. She turned on her most innocent smile. Sneaking around in her teenage years, hiding her wicked streak had paid off. "No, we decided to make margaritas, and then—wouldn't you know it?—we couldn't find tequila. And typically, when I finally found a bottle, it was on the top shelf."

"And you needed Alex to reach it for you," Jessica offered helpfully.

"Yup. He's tall. That's about it."

"And the door blew closed, and the closed-in room made you both flushed and short of breath?"

"It was a really high shelf," Alex offered.

"Sure." Jessica wasn't stupid, and Alex knew that she also wasn't convinced by their lame excuses. Alex didn't know how to make her forget about what she was probably thinking.

The three of them shared a quiet, tense moment, and Alex's eyes widened when Rafael came up behind them. "What's going on? I was wondering what happened to those beers you were getting."

Alex, Maria and Jessica all looked at one another. Maria smiled and held up the bottle. "It's margaritas instead," she explained, pushing past everyone else and walking into the kitchen. She looked over her shoulder and frowned when she saw the questioning look that Rafael shot at Alex. They maintained eye contact for a moment before Rafael moved on and left the room without another word.

Alex hung back from the group and mentally scolded himself. It had been stupid, risky. Having sex with Maria in the pantry, not far from the rest of the family, had been dangerous. Anyone could have walked in on them.

As Maria poured and passed around glasses of margaritas, he thought about how Mr. and Mrs. Martinez had stepped in when he was a child. They'd invited him into their home, accepted and loved him, saved him from a life in the foster care system. He repaid their generosity by watching the delicious curves of Maria's ass as she moved.

He wanted Maria with every part of him, and when he looked at her, desire flooded him, filling his entire body, so that it was difficult to move, to breathe, to do anything but hold her, consume her. But she was so good. Too good for him. He would only hurt her, and he knew that he should keep her away. Admitting his feelings for her could make his entire life implode. He could lose everything. He looked up at the family home. He could lose the only people he'd ever called family. They'd been his saviors. He owed them better than betrayal.

He caught Maria's gorgeous brown eyes across the fire as she smiled at him. He smiled back. His chest tightened with emotion that he'd never experienced before. Maria saw the best in him, always. And something changed when he was with her. But still, it wasn't right. She needed, *she deserved*, better. And even though it would kill him, he vowed to himself to stay away from her.

He couldn't take it anymore, so he stood. "Thanks for everything, once again. But I'm going to head home. I've got a few things to do tonight." Turning his back on the group's objections, he waved and made his way to his car, not stopping to say goodbye to anyone else, lest they see the guilt written on his face. But Maria stopped him before he reached his car and made his escape.

"Hey, Alex, wait up!" she called.

He turned and couldn't help the smile that formed on his lips when he saw her. He was headed for dangerous territory.

"What's going on? Why are you leaving?"

"I have to."

"How about I come over tonight?" she asked in that mischievous tone of hers.

It was his chance to say no. To put some distance between them. The list of reasons why they shouldn't be together going through his mind: she was so much better than he was, she was too good for him, he was a piece of shit who had betrayed his only family. If Maria got any closer to him—to the *real* him—she wouldn't like what she saw anyway...

Alex cursed his lack of strength when he nodded.

"I'd like that. Even though I don't think it's such a good idea."

"Why not? I've got some *very good ideas* for us to try."

When Alex looked down into her dark brown eyes, he saw lust and mischief. And he knew he wouldn't, couldn't, resist her. There was no way he didn't want to be with her. "I'll see you at nine?"

CHAPTER TWELVE

IT WAS 9:02 when Alex heard the elevator open in the foyer of his penthouse. He'd long since given Maria the key card for the elevator and permission to come and go as she pleased. He met her in the foyer, and without even saying hello, he lifted her so that she wrapped her legs around his waist. He couldn't wait another second. He needed Maria—right there, right then. With an outstretched arm, he swept clean the small table in his foyer, sending a stack of mail to the floor, and he perched Maria on the edge. He stood between her spread knees and was grateful that she was still wearing her skirt.

While Maria unzipped his pants and pushed them over his hips, he reached into his pocket for the condom he'd put there earlier. It took only a matter of seconds for him to cover himself, and push Maria's panties to the side. In a couple of thrusts, they were both breathing quickly, and Alex could feel her heart pounding against his chest, in time with his own, as he brought them both to the edge, where he threw himself over with a low groan and a shudder, and she clenched and tightened around him in her own release.

* * *

A couple of hours later, they lay on their sides, facing each other in the center of his king-size bed, his thin white bedsheet draped over their legs.

"Raf asked me to be his best man."

"That's typical. You're lying in bed with me, and you want to talk about my brother," she laughed. "But I know. He told me earlier."

He smoothed his palm over the delicious curve of her hip. The shape of her made his mouth water, and he recalled dragging his tongue up her torso, tasting her. He sighed. "He's my best friend, and this is how I repay him."

"You need to get over all that. This isn't wrong if we both want it. I like you. We're good together. I mean, you want it, too, right?"

"I do. I like you, too."

"Does this mean I'm your girlfriend?" she whispered as she leaned in, conspiratorially.

"Maybe," he said, his tone turning playful. Then he sobered. "You'd be my first."

She pulled back. "What? You've never had a girlfriend?"

He shrugged. "Nothing that lasted beyond a couple of dates, or late-night booty calls." He dated women, slept with them, but he'd never had a real relationship with any of them. He'd always made it clear where he stood, and if they couldn't deal, he would cut out.

"Not even as a teenager? There was no puppy love? There was no girl you fell head over heels for?"

He tried to seem unaffected, and to be honest, Alex had never analyzed how he'd felt about it. But the sad look in Maria's eyes told him that maybe he'd missed out. He looked away. "No. When I started having sex, I realized where my talents lie, and it wasn't in relationships." He smiled. "I'm not a serious commitment guy. I figured that if I can show a woman a good time, then she didn't need anything else from me." What Alex left unsaid was that he never let anyone get close. What would happen if they did, and they didn't like what they saw? No one else had.

"That's really sad, Alex. You've never experienced that new love feeling. Being so infatuated with someone that it hurts."

He looked her over—she was so beautiful, naked in his bed, his sheet lightly covering her hip. There was something so pure and loving in her gaze, his chest clenched, and he felt like he could barely breathe. "I don't know what this is," he whispered. "But is it painful when I can't touch you? Then, yeah, I'm feeling it right now."

Her response was a simple smile, and without saying anything further, she turned around, facing the wall, pressing her ass into his crotch and leaning against his back. His arms automatically wrapped around her, and he held her close. She was so warm and soft against him, and he could feel her heart beat. Or maybe it was his. They were so close, wrapped up in each other, that he couldn't tell.

And that was how they stayed until the sun rose the next morning.

CHAPTER THIRTEEN

ALEX WOKE UP the next morning, naked, and his sheets tangled around his limbs. When Maria stayed the night, he always slept better than ever. He reached out for her, but found his king bed empty. He'd become so accustomed to having her there that her absence made him miss her. Pushing back the sheet that was strewn over him, he retrieved his pants from the floor and pulled them on.

The smell of coffee made its way through his open bedroom door, and he followed it to the kitchen, where he saw Maria, wearing one of his shirts, standing in front of the stove he never used.

"Morning," he said, making his way to the coffee maker.

She watched him over her shoulder with a smile on her face. He kissed her.

"You really need to buy some food," she said, pushing scrambled eggs around in a frying pan he didn't know he owned. "The only thing you have are eggs, milk and coffee."

He shrugged. "I think there's an apple or something in there, too."

"What if your bourbon and cigar stash was as empty as your fridge?"

He gasped in mock horror. "Why would you say something like that?" he laughed and, grabbing her by the waist, pulled her to him. "How long have you been awake?"

"Not long. I was kind of hungry and was dying for a coffee."

"I don't think a woman has ever cooked me breakfast."

"It's just eggs."

He kissed her, slow, and their tongues slid together leisurely. "It doesn't matter." Holding her, he could definitely get used to lazy Sunday mornings in the kitchen. "So, what are your plans for today?" He toyed with the buttons on the shirt—his shirt—that she wore. "I hope they involve not wearing clothes."

She frowned. "That would be amazing, but I have to head to the community center. How about you?"

"I'm meeting Alana later to go through some stuff for the hotel later this afternoon. But until then, I'm free."

"Why don't you come with me?"

"What?"

"To the community center. It's always a lot of fun. And then you'll get to see what I do when I'm not an office lackey."

"Is that all you think you are? You're more than a lackey."

"I do the coffee runs and make copies. Sure sounds like a lackey."

He reached out and cupped her jaw. "You have become an integral part of our office. It wouldn't be the same without you."

"It's nice of you to say, but you only think that because you think I look great in a pencil skirt."

"Well, you do," he maintained.

"But there's so much more I could be doing. That we all could be doing. There are a lot of communities in this city that need help."

"We have The Brotherhood's charitable foundation. We donate regularly to various charities in the city."

"I know, and you guys have contributed so much to the city, and I don't want to tell you how to spend your money, or how to help people. Money *is* a huge help, but you aren't on the front lines. There's more to charity work than writing a check. You don't physically see the difference it makes in people's lives."

She was right. While they donated a huge portion of their fortunes to local and international charities, he'd removed himself from the life he used to live. He'd forgotten the days he'd spent at rec centers, hiding out until it was absolutely time to go back to his house. And he suddenly couldn't think of a better way to spend a Sunday morning with his clothes on. "Sure. That's sounds like fun. I'd love to go."

Maria watched Alex as he played basketball with some of the older kids. Even though he towered over all of them and could reach up and touch the lowered hoop, he still acted as if the kids were giving him a run for his money.

Her friends and colleagues Beth and Anna came up beside her and watched Alex roughhouse with the kids. "Is that the reason we haven't seen you much lately?"

"I'm really sorry I haven't been around. I've been working."

"So, you guys are dating?" Anna asked, nodding at Alex, as he made his way down the court.

"We're definitely doing *something*." She wasn't worried about telling her friends about their relationship. "But we're keeping it on the down-low for now."

Anna shrugged. "He's cute. He's generous, too."

Maria's eyebrows drew together as she turned to her friend. "What do you mean?"

"Here, look at this." Anna passed over the check that bore Alex's signature and a large five-digit donation.

"He gave you this?" Maria asked, looking from the check back to Alex on the basketball court.

"Yeah, on the condition it be anonymous. He wouldn't even let me take his picture. He said the place was all too familiar to him."

"Well, it's really going to come in handy. There is a ton of great things we can do with this money," Beth said.

Maria looked back at Alex, who let a boy get past him with the ball and shoot a three-pointer. They all

cheered. He may have looked tough, with his tattoos and ever-present scowl, but Alex was such a
sweet man, and she wondered what he'd meant by
the place being familiar. He'd come to live with her
family when he was young, but no one had ever told
her why, or what his own home life had been like.
Her heart clenched, and the realization hit her. She
was falling in love with Alex Fischer.

"You know, I'm due for a break," Beth said. "Want
to grab some food in the canteen?"

"Yeah, let's go. Anna, you in?"

Anna shook her head. "I just ate, and I've got
some paper work to take care of. You guys have fun."

Maria and Beth walked down the hall to the community center's lunch room. Because it was after
lunch, the room was empty, and they both selected
cans of soda and ice cream sandwiches from the
small canteen before sitting at a table that was built
for children.

Even though they were roommates, with all the
days that Maria spent at the office and the nights she
spent with Alex, they barely saw each other anymore.

"How's it going?" Beth asked. "Work and everything?"

"Really good so far." Maria frowned. "But I'm
getting tired. I've just been so busy lately."

"With work?" she asked, her eyebrow raised. "Or
with *Alex*?"

Maria looked away. "The Constitution says that
I don't have to answer that question," she said with
a giggle, as she unwrapped her ice cream sandwich,

noting the way her heart pattered in her chest at the mention of Alex's name. She felt her lips creep upward in an uncontrollable smile.

Beth looked her up and down. "Well, whatever you're doing certainly looks good on you. I don't think I've seen you smile like that in a long time."

Maria shrugged. "He makes me happy. It feels like I've wanted him for such a long time, and now that we're together, it's even better than I thought it could be."

Beth cocked her head to the side and watched her for a moment. "This is serious, isn't it?"

Maria's nod was a small, subtle movement, but she didn't elaborate.

Beth looked around to make sure they were alone and leaned across the table. "You're not going to share any details about whatever you've got going on with Mr. Tall, Dark and Edible?"

Maria tried to maintain her poker face, since she and Alex had decided to keep their relationship a secret, but she couldn't hide it from her best friend. "It's complicated."

"Ooh, sounds juicy."

"He doesn't want Rafa to find out, and because he's *technically* my boss, we've been keeping it kind of secret."

"Even juicier. And how is he?"

"He's well."

"Girl, you know that's not what I meant."

Maria winked. "It's really good. He really is

amazing in bed. But that's not all. He might look like a tough guy, but he's sweet, kind. I really like him."

"I'll bet he is."

"And that's all you're getting."

Beth huffed out a dramatic breath and sat back in her chair. "And seeing as how you aren't going to share any juicy details. I guess we should just sit here and eat our ice cream. I'm sorry, but I do need to make this quick. I volunteered to clean out the equipment room. It'll probably take hours."

Maria frowned again.

"What's wrong?" Beth asked.

"Nothing, really. I'm so grateful to have a job, but I really do miss working at the center as much as I used to. I'd love to go back and help you."

"You still come by when you can."

"But not as much. I'm doing office work for rich businessmen. It's a nice placeholder, but I'm not doing anything to help anyone. While I know I'm important to the team, it's not exactly fulfilling work."

"We miss you down there, too. So do the kids. Maybe you'll find a way to do both. Oh there's some news: Anna is stepping down."

"What?" Maria couldn't believe that the dedicated center coordinator would ever leave.

"She's moving to Tucson to be closer to her family. But you know, that means there's a position open," Beth said helpfully.

"Good to know," Maria said, sadly. She knew that she was qualified for Anna's position, but it didn't pay much. The salary wasn't anywhere close to what she was making at Collins/Fischer. It would just cover her bills and not allow for luxuries or savings. But it was a job she really wanted, one she would be good at. "If only there were enough hours in the day to do both, right?"

CHAPTER FOURTEEN

ALEX AND ALANA were quiet but cautiously jubilant as they left city hall with Jessica. Throughout the week, they both had individually met with most of the city councillors and members of the community and assured them that there would be nothing *too* lascivious happening at the Hedo, and even though there were still a couple of holdouts, they were confident that they'd made their case. Now they just had to wait for their new permit application to go through.

"Thanks for everything, Jess," Alex said, turning to her. "I'm sorry any of this had to blow back on you and your career."

She waved him off. "I've handled a little bit of scandal before—I can handle it again. Plus, I know neither of us has done anything wrong. It's business as usual. And Neil is fast-tracking your permit, so we should definitely know something by the end of the week."

"We appreciate it." He looked up and saw Councillor Perry, an old man who had served on council for decades. He was known to be strict, firm and quite conservative. He was the last councillor he wanted to talk to. "Ladies, excuse me for a moment," he said, breaking away. "Councillor," he called and jogged up to him.

The other man stopped as he was leaving the building. "Yes?" His thick eyebrows knit together as he frowned.

Alex extended his hand. "Alex Fischer, from Collins/Fischer."

Perry just looked at his hand instead of shaking it. "Yes, I know who you are."

Alex had dealt with difficult people in the past, and the councilman's rebuke did nothing to throw him off. "I was hoping to speak to you today. But you weren't in your office."

"Is that so?"

"Yes, we wanted to assure you, and address any concerns you might have about our proposed hotel."

"Ah yes, the brothel you want to open on the Strip."

Alex felt his cheek twitch. "It won't be a brothel."

"You want to bring filth to the heart of our tourism industry."

Alex was taken aback. "We're not proposing to do anything that tarnishes the name of Sin City," he said, using Las Vegas's nickname for effect.

"No, of course you wouldn't," the geriatric asshole said, looking Alex over.

"Do we have a problem, sir?"

"No problem. I know all about you. You were just an inch away from spending your entire life in the system. I looked into the pasts of you and your partner, Brett Collins, when the proposal passed over my desk. Collins is an addict and you're a poor foster kid who got lucky, but still looks like a thug."

Alex had to literally bite his tongue to stop himself from saying something that he would regret. The old fucker could say anything he wanted about him, but not his friend. He and Brett had both experienced their troubles in the past, but those were behind them now.

"Look at you, with all of those tattoos. You want to be taken seriously in this community? Maybe you should have made better choices."

Alex stepped back from the councillor before he found his fist connecting with the man's eighty-year-old jaw. "I can see we aren't going to change your mind on this. We were hoping for a consensus with city council. But with most of your colleagues on board, we'll just go around you. Thank you for your time."

As he walked back to where Alana stood with Jessica, he thought about what Councillor Perry had said to him. But it was his own near-violent reaction to the old man that had disappointed him the most. Maybe the councillor wasn't wrong. Maybe Alex was still the same thug he always was. Maybe he hadn't changed as much as he'd thought.

Alex rejoined the women in time to hear Alana say to Jessica, "We were going to head over to club, want to join us?"

"No, I've got a meeting to get to, but thanks,"

Jessica said. "And Rafael and I have dinner plans later."

"I definitely need a drink after today. You don't know how many of those guys asked me if, and how, I would personally welcome them to Di Terrestres," Alana said, pulling out her high blond ponytail and fluffing her hair as they headed for Alex's Jag. Alex's eyes narrowed in a glare, and she waved him off. "Don't worry, lascivious assholes are nothing new. I know how to take care of them."

"What did you say?"

"I tell them that I would be glad to welcome them and their wives anytime. You should have seen their faces."

Alex laughed. As a woman in their business, he knew Alana put up with a lot of sexism and other bullshit. But she did know how to take care of herself and wouldn't have any of them interfering on her behalf. "Still not cool, though."

"I know, but Viagra-popping post-middle-aged men are the least of my worries. Let's just focus on Hedo for now. What did Perry have to say?"

"Nothing encouraging," he muttered. "Maybe you would have had more luck."

"God, how many more stumbling blocks are we going to have on this hotel?"

"This isn't a stumbling block. We don't need him. Hopefully this will be all. Once the permit is straightened out, we can get the crews in immediately." Alex unlocked the doors and they both got in.

"That's optimistic of you," Alana said.

"Some days, optimism is all I've got." The thought of settling at their usual table at Di Terrestres got him thinking. He felt raw thinking about his troubled past, and even though he owned the place, he suddenly didn't feel like he fit in at Di Terrestres, as if he didn't belong there. He turned to Alana. "You know, I don't really feel like heading to the club tonight. Want to go somewhere else?"

"Yeah, what did you have in mind?"

"How about a bit of a blast from the past?"

When Alex headed toward the university, Alana started to laugh, knowing exactly where he was driving. "It's been a while," Alex agreed. He made a couple of more familiar turns, but ones he hadn't taken in years, and parked his car in front of the dive bar where they'd shared many a pitcher of beer while in grad school.

"Think your car will be okay here?" she asked.

"I'm sure it'll be fine."

They walked inside and while Alana found a table near the back, Alex went to the bar and ordered them a pitcher of beer.

"I know it's Thursday, but it's not like we had any downtime this weekend, so what the hell?" he said, expertly pouring each of them a mug of beer. He'd worked at the same bar, putting himself through college.

Alana accepted her glass and took a sip. "Sounds good. We'll get a cab home. And it's been a while since we've had any time to chat."

"What do you want to chat about?" He dragged

a tired hand across his face. "Anything except for work, please."

"Well, if we aren't talking about work, that narrows the list of topics considerably. Movies?"

"Who has time for movies?"

"Pets? No," she corrected herself. "Neither of us has a pet. Politics is exhausting. We can gossip about our friends, I guess."

Alex laughed.

"That leaves sex, I guess."

He sobered and said nothing. Talking about sex meant talking about Maria.

"I haven't seen you at the club lately," Alana told him. She ran the place and had her eyes on everything that happened there. "That could mean one of two things: you're in a relationship, or you're bored by what we offer, which I know isn't possible. How's the love life?"

Alex snorted into his glass and drank without answering, but Alana had honed in on it. He and Alana had always connected, since they'd met in college. Things had always been platonic between them, and they'd been each other's sounding board when it came to matters of the opposite sex.

"That bad, huh?"

"You have no idea," he muttered. "What about you? Let's talk about your love life."

"That's a short, boring conversation."

"No obsessed suitors darkening your door?"

"Hardly," she scoffed. "Thank God for the club, or I wouldn't have any sort of physical release. And it doesn't help that I've been sleeping in my office bedroom most nights."

Alex felt bad. Alana's workload had increased significantly since they'd started work on opening the hotel. It seemed that his venture, his pet project, was adversely affecting his friends. But if he needed to, he could handle the work on his own. "If you need to step back, just let me know. I can deal with the hotel stuff. You've got a lot on your plate right now."

"No, don't worry about it. It's not like there's anything else better to do in Vegas." She put her elbows on the table and leaned in.

"Yeah, boring ol' Las Vegas, with no shortage of people, shows, concerts, attractions…".

She laughed. "Shut up. I don't want to talk about it. Don't worry about me, or my workload, or my sex life. So, what's going on with you? You're more sullen than usual."

He needed to tell someone; maybe Alana would understand and provide a little insight into the mess he'd made of his life. "You called it. I am seeing someone, but it's doomed from the start. It's not right, and I know it."

"Well, I can't say I'm not intrigued. What's going on? Nothing sketchy or illegal, right?"

"Illegal? No. Sketchy? Most definitely."

"Okay… Lay it on me."

"It's Maria. We're sleeping together."

Alana's eyes widened for moment, and then she nodded in understanding. "You know, that night at Di Terrestres, I knew something was up with you guys.

But man, forget for a second that she works for us. She's Raf's sister. He doesn't know?"

"No. He might have had some idea something was going on last weekend." He remembered the wary way Raf had looked at him after they'd almost been caught together in the pantry. "I think he thinks that something is up. He's going to kick my ass if he finds out. And not to even mention what Brett will do when he finds out what I'm doing with our new assistant. Although, I'm sure he suspects something is going on."

"I wouldn't worry about Brett. He'll probably just give you a good scolding. Raf will *at least* kick your ass, though. Just so you know, I'm not going to tell either of them. But if you're just messing around with her—"

Alex glared at her.

"Is it more than that?"

"Christ." Alex drank from his glass. "I don't know. She's so fucking good, you know? She's this amazing person, and she's so pure, and full of life and optimism."

"She is."

"And I'm a mess. Why couldn't I just go back to living my life the way I used to? Work, gym, clubs, sex, repeat. It was so easy, mess-free. But Maria's thrown a wrench into all of it. I just find myself wanting to be with her all the time."

"That's kind of fucked up, Alex. Sounds kind of like the L-word, though."

"I don't know."

"And you're not going to tell Raf?"

"I need to. But I have no idea how. You know how protective he is. He's trying to focus on his run for Senate, and I can't afford to drive a wedge in the group while we have so many things going on. We need to be united on every front. You don't need to tell me that it sounds like a cop-out… I know I sound like a goddamn coward."

Alana seemed to accept that, because she sat back in her seat and looked around the bar. "Man, so much has changed for us since the last time we were here."

Alex nodded. The Brotherhood had traded in the beat-up booth at a college bar for their table at Di Terrestres. Alex looked at his rough, tattooed hands. Maybe Perry was right. Maybe he hadn't changed. Maybe he was the same poor punk he'd always been. He couldn't hide himself behind the steering wheel of a luxury car or an expensive suit. "But it doesn't feel like we've changed, does it?"

Alana leaned in, as if sensing his melancholy. "What's up?" He shook his head and tried not to answer her. But she didn't let it go. "Talk to me, Alex."

"I don't know. Maybe I've been doing a lot of soul-searching and all that. My relationship with Maria, and with what Councillor Perry said to me today, I've just got a lot on my mind."

"What did he say?"

"He just said out loud what I've always suspected— I'm still just a thug in a suit." He looked down at himself. "This isn't the real me."

Alana's face softened. "Come on, man, no. That's

a goddamn lie, and you know it. We're all a part of The Brotherhood, despite our backgrounds. You might have had a rougher start than the rest of us, but you've also worked harder than anyone I know. Don't listen to what some old, ignorant tool says. You're a good, intelligent man. And you're a shrewd businessman who got where he is with hard work, no matter what tattoos you have on your skin."

"I know that, but sometimes it's just hard, you know? Just feeling like I don't belong. And I feel like people can see it."

"Imposter syndrome is a cruel bitch, Alex. I have a theory that nobody feels like they belong all the time. Especially since we were so successful early in our careers, people didn't believe we earned it. But we did. Don't think for one second that you don't deserve this life. We all do." She looked at their empty pitcher and grasped the handle. "Next round is on me."

After several hours, and a couple of pitchers, Alex sat back in the booth. Their agreement to not talk about work didn't last for long. They'd scrawled notes on several napkins and had brainstormed their way through some design and structural issues that they might run into.

Alana waved one of the napkins. "We should really do most of our work here," she said, her voice slurring a little. They were both feeling the buzz, but they were confident with what they'd accomplished.

"Well, it worked for group projects in college,"

Alex added. "It was nice to get back to basics at least for an evening."

Alana yawned. "But now I'm tapped, man. I'm going to call a car." She pulled out her phone and typed a quick message to one of their drivers. "You coming?"

Alex thought about leaving, but he wasn't ready yet. He knew it was too late to call Maria, so leaving would mean going back to his cold, empty condo. He shook his head. "No, I might stick around a little longer."

Alana's concerned gaze irritated him. "You sure? Is everything all right?"

"Everything is fine. I just want to sit here for a bit. I've got some thinking to do."

"All right, hon." She put a friendly hand on his shoulder as her phone buzzed. "And that's my ride." She patted him on the back, as she stood. "We'll talk tomorrow."

Alex nodded and watched his friend stride to the door. He could have left with her, but he didn't want to, the vast emptiness of his condo becoming less and less appealing with each day. It dawned on him that that was the reason he spent so much time at the office, and why he often found himself taking on many projects at once, ones that took most of his time. But now he was on his own. And he could relax in the once-familiar environs of the dive bar where he'd spent so much time during college.

Things hadn't changed here. But he had, hadn't he? No matter what happened in his life, the luxuries and the fancy things he'd amassed, the accolades and success, he couldn't escape his past and what he was. He looked down at the tattoos that covered his hands—*work* and *play*. No matter what Alana had said, he didn't always feel like he fit into the world of The Brotherhood. Part of him still felt like the same street punk who had received a lucky break. As the melancholy set in, he wanted something stronger, darker. He signaled to the waitress and ordered double Jack Daniel's. Then, he put a $100 dollar bill on the table and asked her to bring the bottle.

Maria was in bed when her phone rang. "Hello?"

"Maria? Hi, it's Alana."

Maria pulled her phone away from her face and looked questioningly at the screen. "Alana, what can I do for you?"

Alana hesitated. "I know it's late, and this is kind of awkward. But I was just at a bar with Alex, and he stayed behind. I'm worried about him, and I was wondering if you could go and check on him. I'll send my driver over for you, if you can drive him and his car home?"

Maria sat up in bed like a shot. She didn't want to think too much about how Alana knew to call her. Alex must have told her. "Yeah, of course. Thanks for calling me." She gave Alana her address and hung up the phone. Maria quickly got dressed and grabbed her purse just as the town car pulled up in front of her building.

Once settled inside the car, she picked up her

phone and dialed Alex's number. Several rings went through before he answered.

"Hey, babe." His voice was deep and dark, and a little slurred. "What are you doing awake?"

"Are you okay?"

"I'm just great." The low tone of his voice contradicted his words.

"What's going on, Alex?"

"I'm just having a few drinks."

"What are you doing there? Is something wrong?"

"Nah, I'm fine. I'm always fine."

"Alex, stay where you are. I'm coming to get you."

"No, Maria, don't—"

"I'm on the way. I'll be there soon."

When Maria made her way into the bar, it wasn't hard to find Alex. He was sitting alone in a booth, a bottle of Jack Daniel's and a glass in front of him. His white shirt was open at the collar and his tie had been discarded, the gray ink of his tattoos sneaking up his neck, his sleeves rolled up. She knew that his clothing cost at least a couple of grand, but she never would have guessed the dangerous-looking man in the booth was a partner in a multimillion-dollar firm. He looked like a complete badass, able to fight anyone in the bar, as he cradled a short glass in one large hand and held a cigarette between two fingers of the other. He downed the whiskey in one swallow and poured more from the bottle. His slump did nothing to mask the shrewd intelligence behind his eyes or the power he commanded.

She sat across from him, and he looked up at her. "This is no place for you," he told her.

"You're telling me. Yet you're the one who left your fancy car outside."

He flicked the ash from his cigarette in the ashtray. "I fit in here better than you know."

She held out her hand. "Give me your keys."

He scoffed. "Why?"

"Because we're leaving."

"No. I'm fine here."

Maria looked around. She'd known Alex for years, but she'd never seen him act like this. His eyes were hooded and dark, not meeting hers. "Alex, you're scaring me. What's going on?"

He said nothing. But Maria found the strong, silent stereotype exhausting. As he lifted his arm to drink from his glass, she snatched it from him and dumped its contents into the ashtray that held the remnants of several Marlboro Lights from the rumpled packet that also sat on the table.

"What the hell?" he said, his voice raised in irritation.

"If you don't want to talk to me, fine. But if you think I'm just going to sit here and watch you drink yourself into oblivion without telling me what's going on, you've got another think coming. Now stand up and walk out with me, and I'll take you home."

Alex glared at her, but she didn't waver. She knew that not many other people had ever spoken to Alex like that. But she didn't care. Finally, he sighed and stood, laying his keys on the table in front of her. "Fine. Let's go."

He seemed to be able to hold his liquor, and was somehow steady as they made their way to the door. He got into the passenger seat of his own car as Maria settled in behind the steering wheel. "Hmm, I might have to drop you off and take this baby for a joyride."

"I don't think so, babe. Just because I love you doesn't mean I won't spank your ass for driving my baby."

Maria blinked at his admission and turned to face him. His eyes were closed, and his head was turned away from her. "What was that?"

"What was what?" he asked, his voice slurred. He looked ready to pass out. It seemed his little declaration might have been made under the influence of alcohol or fatigue.

"Nothing."

He didn't respond, but he moved the seat to make room for his long legs and leaned it back so that he reclined at an angle. Maria took her eyes off the road long enough to sneak a glance at him; his head was against the headrest, and his eyes were closed. His breath was steady. He was asleep. Her house was closer, and she was also tired and not looking forward to the Las Vegas Boulevard traffic. She turned in the opposite direction of the Strip and headed instead for her own apartment.

After the short drive, she parked in the spot next

to her own car and shook him awake. "Alex, we're here."

He mumbled incoherently, and then his eyes popped open. He looked out the windshield. "This isn't my building."

"It isn't. I didn't want to deal with Strip traffic, and you were asleep, so I brought you to my place. It's only fair, right? I'm always at your condo."

"Yeah, fine." He scrubbed his hand across his eyes and looked around the parking lot.

"This isn't a great area, you know."

"It's not that bad," she said, getting out of the car.

"Why are you living here?"

"Because it was reasonably priced and Beth needed a roommate. And plus, it's near the community center."

"Yeah, and that's the problem," he mumbled.

Her mouth dropped. "Oh my God, you're such a snob." She opened the door to her small apartment, guided Alex inside and closed it after him.

"I'm not a snob," he told her. "Make sure you lock it."

She flipped the dead bolt and dragged the chain into the lock. "I always do. And you are a snob. Just because this is a low-income area, it isn't a crime-ridden hellhole. The people are nice here. They're just trying to get by and live their lives. We all look after each other. I never thought you would be so far removed from the real world, sequestered in your luxury penthouse and office tower."

He stopped walking and watched her. "I'm not removed from it. I just know that you deserve a great place to live."

"This is where I live. I like it here. And you can't change that."

"Okay, I'm sorry. What if we gave you a raise? You could get a better place then."

"A raise would be nice, but I'm not moving. Remember? I like it here."

"Raf and your parents know you live here?"

"Will you let it go? Yes, they know I live here. They don't love it. But..." She shrugged. "What are they going to do, tell me I can't? Like that wouldn't make me move to a way worse neighborhood out of spite."

"You're so stubborn," he muttered as he walked in after her.

"Takes one to know one."

Alex let her lead him through her apartment to her bedroom. He kicked off his shoes and flopped down on her bed. It was much smaller, and lumpier, than the king at his home. But it smelled like Maria, and that made it better than anywhere he'd ever slept. He allowed himself to sink into it, even though it barely contained him as his feet hung over the end.

She followed him onto the bed and lay next to him. He wrapped his arm around her and took the glass of water she offered. "Thanks, Maria. For everything."

She waited until he drained the glass before she asked him again. "So, do you want to tell me about what it was that took you to some shitty dive bar, downing Jack Daniel's and chain-smoking Marlboros?"

"I'm never drinking with Alana again," he said with a chuckle. "We just went there to have some drinks after work, and then we got carried away with some design ideas. We actually got a lot accomplished. She called you, didn't she?"

"She did. And I'm glad. You told her about us?"

"Yeah, I know we agreed to keep this secret, but I had to tell someone. I was hoping she'd give me a little insight."

"And did she?"

"A little. She agrees that Raf will kill me if he finds out." He pulled Maria closer. "But it was a good night. Felt like we kind of went back to our roots a bit. That was our bar during college. It was kind of nice to go back in time a little. At least for a couple of hours."

"I remember you from back then. You've changed so much."

He shook his head. "Maybe in appearance. I haven't changed so much. I'm still the same lost, troubled punk I always was. I can put on a suit and drive a nice car, but I haven't really changed. As much as I thought I might have."

"That doesn't mean you aren't a good man. You were one then, and you sure as hell are one now."

"I'm not. I had a lucky break when your parents took me in. If they hadn't, who knows where I would have ended up?"

"I think you would have turned out fine anyway. You can't fake ambition. I see kids all the time, coming from families like yours. It's so hard to break the cycle, and so many get lost in it. You persevered. That's incredible. I'm proud of you."

"Your family pulled me up and gave me the chance. You're so fucking good, Maria." He sighed. "You're so pure. What are you doing with me?"

"You're a good guy," she told him. "You're kind, you make me laugh, and you're really good in bed."

He pulled her to him and chuckled against her lips before he kissed her.

She pulled away, scrunching up her nose. "You taste like whiskey and cigarettes."

"Before tonight, I hadn't smoked a cigarette since college—I was feeling nostalgic. I'm sorry." He moved to get up. "Do you have any mouthwash?"

"In the bathroom. But don't be sorry. You always taste good." She wrapped her arms around his middle and pulled him closer. She felt him stiffen, as if her physical affection hurt him for a moment. She unbuttoned his shirt and traced the swirls of gray ink that covered his body. He was so sexy.

"Do you know why I ended up living with your family?"

She shook her head. "I don't really remember. I was only two. But I asked one day when I was a little older, and Mom and Dad explained to me that you would be staying with us. I learned later that your mother had died, and your dad was in jail. But no one ever explained what had happened."

"My parents were junkies and fought all the time. I don't even really think they knew I was there half the time—they just focused on chasing that next high. I always told myself that I wouldn't be like that. One night I remember they were fighting, and it went too far. My dad pushed my mom down the stairs, and then went out to get high. He didn't care that I was eight and still at home. He just left me. The next morning, she was still at the bottom of the stairs when the cops busted in. Apparently, he'd been arrested after breaking into a convenience store, and he broke down and told them he'd killed his wife. He still didn't mention that I was there, and the cops were surprised to find me."

"Oh God. Alex." Her heart broke for him, as a man, as a child who'd experienced so much trauma and had suffered in silence. She wondered what would have happened if her family had not opened their door to him. She knew he'd studied hard in school and managed to secure a scholarship for college. He'd succeeded in life in his thirty-two years, despite all the odds that had been stacked against him. But he was still so alone. He had his friends; he had her family. But no one looked after him.

"Your parents were kind enough to take me in. And that's why this is so hard for me. You see that I owe my life to your family. They saved me from the system. Lying in your bed feels like such a huge betrayal to the people who saved me."

"My family loves you. You were a welcome addition to our family. I can't imagine our lives without you."

"But I know that I was just one misstep away from following in my parents' footsteps. I got lucky."

"You've worked hard. You deserve everything you've gotten."

"And those kids at the community center…"

"That's why you donated the money, isn't it?"

"Thank you for taking me there. I know what kids like that go through. I know we have a philanthropy branch of The Brotherhood. But I've removed myself so far from kids like the ones I met. I want to get more involved."

"I'm glad to hear that. They really liked having you there."

He reached out and cupped her cheek. He drew her near and kissed her. His kiss was a light touch, but it possessed every bit of fire and passion that it always did. He pulled back. He had a meeting to get to and he had to go home and shower. But he was reluctant to pull away. Every time he touched her, he found it harder and harder to stay away from her.

It was a new feeling for him. With women, he always felt restless, ready to bolt whenever he was given the chance. But with Maria, he couldn't bear to part from her. He couldn't pull away. It physically *hurt* him to pull away from her. He'd never felt like that before. It confused him, threw him off-balance. He didn't get it. Maria was different, and part of him thought it was terrifying.

They lay together in silence for a moment. What could she be thinking about the things he'd told her? He'd never told anyone but Raf and his parents about the circumstances that had brought him to their home. He didn't say anything; his eyes were fixed on the ceiling, his mouth set. Maria suddenly placed her hand on his jaw, and that got his attention. His arm around her waist tightened, and he looked down at her.

She rolled over on top of him, straddling his hips, and let her fingers follow a path down his chest until they settled on his belt buckle.

"What are you doing?" he asked, eyeing her.

"Showing you that you're good and deserve love. You're a good man. I want to take the pain away."

"I'm not feeling too much pain right now."

"And you won't." She leaned over him and brought her lips to his ear, her voice a throaty whisper. "I want to taste you, Alex. I want to feel you come down my throat." She straightened, and as she unfastened his pants, she looked him in the eyes. "Are you too drunk for this?"

"Never too drunk for you. But you don't need to do this, Maria."

"I want to." She loosened his pants and pulled them down, along with his boxers. Despite his drunken state, he still managed to watch her, not wanting to miss a second. His cock was hard and stuck straight up. She grasped him, leaned in and started at the base, dragging her tongue upward, until she reached the throbbing pink head, which she took into her mouth.

Maria's mouth was heaven. He moaned, and she took him deeper, fisting her fingers at the base, while her lips drew up and down over him. He raised his head from the pillow and watched her as she continued her up-and-down motions, sucking in her cheeks as she took him deeper and deeper, allowing him to hit the back of her throat, until she could take no more. With her lips resting on the base of him, Alex stilled and tried to stop himself from pulling back and thrusting into her again. His breath was ragged as he tried to control himself.

Maria moved her head up, slowly, torturously so, until just his head remained wedged between her soft, lush lips. She swirled her tongue around it, and Alex shuddered.

She lifted her head and looked up at him. "You know, Alex, I never used to put much thought into blow jobs. It was always just a precursor to the main event. But with you?" She dragged her tongue up the sensitive underside of his dick. "I love it." Another lick. "Every part of pleasing you fascinates me. Your taste, your smell, the sounds you make, the way you trust me enough to give yourself over to me. You make me feel powerful."

Her words were a shot to his heart. Their eyes connected over the length of his torso. Goddamn, he could love this woman. It hit him—he *did* love her. The realization made him tense up, and Alex could feel his jaw set hard, and a muscle tick in his jaw.

"Baby, relax, okay? Just let go."

He reached down and traced her jaw with his fingers. "Why don't you come up here?"

She placed a kiss on the head of his penis and ran her fist lazily up and down his length. He pushed his hips up in response. "Are you going to relax for me?"

His chuckle morphed into a moan. "I'm not sure how much more relaxed I could be." But he groaned and put his head back into the pillow when she increased the speed of her fist, pumping up and down. She added her mouth, and he moaned his approval and put a coaxing but supportive hand on the back of her head. Urging her to take only what she could.

But apparently she wanted all of him.

His breathing increased, and his movements stiffened; she knew he was close. He put his fingers on her cheeks, trying to push her away. "I'm coming, Maria."

She hummed, urging him to finish, and she increased her pace.

"Oh fuck!" he shouted, as he pumped his hips, filling her mouth with his seed. She took every drop, then crawled over his body and settled next to him in his arms.

He kissed her forehead, and she smiled and snuggled closer. She felt happy, content and safe in his arms. He reached out and turned off the lamp, blanketing the room in near-darkness. "Thank you," he whispered in the silence.

"For what? The stellar BJ?"

He laughed. "For everything. For letting me vent,

for coming to get me at the bar. For not putting up with my bullshit. And the stellar BJ."

"It's all my pleasure," she told him. "Thank you for sharing your past with me. And I will listen to you vent and put up with your bullshit whenever you need it, okay?"

CHAPTER FIFTEEN

A COUPLE OF hours later, Alex and Maria were squeezed together on her much smaller bed. Even though Alex's penthouse was luxurious and held every comfort, she loved being with Alex in her space. In her tiny room, on her tiny bed, where his feet hung off the edge. But he didn't complain. He just held her tighter. Wrapped in his arms, she drew circles in the chest hair that covered his hard pecs. When she got to his nipple, she grazed her nail over the tip. He hissed.

Maria's mind drifted back to driving him in his car. She remembered what he'd said in the car. *Just because I love you...* And even if he didn't remember saying it, she couldn't ignore the full feeling in her heart when she'd heard the words. Her chest tightened with emotion, and she felt light. She was in love with Alex Fischer.

"I love you, Alex," she whispered in the dark. When he didn't respond, she continued, not wanting to look at his face, afraid she would see the rejection or fear etched on it. "I don't need you to say it back or anything," she finished quickly. "I just want you to know where I stand. I love you."

He didn't say anything for a long, drawn-out moment. And when she mustered the courage to look up at him, he was looking down at her. "No one's ever said that to me before."

He told her that he'd never been in a relationship before. But his response still surprised her. "I know you've never been in love. But a woman has never told you that she loves you before?"

He shook his head. "No, that's not what I meant. I mean, *nobody* has ever said it to me."

Her heart split in two for him. She pushed up so that she lay on his chest. "Nobody? Alex, oh my God. I love you."

He pushed his fingers through her hair. "Maria, you're too good for me. I don't deserve your love."

She felt the tears pool in the corners of her eyes. "Alex, you deserve love. You deserve happiness. You're worthy of love. And if you can't say it back, that's okay. I understand." She took his face in her hands and forced him to look at her.

He smiled down at her. "I'm not sure if I know how to love. I've spent so long keeping people away figuring that maybe if I showed them the real me, they wouldn't like it."

"You've shown me what you are. And I'm not going anywhere. There's nothing to loving, you know. It's just about letting yourself feel what's in your heart." She placed her palm over his chest. She could feel his heartbeat. "Love is for sharing, not hiding. Don't be afraid of it."

"Maria." He sighed and pushed her hair over her shoulder, caressing her skin. "You told me that I didn't have to say it, but I will. I love you."

She couldn't stop the smile that formed on her lips. It wasn't just Alex's declaration of love for her, but the fact that she'd broken through his tough, hard exterior. She pulled in closer to him, and his arms tightened around her again. Maria closed her eyes, inhaling his scent, and realized that she could still taste him on her tongue. She heard his breath grow heavy and even. She looked up at him and saw that his eyes were closed and he was asleep. Maria smiled, content, never wanting things to change. Completely surrounded by him, she closed her eyes and let herself drift off to sleep.

CHAPTER SIXTEEN

FROM THEIR USUAL table perched high above the rest of the club, the five original members of The Brotherhood, along with Rebecca and Jessica, watched the people below as they mixed and mingled, touching and flirting, as waitresses in short gold dresses passed throughout the room with trays of drinks.

The place was near capacity, and Alex knew that hundreds more wanted memberships, wanted to be part of the experience that they provided. But more often than not, Di Terrestres was full, and the suites and demo rooms had waiting lists. The Brotherhood had to get to work on Hedo. Every day that their hotel wasn't open was costing them thousands of dollars in lost revenue.

"We really need to stop dicking around and get Hedo off the ground."

"And we will," Alana assured him. "With the permits in line, and everything going our way, we've got crews working around the clock. It's a priority right now. We'll get there. And it'll be soon."

"I know, but the issues and delays we had were

frustrating. It'll be good to be finished." He turned to the rest of the group. "And it's going to be amazing. Alana's designs are awesome!"

Alana blushed. Alex was glad that she'd had the chance to use her creativity to design the hotel. Even though she was the manager of their restaurants and club, she was an incredibly talented interior designer, and she didn't often get to display those skills. "Thanks, but I can't take all the credit. It really was a collaboration, though."

"It's going to be one hell of a venture. Las Vegas has nothing else like it," Gabe added.

"You got that right."

"And guys, thanks for giving Maria a job working with you," Rafael said. "Although I had dinner with her the other night, and she was exhausted. You must be working her to the bone."

Alex coughed into his glass in surprise, nearly choking on his drink.

"Yeah, you're really *rubbing off* on her," Alana added casually, lifting an eyebrow at him. She was the only one at the table who knew Alex's secret, and she was having fun with him. But thankfully, the subtext was lost on Rafael, who was already on his phone, his thumbs moving rapidly over the screen.

"Your birthday is coming up," Brett said. "What do you want to do?"

Alex had been so busy that he'd almost forgotten that his thirty-third birthday was coming up later in the week. "I don't want a fuss or anything. It's just a birthday." But in an instant, he pictured himself having a private celebration with Maria, naked in his bed. But his friends clearly had other plans.

"We could have a party here," Alana said. "I can talk to one of the event coordinators. Get some performers. Invite your nearest and dearest."

Alex's "nearest and dearest" were the people sitting with him. Minus one: Maria. "Nah, guys. We can do something quieter. Let's get dinner somewhere or something, if you insist on celebrating. We'd have to shut down for the night. We'll have to make it up to our clients. Think of the lost revenue."

"Dude, not everything is about money," Brett said.

"Come on, it'll be fun," Alana implored.

Alex looked around the table and saw that all of his friends looked excited, and he realized that it would also be a fun break for his friends...his birthday gave them the perfect excuse to cut loose. He could tell that they all needed it as much as, if not more than, he did. "Okay, sure." He threw up his hands. "Let's party."

The tabled cheered, and Alana started talking about things they could do for the party, but Alex's attention shifted to his phone. Maria had sent him a photo of herself. Nothing dirty or salacious, just a picture of her in her apartment. The accompanying message read, Miss you.

He missed her, too. He looked up at Brett and Raf, sitting with the women they loved. Touching, kissing, whispering to each other. He wished that Maria was sitting next to him. He wanted to take her out, show her off, be able to kiss and touch her whenever he wanted. It was time to tell the truth. He wanted to announce it to the table, to Rafael, but not without talking to her first. It was time for him and Maria to have a serious conversation.

"So what type of outfit are you looking for?" Beth asked as they both riffled through nearby racks.

"I want something that will absolutely destroy Alex's life," Maria told her. The night before, Alex had come over, and he'd told her that he would be having a birthday party at Di Terrestres.

"I can't believe that you don't have anything to wear," Beth said.

"Well, I don't. I pored over my closet this morning, and sure, I have lots of club clothes, but I don't really have anything that says 'birthday party at my secret boyfriend's sex club.'" She wanted something sexy, but also something that would blow Alex's mind.

Beth laughed, still flicking through hangers. "I'm pretty sure he wouldn't care if you showed up in a paper sack."

"That doesn't mean I have to," Maria said with a giggle.

Beth gasped. "I think I've found it," she said, pulling a silky rose-gold dress from the rack.

Maria looked it up and down and took the garment from her friend. "Wow." She looked at the price tag. "Wowww." It was more than she'd ever spent on an article of clothing. "I don't think I can."

"Just try it on," Beth urged. "You want something

that will drive him crazy? This will. Just treat yourself, and him."

Maria sighed, drawing her fingers over the silk.
It felt incredible, more decadent than anything she'd
ever felt. "All right. I'll try it on."

She walked into the changing room, and Beth
followed, as was their custom. They didn't think
it strange undressing in front of each other. Maria
quickly stripped off her T-shirt and jeans and pulled
the dress over her head. The garment was small, the
silk thin and extremely low-cut, and she wouldn't be
able to wear a bra, or anything else underneath it. But
the silk was smooth and cool, and tickled her skin,
causing her nipples to bud. Ignoring Beth's low whistle, Maria looked in the mirror. The dress was posi-
tively scandalous. Thin spaghetti straps held it on her
shoulders and the silk wrapped around her, forming
a low, plunging neckline between her breasts and an
almost indecently high slit on one thigh, but asym-
metrical, making it hang slightly longer in the back.

When Maria turned back around to face Beth,
her friend's mouth hung open. "Oh my God, that is
stunning."

She turned and checked herself out in the mirror.
The expensive silk felt like a dream against her skin.
Beth was right, it was stunning.

"That dress will one hundred percent make him
drool."

"As long as he doesn't do it on the dress." She fin-
gered the equally scandalous price tag. "But, God,
the price, though."

Beth waved it off. "Come on, splurge a little. What's the good of having that fancy job if you can't treat yourself from time to time?"

"It is his birthday," she reasoned, looking at her friend in the mirror.

"And it's at that club of his. If you can't be a sex goddess at an erotic club, I don't know where you can be."

"True." She knew that Di Terrestres had a more formal dress code, but she wasn't sure how it would go for his private party, although Alana had told her that she could expect it to be sexy.

"My brother is going to be there, though. I know he's going to freak when he sees this. He might throw a blanket over me."

"Maybe he'll finally get it through his thick head that you're a gorgeous, vivacious woman, and not just his little sister anymore."

"I wouldn't hold my breath on that one," she said with a laugh, and she gave one final twirl in the mirror. "You're still coming with me, right?"

"Yeah, I wouldn't miss it. I like Alex, and I really want to get a look at the club."

Maria turned and checked out her butt in the dress. Just as good a view from the back. She was satisfied by it, but she frowned.

Beth didn't miss it. "What's wrong, hon?"

"I was just thinking how great Alex and I would look together. Me wearing this, and him wearing whatever he's wearing. But we can't. We won't even be able to kiss or touch each other." She shrugged. "I just wish were like a regular couple."

"So, is Alex afraid of Rafael, or something?"

Maria shook his head. "He's not afraid, even though he knows he's due an ass-kicking from my brother. But he's trying not to distract Rafa from the campaign trail. He wants to keep him focused. I know he's right. But it's frustrating sometimes."

"Does that bother you?"

"Yeah, it kind of does. I love him. But it's a tricky time to come clean with Rafa. And I don't want to push Alex to do anything he doesn't want to do. So that's why we're still keeping it a secret."

"Have you told him that?"

"No."

"Why don't you tell him that you want to come out as a couple?"

"Because part of me is enjoying the secrecy. Sneaking off together, all the private glances and touches. But I don't know how long that will be enough. And I don't want to add anything else to his plate, either. He's got so much going on with the new hotel that I don't want to add any stress."

"If it's a big secret, doesn't that make it hotter?"

She smiled. "It really does. And maybe that's enough for now." She brightened, looking at herself in the mirror. The silk dress was sexier than anything else she'd ever owned. She knew that Alex would love it, whether he could show it in public or not. She turned back to face Beth. "Anyway, I'd better buy this dress before I change my mind."

Maria paid for the dress, cringing slightly as she swiped her credit card, and she and Beth left the upscale shop and walked out into the pedestrian mall, doing their best to dodge the crowds of tourists sightseeing, gawking at the designer labels, doing their best to leave their casino winnings within the Vegas city limits. Like most locals, Maria normally avoided all things the Strip, but she always enjoyed people watching, and Las Vegas Boulevard was the place to do it.

They strolled around the promenade, catching up, stopping at shops. Maria had already spent more on one item than she ever had in her life, but when they stopped in front of Agent Provocateur, Maria knew she had to go inside.

She and Beth giggled as they looked through the racks, holding sheer lingerie against their torsos. She picked up a low-cut lace bodysuit. "Think this will work under my new dress?"

"Girl, I'm not even sure you could wear underwear under that dress at all."

"Not that Alex will complain," Maria murmured, and turned back to return the garment to its place. But instead of seeing Beth, she saw Rafael and Jessica.

"Maria," he said, not letting on whether or not he'd heard what she'd just said, and she wasn't sure if his strained expression was from the fact that he'd just heard Maria admit that she was sleeping with his best friend or because he'd caught his sister in a lingerie store. Maria could feel the color drain from her face. "Doing some shopping?" he asked.

"Yeah, I needed to pick up a new dress. For Alex's party," she said, testing him to see if he'd heard her say his name earlier.

Jessica eyed her shopping bag. "I can't wait to see it."

"Anyway—" Rafael nodded at the items Jessica had bundled in her arms "—we should be leaving."

"In a hurry to get that lingerie home, Rafael?" Beth teased, coming up behind Maria.

"Is he ever," Jessica said with a laugh. Rafael rolled his eyes. "We just got a pole installed at his place." She winked. "I'm looking forward to trying it out." Until recently, Jessica had made a career out of stripping. She'd even won awards for her pole-dancing skills.

"You mean *our* place," he told her. Maria smiled as she saw the love that her brother had for Jessica. It was reminiscent of the way Alex looked at her. Again, Maria faltered, and she felt a sad smile form on her face, not being able to be publicly affectionate with the man she loved.

"Anyway, we're leaving," Rafael confirmed, taking Jessica's arm and gently leading her to the cash register, obviously eager to get his fiancée back home.

"So are we," Maria said, turning in the other direction. She'd already spent so much money on her silk dress that there was no way she could justify spending hundreds more on lingerie. "We'll see you tomorrow at the party."

Once they were outside, Beth turned to her. "Oh my God, do you think he heard you talking about Alex?"

"I don't know," Maria said. She glanced over her shoulder and saw Rafael watching them.

CHAPTER SEVENTEEN

ALEX PULLED HIS shirt over his shoulders and started buttoning. He grinned at the scratch marks that Maria left etched on his chest. God, he loved that bad side of her. He heard her throat clear behind him and turned to see her step from his bathroom. She was wearing a silk dress, if she could call it a dress. The rosy cream-colored material, which contrasted beautifully with her dark skin, barely restrained her delicious curves. It was obvious to him that she wasn't wearing a bra. On her feet, she wore precarious strappy gold stilettos that buckled at her ankle, and he immediately imagined her wearing those shoes, her legs wrapped around him, digging the heels into his ass as he thrust into her. He'd have to make sure she kept them on when they got home. He let out a low whistle. "You're stunning."

"You like my dress?"

"Calling it a dress is a little generous, don't you think?" He walked over to her. "You think I'm going to let you leave the house like that?"

"You think I'm asking your permission?" she countered.

He chuckled and turned away from her, picking up a bag from his dresser. "I don't know how I'm going to enjoy my birthday when my dick is already this hard from just looking at you. But as long as you're going to be torturing me all night, I'm glad I bought this."

"Why are you giving me a gift on your birthday?"

"You might call this something for me, too." He winked.

She took the bag and reached into it. He smiled as she pulled out the small handful of lace. "What's this?" She held the panties up, and her eyes widened when she saw they were crotchless, but for the string of pearls that connected the front and back.

He'd picked them up at a sex shop on his way home from work. He couldn't wait for her to put them on. He wanted to know that every step she took that night would send ripples of pleasure throughout her body, and it would be caused by him. "I want you to wear them tonight."

"Oh really? What if I'd already committed to not wearing panties tonight?" She lifted the hem of her skirt, past her hip, revealing her tattoo, but still covering her pussy, teasing him with nothing but bare, smooth, golden skin.

His groan was pained. Why had he agreed to a birthday party at Di Terrestres? He wished that he could just stay home and wrap himself up in Maria. He went to her and brushed his hand over her hip, under the dress. The material grazed his hand, but its softness was nothing compared to the feel of Maria's skin. "Do we have to go?" he asked, burying his face in her neck. "I'd rather we stay home."

"Are you asking if we have to go to your birthday party?" she asked, pushing him away. "Yes. I think people might wonder where you are by the time the cake comes out. It's just for a couple of hours. And I'm going to be the one wearing these," she said, stepping into the lace panties. She pulled them up, and a wicked smile adorned her lips when they settled into place, the rope of pearls nestling against her clit. He knew that by the end of the evening, she would be wet and needy. "So, here's the deal. I'll wear these," she said with a whisper. "But you don't get to touch me until the evening is over."

He raised his eyebrow, seemingly intrigued by her offer. He reached for her, but she moved back, out of his reach. "Not many people give me commands," he told her.

She smiled. "I know. But I'm different."

"You certainly are." He regretted that they had to arrive separately, and that she and Beth would show up just after he did. He wanted her on his arm. He wanted to show her off. Several times that week, he'd tried to tell Rafael that he was in love with Maria, but every time, something had interrupted him.

He snaked his hands under the silk of her dress, and cupped them over the lace that stretched across her hips. He gripped the lace and jerked the panties up a little farther, making her squeal in surprise as the pearls lodged themselves between her labia. Her brown eyes turned black with desire, and using his pinkie, he traced the edge of the lace and was satisfied by her lustful gasp when he hooked his finger underneath the material and pulled, causing the pearls to move against her most sensitive flesh.

His lips grazed her ear, and he whispered, "So tonight, when you're walking around the party, dancing with your friend, every time you move, how will you feel knowing that I'll be watching you, knowing that you can feel those pearls in your pussy, wondering how long it'll be before I sink deep inside you?" He pulled the panties again. And she hissed. He moved back and let her straighten her clothing. "The sooner I get you home, the sooner I can completely ravish you. Let's go."

She hummed in approval and closed her eyes, leaning into him, as if savoring their nearness before they were scheduled to leave.

"But before we go, there's something else," he said.

Her eyes flew open at his tone. "What is it?"

"I want to tell him about us. Rafael. I'm tired of hiding this."

"Really?"

"Yes. I've almost told him a couple of times now. But I needed to talk to you first. Are you ready for it?"

"Yeah, but what about all the reasons we had for keeping it secret?"

"Fuck it. This is too important. You're too important. I love you." He relished saying the words. They had become easier to say each time. But even though he'd never known love before, he knew that Maria was the most important thing to him.

"I love you, too. And I'm ready. I don't know why I thought we needed to hide."

"You're the best thing that's ever happened to me. I know I don't deserve you, but I want be able to take you out, show you off." He put his arms around her again. "Even if Raf decides to never speak to me again, even that will be worth it. We need to do this." Maria smiled, and Alex realized that he wanted to put a smile on her face, every day. "I love you," he whispered, cupping her face in his palms and drawing her nearer for a kiss. His lips grazed hers, and his phone vibrated on the dresser. Alex knew without looking at it that it was his driver, coming to take him to the club, and Maria to her house to pick up Beth. "You've got to go."

Even though her brother owned the club, and Alana had added her permanently to the guest list, Maria had only been to Di Terrestres once. That night was still at the forefront of her mind, and her loins. It was the night that she and Alex had first been together. That night at Di Terrestres had marked the beginning of the most incredible relationship she'd ever had. The attraction between them had been potent, combustible enough that it almost destroyed them, and now this night at the club, they would tell Rafael about their relationship.

She and Beth walked in together, and the vibe at the club was much different than it had been that first

night. The music was heavier. Alex's favorite hip-hop
tracks pulsed from the speakers, played and manip-
ulated by one of the country's hottest DJs. Scantily
clad men and women danced, gyrating, on platforms
along the walls. For Alex's birthday, Di Terrestres
had turned into one of the hottest nightclubs she'd
ever entered.

A hand cupped her shoulder, and she turned
around to see her brother. "I can't imagine what Mom
and Dad would say to seeing you dressed like that."

She rolled her eyes. He didn't know everything
she wore. She thought of the string of pearls that his
best friend had given her, rubbing against her clit
with every step she took. "You don't like my dress?"

"That's barely a dress."

"Well, it's a good thing Mom, Dad and Father
Carlos aren't here then, huh?" Every movement that
Maria made was delicious torture. She tried to keep
it under wraps. But she couldn't keep the grin off
her face. She and Alex had a secret that no one else
knew, but soon, they would tell everyone about their
relationship.

"It feels like I haven't seen you in weeks," Rafael
said. "Not since you started with Brett and Alex.
How is it going?"

"Pretty good. I'm learning a lot and it's great experience. It's really taking away from my volunteer work, but you know, I've got bills to pay." She
shifted, and the pearls slid along her body. She bit
her lip to quell the moan that almost poured from
her mouth.

"You wouldn't have to if you moved back in with Mom and Dad, or me and Jess."

"Yeah, it's not like you guys need your privacy or anything."

"I just hate where you're living."

"I know you do, and I promise, it isn't that bad." Not that she'd spent any time there recently. Most of her free time was spent curled up in Alex's high-rise condo. "If it wasn't safe, I wouldn't be there."

But then her thoughts turned to Alex; her relationship with him certainly wasn't safe. She would never put herself in a position to be hurt, but she knew that if anyone could hurt her, break her heart, it was Alex. And she was a willing slave to her feelings for him, drawn to him—she needed to be with him. But that was what gave her a niggling doubt. It gave him the power to hurt her. To completely break her. Over Rafael's shoulder, she watched Alex as he mingled with the people in attendance. He was so confident and so sure of himself. Even when another woman threw her arms around him. Maria watched as she leaned in and said something in his ear. She tried to tamp down the anger and jealousy that simmered within her. She kept it under control until Alex disengaged from the woman, deliberately putting space between them. She turned back to Rafael and realized she'd been completely oblivious that he was still talking.

"—until the wedding, at least," he finished.

"I'm sorry, what was that?"

He eyed the glass in her hand. "How much have you had to drink?"

"Not nearly enough." Beth came up behind her, holding two champagne flutes, and passed one over to her.

"Is everyone having fun?" Alex came up behind them and draped his arms over both Maria's and Beth's shoulders. Maria wanted nothing more than to lean into him and somehow managed to maintain a distance from him. But then his fingers curled over her shoulder and trailed down her back, touching her so intimately in front of everyone. Marking her as his, reminding her that she was with him, without anyone even noticing. He was teasing her, torturing her, and with every shift her body made, it moved the pearls, dragging them along her most intimate flesh, sparking a fire deep within her. She clenched her thighs together and felt the wetness grow. If she didn't find release soon, she might explode.

As covertly as she could, she looked up at him and saw that he was watching her, his eyes locked on hers. If her panties had had a crotch, they'd definitely be wet with her desire, as moisture began to trickle its way down her thighs. They were ready to tell everyone about their secret relationship, and she was relieved, but that didn't mean the secrecy wasn't still a huge turn-on. She and Alex shared something that no one else did.

"Do you guys want to grab a seat?" he asked, pointing to their usual table.

She might have been in love with Alex, and she relished his lovemaking, but it was dirtier stuff, the toys, the dirty talk, the tricks, that really set her on fire. Her naughty streak hadn't been fed in too long, and Alex was an excellent cook. But while she was wearing the panties for him, she would torture him in the meantime.

They were joined by Alana, Gabe, Brett and Rebecca, and they all took a table above the rest of the party. She sat, and the stimulation against her swollen, needy flesh almost did her in. But when Alex pushed in her chair, it shot vibrations of pleasure that ricocheted throughout her and made her clench her fists as he took a seat next to her. Everyone at the table talked around them. Alex put his hand on her thigh under the table and swirled his fingertips over her electrified skin. She'd made the no touching rule, but she should have known that Alex wouldn't stick to it. And she was glad for it. With his sure fingers on her electrified skin, she was unable to focus on anything but the pounding of her heart.

She took a gulp of the wine that had been put in front of her—the waitstaff at Di Terrestres were really on their A game—and tried her best to remain composed as the pearls moved again. Feeling the moisture, she hoped it didn't soak through her dress. She took a deep breath and looked around at the rest of their group, who were oblivious to her intimate secret, and that Alex was drawing lines with his fingertips on her inner thigh. She bit her lip, and when she thought she might chew through it, she stood, the vibration still shooting throughout her. "Excuse me, please. I need the ladies' room."

Presenting a calm demeanor to everyone else in

the room, she slowly walked out of the room and slipped into the women's restroom. The pearls slid along her slit with every step, and she wanted to cry out from the sensation.

She was surprised when Alex opened the door to the women's room. "What are you doing in here?" she asked him.

"I followed you," he said as if that answered her question, flipping the lock on the door. He stalked to her and put his hands on her hips.

"They're going to wonder where we both went."

"We'll think of something," he murmured against her throat, repeating what she'd said to him when they'd sneaked off at her parents' house. "Plus, the conversation broke up, everyone parted ways. Your friend Beth found a guy at the bar and is chatting him up. No one is missing us."

He whipped her around and bent her over the counter. Her shoes added enough height so that her ass could push against his crotch.

"This fucking dress," he muttered, smoothing the satin over her ass, squeezing her. "Do you know how much you've been torturing me all night? In this dress that shows off every fucking curve. All my favorite things."

"When I picked it out, I knew it would drive you nuts. That was my goal."

"Well, mission accomplished, I'd say."

He pushed her skirt over her hips with one hand, revealing the cream-colored lace that rode high on her cheeks. She felt him run his finger down her crack, against the pearls, and when he pushed them against her back entrance she gasped.

"Did you like that?" he rasped.

She nodded her head, unable to form any words.

He pushed in a little more, and her response was even greater.

He went lower, reaching underneath between her legs to cup her needy flesh. His fingers danced along her seam, tickling, striking the pearls and sending tremors of pleasure that shot from her core and made her arms shake as she held herself up on the counter. She was dripping wet. Using those talented fingers, he spread her moisture around her, and she could feel she was close. He gripped the pearls and pulled them roughly. Her already needy clit sought the relief, and it was enough, and a thunderous orgasm rushed through her body.

"Maria, I need you so fucking bad," he muttered. As she came down from her orgasm, he lowered the straps from her shoulders, pulled the flimsy satin over her breasts and pushed it down, so it gathered at her hips, and then he squeezed her breasts, pinching her nipples between his fingers. "I want to take every part of you. Bury my dick deep inside you, your hot mouth, that sweet pussy, tight ass. I want to slide my dick between these tits and come all over your chest. I want it all." He groaned and leaned over her, his warm, strong chest at her now-naked back.

His dirty words, the low timbre of his voice, struck a chord deep within her, plucking at her every desire, and the urgency to feel him inside her deepened. She felt the waves of pleasure as they started low in her core and radiated throughout her, washing over her limbs, until he pressed his still-clothed, rock-hard cock against her ass.

"This will have to do for now." In the reflection of the mirror, she watched him as he unbuckled his belt and lowered the zipper of his pants. He pulled out his dick, huge and hard, for her. He rolled a condom over himself, and in just a couple of seconds he was inside her wet heat.

Maria's moan was loud, and Alex clapped his palm over her mouth and pulled his hips, withdrawing from her, then filling her over and over until her breath became more shallow and her movements more frenzied.

He grasped her hips, his fingertips digging into her flesh, but she didn't complain. She wanted every one of his touches, rough and soft, especially when he pulled her to meet him, all but impaling her with his cock. Her pussy tightened, gripping him in a way that always made him growl out in satisfaction. He pumped in and out of her, their eyes meeting in the mirror. Her breasts bounced with their movement, and he palmed them, pinching and stroking her stiff nipples. She felt so much, and she was again unable to hold on. Another orgasm tore through her and a scream ripped from her lips. If anyone was outside the door, they would have surely heard her.

Maria felt herself clench around Alex's cock, and he came with a grunt through clenched teeth. She felt his spasm as she milked him. He stayed with her until her tremors stopped, before he released his firm grasp on her thighs, and then he stood up straight.

She straightened and fixed her dress. Alex threw the condom in the garbage and zipped himself back into his pants. "Happy birthday," she told him, pulling her straps back to their place on her shoulders.

He smiled and drew her back to him. "Best birthday ever," he whispered against her lips. "Why don't we go find Raf now? Tell him and get it over with?"

Maria nodded. "Let's do it." She opened the door, but Alex had different thoughts, and he took her face in her hands and kissed her, pushing her against the open door. She sighed and kissed him. Maria loved everything about Alex's kiss. The softness of his lips contrasted deeply with the scratch of his stubble. His taste, his scent. She fell completely under his spell every time and let the world fall away.

But it was banished for only a moment, until an outraged male voice broke through her fantasy and brought her back to the real world.

"What the hell?"

CHAPTER EIGHTEEN

FUCK. ALEX PULLED away and put himself between Rafael and Maria, turning to face his friend. He could see the way Jessica clenched his arm, as if holding him back. "Raf, man, this isn't what it looks like." He put out his hand to his friend at a distance.

"What do you mean, Alex? Maria? What the fuck is going on here?"

"Rafa, stop," Maria said, trying to get out from behind Alex's bulk. But there was no way he would let her step between them, into the fray. He knew that neither he nor Rafael would hurt her, but he wanted to keep her away from was about to go down between him and his best friend.

"What's it supposed to look like? It looks like you're kissing my sister. Tell me, please enlighten me, what is going on here?"

"Rafa, let me explain," Maria implored, coming from around Alex's back. The four of them stood in the hallway. Thankfully, they were still alone. But any longer, any louder, they would draw a crowd.

"Maria, stay out of it. This is between us," Rafael

told her, his jaw set, not taking his eyes from Alex. Alex stared back.

"No, it isn't," she maintained. "Rafa, please, just listen—"

"Raf, I know this looks bad," Alex said.

"Bad? Are you fucking my sister?" Rafael shook free of Jessica's hold, drew back his fist, and before Alex could move, it connected with his jaw.

Alex's ears rung but he still heard Maria's scream in the hallway. He turned away and recovered. His jaw flexed. It wasn't broken, but the force behind Rafael's punch could have done some serious damage. Alex watched Rafael, who looked like he still had some fight in him. But Alex stood down. He'd already done enough to the man. He dropped his fists.

Maria stood between them. "Rafa, how dare you?" She slapped his chest. He didn't flinch. Using too much force, he pushed her out of the way. When she stumbled, they both reached out to catch her. Alex met her first, grasping her upper arms, steadying her. And Rafael sneered.

"Get your fucking hands off her." He ripped her from Alex's grasp.

"Don't touch me," she spat out.

"I knew something was going on. But him, Maria? Do you know what he's like?"

"Stop, Rafa. I love him."

"Him? Alex?" He waved a hand in his direction and sneered. "This bourbon-soaked man-whore?"

"Whoa," Alex interjected. His friend's punch had

stung. But his characterization of him had hurt far deeper.

Maria wasn't having any of it. She stood between them and waved her finger in her brother's face. "Don't you *dare* talk about him like that. It's not like that!"

"Maria, do you know how he lives? Parades of women strolling, sometimes in twos and threes, in and out of his life on a nightly basis."

"He isn't like that. We aren't like that, Alex, tell him."

"Yeah, Alex, tell me," Rafael challenged.

Alex took a moment to comprehend the situation unfolding before him. Raf and Maria were fighting. He had become a wedge between them. He'd gotten between the once-close siblings. Rafael had been right. He wasn't right for her. He wasn't anywhere near good enough for her. And while he loved her, and it broke his heart to do so, he had to let her go. He lowered his head, not able to bring himself to look at her. "It's true," he said. He lifted his head and watched her as the recognition of what he was about to do came over her face. It killed him, but he had to go on. "It's all true. This was fun, Maria. But that's it. Your brother is right. It's over."

"Alex," she said, her voice a tortured whisper. "What are you saying?"

"I'm saying it's done. Leave." He had to rip the bandage. The quicker, the better it would be for all of them. He had to hurt Maria so she could heal and find someone she deserved.

She stilled, and he could see the tears pooling at the corner of her eyes. "But I love you," she whispered. "You said you loved me."

He looked from Rafael, to her, to his feet, and fought the urge to pull her into her arms. "Baby, you believed that?"

Rafael started at him again, but Jessica held him back.

Alex saw the hurt and confusion in Maria's eyes, but he looked away from her. He shook his head. Rafael stared at him. Alex knew that he didn't deserve Maria, nor did he deserve Rafael's friendship. He'd fucked everything up. It was best if he stood back, no matter how much it killed him to do so. "Just go."

The roaring in Maria's ears dulled. The gravity of Alex's words finally hit her, and she found it difficult to breathe. "Alex." Her voice was whisper-soft, and she couldn't have mustered a higher volume if she tried.

"Maria, get out of here," Rafael told her, grasping her arm with his fingers.

She broke free. "Fuck you, Rafa," she said, her bottom lip quivering. She turned to Alex. "And fuck you, too, Alex. You're a goddamn coward."

For several moments, she watched as Rafael and Alex stood face-to-face, tense, silent. Rafael then turned and left without a word, and Jessica went with him. Maria walked to the bar, holding the tears back, and found Beth. Her friend was obviously entranced by the man she'd found, but the minute she'd laid eyes on Maria, she walked away from him.

"Maria, are you okay?"

"Can we leave?"

"Yeah, of course, let's go."

They headed toward the exit, but Maria took one look over her shoulder. She saw Rafael, obviously agitated, as Jessica tried to calmly speak to him, and then out of the corner of her eye, she saw Alex. He was watching her from afar. And she'd never seen a man look so alone or so lost.

She stopped walking. "Wait. Just give me a second," she said, and turned and strode toward Alex. She could see the bruise forming on his cheek.

"Maria. What are you still doing here?"

"I don't know. I shouldn't be." She paused. "Do you remember what you said to me that night at Swerve? When you called that guy a loser because he walked away from me without a fight?"

"Maria—"

"No, don't interrupt. Do you remember?"

"Yes."

"I deserve better. I deserve someone who will fight for me. Us. More importantly, I need someone who will fight for himself."

Alex nodded. "You're right. You deserve the world."

"Alex, I don't need the world. I just need you."

"I'm sorry." He shook his head. "I can't give you what you need."

She nodded. "That's what I thought you would say." She took a step toward him and kissed him firmly. Her cheeks felt wet. She wasn't sure if they were her tears or his. "Goodbye, Alex."

"What happened?" Beth asked when she returned. "Talk to me, Maria."

"I'll tell you when we get home. I can't now." Her voice broke in a sob. And as they got into the back of their car, Maria took several deep gulps of air before she let herself collapse against her friend, allowing the tears to fall.

Beth wrapped her arms around her and told her that everything would be all right. That whatever Alex did, he didn't deserve her—everything that a loyal girlfriend was supposed to say.

But even as Maria's heart broke, she realized that it wasn't for herself. She cried for Alex. He wouldn't even try to fight for her, not because he didn't love her; she didn't believe that for a second. He let her go because he didn't believe that he deserved love. And she had no idea how to reach the broken man she loved.

CHAPTER NINETEEN

CHAPTER NINETEEN

MARIA FORCED HERSELF to knock on Jessica's door before she convinced herself to walk away. She wasn't really in the mood to see anyone, but Jess had invited her to one last girls' night at her old place before she put it up for sale and officially moved in with Rafael. Before Maria could turn away, Jessica opened the door and drew her in for a hug. "Maria, hon, I'm so glad you could make it."

They walked inside; she could hear the laughter of the other women and felt relieved. "Rafa isn't here, is he?"

"No, he's over at Brett's. It's fight night. The guys always get tickets and pregame for a bit beforehand. He wasn't going to go, but I made him leave because he was bumming me out."

She felt bad that her own screwed-up relationship had such an effect on everyone around her. "I was afraid that this was an ambush."

"This is a male-free zone—well, except for my friend Ben—at least for tonight."

"Thank God. I don't think I want to look at Rafa at the moment."

"I know. Those guys are so stubborn and hard-headed." Then Jessica smiled. "But I knew something was going on between you and Alex. I just knew it."

"Well, there isn't anything going on now."

"Have you talked to him?" Jessica asked, pouring her a glass of wine.

She accepted it and took a sip. "No. It's been a long week at Collins/Fischer of not talking to one of my bosses. And to be honest, I don't want to think about it at all tonight."

"That's fair, let's just focus on fun…and cocktails."

"I'm in."

The night progressed, loudly and full of laughter. Pitchers of sangria and tequila shots were passed around, and soon the conversation turned, as it always did, to sex.

"And so, I stopped by Rafael's office in only a short trench coat—"

"No! Stop!" Maria cried covering her ears dramatically. "I don't need to know any more details about my brother's sex life than I've already seen," she said, alluding to the sex tape that had leaked and threatened to ruin both his and Jessica's political careers.

The group laughed.

Jessica continued. "Anyway, long story short,

when you only wear a trench coat, make sure you don't get it caught in any doors."

Maria laughed and was glad that she'd decided to go to Jessica's after all. With Beth out on a date, she was grateful to not be spending another lonely, quiet night at home.

"So, what about you, Maria?" Rebecca asked. "Anything new or interesting in your life? I mean, *anything else*?"

As all eyes turned to her, she knew they wanted to know about what had happened between her and Alex. Maria opened her mouth, not sure what to say.

"Well, besides what you have going on with Alex," Alana interrupted.

"What we *had*," Maria muttered, and sipped wine.

"Someone needs to fill me in here," Rebecca said. "Brett gave me a brief rundown, but he didn't have many details. You and Alex were seeing each other?"

"Yeah," Alana answered for her. "Raf has been walking around like a beast, and Alex is sulking in his office."

Maria shook her head. "They're both exceptionally stubborn," she said with an eyeroll. "I don't know, we thought that keeping it a secret would be really fun. Neither of us wanted to upset Rafa while he was campaigning, and Alex was so worried about betraying Rafael and our family. At first it was a lot of fun, but then the secret became exhausting. We'd decided to finally tell Rafa, but he walked in on us before we had a chance."

"Okay, the secret is out," Jessica said with a shrug.

"Why aren't you together now? Rafael knows. He'll get over it, I promise."

Maria's heart clenched in her chest. This was the part that hurt the most. "You saw it. Because Alex pushed me away. But that isn't it. I know he loves me. He just doesn't believe he deserves love. He told me to leave. He won't talk to me. Any work that he needs me to do, he sends through other assistants. I know it's just self-preservation—he's kept people at an arm's length for his entire life. He feels like he's betrayed Rafa, but what do we really have if he isn't willing to stand up and fight for it?" Maria remembered the way Alex had pushed her aside and out of his life. "He's just so fucked up that he can't love himself. And until he learns self-love, he won't let anyone love him, because he doesn't see himself as worth it."

"I've known Alex a long time," Alana said. "He's never been one to express his emotions. But you can tell there's some darkness there. But it all makes sense now. The past few months, I've noticed a difference in him. And I know that it's because of you, and whatever you had."

A silence fell over the room, and Jessica leaned across the coffee table. "If he realizes what he's done, would you take him back?"

Maria pondered her answer, and every set of eyes watched her carefully. "I don't know."

As per their tradition when there was an MMA fight, the guys all gathered at Brett's for drinks and cigars before heading out to watch the main event from their front-row seats. It was always a fun night, but it was the last thing that Alex wanted to do that night. He opened Brett's door without knocking, and Brett was the first to see him. His friend looked him up and down.

"Jesus, you look like hell."

He dropped the case of imported beer on the table and extracted one. "That makes me feel awesome. Thanks."

"When was the last time you shaved?" Gabe asked, stubbing out his cigar and coming in from the balcony.

Alex scratched a palm along his whiskers. They'd been getting unruly, and not even in the ruggedly handsome way that women sometimes found appealing. "Been a couple of days. I've been busy. Maybe it's a new look I'm trying out."

"Homeless guy chic. Yeah, it's all over *GQ* right now," Brett said, and then laughed when Alex flipped him off.

"Maybe it's to cover up the dent Raf put in your face," Gabe joked.

Alex rolled his eyes. The bruise to his cheek had faded. But not the one to his heart. He had a lot to make up for. Maria, Raf. Thankfully, Brett had given him a reprieve. Not giving a him a hard time about sleeping with their assistant and friend's sister.

"Where's Rebecca?"

"At Jessica's house. They're having one last girls'

night there before she and Raf move in together. Maria's there, too."

Alex nodded, and Brett just watched him before taking a swallow from his beer.

"What? I know you want to say something, and frankly, I'm surprised you haven't said it yet."

Brett shook his head. "You really put us at risk, professionally, starting a relationship with our assistant. It definitely should have been cleared with HR."

The impact on the company was frankly the last thing on his mind. But he saw Brett's point. They'd worked for so much, but if it had gone sideways in another direction, it could have ruined the company. "Yeah, I know. It was stupid."

"No, it wasn't stupid." Brett sighed. "Think about how much you were on my ass when Rebecca and I started hooking up. Or Raf and Jessica. Love makes you do messed-up things."

"Yeah, and I definitely messed up with Maria."

"What are you going to do about it?"

"What can I do? I'm too fucked up to accept the love of a wonderful woman."

"Love's a hell of a thing, isn't it?"

"I can see why I avoided it for so long. It fucking sucks."

"It does. But when it's good, it more than makes up for the bad times."

Alex could believe that. The best nights of his life were the ones he'd spent with his limbs entwined with Maria's. But no matter how happy those memories made him, the fact that he no longer had her tore his chest apart with despair.

The door opened, interrupting their conversation. It was Rafael, and he walked into the room, looking at Alex. He frowned before moving on to the kitchen without saying a word.

"What is this? You guys can't be in the same room anymore?" Gabe asked them. When neither Rafael nor Alex responded, he continued. "We have too much on the line right now to be fractured. We need to be a cohesive group. You guys need to figure out a way to make that happen. When my parents divorced, my brothers and I had to pick sides. I refuse to do it as an adult."

Brett grabbed a couple of beers from the small fridge under the bar. "Gabe, why don't we go outside for a bit?"

"Sure thing. Let's let these guys fight it out."

Alex walked to the kitchen to talk to his friend, and hopefully not get punched again.

Rafael was standing next to the fridge, staring off into space. The firm set of his jaw told Alex that he was deep in thought. "Hey," Alex said. He opened the fridge and took out a beer and handed one to Rafael.

He looked at the bottle before he accepted it. "Thanks." He looked Alex over. "How's the jaw?"

Alex scrubbed his hand over the lower half of his face. "Still kind of sore, but usable. The bruise has faded, at least. How's your fist?"

"About the same," he said, flexing his knuckles. "I'm sorry I punched you."

Alex shook his head. "I don't think you're that sorry."

"Okay, I'm not," Rafael admitted, and then he frowned. "Dude, she's my sister."

"I know."

"How long has it been going on?"

"A couple of months."

"And it was serious?"

Alex nodded. "It was. But there's always been something between us. We just couldn't ignore it anymore. But I know that I should have been honest. I need you to know that I never pushed her to do anything. Everything that happened between us, we both wanted."

Rafael seemed to mull it over. "I'm sorry for calling you a—what was it?"

"A bourbon-soaked man-whore."

"Yeah, that was uncalled for."

"It's okay. You weren't wrong."

"I still shouldn't have said it." He paused and faced him head-on once again. "You're not good enough for her, you know."

"You think for a second that I don't fucking know that?" His heart ached at the thought. "I know that she deserves better, and I wanted to be the man she needs. But I couldn't."

Rafael nodded. He blew out a heavy breath. "Man, you should have told me you were dating my sister. It would have definitely softened the blow."

Alex flexed his still-aching jaw. "You mean the one to my face? I know we should have told you.

We were going to. But you walked in on us first. If it matters now, it wasn't just the sex. She isn't like the other women for me. It was more than just a casual hookup. It was always more than that. I didn't mean to fall in love with her. I tried my best not to."

That made Rafael pause. "You're in love with her?"

"Yeah."

"Meanwhile she's pissed at both of us."

Alex knew why she was mad at him. "Why is she so mad at you?"

"Because according to her, I'm trying to run her life, and she's mad that I punched you. Apparently, she thinks I overreacted." Alex laughed. "And she's mad at you because you're a coward."

"Yeah, she told me the exact same thing." She'd been right. He was a fucking coward.

"Are you going to fight for her?"

Alex felt his heart rip apart as he pictured the look on her face when he'd told her he didn't love her. That was hurt that he'd caused her. He'd put that pain on her face. Maria deserved better than him. "No."

Rafael looked surprised. "Really?"

"It's for her own good. I have to let her go."

CHAPTER TWENTY

EVEN THOUGH HER head was heavy and foggy from the night before, Maria's hangover had mostly dissipated. And she still made it to the community center in time for her volunteer duty. All morning, she'd felt a little behind, as if she were moving in slow motion. She'd drunk too much at Jessica's the night before, and she was feeling the aftereffects of the alcohol.

But after going to bed the night before, she'd made a decision. It was time for a change. For her to get back to basics. She wasn't happy as an assistant for a couple of rich guys in an office tower. She looked around the community center. This was where she belonged. Her little foray into the corporate world had been fun, and she'd gained so much valuable experience. But it couldn't continue.

Maria entered the main day care area. After providing breakfast, the staff organized activities for the neighborhood children. Maria headed over to one of the tables. The movement made her head hurt. She sat next to Henry, one of the underprivileged children who came to the center while his mom worked.

He was drawing a picture of three people. "That's fantastic, Henry. Who is that?"

"That's me and my mom," he told her, and then he pointed to the third figure. "That's you."

Tears welled in Maria's eyes. Henry was always such a sweet, sensitive child, and since Maria's very first day at the working at the center, he'd latched on to her. That she warranted a spot in a picture next to Henry's mother, a single woman who worked two jobs to provide for him, made her heart surge. He spent a lot of time at the center, and Maria wanted to do anything she could to ease their burden. Henry finished his drawing with one final stroke of black for Maria's hair and passed it over to her.

"Is this for me?" she asked, her headache forgotten. "It's wonderful. I'm going to put it on my fridge at home."

He smiled and reached out for a hug, which Maria gladly obliged. Those were the moments that made the tough job and low pay more than worth it.

"You like it?" He looked up at her, his brown eyes large.

"Of course I do," she assured him. "Thank you so much."

The hours she spent at the center as a volunteer were some of the best in her life. It wasn't always as challenging as some of her humanitarian work in war and disaster zones, but she loved it there, meeting new people, helping them find the services they needed.

Maria looked up and saw the door open. It was

Anna, her friend and the director of the center. "Henry, I'm going to go talk to Anna for a little while. Why don't you go play with the other kids outside?"

"Maria, it's good to see you back here. We've missed you."

"I've missed it, too. So much. And that's kind of what I wanted to talk to you about. Beth told me you're heading back home."

"Yes," she said. "I missed my family too much. So we're Tucson-bound in a couple of weeks."

"I would like to apply to be your replacement."

Anna looked her over. "That's good to hear," she said, smiling. "Let's go into my office. We can discuss some details."

Maria took a deep breath and raised her fist. She hesitated and then knocked rapidly three times on Brett's door.

"Come in."

She pushed open the door and saw that Alex was seated across from Brett's desk. His posture stiffened, and she looked away from him and focused on Brett.

"You're both here," Maria said. "That's good."

Brett looked up at her and folded his hands on the desk in front of her. "Maria, what's up?"

"I just wanted to give you this," she said, handing over the envelope that she'd been looking at all day.

Brett's eyebrows knit together as he accepted the envelope. "What is this?"

"It's my resignation."

"What?" Brett and Alex said together.

"It's my two weeks' notice. I don't think I can work here anymore."

"Maria," Alex said. "Is this something we should talk about?"

"No, I don't have anything to say to you. It's just the right time. A position at the community center opened up, and I interviewed for it and got the job."

"Congratulations, I guess. But is there anything we can do or say to make you stay?" Brett asked.

"No, really. It has nothing to do with you, *either of you*," she clarified, with a look in Alex's direction, "or the company, and I'm so grateful for the opportunity you've given me here. But I need to get back to what I'm passionate about. My work at the center, helping people."

"I can't say I blame you for that. But we'll definitely miss you."

She nodded, and started to turn. "Okay. Well, I'm going back to my desk. Let me know if you need anything."

"Maria, wait!" Alex jumped up and chased her out the door. He caught up to her outside in the hallway. "Don't do this," he said.

"Don't do what?"

"You don't need to quit."

"That's where you're wrong."

"If this is about what happened between us—"

"Yes, Alex, it's the hardest thing in the world, seeing you every day here at work, when all I want is for you to put your arms around me, kiss me. But you can't do that right now. Rest assured, though, the decisions I make have nothing to do with you. I'm doing this for me. I'm moving on. And you have to accept that."

Alex rubbed his jaw with his palm. His eyes were tired. He looked miserable, and for a second, she wanted to console him. But she held herself back. He'd broken her heart, and even though he'd pushed her away, she knew it wasn't what he wanted.

She thought he would confess his love. Tell her to stay, and that he wanted to be with her forever. "Is there anything I can do to get you to stay?"

"You want me to stay? At Collins/Fischer? Or with you?"

"The job," he said, after a long pause.

If her heart hadn't already been shattered by the man in front of her, she might have felt something besides the dull ache in her chest. So Maria swallowed her sob and turned away from Alex. Probably forever.

Alex walked back into Brett's office and sat heavily back into his seat. He looked at the stacks of papers in front of them. They had been in the middle of a meeting. "Where were we?"

"Good question. I just lost the best assistant I've ever had. What do you have to say about that?"

"Not a goddamn thing," Alex said, his lips folding into a grim line. "Can we just get back to work?" But instead of sitting, he made his way to the wet bar and opened several drawers. "I know you're sober, but why don't you keep any booze in here?"

"The good stuff is in the cabinet to your left," Brett told him. "For just such an occasion."

Alex grabbed the first bottle he saw, unscrewed the top and raised it to his lips.

"Dude," Brett said, with a concerned edge to his voice. "Take it easy."

Alex looked at the bottle in his shaky hands. He needed to get himself under control. And booze wasn't the way to do it. But he'd so royally fucked up his entire life by letting Maria walk away. He wasn't the man he wanted to be; he was quickly morphing into the man he'd fought against being his entire life—his booze-and-drug-addled father. But most important, he wasn't the man Maria needed. He needed to work on himself before seeing her again. Taking several deep breaths through his nose, he capped the bottle and took a bottle of water from the fridge. He returned to where Brett sat at his desk. "Can we get back to work now?"

"Yeah, sure. Is there anything you want to talk about first?"

"Not right now. No."

They worked in silence for a few minutes. Alex managed to focus on the task at hand, and he felt calmer as he looked over Collins/Fischer's projections for the next few years. The numbers were encouraging, but they did little to lift his mood. He was starting to realize that maybe money and success weren't everything. "Christ, look at these numbers. We've definitely made it."

"I think we're a few years past actually 'making it,' don't you think? We're doing very well."

He thought of the wealth that he and Brett had amassed. They had everything they could ever need. More than most others had. He had an idea. "Even after we reinvest in The Brotherhood's other ventures, and cover the operating costs for Hedo until it turns a profit, we've still got quite a bit of capital here. Any ideas of how to use it?"

Brett shrugged. "I haven't thought about it. Why do you ask? Do you have an idea?"

Alex nodded. "I think I know."

CHAPTER TWENTY-ONE

Six months later...

FROM HIS VANTAGE point high above Hedo's open-air lounge, Alex watched the partygoers frolic below them. Months and months of meticulous planning, logistics, meetings and hurdle-jumping had paid off, and the hotel was finally up and running.

He was more relaxed, but it wasn't only because of the hotel; Alex was in a much better place, mentally. He'd been spending time with a therapist, working through his issues that stemmed from childhood, and he'd tried his best to mend his relationship with Rafael. He'd even cut back on drinking, realizing that he'd used sex and alcohol to fill the void his upbringing had left within him, until Maria had come along.

Maria. He hadn't seen Maria in a couple of months. He didn't feel he could. Not until he worked out his own issues. He'd wanted to see if she would move on with her life. It was what she deserved, to find someone who wasn't so screwed up. But from what he'd heard, she hadn't.

Brett and Alana joined him and looked down at the party that they'd yet to join. "We did it," Brett said.

Alex took a deep breath. "Yeah." He found it hard to take part in the revelry. He was distracted, nervous. And he didn't get nervous. His normally razor-sharp focus had waned. During the course of opening the hotel, he'd almost lost everything—his best friend, the love of his life.

But he had a plan. A way to make it right, provided, of course, that Maria would even speak to him. He clutched the small velvet box in his pocket and hoped that his late gesture would be enough.

Rafael walked up to him and passed him a short crystal tumbler, and he drank the high-priced bourbon. He and Rafael were still friends, but something had changed between them. As if Raf still held some resentment or distrust. And Alex knew that it could have been avoided by staying away from the man's sister, or at least being honest about their relationship.

"So, you're actually doing this?"

"Yeah. As long as I have your blessing."

"You've got everyone's blessing. Just make it right with her, and don't screw it up this time, okay?"

"I'll do my best."

"She's a tough one. You're definitely going to need to grovel."

"How much do you think it'll take?"

"How much you got?"

"I'll do anything to get her back."

"Good luck," he said, patting him on the shoulder.
"Thanks."

"We should get down there," Alana said, coming
up between them, taking both men by the elbow and
steering them toward the elevator. "Let's go revel in
our new success."

Maria sat at the bar, staring intently at her phone
screen. Alex had asked her to meet him there. She
hadn't seen him in a couple of months—they hadn't
even crossed paths. Apparently, he'd been busy getting Hedo off the ground. She looked around. The
place was spectacular. The Brotherhood had taken
his vision and done an amazing job. Pride surged
through her, as she took in all of the partygoers. Just
like the rest of The Brotherhood's ventures, Hedo
was sure to be a success.

Maria wasn't sure why he wanted her there, especially since he'd spent the past several months avoiding her. She'd tried to move on—see other people,
but they weren't Alex. He'd still been the one to consume her every fantasy when she lay awake in bed,
unable to sleep without him by her side.

Alex had yet to show up. But there was no doubt
his staff had already told him that she'd arrived.
She'd heard from Rafael that Alex was doing better
lately. He'd been seeing a professional and cutting
back on his drinking. And she was proud of his progress. But that didn't quell the hurt that tightened her
chest every time she thought about him.

"Thanks for coming." She heard his voice behind her. "We really need to talk."

Swiveling around on her stool, she turned to look at him. "It's been a while." She paused to soak in the sight of him. "What did you want to talk about?"

He sat beside her, and they turned to face each other. "I've missed you."

Maria had missed him, too. But she wouldn't say it. She'd laid it on the line for him so much already. She had some pride. He had to meet her halfway. She wanted to crawl into his lap and feel his arms wrap around her again, but she simply nodded, remaining cool. "What did you want?"

"I want to apologize."

"Really?"

"Yeah. I made a mess of everything. And I hurt you. I'm sorry."

She looked around the crowded, lively room. "Should we go somewhere private?"

He shook his head. "Nope. I'm done hiding. I'm not afraid. I don't care who hears me say any of this."

"Oh really? Why shouldn't I just tell you to go fuck yourself?"

"I couldn't blame you if you did. But I'm hoping you'll hear me out."

"And if my brother sees us? Will he want to punch you again?"

"Me and Raf have come to terms. He says that if I screw it up, or hurt you again, then we'll have problems again. Otherwise, we have his blessing."

Her eyebrow raised. She tried to not let on how

his words stole her breath. "And do you think you can do that, not screw it up?"

"I can try. I can't promise that I won't be stubborn, or bullheaded, but you wanted me to fight for us. I will. Every day. But I can't do it alone. We both need to fight for us. I love you. I always have, and I've never stopped. I want to be the man you think I can be. I want to make you proud. But I need you with me. If you'll have me."

"Alex, I still love you, too. You really hurt me, but I don't think it's anything compared to how much you hurt yourself. I always saw the good in you."

He pulled a velvet box from his pocket. Her heart sped up into overdrive. "You've always been my family," he told her. "And I want to make it official. I've never loved another person the way I love you. Marry me."

"Alex."

"It doesn't have to be now, or anytime soon. But I want you to know that I'm in this for the long haul. I want to be with you for the rest of my life. If that's what you want, too." He kept going, and Maria barely processed his words. "I know that I don't deserve you, and I have a lot of work to do to make up for everything. You make me a better person. And if this is moving too quickly, I understand. I'll put this ring away and give it to you when you're ready. But I will do anything to keep you by my side. We don't have to get married or even engaged right now. But I want you to know that I need you in whatever future we can have together."

"How can I trust that you won't push me away? You shut me out. Do you know how much that hurt me?"

Alex nodded and looked down at his hands. "I thought I was doing the right thing, for both of us. But looking at you and telling you to leave was the hardest thing I'd ever done. Staying away from you was torture, and I'll never be able to make up for hurting you like that. I promise I will spend the rest of my life trying. But I'm hoping you'll give me the chance."

Those were the words that Maria had wanted to hear for six months. She wouldn't forget the pain she'd experienced, but being away from Alex had convinced her that she was at her happiest when he was by her side. They could try again. They could make it work.

"I'll wear your ring, Alex. I want to be with you forever. I want to marry you. But not yet. When we're both ready. We have a lot of work to do to get there, though. I'm ready to forgive you, but not forget what I've been through."

"I know. And I'm ready for the challenge."

"Me, too." She smiled. "My family will be thrilled when we tell them."

"Yeah, they were thrilled," he said with a smile.

She was shocked. "Did you tell them?"

"I asked your parents. Formally. And I told them everything—sparing the obvious intimate details, of course. A traditional family like yours, I knew that it was the only way. They were surprised, but happy."

"I know they must have been, because they love you."

He slipped the ring on her finger. It fit perfectly. "There's something else."

"What is it?"

"I've got some news about your community center."

"What do you mean?"

"It's come under new management."

She cocked her head to the side, trying to interpret his meaning.

"Just listen and let me tell you," he said with a smile. "Me and Brett have decided, and with contributions from the rest of The Brotherhood, Collins/Fischer is dedicating ten million a year for a foundation to help the people of Las Vegas. We've bought your community center. We're making the building bigger and upgrading the facilities. It's going to be amazing. And we want you to run it."

Maria blinked. "Wait, what?" She almost had whiplash as she tried to process what he was telling her. "You're piling a lot of information on me right now."

"You know the issues that affect the city, and the people who need help. You'll be on the ground, the front lines, not the office, allocating funds and raising awareness where you need to. Jessica has already committed city hall resources and staff to help you with outreach."

Maria was stunned. Suddenly, within just a few short minutes, she had everything she'd ever wanted. The man she loved and a job that made a difference. She didn't want to move for fear that she was caught in some dream world, and if she woke up, she would be alone in her bed, sad and frustrated at her fantasies.

"Are you serious?"

"Completely."

"Yes," she said, almost breathless. "Yes, to everything. I want to marry you. I want to run your foundation. I want everything to do with you." She leaped over to him and wrapped her arms around his neck, and he held her by her waist and lifted her to a standing position. Maria pulled back. "I love you, Alex."

"I love you, too."

Maria looked into his eyes, and then around the full club. He'd almost made her forget where they were. "We'd better get back to the party. We've got a lot to celebrate."

* * * * *

COMING SOON!

We really hope you enjoyed reading this book. If you're looking for more romance, be sure to head to the shops when new books are available on

Thursday 21st February

To see which titles are coming soon, please visit
millsandboon.co.uk/nextmonth